Harry, Revised

Harry, Revised

A Novel

Mark Sarvas

BLOOMSBURY

Sarvas

Published by Bloomsbury USA, New York
Distributed to the trade by Macmillan

A brief excerpt of Chapter Three appeared in 2004
in *Pindeldyboz*, an online magazine

4983 421

All papers used by Bloomsbury USA are natural, recyclable products made
from wood grown in well-managed forests. The manufacturing processes
conform to the environmental regulations of the country of origin.

Library of Congress Cataloging-in-Publication Data has been applied for.

ISBN-10 1-59691-462-9
ISBN-13 978-1-59691-462-9

First U.S. Edition 2008

1   3   5   7   9   10   8   6   4   2

Typeset by Westchester Book Group
Printed in the United States of America by Quebecor World Fairfield

For my parents

One

In which our hero orders a sandwich and is late for an appointment

HARRY RENT USED to fiddle with his wedding ring, now he fiddles with the space it has left behind.

He fiddles by running the tip of his thumb along the underside of his fourth finger. He fiddles with it idling at a traffic light. He fiddles with it when addressing his attractive assistant over the intercom, asking her to send in his next patient. He fiddles with it waiting for change at the grocery store. He fiddles with it both absently and consciously. Consciously, to be certain it's gone. As for why he fiddles absently, he's not yet sure.

Presently, he's fiddling with it at a luncheon counter. He's surprised, but no more than vaguely, by how natural its absence already feels. The rest of his allotment of brainpower is split between despairing over how completely his new gray Italian suit fails to make him resemble the dashing model in the magazine ad—it hangs limply on his body, draped in woolen defeat—and trying to ignore how maddeningly nervous he feels sitting here on this stool, fiddling with a ring that's no longer there, waiting for his waitress to turn her attention to him.

There's an excellent chance that this unplanned lunch stop is going to make him late, and although he minds, he can't quite bring himself to forgo the stop. (Even as he recalls the sepulchral tones of the unctuous Tony Glide advising him that "things at Flavin and Makepeace run like clockwork," so punctuality is strongly advised.) He notes this, it registers that he ought to mind, and he wonders why he doesn't. He does this a lot, this strange circular thinking, Harry the Ouroboros, watching himself watching himself watching, often emerging many minutes later, foggy-headed and thick-tongued as if waking from a deep sleep. Wondering *what the hell just happened*, knowing only that another little piece of time is lost forever.

And now he's done it again, and all that alerts him to this fact, that brings him back to the moment, is the plume of perfume left behind by his departing waitress, and he realizes that he's once again missed his opening because he's been lost somewhere in Harry-land. He sighs with gathering desperation, the lateness of the hour beginning to weigh on him, and he glances down once more at the menu, on a futile hunt for something to eat. But Café Retro's forced good cheer and whitewashed surfaces meant to evoke the 1950s leave him cold, as do the Chuck Berry selections in the jukebox and the menu consisting largely of deep-fried this and sugarcoated that. Now, as he's debating the relative merits of the Kitchen Sink Chili over the Atomic Sloppy Burger, while carefully trying to negotiate the hot-fudge stains left on the menu by a less fastidious predecessor, some primeval instinct kicks him—nostrils flare slightly, adrenaline flows, hairs stir on the back of his neck, pupils dilate, and some infallible whisper in his ear advises him, *Look up, Harry. Lift your head, my man. Your moment is nigh.* And the head is lifted because who is Harry to countermand such fundamental, ageless commands?

"Have you decided yet? Or do you need a few minutes?"

This is Molly. Raven-haired and statuesque, she is twenty-two years old, and this gig at Café Retro is one of several ways she is paying her way through graduate school. She is working on her master's degree in postcolonial studies. The title of her thesis is "Patriarchal Modes in Contemporary Fiction: Just Who the Fuck Is the White Man to Decide What Passes for 'Literary'?" and by all accounts the early draft is a rollicking good read. She has a boyfriend, Bruce, who neglects her, and who she has begun to suspect has at least one other girlfriend. The truth is that she's growing tired of Bruce anyway—the working-class-bad-boy-tattoo thing was fun for a few months, but she's sat through enough French films alone now that reassessment is definitely in the cards. She has a strained relationship with her mother, who lives in Seattle, and is only permitted to call her on Wednesday mornings, by design, as Molly has a class to teach at ten a.m. And she is also all too aware that the man sitting before her strangely fiddling with his left hand, this man who may well be old enough to be her father, has a crush on her, but he's not the first, and such crushes have been a tip boon in the past. Harry, of course, knows none of this. All Harry sees is Molly the waitress, standing before him, waiting for his order.

Nevertheless, it is his moment, the one opportunity he has to ask for something and actually have her do it. Power over women has always fascinated Harry, despite—or perhaps because of—its absence from his marriage. His wife, Anna, was much too successful, too poised, for him to have ever had any power over her. In fact, it was an extraordinarily strange turn of events, he often reflected, that led her to choose him out of the field of suitors blackening her front porch like a swarm of death and dung beetles. But, whoops, Harry feels it coming on, another circuitous detour away from the moment at hand, and so he forces himself back to the present, as he determines how to make the most of this moment, how to play it for maximum advantage, how to *just this once* have a lovely young woman do his bidding.

And, in true Harry-style, he muffs it, a world-class belly flop in front of the Olympic judging committee:

"Boy, it's hard to decide. What do you recommend?"

And it's done, power is ceded, Harry can't grab this moment and run with it, no matter how loudly his desire screams at him. Fiddle, fiddle, fiddle. Patient smile, glancing at her, as though eye contact causes him physical pain.

Molly is both flattered and slightly weirded out to be asked. After all, Café Retro scarcely attracts the kind of clientele that thinks much about what's put in front of them: *Tell me, young lady, what brand of peanut butter does the chef use? I'm a Jif man myself* or *I hope it's genuine Hershey's syrup in the banana split, my dear.* Still, unlike Harry, Molly has definite ideas and tastes and no discomfort expressing them, and thus she doesn't hesitate to go directly to her favorite item on the menu.

"The Monte Cristo. Definitely go for the Monte Cristo."

Disaster. Deep-fried *and* sweet. She couldn't have picked a worse dish if she'd meant to, if she'd had a catalog of Harry's loves and loathes and aimed with deadly, clinical precision at the heart of his culinary Achilles' heel. And now, for a moment, Harry teeters on the verge of exploring the whole "heart of the heel" construction, wondering if that's actually allowed, but the snarling, threatening promise of the Monte Cristo is too strong to permit such reveries. It's inedible, revolting, vile.

"The Monte Cristo it is," he says with what he hopes looks like a suave smile but fears can just as easily be read as murderous constipation.

"Great! If you don't like it, just tell me and I'll get you something else."

"I'm sure it will be great," he says, taking a hatchet to his lifeboat with grim abandon.

She nods, smiling, and is about to depart when she turns back. "Have I seen you in here before?"

Well, no, not in here, not exactly. Harry has passed the front of the restaurant numerous times, paused before the window, gazed in hopelessly, and watched Molly making her rounds. Once he actually worked up the nerve to come in, but sitting in her section demanded more fortitude

4

than the standard model Harry is equipped with, and so he sat in the section that was attended by Lucille, an overweight disciplinarian. Craning his neck helplessly, he withered slowly under Lucille's long, gloomy shadow as he watched Molly gliding effervescently to and fro in her section.

Her question hangs in the air. Harry remembers a sage bit of advice once given to him by another resident during his intern days—if you have to lie, keep it as close to the truth as you can. It's easier that way— less to remember. That said resident was convicted of malpractice and fraud some years later does little to dampen Harry's enthusiasm for his counsel, and so Harry half-nods.

"Passed through once or twice. But I'm not a regular or anything." Tolerable but just barely.

"Too bad," Molly says with a glint of playfulness. Harry's features adjust themselves to accommodate the rush of red that is flowing into his cheeks, and she calculates 15 percent has already leapt up to 18 and is bearing down relentlessly on 20. Harry focuses, returns the serve, and scores, in his eyes, a point:

"Well, if the Monte Cristo is everything you say, I may just become a regular."

And the horrible tactical mistake is at once apparent to him—he has committed himself to a lifetime of Monte Cristos, of returning time and time again and being expected to order nothing else. After all, isn't that one of the great advantages of being a regular—getting "the usual"? *Ahh, here comes Charlie, get him his usual, Frida . . . Good to see you again, Alex. The usual?* And so on. Sure, an occasional *Not tonight, Eddie, I'm feeling footloose—get me a cheeseburger* can be tolerated, but after a while, the universe reasserts itself, and Harry's appearance in the doorway will set the bread in the batter and bring powdered sugar off the shelf. But Harry is careful not to let the shadow of defeat move across his face— it isn't that he's particularly philosophical about absorbing slings, ar- rows, and the rest. Rather, he's too vain to puncture what he perceives to be his best moment thus far, his most suave line of the day, with the appearance of irresolution in any form. And so once again, he studiously ignores where the chips have fallen.

"Excellent," says Molly with a grin. "I'll let the kitchen know that the stakes are high."

The stakes are high indeed, Harry considers, with a nervous look downward at his watch. He experiences a stab of irritation at the realization that time has not, in fact, slowed down on his behalf, and he is now even later than he was moments ago. Worse, the odds are high that this pattern will continue into the immediate future. Events are not moving quickly enough for Harry's taste—a quick tally shows he's exchanged a mere hundred or so words with the Heavenly Molly, a scant return on the twenty minutes he's been sitting at this counter. At this rate, he realizes, his fantasy of a lifetime of sensual bliss together seems several lifetimes away, which represents a few more lifetimes than he has to play with.

But before Harry can unpack all that, as is his wont to do, and delve into this inviting emotional, philosophical, and spiritual conundrum, his attention is caught by the sight of a couple sitting across from each other at one of the booths. He notes them not because they appear as out of place at Café Retro as he does (although they do) or because their whispered conversation, in a backfired attempt at discretion, has taken on a strange, hushed urgency that draws all eyes to it (although it has). What draws Harry's attention is what sits on the tabletop between them, amid salt and pepper shakers, tattered napkins and shriveled straw wrappers that look like discarded snake skins, Sweet'n Low packets and plastic cuplets of creamer, amid various condiments and utensils. Between them sits an urn.

It's clear from the wary expressions on the couple's faces and from the respectful distance that they keep from it that the urn contains human remains.

The sight of the urn elicits a visceral reaction from Harry, an unexpectedly sharp stab of pain in his left side, shot through with nausea and adrenaline as it sets a dark, terrifying thought nudging at him like the head of an unwanted, insistent cat. He draws a steadying breath and—in an unparalleled impersonation of man obviously trying to not eavesdrop—eavesdrops:

"Michael, this is disgusting."

"Would you please keep your voice down, Barb? Everyone is looking at us."

"Everyone is looking at us because there's a goddamned *urn* on the table!"

Point for Barb, thinks Harry. Michael appears to agree, because he sighs and puts the urn under the table.

"Look," he begins defensively, "do you think I was expecting this? It was a simple will reading, for chrissakes. I figured she'd leave me a few of her notebooks or something like that."

Will reading, Harry thinks. How odd. Not words you hear every day.

"Yeah, well, she appears to have left you a little more than that," says Barbara, bristling.

"It's an *errand*, Barbara. She asked me to do an errand. That's all. Whatever else you may be thinking about all this is completely off base. First of all, I—"

But now Michael pauses as his eyes fall on Harry's awkward pose of feigned disinterest. With a scowl, he leans in toward Barbara, and now whatever heated sotto voce negotiations may be taking place are lost to Harry's ears. Harry presses his side, where the stab has become a fading throb, and his febrile mind automatically steps in to try to fill in the blanks, occupying the painfully elongated moments leading up to the delivery of his Monte Cristo (which he now realizes, with creeping horror, he is going to be expected to *eat*).

How much can he suss out from the glimpse he's been afforded? Well, he's pretty certain that Michael and Barbara are married, not especially happily, he suspects, although that may just be circumstantial. (After all, he and Anna appeared quite the happy couple to all those around them.) And it seems equally clear to Harry that the inhabitant of the urn has prevailed upon poor Michael through the agency of a last will and testament to discard or dispose of her in some suitably inconvenient manner over which Barb is now up in arms. The two most obvious questions are (1) who is the "her" in question (Harry pruriently assumes it's an ex of some sort even as he acknowledges it could easily be a friend, a sister, or perhaps dear old Mum) and (2) what, exactly, is the nature of the "errand" she has requested of Michael? Harry realizes that any hope of coming close to the truth on that question would be helped enormously by knowing the answer to the first question, and since neither answer makes itself apparent, his thoughts threaten to return to further contemplation of ham, cheese, and jam. It's a thought Harry finds hard to bear, and so he opts for yet another detour, expertly redirecting his thoughts in well-practiced fashion with a bewildered shake of the head over those who argue so publicly. After all, such public displays would never have occurred to him or to Anna. Even their private displays—save one—were startlingly infrequent and, especially in contrast to Barb's fiery outburst, relatively meek affairs.

The truth is that Harry has simply never been a world-class brawler. Oh, he would have liked to have been a screamer, an arm-waver in the best Burton-Taylor tradition. It's certainly how he imagined himself, a dynamism he fantasized about having that generally eluded him—although *eluded* suggests a chase being given at the other end, some attempt to nab that sucker, and no such attempts ever materialized. Because really, Anna *was* pretty together, right? Everyone could see there was not much to rail angrily against there, so he suspects he would have been accused of just making it up for the sake of the performance. (Not that that sort of behavior is beyond him.) Try as he might, he's unable to remember anything about which he ever felt strongly enough to fight with his wife. There's a curious void where the well of memory should be, and Harry suspects there's something abnormal about this. He tries to will himself to remember, forces himself to pick apart the past, but comes up empty, without so much as dust passing through his fingers, unable to figure out what's responsible for this absence. (Or, he frets, perhaps that's just what he's telling himself, even as he resists a darker, sinister whisper, the hectoring voice that says he's not trying hard at all, and that he knows exactly what he'll find if he does. Such are the daily dilemmas of life in Harry-land, this multiplicity of voices, of endless options infinitely contemplated, never acted upon, always deferred.)

After all, it's not as though there weren't opportunities to fight. There were certainly a handful of occasions when each struck the flinty surface of the other, causing the unexpected spark to fly. But they never combusted. Why? Harry remains unable or unwilling to detect a pattern. Perhaps there simply aren't enough of them for an accurate accounting. But he fears that even with dozens or hundreds to root through like a pig nosing for truffles, he has no real gift for reading between the lines. He's a hopeless literalist and he knows it. He feels that on some level it must recommend him that at least he recognizes this and won't tangle with metaphor or anything remotely stylistic. No "Men are from Mars, Women are from Venus" nonsense for Harry. Men are men. Women are women. It either will or it won't. It is what it is. A rose is a rose is a rose—he's always liked that one. Obvious in a good commonsensical sort of way. A slightly tedious worldview, perhaps, but he can live with that. Harry isn't interested in being flash.

What Harry is interested in being, however, presents another variation on the same elusive problem he's just been wrestling with. Harry finds he's better at defining his absences—self-knowledge through negation or elimination. He thinks that if he could whittle away enough false trails and unpromising detours—I'm not a golfer, I'm not a dadaist, I'm not a plumber, I'm not a cross-dresser (though I have been tempted)—then he could eventually define himself by whatever remains. The flaws of this approach are obvious enough even to Harry, but he's always found it easier to deny, to disavow, and to disengage. He knows that this isn't as it should be, acknowledges it as a flaw of some sort, even as he finds that he doesn't actually feel bad enough about it to do anything differently. Despite his best efforts—which Harry is the first to admit don't amount to much—all roads seem to lead to nothing. Or at most, back to the sofa, to the remote, to—

Okay. Right there. Perfect example. Prime fight potential squandered. But not the standard variation played out in living rooms the world over, angry wives berating their husbands' spastic remote fingers, as they blur past *Star Trek* reruns, cooking channels, and breaking world news with equal disdain. No, Harry's moment of reckoning came when Anna wandered into the living room one Sunday afternoon to find him slumped ungainly in front of a rebroadcast of a recent county supervisors' meeting, dubbed in Spanish, a language with which Harry hasn't even a passing familiarity. And Anna surmised (correctly) that Harry had landed on this channel and simply lost any will to look beyond it. There was no guarantee that any further clicking would be rewarded with any more interesting viewing, and so why not simply stop here? And perhaps what troubled Anna most of all was that, before long, Harry became interested as only Harry could be. He hadn't the slightest idea what was being said, but somehow this bleak little spectacle had drawn him in. Why did he insist on stretching so much out of so little? What was at the root of this almost sinister capacity?

"Really. I'm watching it."

"How can you be watching it? You don't understand a word they're saying." Anna's voice disembodied, as she stood behind him, watching over his shoulder.

"Well, no. True. But look at that guy in the red tie. He's hilarious! He's furious about *something*. No idea what. But I keep waiting to see if he gets his way, if he relaxes at all. But so far the woman in the gray skirt seems to have him over a barrel."

"I think you're just too lazy to change the channel."

"Why should I change the channel?"

Anna was nothing if not scrupulously fair, and she would give every idea its chance before gainsaying it. And so she continued to stand behind him and watch. Trying to see if she could understand. Always willing to try. But as with so many other well-intended attempts, nothing came of this one. After a few minutes, during which the woman in the gray skirt appeared to secure her final triumph over her hapless red-cravated foe, Anna sighed. He felt a gentle kiss on the top of his head, and she was gone.

And that was that. Harry worried that Anna thought he was hopeless, pointless, and not worth engaging and reforming, though he preferred to imagine that she truly loved him totally, selflessly, and could accept any quirk, however banal. As for himself, even if Harry felt anger, he was unlikely to express it. The truth is that Anna intimidated him, scared him a little. Even after eight years of marriage, he never managed to stop feeling outclassed.

It's with a dull clatter now that the Monte Cristo hits the countertop. Harry looks up into the expectant smile of Molly.

"One Monte Cristo for the man in the nice suit."

Harry experiences an unexpected stabbing sensation in his gut. *She likes my suit!*

"Hope you enjoy it." Another smile as she waits.

Oh, God.

She's going to wait while he tastes it. Right here. In front of him. She's not going to move until he validates her recommendation. And now—in all too familiar Harry-fashion—time stretches out, elongating like a thread, or like one of those diagrams of a ray that he remembers from geometry class. He never got rays, what they were for or why he should care about them, but he liked that they started from a fixed point at one end and went on to infinity at the other. It had the best of both worlds, he thought—permanence and eternal movement. Infinity must be a crowded place, he used to think, given everything that goes there—rays, lines, numbers, pi. Time really does slow down, Harry notes, as the first sickly wafts of the sweetened toast reach his nose. They climb into his nostrils and gently but insistently pull his head downward, forcing him to gaze upon what Molly hath wrought.

The Monte Cristo. It fills his plate, steam rising gently from within its folds. A descendant of the *croque-monsieur*, although Harry doesn't know this. He imagines it to be some promotional tie-in from Dumas's day, which gets it wrong by about a hundred years. But he does know the story of the count, of the man falsely imprisoned who reinvents himself and exacts revenge on those who wronged him. That he knows it largely through the Mr. Magoo cartoon and the Classics Illustrated comic book does nothing to dim his enthusiasm. His memory begins to flood with moments from the story—Dantès's discovery of his fellow prisoner and their joint tunneling attempt; Dantès's spectacular plummet from the top of the Château d'If; his first resplendent appearance as the count of Monte Cristo; and the brilliant, systematic culmination of his vengeance. Quite a guy, this Dantès, who could not even be diminished by Magoo's nearsighted bumbling.

Harry has been looking down at his sandwich without touching it for so long that Molly, unfamiliar with Harry's solipsistic tendencies, suddenly determines that he's saying grace over his food. Embarrassed and self-conscious, she quickly and respectfully lowers her head and begins to whisper.

"Our heavenly Father, kind and good, we thank Thee for our daily food . . ."

Startled, Harry glances up at her and realizes that she's misinterpreted his body language, that he's the reason for these devotions. There's nothing for Harry to do but join in.

"We thank Thee for Thy love and care," Molly continues. "Be with us, Lord, and hear our prayer. Amen."

"Amen." Harry mumbles the word unconvincingly, without passion or purpose. But as he looks back up from his plate, there's Molly. Smiling, waiting. Glittering, Harry swears she's glittering. He can't help but smile back at her and then, epiphany. Sudden and unexpected, in the time-honored tradition of epiphanies.

He, too, can be Dantès.

He can remake himself. He will be the count of Monte Cristo to Molly's . . . and now he falters. What was her name in the book? Some kind of car. Well, that doesn't matter now. What matters is that Molly knows nothing about Harry or his life. Nothing about where he's from, what he's done, what he's leaving behind. His tabula could not be more rasa, and rather than muck it up in the usual Harry finger-paint fashion, he has a chance to emerge grandly, to be *her* count. (The fact that Dantès was *unjustly* accused is an inconvenient detail that Harry chooses to overlook.) He's got the means now, and even if he lacks Edmond Dantès's natural brilliance and cunning, he's got a model to follow and Harry's always been good at imitation.

Now something starts to glow, to rumble within Harry, something very much like the beginning of a chain reaction, a little fission of the soul, and for a moment the world feels attainable, and with this wave of confidence he grabs his fork and spears a huge portion of Monte Cristo. He tears into it with an unexpected exuberance, chewing it passionately and viscerally, gobbling the thing up with a vitality that startles him. He grins with delight and Molly reads this as an approval of the sandwich.

"You like it! Excellent!"

She pours him a fresh cup of coffee with a home-run smile, and in that smile Harry perceives a bond of some sort, or at least a suggestion of one. As he smiles back at her, he takes another forkful of the sandwich, which could be sawdust for all the attention he's paying it, and he lets himself imagine how it will be with her . . .

He'll have to come back, of course. In his mind's eye he imagines a half dozen return visits, imagines Molly happier to see him each time. They exchange pleasantries, which, over time, take on a more personal cast. He learns the details of her life, asks after her mother, her friends, whatever it is she does when she's not working here. She laughs at his jokes, admires his clothes, asks him if he's been working out. Soon thereafter, the confidences begin. She expresses her disappointment in the men in her life, complains about their shallowness, and how she longs for a man of substance, someone who's not a kid anymore, who knows who he is, you know? And Harry will understand and offer advice and startle her with his wisdom, with his decency and clarity of self. He'll always know just what to say to her, just what she needs at any given moment. He'll begin to surprise her with little gifts—nothing extravagant and always tasteful, calibrated to demonstrate perfectly how closely he listens to her. Two weeks after she expresses nostalgia for a picture book from her childhood, Harry will hand her a copy of same. When she mentions in passing a preference for an unobtainable import version of her favorite world-music group, she will miraculously be offered a copy within days. Then he kicks it to the next level, begins to anticipate her, read her taste, venture into territory unguided and surprise her with his sensitivity and perception. It's right around now that she admits she's become attracted to him—yeah, she knows he's older than she is, but that's becoming part of the attraction for her: a sensitive daddy who will fuck her. His heart will skitter when she utters the word—Harry likes to imagine that she's gotten a hidden, dirty side—and he'll gulp and look away in a manner that she'll find charming. That's when she'll reach out, lift his face toward her and give him a kiss. It will be a hurried one—they're still in the coffee shop, after all—but with the sweetness of her lip gloss and the hint of the tip of a tongue, Harry knows he's standing at the threshold of bliss. The proper kiss will come later in the day—he'll be waiting in his car for her to get off, knowing that she'll be looking for him, imagining her consumed with him, and when he steps out of his car, she will race into his arms and pull his mouth hungrily against hers. He'll invite her away for the weekend, take her somewhere with style and elegance, remove her from the world of Café Retro and dazzle her with his charm and attention. He's thinking about Napa, a nice Victorian inn right on the outskirts of town. She'll lean her head on his shoulder for the entire drive and never want to leave the room. They'll make love before the fireplace, toss on robes when room service knocks, and giggle once they've left. He'll invite her to come live with him—her place is so small, after all, even if it's perfectly, charmingly laid out. With tears in her eyes, she'll accept, telling him that he's the man she's been waiting for, dreaming about. They'll marry—he'll propose back in their charming room in Napa, back in front of the fire. Or wait. Better still. In Dublin. He'll take her to see her ancestral lands (Molly, she must be Irish), and as they stroll along St. Stephens Green, he'll ask for her hand. She'll cry again when she accepts. The wedding will be small and tasteful. Max the podiatrist will stand as his best man, Molly's virginal sister will be her maid of honor. A few weeks after their honeymoon in Venice, Molly will tell Harry that she's pregnant. He'll touch her stomach gently, tears welling up in his eyes, when—

"Dammit, Michael! She's *dead*. I'm not!"

Barbara's fury has slammed the covers on Harry's storybook, and he's disagreeably surprised to find incipient tears in his eyes. He wipes them away, hoping no one has seen him sniffling at his own daydreams. He watches as Barbara collects her things and storms from the café. He and Molly exchange a puzzled glance, and then Harry returns his attention to Michael, who reaches awkwardly under the table for the urn, which he places under his arm like a child carrying his schoolbooks, and hurries from the restaurant.

Again the urn. Again that strange admixture of nausea and adrenaline. Of terror. Suppressing the pain that has returned to stab at his side, he looks at his watch.

"Shit," he mutters. He looks up to Molly. "I have to go, I'm late. I'm sorry. It was really delicious."

"I'm glad you liked it," she says with a smile, clearing away the plates and pocketing her 35 percent tip. "Come on back sometime and have another."

Harry sighs blissfully. "Science hasn't discovered the force that could keep me away," he says. Actually, it's what he imagines himself saying, but all he can manage is a mumbled "Will do."

He stands and brushes off crumbs and powdered sugar from his suit. It's bad enough that he's going to be this late, he needs to be presentable. As he exits the restaurant, he prays that, for once, traffic will cooperate with him.

After all, it would never do for a man to miss his wife's funeral.

Two

In which our hero attends a funeral

Amid the quiet, respectful murmurs of the other mourners, in the subzero darkness of the air-conditioned funeral parlor, the casket looms immovably, devouring Harry's field of view. ("Oh, we don't call them *coffins* anymore," he'd been corrected by Tony Glide, the overgroomed, overmanicured, overperfumed mortician of Flavin & Makepeace. Glide was of a type equally at home purveying coffins and caskets or plots of Florida real estate, and the only thing that appeared to disturb his imperturbable salesmanship was Harry's resolute refusal of all the familiar comforts of mourning. "Handkerchief, sir?" "No, thanks." "Water? Something to eat?' "Nope, fine." "Do you need a moment alone?" "Don't think so, thanks." And on it went, until he simply stopped offering, mistaking Harry's reticence among strangers—among everyone, really—for callousness. Now Glide lingers at the side of the proceedings, monitoring movements and needs, a lean and hungry look in his eyes.)

It's a bronze job, the top of the line, no expense spared, as Harry knows he'll be judged on a whole host of criteria, so there's no point slipping up here, right at the beginning. It's closed, necessarily.

Harry is fussing with his hands. This business of what to do with one's hands has always vexed him, a creeping awareness of ungainly appendages. He always finds them in the wrong places—caught in closing doors, oddly raised in photographs, trapped beneath his sleeping wife—and today is no exception. His favored position, hands in pockets, strikes him as a bit too casual in light of the proceedings. He tries clasping them before his midsection, but that feels ridiculously pious. Hands behind his back feels too martial, more honor guard than husband. And so, as he has done so often in the past, he settles for dangling them limply at his side, streamers abandoned by the wind.

With the matter of the hands settled, Harry returns his attention to the casket. He knows he should be thinking about his wife instead of her container, but, as before, something holds him back, an amorphous terror, an obstacle thwarting his attempts to bring Anna into any kind of relief, and he finds himself contemplating, instead, pillows. Reviewing casket options with Tony Glide, Harry could not get past the question of the pillows.

"You have several options in your range," Glide explained. "I'm rather fond of the Eternity series—the mahogany version is the preferred model for statesmen and celebrities. But if you want to go top-of-the-top, there's really only one choice."

"What's that?"

Glide slid a glossy photo brochure under Harry's nose.

"The Horizon. It's our semiprecious bronze model. It has one great advantage over its lesser wooden brethren."

"What's that?"

"Decay. It won't."

Harry nodded, impressed, and decided that the ten-thousand-dollar price tag was a small amount to pay to ensure a dry, dirt-free eternal rest for Anna. He didn't have any strong religious or spiritual leanings, but on the off chance that Anna was in fact looking over the proceedings, he imagined the choice would satisfy her. Anna's parents—gone nearly five years now, Harry reflected with relief that still felt fresh—had always expressed themselves through displays of cash. When Anna's older sister, poor thwarted Claire, divorced her first of three husbands, their feckless father consoled her with a T-bill. Fondness-as-finance was the lingua franca of the Weldt family.

As Harry thumbed through the brochure for the Horizon semi-precious bronze, he noticed the pillows and the plush lining of the casket. "That's an awful lot of pillows, isn't it?"

"We want the departed to rest comfortably on their journey through eternity."

Harry nodded gravely even as the simple logic of the following statement echoed within: "What comfort? She's dead." He fought to keep the statement within, but as similar thoughts often had in the past, it pried his teeth open and made a mad dash for freedom, catching an unsuspecting Tony Glide upside the head. Glide's preternatural smoothness momentarily disrupted, he could do little more than offer a startled "Eh?"

"What I mean is, well, she doesn't really feel the pillows, does she? It just seems odd. Like it's more for us than for her."

Glide recovered his game and parried, "We find that the grieving process is a collective experience, and that mourners are comforted by the appearance of serenity."

"Oh, okay." Harry paused long enough to let Glide think he had scored his point, then piped up, "Only, you know, it's going to be a closed coffin."

"Yes." Glide did not see the point.

"So no one will really know whether there are pillows or not."

Battling Harry on principle and unwilling to concede anything, an arctic "True" was as far as Glide would go. There the matter seemed to rest. But later, when Harry handed over his check, he asked, "So, you do put the pillows inside? Even though it's closed?"

"Yes. Of course."

"But nobody can see them. Or know they're there."

"We know they are there. Anna knows they are there." On the latter point, Harry remained unconvinced.

And so the Horizon bronze semiprecious it was, replete with pillows, and now, standing before the massive, glittering torpedo, Harry is confident that it is a display of extravagance that the room will respond to. But the pillows have returned to lick the back of his brain. With the same unpracticed flourish with which an inexperienced diner summons a waiter in a fine restaurant, he beckons Tony Glide, who sleekly attends Harry, his steps across the room unobtrusive in a way that can only be achieved through years of practice, efficiently slicing a path to Harry without disturbing the grieving of the other mourners.

"Yes, Mr. Rent," he says, in a perfectly modulated whisper, never overbearing in its solicitude. "Can I get you something?"

"So, look, the pillows. What did we finally decide?"

"I beg your pardon, sir?" Glide can scarcely conceal his surprise.

"What did we go with? They're in there, right?"

Crimson inches upward from Glide cheek to Glide forehead. "Of course, sir."

"Because, you know, no one can see them."

"I assure you, sir, they are there."

Harry nods, more or less satisfied. "Nice ones?"

"Lovely ones, sir."

"What color?"

"Excuse me?"

"What color are they?"

"Beige Quietude."

"What?"

"Beige Quietude, sir."

"Quietude's not a color."

Glide is losing his patience now. Harry is bearing down on his well-practiced reserve like the proverbial thousand drops of water.

"It's a proprietary line, sir."

"Oh. It's just—"

Glide graduates from impatient to curt. "This is isn't the time for this, Mr. Rent."

"But—"

"That's all, sir. And you have jam on your tie."

"What?"

"Jam. On your tie."

Glide secures his victory by pointing to the Monte Cristo footprints. Harry grimaces. *Shit.* He pulls out his tie and begins licking and rubbing it, trying to remove the stain.

Glide pats his arm. "Come on. I'll give you a clean one."

Harry looks up with surprise. "A spare tie?"

"Yes. Sir."

"You guys think of everything."

"Follow me to the office, Mr. Rent."

"It's not Beige Quietude is it?"

"No. It's not."

In the white porcelain glare of the bathroom, Harry, collar up, examines the stain on his tie. It's completely ruined, the sticky strawberry ejaculate having landed squarely in one of the white patches of the tie's Mondrian-like pattern. Nothing to be done. He sighs with disappointment—the tie was a present from Anna. No special occasion, just one of the everyday favors that she bestowed upon him with regularity, unimaginative but well meant. Ties, pens, cuff links, picture frames, wallets, the entire men's accessories counters of some of the best department stores in the city found their way into Harry's cluttered nightstand. Although they all previously tended to blur into a single accessorized lump, Harry is now conscious of each item's talismanic value and is reluctant to let any of them go.

He gently drapes the limp, wounded tie across the sink. He removes Tony Glide's replacement from its trifold plastic wrap and hangs it around his neck. No Windsors or half-Windsors for Harry. He's always suspected that his smallish face and indistinct features disappear against the chunk of the Windsor knot. Instead, he does his best to execute the familiar four-in-hand: the broad end passed over the shorter end, looped through; a tight, small, unprepossessing knot. But to his surprise he fumbles the knot, and only this disruption in a familiar pattern he's executed most mornings of his adult life alerts him to the fact that his hands are shaking. With detached fascination, he watches the tremulous dance at the end of his arms. He clasps the rim of the washbasin to steady himself.

Harry turns his back to the mirror and leans against the basin, going to great lengths to avoid making eye contact with himself. He can't bear the prospect of the face he knows all too well in all its ordinariness. A goatee that's begun to give up flecks of gray hiding a weak chin, providing the illusion of cheekbones. Cool gray eyes beneath a loose tangle of hair that's probably longer than is fashionable for his age or appropriate for his profession. The most obvious blemish, at least to Harry's eyes, are his lips—thin and drawn tight, even when he's relaxed or amused. He's always felt they make him look untrustworthy. Although over six feet tall and thin (but for an unfortunate marsupial paunch), Harry's never possessed anything that might be confused with grace. His movements are always awkward and tentative, and he wears his clothes—even today's resplendent gray suit—as though they were dropped onto his body from overhead.

He raises his hands from the basin and checks for tremors. Caltech seismographs twitch in agitation. *Shit.* He tries the four-in-hand again, without success.

"You never could tie a knot for shit, Harry."

Max the podiatrist steps over to Harry, turns him around, stands behind him, and, like a father teaching his son, begins to assemble the four-in-hand.

"No Windsors, Max."

"I know, I know. I never understood why you liked this *farkakta* knot so much."

21

The men stand in silence as Max expertly weaves the knot. Although at seventy Max is nearly twenty-five years Harry's senior, he's been his closest friend since they met during Harry's intern days. Silences mark their odd friendship, dotted with Tourette's-like bursts of obscenity from Max, so it's not unusual that they now stand wordlessly in the bathroom. As Max busies himself with the tie, Harry is surprised to find his thoughts drifting back to Molly. The sheer inappropriateness startles him, and he promptly banishes her from his mind—but not without lingering for a moment on the detailed latticework of the tattooed wings he'd glimpsed at the base of her bare back.

Max turns Harry to face him, to consider his finished product.

"It'll do."

"Thanks, Max."

Max waves away the thanks and picks up the damaged tie, scrutinizing it. "What's this, ketchup?"

"Jam."

"Jam? How the fuck?"

It's Harry's turn to wave Max away. "Long story."

Max nods. "How you holding up, kid?"

Harry shrugs from somewhere deep within his suit. "Okay, I guess."

"You guess?"

Harry nods and hesitates. It's clear to Max that something is troubling his friend, but their history is built on accommodation, on staying out of each other's way, and so Max waits until Harry is ready.

At length, Harry asks a question. "Did you . . . How did . . . What was it like when Doris died?"

Max can't conceal his surprise at the personal question. In the time-honored male tradition, their friendship has been long on jocularity and short on reflection. Max considers a moment before replying.

"Um, how did I feel? If I couldn't smash it with my bare hands, I better fucking be able to drink it is how I felt."

Harry nods. He would like nothing more than to tell Max how terrified he is by the lacuna in his heart where grief and memory and sorrow should be, but which is instead filled by inappropriate thoughts and un-accountable behavior. That he can't understand this blank nothingness that suffuses him and actually has him beginning to fear for his mortal soul (insofar as he understands the idea). He's sure something is wrong with him, something is broken, and he worries it's beyond repair.

"Yeah. I'd like to smash something, too," he says unconvincingly, when all he really wants is to *want* to smash something.

Four-in-handed Harry assumes his place of mourning in front of the casket. He lowers his head with appropriate solemnity as he reflects on his exchange with Max. He envies Max's response to the loss of his beloved Doris—a former patient whose large, knuckled toes Max found eternally attractive. Harry wishes that he could borrow it some-how, use it as a template to make up for his shortcomings. As he glances around the room, Harry suspects, a little defensively, that his lack of the visible markers of grief is beginning to discomfit his fellow mourners. It's true that no river of tears has flowed down Harry's cheeks. But who's to say what that means? For all anyone knows, Harry might be one of those rock-ribbed introverts, his placid façade covering a tem-pest of explosive feelings.

Harry's proposed self-portrait fails to convince even himself. Where grief should reside, there's neither introversion nor explosion. The only emotional response Harry can divine within himself is this incipient terror. But before he can probe its nature, Harry is disrupted from his thoughts by the sniffling presence at his side of Beatrice.

"Oh, Harry . . . I'm so . . ." She dissolves into tears on Harry's shoulder as he embraces her stiffly. She'd worked with Anna in the In-ternational Mergers department before Anna left the firm. Harry's al-ways felt uneasy around Beatrice, a severe case at the best of times, and this is far from the best of times. She reminds Harry of Mrs. Girardi, his fourth-grade teacher, a squat, wide, tightly bunned bulwark against pleasure in any form. Decked out in mourning garb, she's a bleaker, more forbidding figure than usual, Torquemada in tights. But there's something pitiful about her today, something that calls out for comfort, and Harry obliges, lest he impair her mourning in any way. He settles for patting her shoulder kindly and whispering in her ear, "Anna thought the world of you." Beatrice nods thankfully and, with a kiss to his cheek, trundles off.

Harry can't help but feel inadequate as her ostentatiously moist display of grief seems to underscore his own emotional parsimony. But it gives him an idea. Perhaps he can latch onto and absorb a bit of the free-floating grief in the room and jump-start his own stalled engine. He decides to test his theory on Aaron and Mia, who now approach him tentatively. He's probably exchanged no more than a hundred words with Aaron before this moment—Aaron's wife, Mia, a scarlet-haired, black-lipsticked wraith who was Anna's assistant, is the bit of connecting tissue there. Aaron's a big, dumb, slow-moving iceberg of a man, in whom Harry doesn't expect to find much useful emotion on display. He's surprised, however, as the couple gets close enough for him to note Aaron's red-rimmed eyes.

"Harry," Mia whispers, and throws her arms around him. He can feel her slender, birdlike frame vibrating with sorrow against him. He puts one arm around her and takes Aaron's extended hand with the other.

"She was a great lady," Aaron mutters huskily. "A great lady." Mia's vibrations amplify at Aaron's words, and Harry stands there blankly, stricken. He expected Mia to be distraught, but Aaron? Harry stares as the big man shakes his head slowly from side to side.

"She was the best, Harry. It's not fair. It's not fair," he mumbles. Mia puts a consoling arm around her husband and moves him away, but Harry wants to stop them. He wants to slice them open, somehow, and extract their memories, their pain, their loss, and transplant them within himself. It's maddening to him, impossible to understand. He's not a vacant person, he certainly loved his wife. So why can everyone in the room give voice to their loss except him? A certain level of numbness is understandable, but what is this blank, thrumming terror that blocks his every effort to summon up Anna's essence?

Harry shuffles slowly back to his spot before the casket, unable to bear any more grief that's not his own. He stands ramrod straight, rivulets of sweat dripping down his neck, along his spine, collecting at its base. Muscles in his back and thighs begin to ache from holding this mourning pose. The thudding roar of blood pounding in his ears casts an acoustic blanket over the room's choked sobs. As Harry's eyes flit from face to face, envy and self-pity pool within. There're Regina and Howard, his normally invisible neighbors, eyes downcast, cheeks damp; Deb from Anna's on-again, off-again Italian class, clutching herself, rocking back and forth quietly; Alex, Emily, Steven, and all the rest of them, communing with their memories of Anna: school memories, work memories, travel and leisure memories, golf memories, cycling memories, all intact with their suffering. How he would like to take his place among them, wallowing in loss instead of standing here, empty and terrified, his wan attempt at transference a miserable failure.

Harry sighs, trying to come to terms with this dislocation. With no sense of time or place, no freight of memory, he's nothing more than a sweating man in a suit at a funeral. He shrugs inwardly. Perhaps that's all he's meant to be. What do they all want from me anyway?

What do you want from me, Anna?

He looks up to find Tony Glide's eyes darting discreetly away. Harry's reminded of all his years of covert girl-watching, appraising glances timed to avoid eye contact. Okay, Glide, I'm onto you. Harry lowers his eyes, gives Glide a moment to return his attention to him, then flings his eyeballs in Glide's direction. Nothing. Glide is consumed with an examination of the flower arrangements. Smooth. A slippery customer. Harry turns away again, this time toward the cross on the wall, suggesting prayer or religious devotions of some sort. A longer interval and then a whip-crack turn of the head. Success. A busted Glide again directs his eyeline elsewhere, a moment too late.

Why the interest? Harry wonders. What's he watching for? And then an idea takes hold of Harry: *the pillows. The motherfucker is jamming me up on the pillows.* Somehow, Harry has achieved absolute certainty that Anna is lying in an unpillowed casket, and the thought crowds out his unease, his anger, his terror, everything. He glances up at Glide, an animal flare behind his irises. Glide must smell this new, feral aura because he gulps nervously, moves away, and busies himself arranging chairs. You son of a bitch. Beige Quietude my ass.

Harry's entire being collapses into a single idea: open the casket. He won't rest, he *can't* rest, until he's pried open the lid and looked inside and beheld a sea of Beige Quietude with his own eyes. How to accomplish this? Harry considers that he has three options: clear the room; wait until later; or open it now, in plain view. The proximity of the mourners, far enough to grant Harry his privacy but close enough to convey their intimacy, precludes an inelegant lunge to the lid, even as the drawbacks of this approach are clear—this is an attack without an exit strategy. Finally, inspiration strikes.

Harry approaches the casket reverently and gently lowers himself to his knees before it. Assuming the position of many a nighttime prayer against the foot of the bed, he clasps his hands, leans them against the lid of the casket, and bows his head, thumbs pressed to forehead. A surreptitious glance to the left and to the right suggests that the gambit is working. Mourners have given him a respectful distance. Harry continues in faux prayer for a moment to allow the novelty of the view to wear off, for attentions to wander away from him. After a decent interval, his right hand disappears from view while his left maintains its mock-prayer position. Angling his body to cover his movements, he finds the lip of the lid and wedges the heel of his palm against it. His body strains as he tries to lift the lid. Nothing. The Horizon semiprecious bronze is one heavy mother. Harry feels the flush of the effort reddening his cheeks and ears, this heaving breath and trembling effort mistaken by the others as the overdue tidal wave of grief. Harry regroups and makes another lunge, his body straining like an Olympic weight lifter. A ray of success breaks the clouds and the casket lid squeaks promisingly. Harry's face gleams with sweat as he pushes along, Herculean, unwilling to surrender. Avoiding looking at Anna, he feels a wave of relief at the first flash of Beige Quietude—

"Harry?"

Startled, Harry drops the lid shut and looks up into the bewildered eyes of Claire, Anna's older sister. "What . . . are you doing?" she asks in a hushed, wounded whisper. Harry clears his throat with embarrassment and tries to rise nonchalantly but can't, his nonchalance undermined by the fact of his necktie stuck underneath the casket lid. Held beyond death do us part to his departing wife. Dignity being well out of the question, he sighs and yanks the tie free.

"It's their tie," Harry says, by way of helpless explanation. "The funeral parlor gave it to me."

He winces, in anticipation of Claire's reaction—Claire, ever the more voluble of the Weldt sisters—but there's a vacancy in her eyes, her normally unruly spark absent. Harry suspects she's on a mild sedative, and it's left her diminished in every way. He feels a surge of pity for her, Claire the second-rater, Claire the Other Sister, Claire the thrice-divorced depressive. Claire the medicated and helpless. She's all that remains of the Weldt family, and he can't imagine how she'll function without her sister. He extends a consoling arm toward her and is startled when she flinches, pulling herself just beyond his reach. She clutches herself, eyes downcast as she shivers.

This is a shock to Harry. He and Claire have always been close, bound by their shared rejection by the elder Weldts, her mother's in particular. Over the years they'd formed a bulwark of commiseration against her reproaches, flailing in the long shadow of Anna's seemingly effortless perfection. A harmless conspiracy of two, the charter members of the Fuck-up Club, as Claire liked to joke. But there's nothing binding them today.

"What happened, Harry?" There's a robotic flatness to her voice, a complete lack of inflection.

"You know what happened," Harry answers, as softly and as kindly as he can. "Her heart . . ."

Claire hangs there, unmoving for a moment, as if the effort of processing his answer consumes all of her available energy. Presently, she moves slightly, raising her head.

"Why, Harry? I don't understand."

"I don't know, Claire. Everyone missed it. She was so fit and . . ."

She shakes her head slowly. "Why, Harry?"

Claire's uninflected relentlessness is starting to unnerve him. And it begins to dawn that it's a different *why* after which she's inquiring.

"Why, Harry? Why was she there?" Her eyes imploring, uncomprehending.

Harry's mouth dries. He says nothing.

"Why, Harry? Why *plastic surgery*? I don't understand. Please. Explain to me." Claire's tone isn't insistent or demanding so much as plaintive, not much more than a whisper, and Harry would like nothing more than to set her at ease, even as he knows he can't tell her what she most needs to know. Harry wants to say something, anything, wants to speak up but can't. The words pile up, backlogged in his throat like cars on a rain-slicked freeway. It's a strange, enervating paralysis that suffuses him—thoughts careen and collide in his brain but no amount of effort can move his lips. Claire reads this helplessness as vacancy and thunderclouds of tears gather darkly in her eyes.

"Did you do something to her, Harry? Please . . . Help me . . . I don't understand. Harry, *I don't understand* . . . "

Uncomfortable mourners edge away from the tableau, easing toward the safety of the exits.

"Claire . . . I'm sorry. I am." The empty words pop like lightbulbs falling to the floor.

Claire lowers her head again, and now the storm hits and the sobs shake Claire's body much as Harry imagines the defibrillators shook his dying wife. Glide materializes at her side, his mortician's ESP infallible, and he expertly guides her from the room, away from Harry, away

28

from the departing mourners, away from the Horizon semiprecious bronze. Her mumbles drift back into Harry's buzzing ear . . . "I don't understand . . . I don't understand . . ."

Harry looks around the room, which is now empty except for Max. Harry finds his voice at last.

"Jesus, Max, she doesn't think this is my fault, does she?"

Max looks at his friend with an infinite sorrow, pats Harry's arm, and heads out of the room, leaving Harry alone with Anna to experience a distantly familiar sense of falling away, something he's felt once before, as though the structures beneath his feet that hold him in place have dissolved and given way. As he feels himself plummeting into a bottomless fissure, he flails desperately for help, and his slippery grip fastens once again on Edmond Dantès. How many years did he spend tunneling his way to freedom—ten, twelve, more? Now Harry sees he's going to have to do the same thing, to find a way to dig himself to freedom. Wrongly accused, Dantès escaped. Harry, too, will escape since these charges are equally specious. Why would anyone blame him? What legitimate reasons could any reasonable person have for thinking this was Harry's fault?

After all, he wasn't the surgeon, wasn't advising, wasn't present in any way. All he got was a phone call. Could he please come down to the hospital right away? The details of those first hours and everything that followed are hazy. It's been only a week since the call—they'd had to wait for an autopsy—but Harry lost his grip on recall within days. The shards that still catch and reflect memory include these:

Harry left his office within minutes of receiving the call, not without some foreboding but far short of dread. As the Jaguar drove itself to the hospital, he tried to think about the possibilities—the procedure was simple enough, done daily in this city. The doctor was an experienced hand, had come with the best references and the mightiest fees. Perhaps there was a financial question. Something to do with insurance?

At the hospital, Harry was guided into a quiet carpeted room. The carpet sparked the first hint of dread. Tile and linoleum are the working surfaces of hospitals. Carpeting is something different. Bad news. Before Harry could run away with himself, Dr. Gustav Couteau stepped into the room. Harry hated him immediately, all six-foot-four-square-shouldered-salt-and-pepper-bearded-soap-opera-doctor-babe-magnet of him. Harry felt himself shrinking, diminishing rapidly in Dr. Couteau's formidable shadow. Some desperate face-saving measure was called for.

"Capped teeth?" blurted Harry.

"I beg your pardon?" asked Dr. Couteau, a trace of a European accent nibbling at his *r*'s.

"Are your teeth capped?" Harry repeated, losing steam. Nothing derailed him as effectively as direct incomprehension.

Dr. Couteau forced a sad smile and spoke with practiced kindness. "You have a sense of humor, Mr. Rent. That's good, I hope it will provide comfort to you in difficult times ahead."

Played out, face lost, Harry waited for more.

"I am so very sorry to have to inform you that your wife died an hour ago."

(The moment of closing.)

"I can assure you she did not suffer. She was under general anesthesia at the time."

(The spaceman snipped off from his EVA. The child at the mall staring at a sea of adult kneecaps he doesn't recognize. A one-man Donner party.)

"She appears to have suffered massive cardiac arrest, which is surprising for a woman of her age. Were you aware of any existing conditions?"

Harry shook his head dully. "Conditions. No."

More questions followed but Harry remembers none of them. Nor does he remember how he found his way home. Nor does he remember the calls, the visits, the outpouring that followed in those first days. He doesn't remember the bottles of vodka consumed, the appointments missed, the cleaning lady's look of horror at the piles of soiled clothes and filthy dishes in the sink. Above all, he doesn't remember the suffocating guilt and shame, the almost unbearable sense of dislocation, the sheer unimaginable prospect of continuing with daily life. It's as though, the moment he'd crossed the threshold into a world without Anna, he no longer had use for memory and opted to do without. Because he remembers almost nothing at all until the moment he pulled his resplendent gray suit from his closet and took a seat in Molly's section of Café Retro. And although he welcomes it, it's not a forgetfulness he trusts. It's a void that fails to convince.

Three

In which our hero loses something of great value

SEVEN YEARS INTO Harry Rent's marriage to Anna Weldt, Harry has embraced the consolations of routine. The agency knows what kind of girl he likes—young but not too; buxom but not too; blond but not too. The girls working the phones call him the Not Too Guy. Harry doesn't know this, of course, but if he did, he'd probably be impressed with its economical correctness. He's never been one to fight the truth, and he'd see his truth summed up with elegant simplicity. The Not Too Guy, indeed.

The other details of the script are similarly unvarying. He always meets the girl in the same hotel (but not the same room—Harry's not fetishistic about it). He always takes his appointments at the same day and time—Thursdays at two thirty. (It's the day Anna and Claire have their weekly lunch, so he's unlikely to have to account for his absence.) He always removes his wedding ring. (He tells himself it's out of respect for Anna, but the truth is he's terrified of being identified as a potential blackmail target.) He applies himself diligently if without passion to the same position for the same amount of time, then takes the same route back to the office, feeling guilty and despising himself all the way back. Promising himself "never again," even as he already feels a frisson of arousal toward the following week.

Today it's Anastasia, an Eastern European—he can't quite place her; Poland probably, but there's been an influx of Serbian girls lately. Maybe even Ukraine. He's more perturbed by her name—much too close to *Anna* for his comfort.

"Um, do you mind if I call you something else?"

"You call me anything you want, baby," she says with appropriate fecundity. "I undress?"

Harry nods nervously. The nervousness is another recurring feature of these visits. He's lost count of how many squalid little lays like this one he's partaken in—dozens, probably—and yet each time, his heart races, his hands shake, and he's sweaty and pale. He remains eternally convinced that this is the one that goes wrong. This is the time she's actually a police plant. It's only once the money is handed over and the doors haven't crashed open that he'll begin to relax.

"Donation's on the pillow," he mumbles. She smiles and scoops it into her purse, then disappears into the bathroom.

Harry waits, on edge. Once an appropriate interval has passed, he sighs and sits down on the bed, loosening his tie. He can hear Anastasia preparing in the bathroom and marvels at the amount of time these women spend getting ready. Not women in general—Harry kind of understands that one, or at least accepts it as going with the territory. *These* women. The fact is, she's not required to do much more than strip down to lingerie, perhaps apply a dab of perfume to cover the lingering scent of the last customer, and then down to the transaction we go. But for some unfathomable reason they spend much more time stripping down than they do dressing to leave. Getting out of the room is a task usually performed in the skinny side of a minute.

Now, before Harry can get too far down the road analyzing the number of steps involved in each action, undressing and re-dressing, Anastasia emerges, ready to go to work. She's wearing the Standard Getup, something straight out of Introduction to Hooking 101—push-up bra, garters, heels. Unimaginative but effective, at least for Harry, who's feeling a mild stirring. He focuses on her impossibly deep cleavage, created by clashing mounds of silicone, rather than the incipient signs of cottage cheese making tentative inroads across her thighs. Too many pierogies, he suspects.

She straddles his lap, strategically presenting her breasts at mouth level.

"So you tell me how you like it."

Harry nods. "This is fine." He tentatively puts his arms around her waist and is about to brush his lips against the taut flesh across her bosom when there is a knock at the door. Harry flies into the air as though the bed has just kicked him off. Anastasia bounces with a resplendent thud against the armoire and falls to the floor, sprawled in scattershot repose. The words *What the fuck?* make a valiant effort to leave her throat but are stopped by Harry's terrified finger to the lips.

"Who is it?" asks Harry, his voice skittering across octaves. There's no reply, so he tiptoes to the door and peeps through the peephole. He's disconcerted to find that he can see nothing—something appears to be stopping up the eyepiece. A strand of irritation invades his terror. "Who's there?" he insists, with no greater success. His mind channel surfs the possibilities: prankster children staying in the hotel? Anastasia's jealous beau or pimp? (Do they actually have pimps anymore? Harry wonders, but stops himself with an uncharacteristic display of self-control.) Perhaps Podiatrist Max has followed him to his love lair? Or— the worst of many unlikely scenarios—it's Anna? Something resonates with him on that one, and for no good reason whatsoever, the notion that Anna has found him out settles on his heart like a lead cloud.

In the time it's taken him to tango through this thicket, Anastasia has helped herself to her feet and brusquely shoved Harry from the peephole. She squints through the opening.

"Is nobody."

"What?" Harry looks for himself. She's right. Is nobody. "Probably just some kids," he mutters. They return to the bed, but whatever trace amounts of eroticism might have been in evidence at the outset have quit the premises. Anastasia presents herself mechanically to Harry, who feels like a man holding a bouquet of dead flowers. She is struggling with his resistant zipper between her teeth when there's another knock at the door. This time—the memory of her free fall still fresh—Anastasia leaps away from Harry before he has a chance to rise. But Harry surprises her and stays rooted to the bed.

"Who is it?" he asks tentatively, as though trying on the question for size. There's no answer. Harry shudders, at a loss. He's so far off the chart of his routine that he can't fathom a next move. He turns his pale visage to Anastasia, seeking counsel and comfort. She rolls her eyes and, as she has many times before, reminds herself just what sort of man pays for sex. She sighs and makes for the door, but before she can reach it, an unexpectedly fleet-footed Harry is interposed between them. He looks through the eyepiece, to be greeted once again by the same black nothingness, only this time he's momentarily convinced he can make out the outline of a thumb—as though someone has blocked the eyepiece with a finger. This sets Harry's heart clattering.

"There's someone out there," he hisses to Anastasia.

Anastasia is unperturbed. "So? We in here." She'd be filing her nails if she had an emery board. Harry considers the inarguable logic of this for a moment. A dead bolt and a well-stocked minibar can probably hold off all manner of unexpected guests. For a moment his mind skips ahead and it's Harry Siege, Day 12. The hotel room has grown rank, filled with soiled sheets and damp towels. The gutted minibar's door swings open forlornly. The chips are gone and the M&M's have been apportioned out via color coding—reds on Monday, yellows on Tuesday. Save the greens for celebrating when it's over. Supporters line the balconies across the street, FREE HARRY banners flapping in the wind even as the Evil Finger continues to block the peephole. The adventure unfolds in Harry's fevered brain and he's drifting with it—

Another knock. Startled back to the present, Harry surprises himself by whipping the door open in irritation to find two uniformed police officers, the hand of the Short, Square, Bullheaded One hanging in space where the eyepiece was located just a second earlier. The bolt of annoyance that fueled this brave if wrongheaded gesture dissipates at once. Harry feels his knees go gummy. His lunch starts edging its way back into his esophagus. He grabs the doorframe for support.

"Can I help you?" he asks with as much dignity as the situation allows.

"Why don't you step inside, Mr. Rent?" This is from Tall, Gaunt One, and Harry can't help but think of Picasso's sketch of Don Quixote and Sancho Panza. Repressing a potentially catastrophic urge to laugh, Harry nods and backs into the room. They follow him and Sancho closes the door behind him.

"The hotel management does not appreciate this kind of activity," Quixote informs him. "ID please?"

Harry's trembling fingers can barely extract his driver's license from his wallet as he reflects on this odd assertion. The hotel management has been allowing this activity for months, he thinks. In fact, their doorman put me in touch with the agency, he remembers. However, it occurs to him that this is not his ideal defense, and it may be the wrong moment to deconstruct the hotel's unexpected volte-face in matters of consensual adult activities. He hands his license to Sancho, who takes it and disappears, talking into his radio.

"Officer, listen, I'm awfully sorry. I've never done this sort of thing before." Harry shakes his head. "It was a stupid thing to do." He's been in enough traffic stops to know the formal steps of the Attitude Test. Be helpful and deferential, express contrition, and most officers will leave you alone. He knows that the lives of low-ranking fuzz like these are ruled by paperwork, and arresting him would constitute more typing than he's worth. Provided he hasn't drawn a cop with a mean streak, things should go his way.

And indeed, Quixote seems to be buying Harry's patter, recognizing his appropriate if workmanlike rendering of the Abject Collar. Sancho hands him back his license—no priors for Harry. He's a model citizen and he knows it. And although it's likely to save his ass here, he's aware of a vague irritation. Once again, he's the catch who gets thrown back in. Still, it looks as though Harry may get through this one, when the pair turn their attention to Anastasia.

She's located her nail file and now has an activity to match her mien—bored, impatient. Harry begins to perspire gently, wondering if they've heard of the Attitude Test in Poland or Serbia or Ukraine or wherever. I mean, we're talking the land of Stalin and the KGB, he thinks. Sure, she's too young to remember any of that, but there must be some primeval bit of genetic coding in all Eastern European immigrants that tells them how to behave before authority figures.

If there is, it's a recessive trait in Anastasia, who counters Sancho's request for ID with a tart "We did nothing. We sit. We talk." She indicates her flimsy garment. "I give him little show. Not against the law."

"Ma'am, please just show us some ID."

"Are you arrest me?"

"We can arrange that, if you like."

Harry can't believe his ears. He's paid this woman four hundred dollars to fuck him but this is not what he had in mind.

"Jesus," he says to her, "they're being nice. Just show him your ID."

She snorts, dismissing Harry thoroughly, permanently, absolutely. She turns on Quixote.

"This free country, no? If I want show sad, lonely man my titties, why you care?"

Harry's head sinks into his hands. He's already resigned to his arrest and wondering whom he can call to get him out. He's got to find someone who has sufficient means to post his bail but who will keep his secret. Now, at the thought of a night in jail—impossible to explain to Anna—he loses it.

"*Jesus, you idiot!* Just show him your damn ID! What's the matter with you?!" He sits down on the bed, trembling. He turns to the officers. "I'm sorry, guys. She has nothing to do with me."

Quixote and Sancho take in the scene for a moment—the trembling john, the defiant hooker—and do a quick bit of calculus based on the law of diminishing returns. Quixote addresses Harry.

"We'll let you off with a warning this time. Next time, rent some porn, okay?"

Harry nods gratefully. Sancho turns to Anastasia and tosses her clothes to her. "Get dressed, and get lost." They watch as she wriggles hurriedly into her skirt, garters carelessly flapping on the outside like streamers on a Chinese parade float. Hurling a string of Slavic invective, she storms out of the room, past a few curious noses protruding from adjacent rooms, and is gone in a puff of cheap perfume. The officers appraise Harry with equal parts scorn and pity as they close the door behind themselves.

It's in the bathroom, after he cleans the last of the vomit from his collar, that Harry begins to weep.

And it's as he's finishing up the last Scotch in the minibar that he notices he can't find his wedding ring.

Harry fiddles nervously with his naked ring finger as the sounds of excavation drift up from behind the counter. A colony of eggshell ring boxes and packing materials accrues piece by piece on the glass counter, passed overhead by a tiny, wizened hand.

"I remember that one. Very nice model. Sold a bunch. Too bad discontinue."

At length, Mai Lin Goldberg sighs and emerges from behind the counter. A tiny Chinese woman of sixty-seven, Mai Lin changed her name to Goldberg a dozen years back in a misguided attempt to secure "street cred" in the jewelry district. And although she didn't fool any of her peers (her sketchy knowledge of the Torah was a source of much unintended mirth), it had an effect on her clientele. "People want Jewish jeweler," she would shrug by way of explanation. "Just like doctor. I do for customers. Make the goyim feel better." Within a week of the name change, sales doubled. The photo of the absent Mr. Goldberg that she kept in the ornate, silver-plated *Birkat Habayit* frame was actually a picture of the Rebbe Avram Moskowitz, clipped from an old issue of the *Queens Jewish Bulletin*.

Harry and Anna have been loyal customers for years, so Mai Lin's gone the extra mile in her search, and it's with what appears to be genuine disappointment that she comes up empty. "Sorry," she says, shaking her head. "No more."

Harry grinds his teeth and holds back tears of anger as he kicks himself for this rare, unaccountable burst of individuality. If only he'd opted for the standard-issue gold or platinum band, he'd have been home hours ago. Instead, having been seduced by the Everhappy Eterna Comfort Band™—a gaudy assemblage of gold and platinum weave with diamonds and "Etruscan-inspired engravings"—Harry has spent the last four hours standing before a variety of counters and jewelers, attempting to describe the missing ring to an assortment of shrugs and shaking heads.

"Never heard of it."

"Might have had something like that last year. Didn't sell."

"I need a better description—that could be anything."

The worst ones, though, were those who thought they had it.

"Sure. I know the one. Gimme a sec."

The jeweler would reappear with his offering, glittering against a black felt pillow, assuming his best courtier pose. Harry's heart would climb in anticipation, then belly flop back to earth at the sight of the thing. A sad shake of the head and he'd turn to leave.

"Wait! I can give it to you for a song."

He'd done everything he could to avoid visiting the family jeweler. He'd even considered calling Claire for help, as she was well placed to sympathize with his self-made troubles and had come to his rescue on previous occasions. But the particulars of this problem made her an unlikely ally, and as the afternoon ran out, it became clear to Harry that the call to Mai Lin could not be avoided. So he planned his story and hoped he could rely on her discretion. He wasn't disappointed. Mai Lin Goldberg had seen it all.

"It slipped off while I was scrubbing the toilet," Harry had explained, wondering if his pale, sweaty face was betraying him. "It was just an accident, but Anna's superstitious, you know. It would really upset her if she knew I lost it."

Mai Lin nodded comfortingly and patted his arm for assurance. "We find you ring," she said with a conspiratorial grin. And for the first time all day, Harry had felt reassured, had even begun to relax. Until this final, catastrophic shrug of defeat.

"I sure I had . . . ," Mai Lin says to the air, performing a mental inventory of possible hiding places. She sighs, disappointed. "I make you copy—take . . ." She counts days on her fingertips. "Six days."

Harry slumps onto the stool, and now despite his best efforts, the tears begin to collect. He is going to be found out and there's nothing he can do to save himself. He looks around the bustling mart at deals being struck at the other counters: young couples selecting engagement rings as they struggle to match low budgets with high hopes; grandmothers selling off their courtships, converting memories to food and fuel; indignant divorcées learning the truth about the quality of their testaments; beginnings mingling with endings, hope and desperation all around him, and he can't believe there's no hope to be had for him. But just as he lowers his head into his hands with a whispered "Shit," Mai Lin springs to life.

"Wait a minute! Have old display. Back in stock. Maybe—no promise. Wait here."

Harry nods glumly as Mai Lin goes off to have a smoke in the stockroom, a copy of the Everhappy Eterna Comfort Band™ safe in her pocket where she tucked it within seconds of receiving Harry's frantic phone call. As she smokes, she remembers a saying her mother told her: "You don't boil a frog by throwing it into a boiling pot; it will jump right out. Put it in a pot of cold water and slowly turn up the heat."

When she returns, Harry fails to notice that she smells of stale cigarette smoke. He fails to notice that she's been gone a relatively short time, and that not a hair is out of place—in short, there are no visible signs of an exhaustive search through a stockroom. He regards her indifferently. For the first time today, he has not allowed himself to feel any hope, so it's a near body blow when Mai Lin reverently places the Everhappy Eterna Comfort Band™ on the counter, gleaming against a wine-dark sea of felt.

Harry doesn't leap or shout out.

Harry doesn't burst into tears.

What Harry does instead is this:

Harry faints.

Harry opens his eyes to find a dozen bearded men standing over him. He blinks his eyes clear and warily nods hello. A relieved smile is relayed across a dozen pairs of lips like a stadium wave. The men promptly disperse like a football huddle. Mai Lin helps a nonplussed Harry to his feet.

"They afraid you sue. But you okay. Yes?"

Harry nods uncertainly but now he's remembered the ring.

"My ring! You have it!"

"Yes. Good news, no?"

Impulsively, Harry hugs the little woman. "Great news!" Mai Lin wriggles free and returns to the business end of the counter. As Harry pulls out his wallet, Mai Lin prepares an invoice that is triple the original cost of the ring. She presents it to Harry, who is startled by the number of zeros he's looking at. Harry, after all, is unaccustomed to being at the mercy of another. Although he's something of a naïf in the ways of the world, he's generally managed to keep himself out of the clutches of those who would do him harm. Until now.

"Um. Wow. That's a little expensive, isn't it?"

Mai Lin does a credible impersonation of surprise, takes the bill from Harry, and glances it over. "Looks okay." She hands him back the invoice and smiles.

"Well, it's almost—what?—triple what I paid for it."

Mai Lin offers up an understanding, sympathetic head bob. "Inflation. That was eight years ago."

"*Three hundred percent* inflation?!" And then, ever so slowly, it dawns on Harry. He's being worked. She has him in the crosshairs, and the fact that he deserves it, that he's earned it, doesn't make it go down any easier. He scowls as he hands over his credit card.

"Shame on you, Mrs. Goldberg. I thought we were friends."

These will turn out to be the most expensive words Harry has ever uttered.

Mai Lin looks at Harry with disbelief and swipes the Everhappy Eterna Comfort Band™ from view. Harry, clearly, doesn't know the rules of the game. You take your hiding with good grace. You never—*ever*—put your benefactor on the spot. It's messy, ugly, it wounds the pride. And what is a Chinese Goldberg, after all, if she hasn't got her pride?

"Shame on me? Shame on you, Mr. Rent." She does a mincing impersonation of Harry. " 'I lost in toilet.' That some kind of bullshit. I bet I know where you lose it. Shame on *you*." She drops the ring into her pocket. "Not for sale."

It's a riveting performance, scaling heights of indignation that she doesn't really feel, even as she totals up the mental adding-machine tape—here's a chance to move those horrible platinum eggplant earrings and that glittering monstrosity of a charm bracelet that has been languishing in the case since last holiday season. Before Harry finishes his round of abject mea culpas he's saddled with an additional five figures' worth of inventory that Mai Lin had despaired of ever moving. "Make nice gift for Anna," she says as she wraps the numerous purchases. Harry's been flayed and she's done an expert job, admirable in

its efficiency, leaving little more than bone and tendon to hold him together. But as he leaves burdened with his loot, the Everhappy Eterna
Comfort Band™ is safely restored to its rightful place, albeit loosely, the
ring being a half size too large and the remains of the day being too
short to size it properly. For the entire drive home, he rubs his thumb
reassuringly across the bottom of the band, the metallurgical equivalent
of pinching himself to make sure he's awake.

Harry is awake. He's done it. Never again, he swears to himself,
believing that this time he means it.

And now here's Harry, irrepressible, nosing his car through the curves
and up the hills as he winds his way above the smog and toward home.
He knows the road intimately and normally only applies part of his
brain to the drive; it's become reflexive after all these years. But every
now and then, when Harry finds himself feeling particularly alive or
vital, brimming with an odd and uncharacteristic flash of purpose, he
speeds through the curves, as he's doing now. He's pleased that the ordeal of the ring is behind him, he's free, safe and clear, and now he begins to look forward to getting home and seeing Anna.

He's focused on the road, the power of the vehicle moving through
his fingertips resting on the steering wheel. He slows a bit as he reaches
the crest of a hill—there's a sharp switchback on the other side—and
once he sees the empty road before him, he guns it through the curve
and down the hill. The drop in his stomach is a pleasant sensation, re-
minding him of countless childhood roller coasters, and he grins contentedly. Harry is at the wheel, and he knows the way. It's as he likes it.
All is well.

He pulls into the driveway and stops the car. Home.

The house is a white box on stilts with lots of windows, perched on a
hillside. Ocean views on the rare clear days. The nearest neighbor a good
hundred yards away on every side. Not Harry's taste, but taste is never an
issue with Harry. He can't be said to have taste, so much as a clot of
loosely held leanings, any one of which can quickly be negotiated away

and are, almost daily. He'd leaned, for example, toward a convertible Saab, but Anna suggested that the Jaguar might paint a more comforting picture for his patients, and in the end Harry didn't feel strongly enough about either car to object. In the case of the house, Anna was paying for it, so Anna did the choosing.

Now he closes the door of the Jaguar and bounds toward the steps, ungainly and energetic, like a poorly trained Labrador puppy. As he grabs the door handle, he's reminded of the day's contretemps—the loose ring clinks against the doorknob and slides along his finger—but the unwelcome memory is swamped by more primal responses. Home. Safe. Wife. Good. Life. Yippee.

"Hello? Anyone home?"

Harry's voice bounces off the hardwood floors. The space is large, airy, and bright. The cool minimalist elegance has always left Harry feeling unsettled, as though a challenge has been issued to which he's failed to rise. His few, wan attempts to engage the space have all met with deafening indifference. The occasional stray personal touch or modification would eventually disappear, quietly relegated by Anna to a storage room downstairs, although Harry could never fully convince himself that the house itself hadn't swallowed up these mild assertions of self.

"Anna?"

There's no response. The bedroom is empty but her work clothes—a dark suit, a cream blouse—are draped over the back of her bedside chair. Harry heads out of the bedroom and across the dining room, then finally spots her sitting out on the balcony reading *Madame Bovary*.

He stops for a moment and regards her through the sliding glass door. Her dark hair is pulled back tightly in a ponytail, and he admires the strong line of her neck as her head hangs downward toward her book. She's always had regal lines—a strong jaw, angular cheekbones, a face with a pedigree, a pedigree that can leave Harry feeling diminished.

But at the moment he feels a surge of affection for his wife and expertly swats away that dark voice that berates him for his foolish extracurricular activities. I'm here now, aren't I? he thinks irritably. This is what counts. The rest is, well, it's an aberration. I'm done with it. Or it's done with me.

But the voice will not be stilled so easily. And as Harry stands there, the memory of Anastasia's head bobbing over his zipper flashes into his brain, and the affection is shattered by a sweaty wave of guilt, remorse, and shame. You're such a fool, he tells himself, heart pounding (with which voice, he's no longer sure). Whatever the shortcomings of your marriage, whatever uncertainties Anna has struggled with—and she *has* struggled, you know she has—whatever she may have done, you've watched her reproach herself for her judgments. Is this really the way you think she should be treated? You don't deserve her, Harry. You don't deserve shit.

"Harry, are you okay? You look awful."

Anna's voice snaps Harry out of his reverie. He finally notices his wife standing before him and smiles weakly.

"I'm fine. Hi."

He throws his arms around her and embraces her, holding her perhaps a bit more tightly than usual.

"Hey. What's the matter? You're pale. And you're soaked." She places a hand on his forehead. "Do you have a fever?"

Harry shakes his head. "No. I'm fine, really. Happy to see you."

She smiles at her husband. "I'm happy to see you, too. I was starting to get a little worried. It was getting late."

"Traffic was a nightmare," Harry answers, recovering himself gradually. Steadying. Calming down.

"Yeah, same here. I could have walked home across the hoods of all the stopped cars."

But Harry's not listening. There's something he finds he'd like to try to say. He steadies himself for what feels like a necessary revelation, something that's been building up and refuses to be contained any longer.

"Anna—"

"Wait." She turns and runs off. "Just a second. I almost forgot, I have a surprise for you." She says the last sentence from the bedroom, to where she's hurried off.

Whatever Harry is trying to say to Anna isn't going to come out in time and, knowing Harry, would probably have been insufficient if it had. He knows this and still he labors. "Anna, listen I—"

"Did we forget something today?" Anna asks from the bedroom.

This unnerves Harry, who lives in perpetual terror of missing important dates—anniversaries, birthdays, deaths. He does a frantic tear through his mental calendar but comes up empty. The nearest possibility is weeks away.

"I don't think so," he says uncertainly. "Claire's birthday isn't for—"

"No, silly," she says playfully. "Not a birthday." She hurries back to him, hiding something in her clenched fist. "You forgot your—"

The next word—*ring*—never makes it from her lips. Only now does she notice the Everhappy Eterna Comfort Band™ on Harry's finger. Like a time-lapse image of a flower blooming, her fingers open to reveal Harry's ring. She stares at Harry uncomprehendingly.

"Harry? I don't understand. You have two rings?"

Now his stomach is falling again, as it did in the car on the hill, but there's nothing pleasant about this sensation. He can feel the structure of his life falling away beneath his feet, he's dropping as though the floor beneath his feet has suddenly turned to the stuff of clouds.

Now Harry is outside himself. Watching himself watching himself watching. These are some of the things that pass through his mind:

One of the patterns visible in the wood of the dining room table looks strangely like Ringo Starr.

There's that mechanical pencil, still under the couch, where it rolled last summer.

The chipped paint on Anna's toenails. That her right big toe is slightly larger than her left.

The Everhappy Eterna Comfort Band™, slick with perspiration, is sliding off his finger.

He's hungry. And strangely in the mood for pepperoni pizza.

He can't remember what he had for dinner last night.

He still hasn't had the rattling sound in the Jaguar looked at.

"I don't understand." An insistent plea.

And reflexively, Harry's lips part with the beginnings of a lie. But something stops him, that same urge that nearly found voice moments earlier. He knows he could make up a story on the fly, something about mislaying the original and not wanting to worry Anna. But Harry has a sense that it's time, after far too long, to simply tell the truth. To take his lumps, come what may. To have what might well be the first honest moment in seven years of marriage, wherever it might lead him.

Being found out, that's not the worst part, Harry now realizes. The anger, the pain, all the things that will inevitably follow this moment, they're just the fallout. This is the worst moment, the flash point, the cataclysm. For as Harry holds the eyes of his wife, he sees confusion in them—genuine puzzlement—and this is the deepest blow: the realization that until this moment it could not possibly have occurred to her that he would lie to her. But, of course, she doesn't know about all the little lies that preceded this grand one, the painstaking edifice of deceit that's about to collapse. He has hurled a brick through her trust, and although he may spend the rest of his life collecting every last shard, massaging the creaky, fractured pane back into a whole, it will always be warped, irregular, distorting the views on both sides.

Four

In which our hero devises a plan

WHO LIVES HERE? Harry wonders, as he looks around his empty house.

The ruined tie from the funeral is jammed into his suit pocket as he hesitates, deflated, in the doorway. Dread holding him in place. The door stands open before him, this despite his lifelong terror and loathing of all forms of flying insects. (He remembers his irritation whenever Anna wandered into the house—often with her arms full of bags—and failed to close the door behind her. He'd leap up from whatever he was doing and race to the door to close it, hissing, "Bugs!") He's unusually aware of his heartbeat, of his shallow breathing, of the fine hairs on his forehead vibrating gently in the breeze. He's aware that he now owns this $2.8 million home on a beautiful Bel Air hillside free and clear. And he'd like nothing more than to close the door, get back into his car, and drive. Where doesn't matter. Anywhere. Not here.

The pressure of the pain in his side is nearly unbearable. His throat is so dry that it hurts to swallow. How can a house seem so empty? So malign? Then he notices the blinking light on the answering machine. Seven messages. Duty calls. Harry steps inside and closes the front door, comfortingly returned to autopilot. For the moment, however, he avoids the answering machine, crossing into his bedroom, where he tosses his coat onto his bed. A small act of rebellion. Anna always liked everything hung up or folded neatly.

Harry would like to be able to cry. He'd like to rage, to scream, to stamp his feet, to do pretty much anything. But the same enervating helplessness that swept over him during Claire's breakdown continues to cling to him like stubborn morning fog. He sits down on the edge of the bed. His eyes fall on the top drawer of his nightstand. He can't bring himself to open it, although he knows perfectly well what lurks within. He can easily envision Anna's years of gifts stowed away, the teeming, living mass of cuff links, tie bars, money clips within rattling insistently like an angry mound of shiny, glistening beetles clambering to get out. But he can't open the drawer, can't force himself to lay eyes upon the one still item amid the cacophony: his Swiss Army knife, a nice one, too—scissors, corkscrew, nail file, screwdriver, tweezers, fork, spoon—all the bells and whistles, none of which have ever been rung or blown. He knows he should try. He should take it in hand and allow its associations, the freighted past it carries, to wash over him and attach him somehow to this moment. But he doesn't dare. He would have to be made of sterner stuff to fight the solitary terror that keeps his hands rooted at his side. And so he sits there, immobile, helpless, the rattle of his pent-up past clattering in his ears.

The tingling heaviness in his hands and feet alerts Harry to the passage of time. He looks up thickly, disoriented, the rattle in his ears replaced by a low-grade whine. It's gotten dark outside. It wasn't dark when he sat down. At least he doesn't think it was. The flash of annoyance he feels at his uncertainty is just enough to bring him to his feet, and he leaves the bedroom in search of a drink. Crossing the empty living room, he passes the blinking answering machine and continues into the dining room. He heads to the glass-and-stainless-steel bar that Anna always managed to keep miraculously free of fingerprints. Smudging the glass front with a shock of guilty pleasure, he looks at the rows and rows of bottles inside, impeccably chosen and maintained but rarely consumed. Having, as always, no strong preferences, Harry selects one of the few bottles that's already open, saving himself the effort of having to open one. (It's always pained him that he doesn't look more at ease opening a bottle. When done right, it can endow the opener with an unassailable air of masculinity. But Harry invariably struggles and flails with a bottle, looking more epileptic than suave.)

Harry pours himself three fingers of bourbon and settles into an uncomfortable, tubular, metal-framed chair in the living room. Ice cubes tinkle decorously in a topaz sea as Harry swirls the glass around, losing himself in drinking ritual, contentedly distracted before the first sip. He wonders if the drink in his hand makes him appear cool in any way. He's always imagined that ordering a bourbon on the rocks scores higher on the Manliness Scale than, say, a gin and tonic or a martini. He's never developed a real taste for the liquor—it still strikes him as harsh and always causes a mild involuntary tremor on the first swallow—but he's aware of its value as an accessory. When he first met Anna, those many years ago, he cultivated the image of a hard drinker, hoping it might help him overcome his mystique deficit. Whenever they met, the tumbler of deep brown liquid was summoned and kept close at hand. Anna's bathroom trips and cell phone calls (especially frequent in those early days of business apprenticeship) were opportunities to surreptitiously dump and ostentatiously refill the glasses. He was certain that Anna must have marveled at his cast-iron fortitude, his limitless tolerance for the hard stuff, but as time went along, the need for props became less, and he slowly stopped ordering the drinks. Only one restaurant, where Harry had established a pattern of regularity, insisted on sending over drinks well past the point that he'd abandoned the charade altogether, and so the lone highball sat at his elbow, ignored through the years. Truth is, two bourbons were all it took to make Harry ill.

But just now Harry would probably welcome feeling ill. He'd welcome feeling anything at all as his eyes drift over the empty living room, taking in the space and marveling at how completely absent from its design he feels. As though he'd wandered blindly into a random house on a random street, for all the connection he feels to this place. Anna liked things cool and minimal—there's a lot of metal and glass, and a decided absence of personal touches—whereas Harry's a bit of a clutter magnet. It's not sloppiness or sloth but rather an abiding sense of never quite being through with anything, never having squeezed out every last drop of utility. And so Harry was given a small room on the lower level of this split-level, hillside frame on stilts to clutter, accumulate, and deface to his heart's content. Now, as he sits in the cool, sterile fluorescent light of the living room, he's aware of the closed room beneath him, feels its pent-up Tell-Tale Heart vitality pulsing below. Seated up here in the chillier climes, he feels like a mountaineer lost on Everest, staving off panic, stumbling helplessly in snow-blinded darkness trying to find base camp.

His glass is empty. How did that happen? He sets it aside—reflexively slipping a coaster beneath it, Anna's countless admonitions still programmed to repeat in a loop in his inner ear—and he feels the cavernous emptiness of the room slowly begin to close in on him, constricting him, shortening his breath. Harry has begun to suspect that it will be impossible to go on living in this house. The silence is total, overwhelming, and absolute, broken only by the memory of Anna's voice bouncing from room to room—he can hear her laughter, her tears, her soft tissue-paper voice, and her occasional exasperated bark, and this layered silence deafens him. It's excruciating and Harry seeks refuge in a second bourbon. Once again he's aware of himself holding the thick, weighted tumbler, although his perception is growing blunted as one by one assorted synapses begin checking out for the night. Shutdown protocols have been instituted, and the offending layers of sound are slowly smoothed away, so that all that remains in the resulting stillness is the mental freeze-frame of Molly's wings.

Answering machine.

No. Not ready yet.

Molly's wings. Harry considers the aptness of his winged angel. He first noted her tattoo peeking out between her short, black T-shirt and low-slung jeans as she reached overhead for coffee filters. The ornate, black lines spanned her tanned lower back, and he imagined cupping her hips with his palms, just covering the tips of the wings, and pulling her toward him. He would have liked to have pushed up her T-shirt to linger more closely on the view. Or better still, to slip her jeans down a bit and pull aside the inverted black triangle of her panties that he could see even now.

A different warmth joins the heat of the bourbon. A dancing Saint Elmo's fire of the groin. He sets his glass aside—no coaster this time, as bourbon sploshes over the rim of the glass onto the side table—and begins to unbuckle his trousers. Harry realizes that he can now masturbate with complete freedom, to his heart's content, in perpetuity— or at least until the cleaning lady arrives the day after tomorrow. The perpetual fear of discovery is lifted, and with a guilty start, Harry marvels at the sheer audacity of whacking off in *this* room, in *this* chair.

. . . Molly . . .

. . . it's rough but not brutal . . . he likes her urgency . . . her need . . . she kisses him hungrily . . . standing in the alley behind the coffee shop . . . her arms wrap around his head . . . yes, to be hungered after . . . she unzips him . . . her skirt already hiked up . . . panties pulled aside . . . already wet so that he slides inside her effortlessly . . . she gasps . . . her eyes widen . . . he pins her to the wall . . . she buries her face in his neck . . .

. . . *Molly* . . . oh, shit . . .

Harry's propensity for disorder stops short of ejaculating all over the floor. He's always kept a Kleenex at the ready to contain his errant seed, but under the diminished capacity of the bourbon he is unprepared for the moment at hand. He reaches into his pocket, finds something, and is about to receive his millions of spermatozoa in safety when he registers what he's holding. His jam-stained tie. Anna's tie.

The moment is blown apart, climax deferred, a Dunkirk of semen. Harry holds the ruined tie in one hand, his shrinking penis in the other. He'd normally be angry or upset, but he settles for the wave of queasy self-loathing that passes over him as he debates whether to start again. Proceeding more out of obligation than desire, he sets the tie aside, rounds up a napkin, and tries to return his thoughts to Molly. But she hangs just out of reach, the presence of the tie banishing her as magically as garlic repels a vampire. With increasing desperation (he's been aroused just long enough that a twinge of discomfort has settled into his balls, necessitating release), he flips through his mental archive of handy pornographic images, flash memories of downloaded porn and hotel-room video rentals. He settles on a threesome with two pigtailed cheerleaders, but before he can get very far his stomach begins to spasm and now the two bourbons are demanding their due. The cramp feels like a spear to his gut, and Harry knows that some vicious diarrhea is only moments away. He's stroking furiously, fighting stubborn flaccidity, the ache in his groin competing with the stabbing sensation in his belly. Finally, with a frustrated cry of "Goddamn it!" Harry wills himself to climax, deriving not an ounce of pleasure from the release, and, clutching the wadded napkin tightly around the head of his penis, races to the bathroom, where the two bourbons claim final victory over his innards.

Weak and shaky, Harry stands over the answering machine. He steadies himself, picks up a pen and a small yellow, ruled pad. Anna always made sure a fresh pad sat beside the phone, and with a pang of sorrow Harry realizes that this is the last pad she will ever place here. He wonders for a moment if he'll continue putting them out or if he should leave this one here, sacred and untouched. He wonders what other last touches lie in wait to haunt him. He presses Play.

There's a long moment of silence in which only a gently rhythmic breathing can be heard. Then Claire speaks tentatively.

53

"Harry?" A long pause. Then a sigh. "Harry, I . . ." A sniffle, followed by the click of a hang-up.

Harry hits the Stop key, unnerved. Despite her foibles, Claire always struck Harry as, in some ways, the more redoubtable of the Weldt sisters, and it's disturbing to see her laid so low. He presses Play and the next message plays.

Like its predecessor, a long silence unravels before a single, whispered question: "Why . . . ?" Again, the click of a hang-up.

Harry hits Stop again. It's too much. He hits Delete, always the brave man in the digital frontier. The counter steps down to 6. He hits Play again.

"Harry . . . what happened to her?" A barely audible whisper.

Click. Stop. Delete. Play.

"Please. Help me understand this . . ."

Delete.

"Harry, what did you do to her? Please answer me . . ."

Stop.

"Why, Harry? Why did this happen? She was beautiful. She was perfect . . ." Tears beginning to overtake her voice.

Click. Delete.

Barely controlled heavy breathing. Bottomless sorrow about to burst into the open.

Delete.

The final message, a piteous wail.

Click. Stop. Delete.

Harry runs back to the bathroom, doubled over in pain, though whether it's from the bourbons or from Claire he's uncertain. Once he's sure he's emptied his bowels even of air, he staggers back out to the living room. There, he's surprised to find one message remaining on the machine. But the light isn't blinking: It's an older message, one he's already heard. Certain, at least, that it won't be a continuation of Claire's pleas, he tremblingly presses Play.

Anna's voice fills the room.

"Hey, love, it's me. I'm running about twenty minutes late tonight, we had an unexpected late conference call. Anyway, I'm on my way, but would you please take the steaks out of the refrigerator? Just leave them on the counter, I'll deal with them when I get there. Love you."

Click. Stop.

It's one of dozens of messages that Anna would leave for Harry. Quotidian, almost banal, the stuff of their lives together. Instructions, usually. Sometimes favors or questions, perhaps a reminder to herself or to them both. Always an expression of love at the end. Harry wants to keep this message, save it, tuck it away safely forever. If it were an old-style answering machine, he'd just pop out the tape. But it's one of those digital wonders, and so after a moment's deliberation, Harry unplugs it. Keeping her trapped but safe. He looks around the room, the combined stench of diarrhea, whiskey, and semen assaulting him, even as he knows he's imagining it. The diarrhea is flushed and freshened by the bathroom's air freshener, programmed to squirt precisely every fifteen minutes. The semen, trapped in the napkin, is long flushed. The whiskey has been mopped up from the side table, the bottle recorked and put away. But the smells overpower him, and so he firmly closes the bedroom and bathroom doors and raises all the windows before easing into bed and burying his face in his pillows.

The next morning, the Jaguar knows it's headed for Café Retro before Harry does. The first indication he has about his destination is an acceleration of his heart, which beats flatly against his chest, like a palm slapping desperately against a thick metal wall hoping to attract the attention of a compassionate jailer. Harry has always enjoyed these moments of anticipation, the gradual build that invariably outshines dim reality. Focusing on a single moment, he marshals all his creative energy to the task of realizing it in the fullest detail—the moment, in this case, being Molly's first sight of him striding confidently into Café Retro, and her unabashed delight at seeing him.

He mentally replays his arrival a dozen different ways, striving to get the timing just right, finding that perfect blend of nonchalance and purpose. Achieving what he feels is suave perfection, he then begins to pair it with a variety of Molly reactions, searching for that elusive perfect fit. First she's clearly delighted to see him, abruptly abandoning a table mid-order to hurry over and greet with him a breathless "Hello." Perhaps touching him, taking his arm to guide him to a seat in her section. Their first contact. Then he scales it back, opting for a more drawn-out but smoldering acknowledgment, her eyes boring through him lasciviously as she refills the chipped coffee cup of one her geriatric regulars. "I've been waiting for you to come back." That's Harry's favorite line, the one he settles on. He's absolutely certain that, as a rule, he fades rapidly from view, like the imprint of a vista that dissolves inside a closed eyelid. There's nothing Harry wants quite so much as to be remembered. To be thought well of.

Inevitably, it's the possibility Harry hasn't considered that greets his arrival at Café Retro. He strides into the café, convinced he's throwing off more light and energy than a supernova, but his conviction finds no takers in the bored faces of the handful of early-morning regulars who sparsely fleck the booths. Derailed and deflated, Harry coasts in on momentum toward his usual seat in Molly's section. He sits at the counter and looks around the room for her, disappointed that she's missed his grand entrance but relieved that she hasn't witnessed his subsequent structural collapse. He's aware that he cuts a uniquely forlorn figure now, as he cranes his neck around the L-shaped room. But his effort is only rewarded with the sight of Lucille limping through the clientele. Harry straightens nervously as she approaches him, her surly eyes barely registering him. It occurs to Harry that he's terrified of this mountainous woman. He winces as bourbon echoes from the night before roil his innards.

"Yeah?"

Harry tries to summon some Dantès-like reserve. "Hey, Lucille. How are you doing?"

"What do you want?" No chitchat today.

"Um, coffee."

She writes his order on her pad, muttering, "High roller," as she limps away. Harry sighs and momentarily considers bolting. Cowardice, his most powerful involuntary reflex, begins to lift him from the stool, but Enlightened Self-Interest elbows its way into the conversation and reminds Harry that he's going to need to be able to return to this place, and he's got a low threshold for awkward encounters. So he sinks slowly back into his seat just as Lucille comes limping back into view. She slides the coffee over to him, spilling it over the edges into the saucer.

"Anything else?"

"No thanks." Harry dabs at the saucer with a napkin. She tears the check off and leaves it beside him and begins to limp off. Harry is terrified of any exchange with her, but his need for information is greater than his fear, so he braves the wrath of Lucille.

"Hey. Where's Molly?"

The mention of Molly's name causes Lucille to stop and turn back to face Harry. The beast roused.

"Molly? I'll tell you where Molly is," she snarls. "She's bailing that worthless piece-of-crap boyfriend of hers out of trouble. Again. Leaving me to handle this whole place on my own. Again. With the ingrown toenail from hell. Not that she cares. Anything else?"

Harry's a bit too stunned to reply. At the mention of the word *boyfriend*, he's experienced a heartbreak that he's convinced is a microcosm of every shattered love he's ever known or will know. He now perceives a Great Wall thrown up around Molly, and Harry's never been much of a wall scaler. If there's no easy door to be found, he's more likely to go around the long way or, better still, turn back to where he came from. He finally shakes his head dumbly.

"Thanks for the concern," Lucille snaps, bearing down on Harry, limping heavily in visible pain. "It would sure be fuckin' nice if just once someone, anyone, maybe considered me and my problems, y'know? That's all. It's not much, right?"

But Harry's only half-listening to Lucille's diatribe, as the crescendo of cramps in his stomach returns to compete with this other, sadder ache in what he supposes is called his heart. Getting to the bathroom is critical now, and Lucille is blocking his way. And so it's more out of reflex than anything else that he mumbles to her, "Call Max," as he tries to squeeze past her.

"What?" Annoyed. Impatient. Moving to impede his path.

"What?" Harry counters effectively, brought back to the present by her harried tone.

"You said, 'Call Max.' "

Harry nods now, cursing his reflexes, having lost interest in Lucille, her plight, and anything not made of porcelain. To extract himself as quickly as possible, he hands her Max's card as he tries again to squeeze past.

"My friend Max. He's a podiatrist. He'll fix you up."

Lucille snorts. "Nice. A Beverly Hills doctor. You think this place gives me insurance?"

The bourbons are pounding against the door. Harry fights to keep the desperation from his voice.

"Tell him I sent you. That you're a friend. He'll figure it out."

There's the first slight crack in Lucille's glacial countenance. "Really?"

"Cross my heart. Now can you excuse me? I really need your bathroom."

Having successfully navigated the third-world toilets of Café Retro, Harry's back on the road, heading to the office. He reflects on recent disappointments. Claire's pleading messages. His onanistic folly. The disastrous state of his stomach. Absent Molly and her felonious boyfriend, and Lucille and her ingrown toenail. The empty house and the empty bed that await his return. Above all, he marvels at how totally without a place to go he feels, this overpowering sense of belonging nowhere. He's never felt particularly at one with the larger world, more a habitué of its fringes than part of its vital center. But he could always count on his tiny archipelago of safety—Anna; Max; Claire; work; the house. But Harry feels as if he's been forced to evacuate his Atlantis, adrift in his eighty-thousand-dollar, air-conditioned, six-cylinder lifeboat, with no real idea as to where to dock this sucker.

Terra firma. What a concept.

He's so spent upon his arrival to work that he fails to notice a battered gray Impala discreetly pulling onto a side street just out of view, where it parks.

Although Harry had pledged to wait a week before returning to Café Retro—best to maintain a nonchalant façade—two days is all he can manage, and even those two are excruciating, little more than waking ticks of the clock. During that period, he's unable to focus on anything for more than a few minutes. Work, reading, watching cable, nothing can shove aside Molly's claim on his imagination. As for focusing on the legal paperwork that Anna's death has generated and which is collecting in fearsome mounds on the dining room table, well, he could sooner run a marathon backward. And so, on Wednesday morning, having ignored the dwindling phone calls from friends with their invitations out and offers of home-cooked meals, Harry instead surrenders to his obsession and returns to Café Retro.

He's so anxious to get a glimpse of Molly, to be sure she's there, that he neglects the particulars of his entrance altogether. It's with record amounts of uncool that Harry pokes his head into the café, scanning the room for Molly. And her reaction when she sees him—she hurries out from behind the counter and runs over to give him an unexpected hug; yes, hug—is rooted in no reality that Harry recognizes. And so he stands there, dumbstruck. Praying that he's not actually drooling.

"Um, hi" is the extent of his verbal prowess.

"*You* are a big sweetie. Thank you!" she says, stepping out of the hug. Harry can still feel the tingling shock from where her small but firm breasts pressed against his chest. Harry would like to say *You're welcome*—even as he's not sure what she's thanking him for. It does seem the thing to do, but this unexpected physical contact has completely shorted him out. Fortunately, Molly's exuberance fills the conversational gaps.

"That toenail has been killing Lucille for ages. And frankly, made her total hell to work with. Your friend took care of everything, just like you said." Her eyes glitter with something Harry can't quite define but which oozes warmth. "Come, sit here." She guides him to a table in her section. "Lunch is on me today."

Finally, Harry is able to stammer. "Oh, no, really. That's okay."

"Are you kidding? That's one of the nicest, most generous things I've ever seen. I insist." She remembers something and smiles at Harry with a wink. "I know. One Monte Cristo, coming right up."

And before Harry can protest, she's gone. But that's just as well—he needs a moment alone, a moment to digest. Because Harry's generally not especially quick on his feet, but he senses that something fundamental has just shifted. There's a great big golden key to the city bobbing into view, and Harry's convinced that, for once, he can figure out how to grab it. He's so focused that not even the thought of another Monte Cristo sandwich disturbs him.

Fact: He did something that helped another person without any particular ulterior motive (other than a diarrhea-induced desire to end a conversation).

Fact: Molly, whose attentions to him have been near nil, hugged him—*hugged him!*—over what she perceived to be his kindness. His selflessness.

Fact: Molly doesn't know the first thing about Harry's life, the circumstances of Anna's death, or that no one who knows him (especially not Claire) is likely to describe Harry as selfless.

Fact: Molly has a boyfriend (and there's still an involuntary stab of jealousy at the thought) who requires a lot of attention and gets himself into trouble.

Fact: Hey, Edmond Dantès helped people in *The Count of Monte Cristo*, even when he did so to serve his own ends, right?

Assembling these facts, Harry comes up with a plan, albeit a Harry Plan, the most noteworthy characteristic of which is usually its ill conception. But as he turns it over in his mind, he sees the possibilities, and they're all good.

He will be Lucille's benefactor.

Like Dantès, he will do his homework first. He'll learn about her life, determine where it's gone wrong, and what she needs to set it right. And then—asking absolutely nothing in return—he will set about making it so. He imagines it's only a matter of time until Molly stops feeling impressed and starts to feel the stirrings of love. And then he can turn that selflessness, that Dantèan focus toward her, and the accumulation of kindnesses will be impossible for her to resist, and she'll be his. (He could, he supposes, cut out the middleman and focus this attention directly on Molly herself, but he decides that echoes his prostitute past too much for his taste.)

It's a long-range plan, to be sure, but Harry's nothing if not methodical—downright plodding when he wants to be. He's willing to work for this one, to wait it out.

As he sits there, turning over the plan in his mind, exceedingly pleased with his cleverness and subtlety, Harry is surprised to find himself looking forward to the arrival of his sandwich.

Five

In which our hero leaves behind the safety of the familiar

IT'S WITH A KNICKER-TWIST of irritation that Harry answers his phone on the fourth ring.

"Harry Rent."

"You owe me eight hundred bucks, Harry."

"Good morning to you, too, Max."

"Don't you good-morning me, you schmuck bastard. What are you doing sending me uninsured waitresses with smelly feet?"

"Come on, Max, she needed some help. It was a good deed." Harry smiles a nervous, guilty smile at his assistant, Nicole, as she drops the day's mail on his desk. Unopened, unstamped, unsorted. She turns on stilettoed heel and exits, allowing him to surreptitiously eyeball her jean-ensconced bottom. He always feels guilty when she's around because he's indulged in the occasional sexual fantasy about her. Harry is mildly fixated on Nicole, or least on the powdered floral sweetness that clings to her, and it's prompted him to make certain clerical concessions.

"Good deed, my ass. It was eight hundred bucks is what it was. Christ, I hate smelly feet." Then, remembering himself: "You holding up all right?"

"I'm fine. And you've been a podiatrist for thirty years. Haven't you acclimated?"

"There are certain things that a civilized man should never have to get used to. That woman's feet could level armies."

"Max, she's a waitress. She's on her feet all day. Where's your sympathy?"

"I can't afford sympathy. How am I gonna be able to retire if I have to keep handing out freebies to your hard-luck cases."

Harry's phone rings. Nicole is supposed to screen his calls, but as with her other administrative responsibilities, this one is a hit-or-miss proposition.

"Yeah, Max, you've been threatening retirement for the last six years. I'm not holding my breath."

"I don't want your breath, I want your money."

The phone continues to ring. Harry sighs with exasperation.

"You need to fire that girl, Harry."

"Max, don't—"

"She's worthless. Totally incompetent. You keep her around so you can stare at her ass. Meanwhile you're filing your own paperwork with the HMOs."

Another ring. Harry tenses, irritated, craning his neck to look through the wedge of his open door. Nicole's desk is unattended. Her framed MBA mocks Harry from her empty workstation.

"Goddamn it," he sighs distractedly. He's completely lost his end of the conversation with Max. "Nicole?" he calls out, hand over his mouthpiece. He's always careful to keep the irritation out of his voice, afraid to upset their delicate balance, which in reality is no balance whatsoever but rather Nicole's total dominion over him.

"Hah," says Max. "She's probably in the parking lot chasing cars. Parked cars."

Harry dreads moments like this one, trapped between unwavering, insistent forces without appealing options. His face is flushed, beads of sweat tickling his scalp. Just as he's decided to put Max on hold, the ringing line goes silent.

"Eight hundred bucks. I'm serious, Harry. And fire her." Max hangs up.

Harry holds the dead receiver in his hand for a moment, then replaces it in its cradle, pulls out his checkbook, and writes Max an eight-hundred-dollar check. He sets it in his outbox, which now occupies the space left behind by Anna's photos. Harry found he couldn't bear the sight of her smiling at him every day, and so now they're tucked away, bottom left drawer beneath the boxes of canceled checks.

He wonders how long the check will sit there before it finds its way to Max.

By late afternoon, Harry has gotten through much of the day's work-load, with little or no help from Nicole, who seems to have developed a fascination with Web sites about midget wrestling. (Harry checks her Web browser's history every night, hoping to find something sala-cious.) Patients needing scanning, photographing, imaging, the com-mitting of selves to bits of film and magnetic tape. Captured, reviewed, filed.

Click. Stop. Delete.

Harry is finishing up with Mrs. Ryerson. She's one of his most profitable patients—a wealthy hypochondriac—so Harry puts up with the nuisance. Her latest perceived ailment was pneumonia, and she felt full chest X-rays were in order. And although Harry is inclined to believe that her real agenda was to show him her new store-bought breasts, he complied, as he always does, and took her X-rays.

Now as he slides them into the viewer, he grimly notes the slightly darkened shade that represents her breast implants. There's no sign of pneumonia, of course, but Harry is astounded at how much of her in-terior space Mrs. Ryerson has given over to these two sacs.

He continues to look at the film hypnotically, until he sees nothing but a blur of grays and whites. These are the moments Harry likes best. Sitting here in the dark, looking through pictures, undisturbed. The spreading tingle of numbness in his rear restores him to the present nearly twenty minutes later, and he returns the Ryerson X-rays to their protective sleeve.

As he slides the Ryerson file back into place, his finger brushes against and then comes to rest on another file. Written on the label in Nicole's ridiculously girlish cursive: *RENT, A.* Almost involuntarily, he pulls out the file, withdraws a sheet of film, and slides it into the viewer. He steps back to regard these familiar bones.

He remembers Anna falling off her bike. Or rather, he remembers her coming home with a badly bruised hip after one of her canyon rides. (Harry had tried to join her once, motivated by a healthy dollop of spousal obligation but not much more. By the third time she'd untangled his pants from the bike chain, it was clear to both of them that she was destined to remain a peloton of one.) She limped into the house carrying her bent bike frame. Her red spandex cycling tights were torn along the right thigh, almost to the hip. She'd swerved to avoid a collision with an exuberant Labrador that was running off its leash, and she'd lost control. Held in by toe clips, she and the bike took a protracted tumble down the canyon trail. Concerned about the possibility of a hip fracture, Harry had insisted on the X-rays.

Now Harry stands in the darkened room, staring at pictures of his dead wife's hips. He traces his finger along the curve of her pelvis and remembers all those nights curled up behind her, his hand hanging limply over her hipbone. This was his favorite of his wife's many curves. Whenever he pressed his hand against it, she felt solid and uniquely his. He places his palm flat against the same part of the image, feeling a strange tightness in his chest. He moves closer, about to rest his cheek against her X-ray when the room unexpectedly floods with light. Startled, Harry reorganizes himself and turns to find Nicole, who regards him with a slightly puzzled expression. She realizes she's intruded on something she doesn't fully understand, but it feels disquietingly inti-mate and the apology dies on her lips. She holds up a clutch of files to explain her presence. "Filing," she says awkwardly. Harry nods brusquely, stuffs Anna back into her protective sleeve, and hurries from the room to avoid the pity and hint of shame that's unexpectedly taken root in her large, aquamarine eyes.

Harry's sitting back in his office, Anna's file on his desk before him, and for the first time that he can remember, he's angry at Nicole. He actually wants to fire her, even thinks of how he might do it, although the prospect of the confrontation makes him feel ill. His eyes fall on Anna's file, and now the pain in his side has returned. His eyes dart around the room for distraction and fall on the check for Lucille's foot-work. Still sitting there. Still in his outbox. A full eight hours later. Al-though this time he's grateful for Nicole's inefficiency. It's reminded him of work undone. It's gotten him thinking again.

Stakeout. One of the quintessential American set pieces, and Harry's done his homework. Absorbed hundreds if not thousands of hours of banal police dramas, enough to know that you need coffee in dispos-able cups, doughnuts, and dark glasses. As he sits in the Jaguar across the street from Café Retro, accoutrements of the trade assembled around him, he marvels at the hint of arousal he feels assuming this archetypal pose. That it's too dark to wear his shades; that the doughnuts sit un-touched—Harry finds the sticky, milky surface of the jelly doughnut repellent—that the coffee is already inconveniently filling and pressing against his bladder diminishes the moment only slightly. Harry feels an unfamiliar power suffusing his limbs—he's used to being naturally in-visible, but to be invisible by choice bestows something on him that's new and exciting.

Almost precisely as the Jaguar's clock flicks to eleven, Lucille and Molly exit Café Retro. They exchange what appear to be brief and ritual good-nights, then Lucille trudges down the street, limping along with a cane, not yet healed from Max's handiwork. Molly is left behind, looking up and down the street, expectancy and disappointment battling for control of her face, and already Harry's off his game. His plan had been simple enough: follow Lucille home, see what could be sussed out about her day-to-day affairs. But Harry didn't expect to see Molly as well, and now he's finding her difficult to turn away from. Lucille continues on her way down the street and Harry's at the crossroads of yet another untenable decision.

Before he can make one move or another, the decision is once again made on his behalf. The flatulent roar of a doctored motorcycle muffler shakes the Jaguar. Harry watches as a leather-clad tough pulls up in front of Molly on a massive Harley. An argument immediately ensues, although it's decidedly one-way as Molly animatedly berates her indifferent chauffeur. Harry takes advantage of the altercation to study his competitor. Bruce is young—Harry thinks probably no more than twenty-five—and has the insouciance of one whose good looks have resulted in a lifetime of being catered and deferred to. Harry recognizes in the long-haired, unshaven, tattooed Bruce that irritating brooding intensity that women seem to melt for. A bubble of hatred bursts open in Harry's chest, and his impression is confirmed as Bruce greets Molly's diatribe with a shrug and kicks the Harley back to life, about to pull away. Harry marvels at the evil perfection of Bruce's timing—Molly calls out to stop him, just as both Bruce and Harry knew she would. Bruce stops the bike but doesn't turn back. Molly hurries after him, climbs onto the bike, and together they scream down Wilshire Boulevard.

Harry's left with a cold cup of coffee in his hands and a roiling hopelessness in his heart. How the hell is he supposed to compete with that? A distant helplessness flares in his belly, and although it feels oddly like an echo—almost a sense memory, pain at a slight remove to the moment at hand—angry tears begin to cloud his vision. He's assailed by this unexpected wave of emotion that seems out of proportion with the moment at hand. The contours of his grand plan suddenly seem thin and foolish indeed.

His plan . . . *Shit* . . . Harry looks up and down the street for Lucille. Fully expecting her to be long gone, he's surprised to find her sitting, waiting patiently at a bus stop. Another item for the constantly growing list of Things Harry Hasn't Considered. It hadn't occurred to him that she wouldn't have a car. This is Los Angeles. Even his cleaning lady has a car.

Still, for once, this has worked more or less in Harry's favor, and he discreetly watches her as she waits. She stares ahead blankly, rigid, looking sadly clownlike in her uniform of thin red and white stripes with wide, white cuffs. No book, no newspaper, no cell-phone chatter. He tries to imagine what she might be thinking about, what those empty eyes of hers see. Perhaps the exhaustion crowds out all thoughts, and she's just sitting there feeling the numb tingle of her limbs. As a few minutes of this pass, Harry grows uncomfortable. There's something disquietingly intimate about this tableau, about staring at this woman in situ, the whole of whose life Harry suspects is captured in those still, blank eyes.

Harry hears the pneumatic sigh of the approaching bus. So does Lucille, and she rises slowly, raising her expansive heft with surprising grace, like a hot-air balloon ascending. She disappears inside and the bus pulls slowly away from the curb. Harry scans the street carefully for police before making a wide U-turn to follow the bus. He's so on the lookout for sirens and lights that he once again fails to notice the gray Impala following him.

Harry has never followed a bus before, and he's having difficulty navigating its unforeseen particulars. The stop-and-go nature of the route presents obvious problems, which are augmented by its sluggish pace. Bus stops situated at the beginnings of blocks leave him in danger of being trapped behind an unfriendly traffic light. Worst, though, is the belch of monoxide fumes that engulfs the Jag each time the bus departs a stop. Harry finally gives up trying to be discreet and settles for sitting on the bus's tail. Each time it pulls away, he lingers for a moment to see if Lucille is among the discharged.

Harry chugs down the boulevard through its polyglot transformations, shop signs in English giving way almost seamlessly to Korean, then overlapping with Spanish before the last Asian characters completely disappear. He's so absorbed by the linguistic colors that surround him that he almost loses Lucille, despite her formidable bulk. His attention has been wandering and there's good music on the radio. (Harry's lustily mangling "Non più andrai" from *Le Nozze di Figaro*.) And his thoughts keep flitting back to Molly's stenciled paramour. Harry surprises himself with the heights of creativity he scales devising fiendishly clever deaths for Bruce. It's as he's caught up in a particularly gruesome scenario involving honey and fire ants that he misses Lucille turning down a side street. Only a glimpse of the receding peppermint stripes of her sleeve momentarily illuminated by a streetlamp saves Harry and sends him into a sudden, careening, ungainly turn down the street after her. Unfortunately, his acrobatics cause Lucille to look directly up at him.

There's an electric moment of what appears to be eye contact, but it's late, it's dark, and Harry's just not sure. He looks away, floors it, and speeds down the street, watching in his rearview mirror as Lucille turns and trudges into her apartment building. Noting the unit—a low-slung, stucco eight-plex—he continues on around the block. He parks the Jaguar out of view, and in the quiet of the car he notices—once again—that his hands are shaking. He rests them on the steering wheel, casting an involuntary glance to the third finger of his left hand where the tan line left by the Everhappy Eterna Comfort Band™ has already begun to fade.

He steps out of his car, double-checking that the alarm is activated, and walks down this unfamiliar street. He's not used to streets that teem so openly with life—his is a world of recessed drives and hedged-in sight lines. As he passes the families sitting on their stoops in the warm summer night, eating Popsicles and mangoes, listening to salsa and rap, he's momentarily pulled by the desire to take a place on one of these stoops, pop a lime into an ice-cold Corona, and inhale the perfume of the jasmine blossoms that sweetens the night. Eyes fasten on him as he walks past, and his hopes of an invitation, in a language he'd be unable to understand, evaporate amid suspicious glances. Harry doesn't belong here. They know it and so does he.

The neighborhood activity thins sufficiently by Lucille's end of the block that Harry can duck into the space between the buildings without drawing too much notice. At first he's elated with himself, dizzy with the danger, when it occurs to him that this sort of thing is probably all too common in this neighborhood, and he's at greater risk from crossing paths with a genuine evildoer than he is from being discovered. Fortunately, it takes little time to find Lucille's room on the ground floor in the rear of the building. The small, barred windows are uncovered, and so Harry's view into Lucille's cramped studio apartment is unimpeded. With a last, guilty look around, he creeps up to the window and peers in.

Lucille's uniform is folded neatly on the bed. The sound of running water can be heard from the bathroom. Harry is shocked by the threadbare, cluttered room. The brown paint has faded and peels in big loose flaps like sunburned skin. Splintered yellow wood can be seen through the thinning threads that hold the dirty cream carpeting together. Harry sees no stove, no dishes, no foodstuffs, but rather a grease-encrusted hot plate on the counter and a single forlorn place setting drying in the dish rack. Three mason jars filled with change—pennies mostly—sit atop a battered folding table littered with disconnect notices. Harry can make out the gas, electric, and phone, all insistent, angry pinks. He can find only two personal touches: a sort of shrine of magazine advertisements taped onto the wall that includes clippings of iPod and sneaker advertisements; and at the base of the plastic lamp at her bedside, a framed picture of a young boy, aged perhaps eight.

Choked with pity over Lucille's impecunious lot, Harry takes out a small notebook and pen and begins jotting some quick notes—*Disconnect notices . . . Picture of boy, who? . . . Wants iPod?* He's so engrossed in his task that he fails to notice two shifts in the night's elements, both of which portend badly for him.

First, the shower has stopped running.

And second, a window has opened overhead.

Harry's unaware of either of these developments, but after a moment he does sense an agitated displacement in the space within, a subtle reorientation of the molecules vibrating in Lucille's living room, and so he looks up from his notebook to find a naked Lucille. Harry is mesmerized by this apparition. By its solidity, its slow-moving enormity. He's never seen naked flesh like this, not even in his examining room. Now, peering through bars at the rolls and rolls of wrinkled fat piled and coiled upon one another, body parts so distended as to be unrecognizable to him, he imagines there's a vagina, an anus, in there somewhere, but he can't conceive of where to begin looking for them. But Harry's fascination isn't prurient. There's something about seeing Lucille in her totality, in her immovable, fixed palpability—there's something quite literally monumental about her, as though recently quarried—and Harry marvels at this strange yet absolute placement. Lucille fully occupies her space in a way that Harry finds strangely familiar and affecting.

He's wrestling with this sensation when a stream of water begins to spray all over him, hitting his head and shoulders, trickling down his neck and back. Water? Rain? No . . . wait. Harry wipes his neck and sniffs his fingertips. Urine.

"Take *that* you son-of-a-bitch, Peeping Tom piece of shit!"

Harry foolishly looks up to the source, and the urine streaming from Mr. Sanchez's penis in apartment three splashes painfully into his eyes. Harry yelps and covers his face and head, leaping back out of harm's way.

Lucille, hearing the noise, looks to the window and screams. She grabs her flag-sized bathrobe and drapes it over her shoulders.

Harry staggers back from the window, hands covering his face, uncertain if he's been seen. Lucille screams again from within.

Mr. Sanchez exhausts the contents of his bladder and shakes his penis dry with satisfaction. "Go peep somewhere else, you sick pervert fuck!"

Lucille comes to the window to pull down her tattered rice-paper blind and scan the alley for her stalker. But the alley is already empty and all that remains is the pungent smell of urine.

Harry walks with rapid urgency back the way he came. Every conversation he passes comes to an immediate halt. Brows furrow and faces grimace as Mr. Sanchez's bouquet fills the night air. Harry's only relief is that the evening's darkness hides the flush of his cheeks. He dives into the Jaguar and doesn't permit himself to relax, to begin to breathe regularly, until he's speeding back down Wilshire Boulevard, and English signs begin to materialize out of the night.

He's so rattled by the evening's outing that he looks directly at the gray Impala in his rearview mirror without noticing it.

"Yes, I'll—"

Hold would have been the next word, but the Department of Water & Power phone operator is faster with her button than Harry is with his mouth. It's the third time in as many calls that he's been placed on hold, and he marvels at the barriers erected between a utility and its customers. Under the circumstances, he's surprised that more people aren't perpetually in arrears like Lucille, whose debts were prodigious indeed, at least by the modest standards of a coffee shop waitress's salary. Nearly $300 in power debt, and a whopping $575 in phone debt (most of it to various chat lines and horoscope services). Given the absence of a stove in her apartment, coupled with the mildness of Southern California winters, the gas bill was comparatively modest—a mere $87.43—but even that seemed beyond Lucille's means.

Freshly showered and in his bathrobe, Harry closes his notebook and sets it aside, the pages crisp and wrinkled by the evaporation of Mr. Sanchez's urine, the ink of Harry's fountain pen a smeared green in places but still legible. He sips from a glass of sparkling water—bourbon is off the menu—as he sits at his dining room table, looking out the window at the fog slithering across the hills upon which his neighbors' homes are perched. Gradually the pinpoints of light from the facing dining-room windows are snuffed out by the thickening blanket.

The operator returns to the phone and gives Harry a confirmation number for the transaction. He reopens the crinkly notebook, jots it down, and hangs up. His mission accomplished, Harry allows himself to luxuriate in his imaginings, anticipating how he'll receive Lucille's gratitude and Molly's growing admiration, when the flaw leaps out at him like a carnival barker. There's no way he can profit from this thousand-dollar outing because there's no way he can point himself out as Lucille's benefactor without appearing to be precisely what he is—someone doing a good deed solely to receive the credit for having done a good deed.

He begins to pace anxiously, turning over the scenario in his mind. It's not the thousand dollars he cares about—although coupled with his check to Max, Lucille is becoming an expensive proposition. Rather, he's anxious to make some sort of progress with Molly. The reverberations of her hug still haunt him and fuel his imagination, and like any addict, he wants more. He's going to have to step into the light a bit, make himself a little more visible if he's to make any substantial gains here. He makes a mental note to pick up an actual copy of *The Count of Monte Cristo* and mine it for inspiration.

But something else has entered Harry's field of vision, an unfamiliar—no, rather, a distantly familiar—sensation that's come out of this latest turn of do-gooding. An odd ebullience is tickling at his belly, an unexpectedly satisfying resonance at having done a good deed. He's made his peace with the notion that this particular flourish will go uncredited, yet he's surprised to find it hasn't diminished his good feelings at all. In fact, Harry actually feels rather like a Good Guy, something he hasn't felt since that first year of his marriage to Anna, when, despite having already won her heart and hand, he delighted in attending her for her sake.

Well, that's something, Harry reflects. At least he hasn't forgotten everything.

Six

In which our hero spins his wheels

FIVE YEARS INTO Harry Rent's marriage to Anna Weldt, he is all too aware of his slowly widening waistline, and although he realizes that Anna cannot have failed to notice it as well, she hasn't yet registered an objection. Harry takes this, if not as approval, then as an implied embrace of the status quo. His belly has been on a steady march outward since the first year of their marriage, and although he's scarcely a candidate for gastric bypass, the ropy muscles and lean, rangy tautness that Anna so enjoyed during their courtship are on the verge of becoming mere memories, a familiar yet distant alter ego found only in curling photographs.

Of course, Harry considers, it's not as though Anna is wholly unaware of what she's feeding him. What sort of metabolic miracles does she expect from him, he wonders, as he loads another helping of her perfectly al dente carbonara (made with eggs, not cream) onto his plate? He concedes that his own lack of self-control might play a passing role in his dilemma, but it would be much easier on him if she didn't ply him with such culinary wonders. By the end of the meal, it's all Harry can do to push himself back from the table and lurch toward the living room, belly straining at his trouser button despite his loosened belt. Flushed, he plops onto the sofa and—Good Lord, he thinks, am I *panting*?—rubs his midsection with satisfaction. He catches sight of his Buddha-like devotions in the hall mirror and feels a shameful jolt at the sight of his profile. He glances back to Anna, who works quietly clearing the table, and wonders how revolted she must be by this change. Beads of sweaty shame prick his forehead, and he swears—absolutely swears—that starting tomorrow he's going to eat a bit more sanely. That this vow is made almost nightly and invariably falls to dust amid morning bagels and cream cheese does little to dampen Harry's conviction that a new day is at hand.

Later that evening, in bed, Harry watches from beneath the sheets as Anna undresses. Unlike him, she remains as lithe-limbed as she was the day they married. Certainly, her patrician WASP metabolism plays no small role, but she's remained active during their marriage, cycling and doing something called "spinning" which Harry dimly understands to involve a stationary bike and loud music. She's even gone so far as to hint that Harry would be welcome to join her. Her hints take the form of rhapsodizing about her spinning instructor, one Robby Geerchyk, whose inspirational and therapeutic values she extols at every opportunity with the mien of an escaped cult member. Harry's found himself wondering from time to time if there is some budding romantic attachment between Anna and Geerchyk, but he's never had the courage to inquire.

Although he always keeps the light low to hide his defects from Anna, Harry feels a mild stirring as Anna slips her diaphanous nightgown over her slender silhouette. He doesn't experience such stirrings often enough anymore, not for his taste or Anna's, but as with all things, Harry hasn't looked too closely at the source of his tapering desire, and Anna hasn't forced the question. Still, he recognizes a window of opportunity when he sees one, and as she slips into the bed beside him, he places his hand on her hips and pulls her closer. With the carbonara still straining at the elastic waistband of his pajama bottoms, he can't help but feel a bit like a troll who has come to ravish the sleeping virgin.

Surprisingly, he gets a slight erotic charge from this idea and lets the scenario take hold as he snarls and roughly paws at his wife's garments. It's clear Anna doesn't share his incipient exhilaration, but she's sufficiently grateful for any signs of sexual life from her husband that she endures his rough penetration from behind and his labored breathing and the dull, sweaty slap of his belly against her muscled back, though it's probably a mixed blessing for both that it's over quickly, Harry being more of a sprinter than a marathoner.

Harry rolls onto his back, wheezing, trying to gauge how disappointed his wife is. True, the encounter hasn't gone remotely as Harry'd hoped, being marked by a higher than usual level of thrashing, panting, and perspiration. But as his heart gradually begins to slow—a bit too gradually, he notes—Harry hopes that the display of desire has, at least, bought himself another comfortable little window of denial in which no uncomfortable discussions need be had. He hops out of bed to empty his bladder, and when he returns, he's surprised to find Anna out of bed, standing there naked, waiting for him. She pulls him into an embrace and lets her hands fall to his stomach, cupping his belly. With a barely audible whisper she says, "We have to do something about this."

Harry looks at her in the room's dim light and nods, then releases himself and slides between the sheets.

"Good night," he says, giving her a gentle kiss, masterfully hiding the shame he feels. He rolls over—it's not uncommon for them to sleep with backs turned—and he lies there weighted under with numb surprise, despite having been fully aware of the situation. Although her tone conveys that it was no easier for her to say than for him to hear, it's as though Anna has violated some long-held covenant by speaking aloud of the matter. This is no good. He wants to hide himself away.

He looks down at his stomach, inhales deeply, and holds it, trying desperately to lower his stomach's profile. But before long he is forced to exhale, and his belly hangs there limply, disinterested in Harry's shame. He presses his hands into his flesh, trying to push his gut back into remission, but it's still no good, and Harry feels ill, sick to his stomach, as though it's only now begun to reject helpings two and three of carbonara.

"Are you okay?" Anna asks softly, her voice betraying familiar regret at, yet again, embarrassing her husband.

Harry nods. "Little queasy . . . that's all."

It's more than that, though. It's every indulged impulse coming back to haunt him; it's the throb of his bloated stomach; it's the feeling that once again his wife is embarrassed by him, as she was once before, on that awful day in Greenwich.

Harry stands in the reception area of Evolution Cycling, clipboard in hand, reading the standard release form and wishing he'd brought his lawyer. Alexandra, the beautiful twenty-year-old who efficiently mans the desk, dismisses the document as "a formality." Harry nods dumbly as he signs the waiver with reluctance as such words as *heart attack* and *accidental death* and *unconsciousness* leap ominously off the page.

The waiting room is pleasant, airy and bright, finished with blond wood paneling and vast casement windows that look out onto a charming commercial courtyard bounded by shops and a café. There'd be something bucolic about the setting were it not for the pulsating beat of amplified Motown and encouraging shouts of "Go! You can do it!" rattling Harry's teeth as he signs. He smiles weakly at Anna and Alexandra as he hands the clipboard back.

"First time, huh?" Alexandra asks. "Don't be nervous. It'll be fun. Robby is a *great* instructor." At the mention of Geerchyk, Anna's head begins to bob appreciatively, as do the heads of several other men and women waiting for the present class to conclude. Claire's snort of derision is the sole dissenting note. She's never cared for Anna's coach, but

Harry begged her not to leave him to face this trial alone, and so she reluctantly suited up in baggy sweats for what she swears is her last appearance in a Geerchyk class.

"Sheep," she mutters.

Harry ignores her and appraises the waiting area, which is filling up as the hour mark nears. This Geerchyk clearly has some kind of following, Harry notes, as his eye ranges over this lineup. He's surprised by how many young and attractive women are present, and how simultaneously distracted and self-conscious he feels. The men are no better, slim and powerful, eyes steaming with purpose.

He watches as Anna chats with the riders, the other regulars. There's clearly a bond here, and he tries to look nonchalant as she introduces him to her cohort. One by one, the testimonials follow:

"First time? Hey, that's great."

"You'll love it."

"It's incredible. Robby is, like, God."

"Just relax and have fun."

They're welcoming and encouraging, but all eyes keep anxiously darting back to the studio doors, which finally swing open on the hour and discharge the previous session's riders.

Harry watches this limp, soggy crew emerge. Men and women, flushed and red-faced, soaked more thoroughly than if they'd emerged from a swim. Harry's struck by the waft of humidity and the thick, pungent perspiration that fills the air. Finally, the exhausted students are followed out by their instructor, yet another stunning young woman whose legs and arms ripple with strength. Harry feels a surge of relief that this woman won't be teaching him—he can't imagine concentrating on his ride watching the likes of her, and she'd make him even more self-conscious than he is. If he's going to go into cardiac arrest, he'd prefer to do it in front of a guy.

Even before the last of the riders has exited the studio, the regulars are filing in, jockeying for position, nearly sprinting for the front row of bikes. Harry stands clear, letting them pass as he peruses the row upon row of spinners. They're malignant beasts, standing in deepening rows like black iron minutemen in formation.

"Let's sit here, Harry," Anna says, picking a bike about three rows back—not far enough in the rear for Harry's taste. But he nods and walks up to his bike, examining it closely. All black metallic angles, still slick with the sweat of its previous rider. Harry winces, and Anna hands him a disposable wipe, which he opens to gingerly wipe the bike down, at pains not to touch his predecessor's perspiration. He holds the used nappy between his thumb and forefinger helplessly, and Anna points to a trash can. Harry deposits it and returns to the bike to find Anna and Alexandra waiting for him, working together to adjust the bike to his measurements and clipping a pair of sneaker cages into place.

"You'll probably need one of these, honey," Anna says, as she slips a gel seat cover over the spinner's saddle.

Alexandra pats the saddle brightly. "Okay, upsie daisy."

Harry undoes his baggy sweats to expose his baggy shorts and ghostly calves. With a final look of trepidation, he mounts the device, and Alexandra busies herself, tightening his pedal straps while Anna expertly supervises.

"This is the main thing," Alexandra says as she makes her final adjustments. "It's your first class, don't try to keep up. Just do what you can—there's nothing wrong with sitting and pedaling the whole time."

Harry nods. "Sitting."

Anna chimes in helpfully, "Try to keep your arms loose, relax your upper body, keep your hips back."

"Hips back."

"Yeah. Listen, Robby can be kind of . . . intense," Alexandra warns. "Don't worry about any of that. Just have fun. You have your towel and your Gatorade?"

Harry nods and smiles wanly. Alexandra winks and disappears. Anna is about to mount her bike when she stops and puts her hand on Harry's arm.

"Thanks."

He nods again and she climbs onto her bike. The entire class is already up and out of the saddle, jogging briskly in place, and Anna quickly assumes the same position. There's a quiet intensity in the room and all eyes are forward on the empty bike that occupies the stage. Besides Harry, only Claire remains in the saddle, spinning her legs without much energy or purpose.

It's a setting worthy of a grand entrance, and Robby Geerchyk makes the most of it, clad from head to toe in black sportswear—skintight riding jersey and tights—and swept-back sunglasses. He nods incrementally at a handful of riders who appear to strain hungrily for his acknowledgment as he strides to his bike. He scans the room intently as he feeds a CD into the sound system. Strange European techno sounds fill the room, and Harry groans, wishing the Motown lady were back.

He watches with grim fascination as Geerchyk fluidly sets his bag aside, slips into his cycling shoes, and mounts the bike, his movements liquid, his steps more poured than taken. Harry takes him in and is impressed, despite his outré musical selection. He has the small, compact build of a cyclist, lean and taut. His hair is black and cropped short, and now that his glasses have come off, glistening gray eyes survey the riders even as they seem fixed on a point of intensity somewhere out beyond the walls of the studio. After a moment of taking in the room, Geerchyk assumes the same standing position as the rest of the class. Harry realizes that he and Claire are the only riders still seated, and so he makes the effort to rise but can't manage the balance and coordination and within a few seconds opts for the saddle. Claire hasn't bothered, wholly unmoved by Geerchyk's mystical presence, and Harry can't help but admire her adamantine unwillingness to be swept along with the crowd. He's always been struck by her independence, however foolhardy it's been at times.

Geerchyk rides silently for several minutes, leaving Harry longing for his predecessor's encouraging shouts. Sure enough, after another two minutes, Geerchyk leans in close to the mike and, with a weirdly monotone intensity that's almost inaudible over the music, says, "Just . . . warming . . . up."

Geerchyk's eyes traverse his riders one last time, and it's clear he's got all the survey data he needs. He leans back into his microphone. "If you need help setting up your bike—"

Harry perks up at the possibility of acknowledgment.

"—you're in the wrong class."

Knowing snickers dot the room. Geerchyk smiles unconvincingly. "Just kidding." No one believes him, not even Harry.

"Add a gear."

And so it continues, Geerchyk riding silently, riders standing and sweating with effort, Harry doing all he can just to push the pedals around as he wonders, This *is Anna's guru? Are these people all nuts?* He looks to Claire questioningly—they've teased Anna in the past about her Geerchyk adulation, but he still can't believe this is it. Claire simply rolls her eyes as if to say, *I told you so.*

He glances up at the clock on the wall and is alarmed to find that only seven minutes have elapsed. Seven minutes! Fifty-three to go, and now Geerchyk spots Harry looking at the clock, and he's reasonably convinced that he's committed a cardinal sin. He reddens and puts his head down, focusing on the pedals strapped to his feet. Sure enough, Geerchyk speaks up.

"Stay *with* your ride, people. Stay focused. Every pedal stroke counts. If you were on an outdoor cycle and you turned to look at a clock, what would happen to you? You wouldn't do it."

We're not on an outdoor cycle, Harry whines within. He looks around the room for confirmation, but Geerchyk's logic seems inescapable to all but him. And still, the riders pedal on.

"Add another gear."

Harry looks down at the knob on the bike. How do they know, he wonders, what a gear is? There are no gears, after all, just variable levels of resistance. Harry contents himself with the notion that they're faking it—just as he is—touching the knob at the right moments without actually increasing its resistance. Once again, Geerchyk seems to read his mind.

"The flywheel weighs thirty-eight pounds . . . that's nineteen pounds a foot . . . you carry more than that when you walk up the stairs. If you sit there spinning away with no resistance, you may look cool"—his tone suggests the contrary—"but you're wasting your time. You're only fooling yourself. Add a gear."

Harry sighs and tentatively touches the resistance knob, turning it slightly, testing his bravery to its modest limits. He feels his pedals slow minutely. Okay, good enough, good-faith effort, he thinks.

"Another ten minutes to the top . . . just . . . warming . . . up."

Ten more minutes of this standing-jog business, so Harry takes the opportunity to check out his classmates. He can't help but fasten first on Excessive Head Motion Lady about two rows behind him, wearing dark sunglasses inside and dramatically flipping her blond ponytail from side to side—if anyone in this room wants to be looked at as much as Harry wants to be ignored, it's this woman. Looking to the front, he spots Fawning Acolyte Guy in the first row, decked out in almost identical black garb to Geerchyk, riding with intensity and staring hungrily at the master for any crumbs of approval. Then there's the team of women riders—six of them decked out in matching cycling jerseys and tights, pedaling in almost perfect lockstep. In the row behind him is About to Expire Old Guy, a gray-haired slip of a man, also in cycling duds, who hunches over his bar, gripping and pedaling for dear life, head rocking as though he's having an epileptic seizure. Harry finds himself hoping the studio has a signed release from this guy. His eyes, at last, rest on Anna.

He can only take her in at an angle as she rides beside him, and he doesn't want to disrupt her ride by watching her too obviously. There's something regal about his wife, with all the good and the bad that the term implies. He's struck by her elegance as she pumps her legs in a single, seamless, continuous motion. Her thick brown hair is pulled taut into a luxurious ponytail that clings damply to her muscled back. Now the grunts of About to Expire Old Guy prompt a Harry thought: If he died here today on this bike, what would Anna remember about him?

What images would she hold in her memory as the years passed? The thought that her lasting memory of Harry might be the coarse troll who roughly penetrated her the night before fills him with a fleeting but genuine sorrow. Anna seems to read his thoughts because she turns, glances his way to check on his progress, and smiles as if to reassure him.

"Back it off. Flush it out."

Harry has no idea what these terms mean, but as he looks around him, he notes that the riders have (a) decreased their resistance and (b) sped up their cadence. Harry triumphantly removes his sliver of resistance but can't spin the wheel any faster than the leisurely pace he's got going. And yet despite his slow pace, Harry is already drenched with sweat, his thighs and calves shriek at him, and his heart is pounding out the back of his head. He's also begun to experience a world-class case of ass-chafe. But Harry is grimly determined—if About to Expire Old Guy can do it, so can he.

"Active recovery. Lower your heart rate with fast turnover. Trust your body, have faith in its capacity to recover."

Harry has no such faith in his body and suspects he'd be a fool if he did. In fact, the only capacity he can consider just now is his newfound thirst for Gatorade, a beverage he's always hated. He's fifteen minutes into the one-hour ride and has already finished his first bottle, and now his bladder is announcing its presence. But he's fairly certain that to leave the bike to urinate would constitute an even greater faux pas than watching the clock. And even worse than the prospect of heaping ridicule on himself is the possibility of embarrassing Anna, a possibility that roots his blistering ass to the saddle.

In that uncanny way she seems to have of reading his thoughts, Anna glances over at him once more. It's got all the hallmarks of another checking-in look—an encouraging smile, a quick wink—but now Harry wonders if there's more to it than that. Is he imagining it or can he detect an undercurrent, a buried plea, ever thought, never articulated: *Don't embarrass me here—please.* Harry would like to think that he's being paranoid—after all, she's been nothing but supportive and encouraging despite his gracelessness on the bike. But Harry can't forget that he's here at her request with all of its echoes and implications. He's been right before about what's remained unspoken, and now he's simply not sure which Anna is riding with him—the one who privately loves and supports him, or the one who has always publicly seemed vaguely ashamed of him. Such uncertainty. It's been his lot for years, and he wonders if his wife finds him similarly unpredictable, though he knows he's flattering himself—he's sure she knows his every move before he makes it, before he himself knows it. Being known so thoroughly by another should warm him, he knows, but it doesn't.

She turns back to the front and he can no longer see her face, so he's left with the dissolving wake of his impressions. As these unhappy echoes subside, he realizes Geerchyk is speaking again.

"Do not quit . . . stick with it. Losers quit. They quit because they think it serves them . . . Because they're afraid . . . of being uncomfortable . . . of failing . . . afraid of what they might find . . . There's so much fear, people. Let it go . . . and find out what lies beyond your fears. Add three big gears and up and climb."

Harry considers Geerchyk's wisdom as the riders around him rise, their cadences slowing under added resistance, defined, rippling calves forcing attached pedals around and around. Despite the stab of irritation Harry feels—he's convinced that somehow Geerchyk's words are addressed directly to him—he acknowledges a kernel of truth in his patter, sees his own fears reflected and amplified through Geerchyk's microphone for all to hear.

"You choose to be fifteen pounds overweight . . . you choose to eat fast food . . . you choose to not ride with enough resistance . . . Everything, it's all your choice, and you can also choose to change . . . But people don't want to . . . It's hard and it's scary and so they stick to what they've always known and nothing ever changes . . . Add a gear."

And now, to his great surprise, Harry begins to feel this unanticipated surge, this sunburst of will that drums up from somewhere within, spurred on by Geerchyk's exhortations, which are beginning to make a kind of endorphin-soaked sense. Harry feels a glimmer of something, a grasping at the change that Geerchyk promises is possible, and that Anna seems to crave.

"That's it, folks . . . don't go easy, don't back off, don't quit . . . push it and remember that change costs . . . it doesn't come for free . . . there's a price and you better be ready to pay if you think you're gonna get anywhere. Add two more gears and hands in three. Five minutes to the top."

Now, as Harry looks between Claire, who pedals at the same laconic pace she began the class with nary a hair astray, and Anna, who has taken on Geerchyk's challenge and is pushing harder, he realizes he has a choice to make, an allegiance to stake out. His natural state, he knows, is more disposed to Claire, and even now that's where his inclinations are leading him. But something pushes him toward his wife, toward her yearning, toward her purpose. He finds that he would very much like to ride beside her, to keep up with her. He has no idea how to do this, but Geerchyk's words have infected him and he makes his choice to follow his wife.

Yes, Harry thinks, with growing excitement bordering on euphoria. I can do this. I'm gonna do it, I'm gonna climb, I'm not gonna quit. He looks around and notes how the riders are positioned—hovering back over the saddle, arms relaxed and fully extended, back flattened almost parallel to the floor. With a near absolute surge of conviction he adds some gears—not the full complement but a legitimate load of resistance far beyond anything he's carried thus far—and he does a workmanlike imitation of the other riders.

He immediately regrets the impulse.

His thighs painfully register their objections almost at once and he's gasping for air, suddenly giving About to Expire Old Guy a run for his money in the First to Die sweepstakes. His only thought is of backing off the resistance knob, but he makes unexpected eye contact with Geerchyk, all black-clad power and fleetness, and he'd swear that he detects a fractional nod of the coach's head. An unprecedented bit of encouragement that steels him to press forward despite his increasingly slippery grasp on the metal handlebars and his now throbbing bladder.

Did Anna see that? he wonders, hoping desperately that she did. He glances over to see what he can divine, but Anna is locked in her own death struggle with her climb. Harry is disappointed that what is sure to be his finest moment of the day has gone unnoticed.

"Two minutes to the top."

The desire to ease the resistance is growing, getting harder and harder to resist. The pain reverberates throughout Harry's body, and now the only thing he can think of is how much better he'd feel if he eased off. He remembers Alexandra's admonition not to try to keep up, and he reasons that for a first-timer he's surely done more than one could have hoped for. But even as he lays the foundation of rationalizations, he catches himself doing just that and finds himself strangely divided, struggling against himself. Geerchyk once again seems to read his thoughts.

"Remember, people, it's mental. Your mind will quit before your body does. Don't let it give in. Be strong . . . One more minute."

Harry glances over at Claire, and the darkness in her eyes suggests that she knows she's lost her ally to the cult. To hell with her, he thinks. So close now, Harry can't conceive of surrendering with a mere minute remaining, although he'd never understood just how terribly, painfully long a minute is. The seconds drag by as he keeps glancing at Anna, hoping she'll look his way, notice his efforts, give him some small bit of validation. But there's nothing and Harry begins to wonder if she's ignoring him. Rationally, he knows she's probably as caught up in her work effort as he is in his, but once again he wonders if his ungainly exertions—a cycling mirror of last night's bedroom contretemps—might be embarrassing Anna. The thought breaks something within and his legs begin to slow, his momentum punctured. Then Geerchyk leans forward in the saddle. "Sprint to the end! Thirty seconds. *Go!*" His legs begin moving in a blur, and an answering anger spurs Harry, and now quite unexpectedly his legs are turning faster than he'd ever imagined they could. The high-pitched whine of the fast-moving chain finally draws Anna's attention, and she's startled at Harry's red-faced pounding.

He enjoys a brief moment of eye contact with his worried wife, which is when it all goes completely to hell.

The sudden burst of speed has caused Harry to brace himself against the handlebars, which are drenched with his sweat. He can feel his hand begin to take flight, but before he can stop it, it's slipped off the front of the bars, causing him to lose balance. As he twists to the right, his foot flies out of the rapidly spinning pedal, and with the last bit of support gone from beneath him, he pitches forward, slamming his crotch squarely onto the resistance knob.

Three days later, Harry finally returns to Evolution Cycling. He's not here as a participant now. Rather, he stands just beyond the courtyard, a bundle of irises—Anna's favorites—in hand. Although it's said that via some evolutionary sleight of hand the memory of pain disappears quickly, the memory of shame is considerably slower to dissipate—if it dissipates at all—and Harry's not quite ready to brave the pitying eyes of Anna's fellow riders and of Geerchyk himself.

Though it must be said that Geerchyk surprised Harry post-debacle. Having passed out from the pain, he came to some minutes later, stretched out on the sticky wood floor of the studio. The other riders had already departed. Only Alexandra, Claire, Anna, and Geerchyk himself lingered behind, administering to him.

"Harry, are you okay?" The first voice, Anna's. Concerned. Nothing but loving.

Harry nodded feebly as Alexandra handed him yet another bottle of Gatorade. "Here, drink this. You need to replenish your fluids."

He propped himself up and sipped from the bottle, avoiding eye contact with anyone.

Anna rose and dug into her gym bag. "You gave me a real scare," Anna whispered. She kissed his head. "I'll bring the car around."

Harry watched his wife silently mouth the word *Sorry* to Geerchyk before departing. Alexandra followed her out, in search of janitorial assistance. An awkward silence pervaded until Harry reluctantly raised his head, looked at Geerchyk, and sighed.

"Guess I really am in the wrong class."

Geerchyk studied him for an uncomfortably long moment and surprised Harry by smiling. Surprised him even further with the warmth of his smile, so far a cry from the cold cycling automaton of the stage.

"You've got heart. The rest comes, if you want it."

Harry nodded, already certain that he'd completed his last spinning class. He sensed that Geerchyk probably knew this, too, but he crouched down and put his hand on Harry's shoulder.

"If you're going to ride—if you're going to do anything, for that matter—do it for yourself. For the right reasons. It's your ride, not your neighbor's, not your wife's, not even mine. She knows that," Geerchyk said, indicating Claire, who remained unmoved by his praise. "It's not enough to know what you want to do—you have to know *why* you want to do it."

Harry nodded again, exhausted, spent, and humiliated. With the freedom of one whose dignity has already been shredded to bits, he asked Geerchyk, "So, by the way, are you sleeping with my wife?"

If he was surprised by the question, Geerchyk betrayed nothing. Instead, a sadly sympathetic look crept into his eyes as he shook his head. "I don't do that sort of thing. And neither does Anna. Don't you know that?" He sounded genuinely surprised.

"Yeah. Sorry. I'm not myself right now." Harry swigged at his Gatorade as Geerchyk patted him once on the shoulder before departing, leaving Harry and Claire alone in the fetid studio. She regarded her brother-in-law with sorrow.

"You poor schmuck," she whispered not unkindly.

Harry couldn't disagree.

He didn't discuss either exchange with Anna over dinner that night as he shoveled helping after helping of garlic mashed potatoes onto his plate. Once the throbbing in his groin had subsided, the only souvenir of his exertions was a ravenous appetite. Anna didn't seem to mind his desperate shoveling down of multiple portions of food. Only when the meal was cleared away did the subject of the day's outing come up at last.

Harry had been dreading the conversation all evening. From the earliest days of their marriage, he'd worried that he was something of a disappointment to his wife, and once that had been confirmed, he'd worked to keep the opportunities to fail to a minimum. And although he knew Anna would never unleash the full brunt of her disappointment at him, he imagined that her disapproval lurked in some hidden place that would one day fill to capacity and finally burst loose with the pent-up letdowns of their marriage. Harry's constant struggle was to keep that holding cell of regrets as empty as possible. But he knew that tonight he'd have to face at least one of them.

"Listen, I don't think the spinning thing is going to work out for me."

"That's okay, Harry. Don't worry. We'll find something else."

And that was that. Harry was surprised by how equably she greeted his news and moved on to other subjects. So, in expression of his gratitude, he's shown up to meet her today, irises in tow. Precisely at the hour, the muffled sound of applause drifts into the courtyard, followed quickly by the dispersing riders. Harry holds far back, just beyond the edge of the courtyard, eager to stay out of sight as the regulars march past. There's Excessive Head Motion Lady, already chatting on her cell phone . . . About to Expire Old Guy lurches and stumbles across the courtyard . . . The cycling team walks out in single file, as if drafting even when walking . . . And Anna pulls up the rear, talking to Fawning Acolyte Guy.

"So how's your husband?"

"Recovering, thanks."

"Guess we won't make a spinner out of him?"

"No, he hasn't got the back for it. He has disk problems, and it just gave out on him."

Harry has barely a second's grace to slip into a doorway so as not to be seen by his wife, disappearing reflexively as he contemplates this lie.

He has no back problems, never has. *Not again, Anna,* he thinks as this new wave of shame washes over him as he stands facing the doorway, back to the street, flowers hanging limply in his grasp. Gradually it dawns on him that Anna's equanimity over dinner probably masked relief. Relief that she wouldn't have to make further apologies or excuses for him. That he wouldn't embarrass her again. Again.

Now, with growing anger, Harry remembers the other time Anna lied about him, the first time, the worst time. But unlike then, when he stood dumbly in the hallway and never mentioned it, something takes over Harry and propels him into the scene. He steps directly into their path and holds Anna's eyes.

"My back is fine," he says, choked, barely audible.

He hands the flowers to his surprised wife, turns, and hurries off, neither hearing Anna's muttered "Shit" nor seeing her drop her head into her hands.

Seven

In which our hero spills blood

ABRIDGED OR UNABRIDGED? That is the question.

Harry stands in the deserted, brightly lit Fiction & Literature section of his favorite chain bookstore, weighing a book in each hand. In his right, *The Count of Monte Cristo* (Penguin, unabridged) weighing in at a formidable 1,276 pages. In his left, *The Count of Monte Cristo* (Puffin Classics, abridged) tipping the scales at a svelte 396 pages. Harry weighs the pros and cons of each, literally as well as figuratively.

He can't deny that an irresistible bit of cachet comes with being an unabridged sort of guy. If depth follows effort, as Harry is reasonably convinced that it must, surely his best hope for a Dantès-esque rebirth must be found in these pages.

But Harry also knows himself, knows the limits of his attention span, and fears that *The Count of Monte Cristo* (Penguin, unabridged) is fated to end up as little more than an impressive desk ornament. And, he reasons, if the story can effectively be whittled down to a mere 396 pages (Puffin Classics, abridged), then how necessary can the rest really be? Harry's a bit under the gun, eager to move along his grand scheme, and he's not sure he's got the time to accommodate what must clearly be nine hundred pages of authorial self-indulgence.

And yet. Knowledge is power and Harry considers the effect of having an additional nine hundred pages (Penguin, unabridged) of power at his beck and call. And what if some essential nugget of wisdom, some brilliant bit of planning, is located in that nine hundred pages somewhere, its value unappreciated by the underpaid junior editor who hacked away to produce the minibook (Puffin Classics, abridged)?

Still, there are practical considerations: transportation, for example. Harry anticipates the inconvenience of hauling around a monster tome (Penguin, unabridged) and realizes that the Puffin Classics, abridged, will comfortably fit in his pocket, his briefcase, and resting on the crest of his belly in bed. To his credit, however, this strikes him as an exceptionally shallow basis on which to choose a book, particularly one with anticipated life-altering effects.

What to do? As he always does when faced with seemingly impossible choices, Harry punts the decision.

"Excuse me. Can I ask you a question?"

Harry addresses this question to the disinterested scraggly goatee behind the information counter. Despite a balmy summer evening, he wears a knit wool ski cap that just fails to cover a variety of eyebrow piercings. A thousand-page tome by a fashionable three-named novelist lies open before him, and he annotates it obsessively and lovingly in a tiny, crabbed script.

"Excuse me."

Goatee looks up with an expression that suggests that the sanctuary of his private study hour has been intruded upon. The energy of a reply beyond him, he settles for a raised eyebrow inviting Harry to proceed.

"Do you think there's a big difference between these?" Harry holds up Penguin, unabridged, and Puffin Classics, abridged, for inspection.

"About nine hundred pages, looks like," Goatee mutters, returning his attention to his literary ablutions.

Thank you, that's helpful, Harry thinks but doesn't say.

"Well, I was hoping you could tell me a little more. I'm having a hard time deciding."

Goatee can scarcely keep the impatience from his face. His eyes flick briefly between the two books. "The long one," he says, before lowering his head again.

"Really? Why do you think?"

Goatee shrugs, indicates the open volume before him. "I like long books."

"Sure, I can see that. But that might not exactly be germane to my situation."

Goatee continues to scribble away, exhibiting no interest in Harry's situation. "The short one, then."

Harry looks down at the volume in hand. "It's just kind of hard to imagine you can tell a twelve-hundred-page story in a four-hundred-page book, isn't it?" Harry's detailed examination of Penguin, unabridged, prevents him from seeing Goatee sigh, pocket his pencil, close his book, and quit the information kiosk. Only when Harry looks up does he realize he has, once again, been abandoned. With the resigned shrug that is as familiar to him as his own voice, he opts to purchase both copies. He knows he's likely to read only the shorter one (Puffin Classics, abridged), but he also knows that the day is sure to come when he will find himself inconsolably curious about what has been elided in the missing nine hundred pages, and for that day he'll want Penguin, unabridged, close at hand.

Standing in the checkout line, Harry scrutinizes the covers. The portrait of Edmond Dantès that coolly regards him from the cover of the Penguin, unabridged, is striking, not merely for the strongly set jawline and thick, wavy hair of the Marseilles seaman. It's the glittering purpose behind his eyes, the sense of an unswerving certainty, that Harry now swears is being transmitted directly through his fingertips, filling him with an unfamiliar strength and determination. His spine visibly stiffens in response, with the effect that his typically ill-fitting suit finds and settles into the previously hidden contours of the man and for the first time appears to fit him properly. He signs the credit slip placed before him with an uncharacteristic flourish, tosses the pen onto the counter with feigned nonchalance, and finds himself making direct eye contact with the salesclerk as he offers up a slightly too loud "Thank you." The salesclerk nods in acknowledgment as she calls, "Next," unimpressed with his transformation. But Harry's not to be dissuaded so easily, and he sweeps the bag containing his books off the counter and strides to the door, then pauses at the sight of Goatee burrowing into his text. All at once, Harry's mouth dries and his heart begins to pound with anticipation. He knows what he has to do. Clutching Edmond Dantès under his arm for strength, he strides over to the information counter.

"Excuse me," Harry says, not quite as forcefully as he'd like, but it's hard to be the count of Monte Cristo with your heart in your mouth. Goatee continues to fetishize his volume. Harry, to his surprise, reaches over and closes the book shut.

"Hey!"

"Don't 'hey' me. I'm a paying customer. And you're here to help me."

Harry turns and heads out to his car. It's not the performance he'd hoped for. He'd considered swearing a bit, perhaps even a physical threat or two. As it is, sweat dots his upper lip and he failed to keep the quaver out of his voice. A comparatively mild censure, to be sure, and looking back from the street, he can see Goatee has already lost himself in his bloated book. But as assertions of self go, it's a high-water mark for Harry, and nothing can dim his giddy pleasure. With a last glance at the cover of the Penguin, unabridged, Harry starts up the car, and he and Edmond Dantès pull out into traffic and head for home, the gray Impala following at its usual discreet distance, unnoticed as always.

Harry steps into his living room, books tucked beneath his arms, and marches past his brand-new answering machine with its insistently blinking *12* but doesn't bother to hit Play. It's been three days of

Claire's entreaties, and Harry's nerves are pretty well shot by her unrelenting presence, her Commendatore to his Don Giovanni. Harry's not unsympathetic to her loss, but, after all, it is his loss, too, and the whole Ghost of Banquo *j'accuse* business is creeping him out, picking at guilty scabs he's desperately trying to let alone. And so, as he has before, Harry sighs and stabs at the delete key a dozen times.

Perhaps he's still flush with the afterglow of his face-off with Goatee. Or perhaps it's the continuing formidable stare that beams out at him from beneath Edmond Dantès's hooded eyelids. But something aligns just so within, and Harry takes another unprecedented step toward controlling his own destiny.

He dials the phone company, propping the phone between his ear and shoulder. He pulls Puffin Classics, abridged, from the bag, sets it on the table before him, and flattens it open to page one, kneading the spine of the book like pizza dough.

"Hi. Yes, I'd like to change my phone number, please."

It doesn't take long. A mere fifteen minutes, including hold time—which Harry devotes to beginning the adventure of Edmond Dantès's rebirth—and it's done. The only phone number he's had for the last eight years, this bit of numerical DNA that tied him to Anna in the dialing digits of all who knew them, has been snipped away. As Harry declines the option of a forwarding message, he experiences the same sort of giddy excitement that he felt back at the bookstore as he realizes that—for the moment at least—he's totally adrift, alone, untraceable. The old Harry Rent is no longer so easily summoned, not that Anna's friends have tried with any diligence. The initial wave of condolence calls has largely faded, replaced almost exclusively by Claire's badgering messages, and Harry can't help but notice, at last, that their friends were, in fact, Anna's friends, and now those friends are gone. Whose doing was that? he wonders. Did Anna try to insulate him from the other parts of her life, for reasons Harry hates considering? Or was he wholly unmotivated to extend himself into her circle—very possibly for similar reasons? It's another for the long list of questions Harry is intent on avoiding.

Harry's giddy solitude doesn't last long. Staring at the silent phone, he becomes increasingly aware of the inert object, imagining it remaining in total silence, never ringing again. Gradually, a sense of being attractively remote and mysterious transforms into a pitched dread of permanent exile.

Precisely three minutes and seventeen seconds after changing his number, he calls Max.

"Hello?"

"Hey, Max, it's Harry."

"Where are you calling from? I don't recognize this number."

Caller ID. Of course. Harry will have to be careful. It's true that total isolation isn't comfortable for him; but nor is indiscriminately tossing out this number. Fortunately, that's been the purpose of this call.

"Yeah, I changed it. I wanted to give it you."

"Changed it? How come?"

"Claire."

"How many?"

"Twelve. Today."

Max whistles a low, impressed whistle. "She always had chutzpah, that one. You *could* take the direct route and actually talk to her."

And tell her what? "Yeah, hey, Max, listen, can you do me a favor?"

"What do you need?"

"Call me back."

"Huh?"

"I'm gonna hang up. Just call me back."

A moment's silence. "Okay."

Max hangs up and Harry considers this odd request. He just needs to hear the phone ring once. To know that he's not irreversibly cut off. A single ring, that's all he needs, to assure him that he hasn't hastily ruptured life-supporting ties, that he won't live alone in silence for the rest of his days.

As he waits, he considers Max's advice about Claire. He realizes that Max is right, but the direct approach has always been Max's modus

operandi and Harry can't pretend to have the . . . the what? he wonders. The courage? The clarity? Maybe it's just the experience, simply
knowing how to walk in a straight line. Harry's not sure what he's lacking, but he knows it's something essential.

The phone doesn't ring back. Harry fidgets, tapping the cover of
Puffin Classics, abridged. It shouldn't take Max this long to call back,
but the phone remains silent and—although Harry's sure he's imagining it—Edmond Dantès's gaze seems to have taken on a malevolent
cast. Harry's heart beats more heavily and he fixes his stare on the
phone, willing it to ring.

"Jesus, Max. What the fuck?"

The silence risks undoing Harry entirely, so he seeks the sanctuary of
the kitchen to occupy his thoughts, a lifelong believer of the watched-
pot theory. He pokes through the cabinets in search of a snack, but he's
too unsettled by the silent phone to entertain any thoughts of food.

He pauses before the spice rack. Row upon row of spices, meticulously ordered by Anna, lined up like chess pieces awaiting an opening
gambit. He's a bit overwhelmed by the sheer variety of them all: rose-
mary, coriander, sage, parsley, oregano, sesame seeds, dill, cumin, bay
leaves, saffron, marjoram. What the hell is marjoram for? Harry wonders. The unbroken seal on the bottle suggests that Anna wasn't entirely sure of the answer.

The sharp ring of the phone makes Harry jump. He slams the cabi-
net shut, races for the receiver, and picks up the handset.

"Hello? Max?" he says breathlessly.

"Of course it's Max. Who else would it be? You said you just
changed the number."

"Jesus, Max, what took you so long?"

"Sorry. I had to take a piss."

"It takes five minutes to take a piss?!"

"At my age, that's grounds for celebration."

"Goddammit, Max. I said call me *right* back!"

"I did. Mostly. Settle down, kid. You okay?"

"I'm fine, Max. Fine. I'll talk to you later."

Harry hangs up the phone—harder than ever before—slumps back into his chair, and begins to calm down. Okay, the new line works, he's made the change, but he's not completely on his own. Life rafts are, after all, indispensable accoutrements for Harry, standard issue, not optional equipment. There are limits to how alone he's willing to feel.

Once his hand has stopped shaking, he picks up Puffin Classics, abridged. Walking past a growing pile of unopened mail that includes entreaties from Anna's lawyer and certified correspondence from her insurance company, he reads about the arrest of his friend and mentor, Edmond Dantès, to build his confidence for a return to Café Retro.

The first thing that surprises Harry is Lucille's mien. He'd expected that, given the lightening of her financial pressures, there'd be a commensurate lightening in her countenance, but he finds something pressed and furtive in Lucille's manner. There's a tension about her that's not all in keeping with her bettered circumstances; nor does it quite match her prior surly self. Harry tries to put his finger on it, and the best he can come up with is that she looks uncomfortable.

And it appears her discomfort is contagious. Molly's normally featherweight grace seems to be muddied underfoot, her shimmering radiance eclipsed and thrown into darkness by the long shadow of Lucille's gloom.

Harry wants to go over to them, to find out what's troubling them so, when he experiences an unpleasant creeping suspicion that what's troubling them, for some unknown reason, is him. He realizes he's been sitting at the same counter spot for nearly ten minutes and no one has offered so much as a glass of water. He wonders if he's imagining it, but then he catches the women huddled, joined by two other waitresses he doesn't recognize, whispering and glancing furtively in his direction. There's a bit of jockeying for position, and finally Molly nods and approaches Harry. The other two waitresses form a human shield behind which Lucille fidgets.

Molly sets her hands on her hips and addresses Harry with authority, but with her voice discreetly lowered. "Can I help you?"

Harry is taken aback by her tone, by the oddly formal request. "Um . . . I was a little hungry . . ."

"I'm not taking your order. I'm asking what you want."

Harry can't quite figure out a world in which these two normally contiguous ideas should be so completely unrelated and is about to say so when Molly cuts him off.

"Look, if you're some kind of stalker sicko, you're going to have to leave. Or I'll have to call the police."

Harry is speechless, overcome with sudden waves of despair and total confusion. He wants to protest. He wants to defend his honor. He wants to rewind the tape five minutes. He wants to not throw up.

"Err . . . ahh . . . ack . . ."

Molly looks at him expectantly, tapping her foot. Finally, Harry manages to squeeze out a shocked "Huh?"

Molly sighs and leans in close. She glances back at Lucille. "Look, I don't know what your personal kinks are, and, frankly, I don't want to know. But Lucille is a person, you know, and we're not going to let you bring any of your sick perv shit in here, do you understand?"

Harry is blinking rapidly, holding back tears, thinking back to the smiling Molly of the Monte Cristo as he desperately retraces the road from there to here. He considers that Lucille might have seen him looking in her window, but he finesses it as much as a sweaty, trembling Harry can finesse anything.

"Perv? Me?"

"Can I ask you something? What the hell are you up to? Paying off her bills like that. It's kind of creepy."

Harry's surprised to have been found out, although he considers too late that it's probably exactly what he would have done in Lucille's shoes—made inquiries, traced credit cards, unmasked his mystery benefactor. Still, it's not quite the reaction he was hoping for, and now

Harry has to improvise, do some world-class shucking and jiving, or this mission is going to be dead in the hangar.

Harry is usually a lousy improviser, lacking the fluid grace essential to making it up as you go, needing carefully studied maps and diligently rehearsed steps lest he find himself tangled beneath his own tongue. But there's something slightly different about Harry this morning, something about having seventy-five pages of Puffin Classics, abridged, under his belt, about feeling the lingering echo of his bookstore rebellion. And so, grasping at mere fog wisps of a plan, Harry looks Molly in the eyes and with all the sincerity he can muster says "You know, you're completely right. I'm sorry."

Of all possible responses, this is the one Molly is unprepared for. Taken aback but cautious, she yields just a fraction, enough for Harry to establish his beachhead.

"Huh?" Skeptical but listening.

"You're right. It does seem kind of weird, but I honestly didn't mean anything by it." Harry presses on, speaking quickly, momentum carrying him, trying not to give Molly much time to think about what he's saying. "I've never done anything at all like that, but when she complained about her foot and about how she couldn't afford a doctor, well, I felt so bad for her, and the truth is I've come to realize that I'm kinda blessed and lucky with my good fortune, and I just got this harebrained idea that I could help out someone who needed it. But I realize now, talking to you, what it could seem like. I really didn't think it through, I just followed what I know was a good impulse in my heart. I'd like to apologize to her. Would you ask her if I could?"

And here's the oddest thing. As he finishes his speech in a breathless rush, he finds that on some level he believes his story. He knows it's been modified and spun just a bit, but there are core bits of what he thinks is probably the truth. He *is* fortunate in his life circumstances, and it really *did* feel affirming to have helped Lucille out, a realization that, admittedly, he only experienced after the fact.

But it goes even deeper than that. Harry finds he feels somehow unfamiliar to himself, surprisingly un-Harry-like, but rather like this new and distinct creation, this odd amalgam of Dantès and Rent. Is that the secret of it all? Harry wonders. Believing your own spin?

Molly has gone back to Lucille and is consulting with her, explaining, pointing to Harry. Lucille seems uncertain, but Molly is clearly lobbying on Harry's behalf. His heart begins to beat faster. Has he pierced the veil of skepticism? He watches them confer, trying not to appear anxious or needy. Finally, Lucille nods and approaches Harry, Molly at her side.

"Yeah?" Lucille asks nervously.

Harry smiles what he's sure is a sheepishly charming smile. His success with Molly has charged him with an entirely foreign feeling that he suspects is what other people call confidence.

"Boy, am I an idiot. I'm really sorry if I creeped you out. I guess the road to hell is paved with good intentions."

Molly smiles at the aphorism, but Lucille looks at him blankly.

Harry presses on. "Look, I really didn't mean anything at all weird by it. I just remembered how unhappy you were about your foot and not being able to afford a doctor, and I just got this crazy idea that I could be helpful. Probably my own ego, too, reading too many nineteenth-century adventure stories and wanting to be a bit of a hero."

Molly can't help but pipe up with interest. "Really? Like who?"

Dantès to the rescue once more. "I love Dumas."

"You're a little old to be playing D'Artagnan, aren't you?" Not without edge but limned with amusement.

Harry makes a mental note to look up who this D'Artagnan is. "I'm eternally young at heart." He turns his attention back to Lucille. "Anyway, it was pretty foolish and definitely ill-considered of me, and I really do apologize if it was insulting or alarming in any way. I promise not to interfere anymore."

Lucille and Molly exchange a look, rating the performance, but

Harry knows he's pulled it off, the way a home-run batter knows when he feels the bat connect with a perfect fastball.

Sure enough, Lucille nods, then shrugs. "Well, thanks." She sighs. "Guess it's kinda nice to be outta the hole," she says grudgingly. "Now I just gotta do something about that shithole I live in . . ."

"How do you mean?" Harry asks with near perfect poise, even as he knows the answer, the memory of his firsthand examination of her squalor still vivid. But the reassurance of his invisibility outside her apartment has instilled him with hitherto unknown levels of confidence.

"Place is a dump. Holes in the carpet. Peeling paint."

"Well, you do have rights, you know."

Lucille's derisive snort shakes her whole body. "Rights. Yeah."

"Really, you do. I mean, minimally, good plumbing, a roof that doesn't leak. But your landlord also has got to paint and maintain the place. It's city law, he doesn't have a choice."

"Yeah, I can spout city law to him as he's throwing me out on my ass."

Now Molly chimes in. "Lucille, he *is* right. I mean, it can be a real pain, but you do have rights." Harry takes the opening and smiles at Molly. To his delight, she smiles back. They're allies now, a team. Another little connection has been forged, and however minute it is, Harry luxuriates in it, dizzied by the rapid and total turnaround in events. He pushes it, binding their little conspiracy a bit tighter.

"You should listen to your friend," he says to Lucille. "She's pretty smart."

Yes, she is. Harry can't possibly know just how close to a bull's-eye he's scored, how totally Bruce fails to acknowledge her smarts, how important it is to have her gravitas acknowledged, how completely working in this café undermines her intellectual sense of self. But he does note Molly's sharp intake of breath as she registers the compliment, and she's about to say something when her cell phone chimes. She pulls out the phone, looks at the caller ID, and scowls. She flips open the phone angrily and turns away from Harry and Lucille with a sharp "What?"

Molly wanders off, phone pressed to her ear, and Lucille can't resist a bit of long-suffering head shaking. Harry looks to Lucille, not going so far as to ask for an explanation, but aligning his eyes in just such a way as to suggest that he's receptive if she wants to unload. Which she does.

"That asshole boyfriend of hers. What a piece of shit."

"Oh?" Harry tries not to appear too interested.

"I don't know why she keeps him around."

Harry impales the worm on the hook and casts his line toward Lucille's gullet. "I don't know, he seems like a handsome kid. You know, if you like that kind of thing."

Lucille shakes her head in such a way as to suggest that Bruce's good looks haven't the slightest hold over her. She sneers at his presence— even though it's only through a cell phone, it's clear that he's unwelcome in any medium—and she weighs whether to open the vault for Harry. Feeling slow-roasted, Harry wills her mouth to move, and before long, without so much as an examining sniff at the hook, she takes the bait, swallowing it whole.

"He steals from her."

Harry can't conceal his surprise. This isn't what he expected. "What?"

Lucille nods through gritted teeth. "First it was just money from her purse, you know, loose twenties. She wasn't even sure it was him. Then bigger stuff—the DVD player."

"Jesus. Why doesn't she turn him in?"

Lucille shrugs. "You've seen him. He's a pretty boy. He charms her, apologizes, says the right things, and she gives him another chance." Lucille picks up a tray and heads to her section. "Either that, or she has a thing for losers. You'd have to ask her."

Harry considers it, watching Molly huddled in the corner with Bruce pressed to her ear. His guilty start—"apologizes, says the right things" struck too close to home—is evolving into a murderous rage that bubbles inside. He wants to tear his rival apart with his bare hands, when it occurs to him that he has absolutely no idea how to do so. He's never thrown a punch in his life and suspects that if he made the effort untutored, he would be both ridiculous and ineffective. But he's begun to realize that with Bruce in the picture this knowledge is increasingly likely to come in handy.

He runs his mental videotape of hundreds of hours of Hollywood punches, bare-fisted heroes dispatching villains with seldom a split knuckle or broken hand in sight, propelled onward through a hailstorm of blows, sweat, and saliva. But Harry's done enough X-rays of shattered fists to know that real fistfights are considerably messier affairs, and he hasn't a clear idea of how to traverse the distance from rage to the X-ray room.

And then it occurs to him. Harry's going to need Max.

Harry knows that Max's foulmouthed bravado landed him in more than one barroom brawl during his medical school days. "Cardiologists are the biggest collection of pussies in the known universe, who think they're king shits because they can carve up a fucking muscle," Max would snarl, invariably with a cardiologist-in-training within arm's reach. "That's all it is, a muscle. Your *ass* is a muscle, you know." As a podiatrist-in-training, Max was considerably less fearful about hand damage in a fight, and consequently the first (and often last) punch was usually his. "None of them could fight for shit," Max would tell Harry years later. "Except the proctologists. That always surprised me. Bunch of tough motherfuckers. Maybe 'cause they were always getting made fun of. One of them beat the living shit out of me for coming on to his girl. I was chatting her up and I asked her if she really wanted to spend a life with a guy whose index finger was always gonna smell of asshole, and *wham*, the son of a bitch dropped me like I was a sack of guano."

Harry's generally suspicious of older men who constantly celebrate the toughness of their youth, but in Max's case the notes seem authentic and on-key. He's confident Max will be a reliable guide through this unmapped landscape. And since Max has reached the age when he genuinely gives a shit about nothing, it's a bonus that he's unlikely to question too terribly deeply Harry's sudden and urgent desire to learn the mechanics of the punch. Which, in fact, he doesn't.

"What in the holy fuck do you need to know how to punch for?"

"I'm in my midforties. It seems like the kind of thing I should know by now. A guy rite of passage." Harry's hoping he won't have to tell Max the real reason behind his request, anticipating Max's usual bit of well-intended but discouraging common sense.

But Max persists. "You wanna kick someone's ass." A note of glee slips into Max's voice. "C'mon, tell your uncle Maxie. Who you gonna fuck up?"

"I'm not going to 'fuck up' anybody, Max. For Christ's sake. There's just this girl . . ."

"You wanna beat up a girl? What kind of sick fucker are you turning into?"

"Jesus, Max, could you please shut up for about three seconds?" Harry is surprised by this hitherto unexpressed bit of forcefulness but barrels on before Max can react. "I'm not going to beat up a girl. There's a girl and she's got this boyfriend who's kind of an asshole. I'm not looking for trouble but, you know, I might find it, and I'd like to know what to do."

Max sits on the line silently for a moment, and Harry wonders if he's irretrievably offended his old friend. When Max finally speaks, his voice is calm and grave. "Nobody's ever looking for it, Harry. Come on up to the house Sunday morning. I'll whip you into shape."

And so it's amid the glare of dewy Sunday morning that Harry and Max find themselves in Max's backyard, dressed in old-guy weekend casual, Bermuda shorts, T-shirts, flip-flops. Max is in lecture mode, which he enjoys.

"First of all, being in a fight is about taking punishment, not dishing it out, understand?"

"Taking it." Harry nods.

"The guy who stands the beating the longest is the guy who walks away when it's done. So don't get any heroic ideas—it's hard enough to even land a halfway decent punch."

"You're kidding. It looks so easy."

"Yep, and that's what you'll be thinking as you hit the ground. You know why you hit the ground?"

"Because . . . I thought it was easy?"

"Because you didn't protect your face. And he threw a sucker punch. Which, by the way, I strongly encourage at every opportunity. So rule number two: Protect your face."

Harry sighs. "Are there going to be a lot of these?"

"Hey, don't be in such a hurry to put your dentist's kids through college. Look, there's a million things to think about—you have to think about height, where your fist is gonna land. Only it doesn't matter because you have no control—adrenaline's high, tempers are cookin', you won't be thinking straight. And then the sound will just . . ." Max shudders.

"The sound?"

"Whaddya think, it's some clean snap or pop like in the movies?" Max shakes his head. "It sounds like a fist pounding a steak. It's fucking disgusting, and when you're busy being startled at how strange and disgusting it sounds—"

"Sucker punch?"

"Exactly."

And so the lecture continues, liberally sprinkled with heroic anecdotes of Max's pugilistic internship, blood-soaked tales of drunken derring-do, but Harry's not listening closely anymore. No, he's marveling at the strangeness of this tableau, wondering how little more than a hundred or so pages of Puffin Classics, abridged, could have transformed him from a man of such banal unobtrusiveness into someone now contemplating so violent a course of action. As he allows himself to be maneuvered into position and posed and propped by Max, who is droning on about fist velocity and angles of contact, he takes stock of this new color in his palette and finds, to his surprise, that he likes it. He'd imagined he would have been offended by the coarseness, the sheer sordidness of the act. But he's taken the first steps toward distancing himself from the Harry Rent who cowered before hookers. And although it's a mere sliver that divides them, it has the potential to become a chasm, a chasm that he increasingly desires to have yawning between the two Harrys. As he fixes his eyes on the far side of that divide, a transformed Harry beckons from what seems an uncomfortably distant vantage point. He seems so far away, so difficult to reach, this new Harry who's a worthy descendant of the adamantine Edmond Dantès. But in the forming of this fist, Harry's reached that point in the journey where the starting point seems equally distant, lost in backward-looking recesses, an undesirable return port. He's compelled onward toward this Harry of definition and solidity and heft, a Harry who wouldn't hesitate to place a firm hand on the shoulder of his foe, the reviled Bruce, and turn him toward himself to deliver the mighty blow he feels collecting in his curling fingers. He imagines stepping up to deliver the punch, and his imagination carries him a bit too far—one step precisely, said step taking him directly into the path of Max's oncoming practice punch.

Max is surprised by the sudden appearance of Harry in his line of fist and can't stop the blow from landing with the dull, wet smack of curled knuckles into filet mignon, although, to his credit, he does try, with the unfortunate effect of wrenching his back, locking him into an arm-extended, punch-throwing position. His cry of unexpected pain accompanies Harry's trip down to the grass, blood flowing freely from a smashed nose.

"Jesus Christ, Harry! What the fuck is wrong with you?"

Harry whimpers, supine on the grass, ignoring the statue of his friend groaning above him. He smears the blood from his nose, but when he stares at his crimson palms, it's not his own blood he sees. For some reason, all Harry can see is the blood that must surely have covered that surgeon's hand, that Dr. Couteau, as he tried to shock Anna's still heart back to life. Harry's fingers, he's now fairly sure, glisten with his dead wife.

Harry rolls over onto his elbows. Cupping his nose in blood-soaked fingers, he moans. Is this all that remains of Anna? This blood? And a houseful of things he doesn't know what to do with? All at once, the impossibility of making sense of his life, of determining his next move, settles into the empty spaces within him, immobilizing him. Over-whelming him at the prospect of administering his future. And for a moment, he's fallen back to the starting line and feels very much the old Harry Rent, helplessly aware of how farcical his hopes of a new self must be, how pathetically his clownish performance must appear to all those around him. Such familiar shame.

He spits blood into his palm and lowers his head. "Max. What am I going to do with all those spices?"

Eight

In which our hero makes a move

HARRY'S MADE IT home from Max's, but it hasn't been easy. There's the intense throbbing of his nose, his slightly blurred vision, the soiled handkerchief pressed tightly (but not too) against his nose. Harry had given up trying to keep the sticky patches of blood from staining the cream leather seats and focused instead on navigating the hills and valleys between Chez Max and home. After what seems an eternity (but was, in fact, nineteen minutes), Harry creeps the car into the driveway. Exhausted and battered. But home. Steeping in relief at his safe arrival. The tension of the day leaves his body in a rush, as he steps out of the car and crosses to his front door.

In this pleasant state of collapsing relief, the sight of stone-faced Claire waiting for him, partly obscured by some bushes, startles him so thoroughly he can barely suppress an un-Dantès-like shriek as she steps forward to intercept him.

"Harry?" Claire steps into view, and all at once the crashing minor chords of the overture to *Don Giovanni* ring in Harry's ears, seeming all too apt to him—the libertine confronted, penance demanded.

Mechanically, he whispers, *"Verrete a cena?"*

Claire stares at him blankly, never having shared her sister's love of the opera. She's dressed inappropriately, as always, trying hard to assume the footprint of someone younger and slimmer. Although it's early afternoon, she's scooped into a too tight black dress out of which her chubby arms jiggle. She totters on improbably high heels as she pushes back damp strands of bottled yellow from her forehead. Harry imagines that she might have been attractive a dozen or so years ago. (He briefly remembers something Anna told him about Claire's penchant for group sex—clearly she has always hungered for attention—but finds the image too unappealing to pursue.) These days, she has the sad air of one who still needs to be looked at long after interest has abandoned her. But where Harry's usually felt embarrassed and even protective on her behalf, now there's only pity.

"You changed your phone number," she says matter-of-factly. "Why did you do that? Because of me?"

She shakes her head, and Harry perceives that something has hardened in Claire since he saw her last. The raft of unanswered pleas have transformed her, giving her a strange new sense of purpose.

"Harry, whatever you're hiding, I'm going to find out." Her tone is utterly neutral but firm, without a hint of menace. "All of it."

She hands him a slip of paper. He glances down at it and beholds his new phone number.

"It took me an hour to get it. Harry, whatever happened, I am going to find out. I can find out from you, or I can find it the way I found this." And now, finally, a hint of threat, of anger suppressed, creeps into her voice, compresses it to a whisper. "She was perfect. If you're the reason she went under the knife . . . God help you if her blood is in some way on your hands . . ." She trails off as she notices the blood clinging to Harry. "Jesus, Harry. What's going on? Why won't you tell me?" She grabs his lapels, gaining force. "Why won't you talk to me? Who's the fat waitress?"

You're one to talk about fat, Harry thinks irritably but doesn't say. He's too bothered by this invocation of Lucille to pause and puzzle what and how Claire knows or thinks she knows. Instead, Harry experiences a brief flair of protectiveness for his charge, something he can't fully understand or explain. He doesn't like this intersection of his lives, of the old Harry and the new. Even as he hasn't yet figured out where precisely he belongs, he does note that Lucille and her travails seem more immediate and real to him than anything else. More than Claire's gradually threatening insistence, more than the unfinished business of Anna's death.

"For God's sake, Harry. Don't you have *anything* to say?"

It's true, Harry realizes. He's said nothing (in English, at any rate). He hasn't felt the need to. He's been strangely comfortable amid his thoughts—thoughts that (and this is something new for Harry) have all been oddly relevant, germane to the moment, not spinning away on some trajectory of distraction as they would have in times past. Harry thinks about this, about his uncharacteristic presence in the moment, and feels as if his feet are not so much planted as rooted into the soil of his home. His place. And when Harry speaks, it's with a voice he doesn't recognize as his own. Where does this deep, confident rumble come from, he wonders. But he won't second-guess it now, he needs it and so he'll ride it wherever it will carry him and knows he'll leave it for later to wonder if it's all merely a blind, a ruse, a narcotic that's keeping him from confronting what matters.

"Watch your mouth, Claire. And mind your own business, please. No one is sorrier about Anna than I am. But I don't owe you anything. It's best for you to leave now."

In the stunned silence that follows—and the shock belongs entirely to Claire; Harry's surprisingly sanguine in his declaration—a sliver of time is lifted up out of their lives and hangs momentarily weightless in the space around them, a moment in which Harry realizes alliances have turned. Claire looks as though she's about to respond but holds herself back. She smells the change upon Harry. Something new and possibly dangerous. Goose bumps appear on her chubby arms, and like a jungle cat that knows it's beaten, Claire wordlessly leaves the yard, her eyes an odd mixture of defiance and sorrow.

Harry emerges from the shower raw from scrubbing. Using brushes, three kinds of soaps, and a washcloth, he's labored long past the point when the last bloodstain spiraled down the drain. Even when the water went from steaming to tepid, Harry remained in place scrubbing dutifully. Not until he'd reduced the bar of soap to a lozenge did he finally step from the increasingly icy stream pelting his scalp. Now his face and neck bark an angry pink, and he's finally convinced that the smell of death no longer hangs about him.

Limbs thick with fatigue, Harry trudges his way across the living room, enjoying the sticky padding of his instep connecting with and then peeling from the hardwood floors. He glances over his shoulder at the line of damp footprints leading back to the bathroom and imagines how Edmond Dantès felt regarding his own footprints in the sand on the island of Monte Cristo, going forth to locate his treasure. But the unexpected ring of the phone prevents any serious playacting from taking hold. Harry is startled and grabs the phone without thinking, without looking at the caller ID, not that he'd recognize this number if he did.

"Hello?" he asks with mild irritation.

"Who the fuck is this?" It's a man's voice. Unsteady, wound tight, perhaps a little drunk—Harry detects a slight but noticeable blurring of word breaks. He's understandably taken aback by the question.

"Excuse me?" he replies, not as forcefully as he'd like.

"I said, who the fuck is this? Where's Katie?"

"You've got a wrong number, pal."

Harry hangs up, angry and shaken. His hand has barely left the receiver when the phone rings again. Harry sighs and answers, "It's still the wrong number."

"How can it be the wrong number? It's programmed in my phone, you asshole. Nice try."

Now Harry is getting angry. Having already stood up to an in-the-flesh Claire, facing down his telephonic tormentor is child's play. "Well then, you programmed it wrong, you asshole," he counters, rather deftly, he thinks.

"Listen, fucktard. Why don't you just put Katie on the phone. I know she's there."

"Listen, there's no Katie here, you understand?"

Now Harry's caller loses it. "Bullshit! Don't you fucking bullshit me because I will come over there myself and kill you both! You put that lying little bitch on the line and you put her on now! You tell her Elliott isn't moving until she gets on the phone!"

Harry suppresses an urge to laugh. "Elliott?"

"Yeah. Elliott. What the fuck?"

The urge wins. Harry laughs. "*Elliott*'s not exactly a name to strike fear into the hearts of men, is it?"

There's a silence on the line, and when Elliott speaks again, it's with subzero steadiness. "Okay. Well, how's *Glock*? As in nine-millimeter. As in cocked and in my fucking hand. Feeling any fear now, fucktard?"

Something unmoors inside Harry and the words come out before he can stop them. "Bullshit. A guy named Elliott wouldn't buy a gun."

And he hangs up the phone triumphantly. Another second, another ring, and Harry's convinced that there's something plaintive about the sound now. He lets the answering machine handle it. Elliott's shrieking rage fills the room. "Oh, yeah? Oh, yeah? Well maybe, maybe, I do have a gun, and, and it's loaded, and you tell that . . . that whore Katie that if she doesn't answer the phone"—and now the shrieks give way to throaty burbles and sobs—"that Elliott is gonna . . . gonna blow his fuckin' brains out . . . right here. Oh, shit, you bitch . . . goddamn it, Katie!"

Harry finds something in Elliott's fissures simultaneously heartrending and disturbing. Feeling uncomfortably the rogue and peasant slave, he picks up the phone, doing his best to calm Katie's aggrieved suitor.

"Listen, Elliott, I really am sorry. But I've only had this phone number for three days. It's brand-new."

There's a long silence on the line, which is finally punctuated by a roiling sigh of defeat. "Shit . . . Katie . . . I waited too long . . . I'll never find her now . . ."

"Waited too long? How long has it been?"

Elliott sniffs wetly and Harry can swear he hears the rough burr of a sleeve being dragged across a nose. "Four years."

"Four years?"

"Yeah."

"You've been in agony all this time?"

"Mostly, yeah. Two summers ago wasn't too bad."

"And you've only just now tried to call?"

"Uh-huh. Look, can I ask you something?"

"Sure, Elliott. You can ask me something." Harry feels his voice belongs to someone else.

Elliott's voice has shrunk, deflated. "I . . . I don't know what to do . . . I mean, this number, that was it. It was like some kind of safety raft for me, like she wasn't *really* gone. All I had to do was get the nerve to call. I know this sounds kinda lame but . . . it kept hope alive, you know? Now it's gone. I don't know what to do."

Harry fumbles, shot through with bolts of shame he doesn't fully understand yet, utterly unable to think of anything to tell Elliott.

"Well . . . um . . . you know, it's complicated . . . I don't know, life is . . . uh . . ." Harry sighs, wanting nothing more than for this call to be over. He grasps at straws. "Well, I'll tell you what *not* to do—none of this gun talk, okay? Seriously, whatever you're feeling, life does improve. It gets better. You get through the dark times. Sometimes, you just have to go through them to get through them, you know?" Here's Harry poaching in irony, marveling at the brittle falseness of the sentiments.

115

"I guess . . ." Elliott sounds unconvinced.

"Look, just promise me—no Glocks, okay? You won't try to get a gun or something crazy like that?"

Elliott sighs. "I can't anyway—I have a history of mental illness."

Harry looks down at *The Count of Monte Cristo* and exchanges a helpless look with Edmond Dantès.

"Look, Elliott, I have to go. Take care of yourself, okay?"

"Yeah. Thanks. Hey, but wait."

Harry sets his jaw and clenches the receiver.

"If I find you've been lying to me, and Katie's there with you, I will come over and seriously fuck up your shit. Okay, that's all. Good night."

"Good night, Elliott."

Harry hangs up the phone exhausted, a marathon runner collapsing at the finish line. He's unnerved by the exchange, though not for the predictable reasons. Sure, it's possible Elliott is a genuine wack job and perhaps Harry's safety is in jeopardy. But he isn't that worried about his physical well-being. It's gnawing concern for his spiritual well-being that's got him on edge.

He walks into his bedroom and sits down beside his nightstand. His heart throbs with dread as he contemplates the still unopened drawer, its job lot of Anna's random expressions of affection still hidden within. He touches the knob of the drawer and begins to crack it open, but the momentary flash of the red plastic of the Swiss Army knife buried within is all it takes for Harry to quickly close the drawer again. He gets up from the bed and crosses to Anna's walk-in closet, where her clothes still hang, untouched. He hasn't been able to bring himself to begin the work of packing her away, erasing these final traces. He pulls a favorite cream blazer of hers close to his face and swears he can smell faint traces of Anna's perfume, hints of French roses. He's suddenly frightened by the knowledge that this fading scent will soon disappear entirely. There's a desperation in his wish to capture it somehow, preserve it beneath safety glass where he can always find it, but he stands there immobile. How is it, he wonders, that four years later

Elliott is a sobbing wretch over the loss of his inconstant Katie, whereas, for all his efforts, Harry can barely bring himself to face his wife's wardrobe, cannot even touch the hunk of bright red plastic in his nightstand for fear of what it will unleash? He returns the blazer to its place, reproaching himself for his cowardice as he closes the closet door behind him.

Evening has settled around the house, rolling into the canyon amid thick, crawling tendrils of fog that finger the bars of Harry's balcony. This is Harry's favorite time of the day, and despite the throbbing of his swollen nose, a brief, genuine feeling of peace washes over him. Puffin Classics, abridged, sits open, facedown on his thigh. He's watched Dantès return to his old life, unrecognized as the count of Monte Cristo, dispensing money and wielding influence. He knows Dantès will achieve his revenge, so it's now just a question of watching how he engineers it. Still, he finds it curious that Edmond seems to be deriving little pleasure from exacting his vengeance, whereas he is still buzzing with newfound strength at having dispatched Claire and Elliott. So, without any sense of foreboding at all, he enjoys this moment, despite the terrifying specter of the Swiss Army knife that whispers to him from his nightstand drawer. Despite that a phone call from Max is about to abruptly terminate his reverie.

At first Harry contemplates ignoring the call, fearing it's Elliott wanting to talk some more. But when he hears Max's voice on the answering machine, he answers. It takes precisely four seconds—the length of Max's greeting—for him to wish he hadn't.

"Hey, that waitress with the smelly feet called here looking for you—you got her evicted."

Miraculously, Harry stops himself at the threshold of Café Retro.

He'd been all set to burst through the doors, hurry to Lucille anxiously, and beg forgiveness. But a Dantèan whisper in his ear brings him up short, and he becomes aware of his panting, of his racing heart, of his sweaty forelocks. And he heeds the whisper and collects himself, wondering, *What would Dantès do?*

Dantès would certainly *not* explode into the café and prostrate himself in abject desperation. No, if he's learned nothing else from his mentor, it's clear that chilly control is all. And it occurs to him that, however inadvertently, he's created another opportunity to be Lucille's savior, and—as a glance through the window confirms—Molly is in the house, so best to make the most of it. He takes a final breath and, convinced that he's ratcheted himself down to a reasonable facsimile of cool, sweeps into the café, taking long strides, hands thrust rakishly into the pockets of his trousers. At the sight of him, Molly hurries over, ashen.

"Oh my God . . . You got Lucille kicked out! She's on the warpath!"

Harry looks over to her section, where the other waitresses avoid her like antelope giving a hungry lion a wide berth. He gulps slightly but maintains his confident air. "Don't worry. We'll sort it all out." He begins to walk toward Lucille.

"Hey, I *really* wouldn't go over there if I were you."

Harry winks at Molly, the very picture of self-possession, hoping she'll be charmed.

"My God, what happened to your nose?"

Harry's fingers fly to his nose. Crap. He'd forgotten all about it. He sighs, deflated—it's hard to be the count of Monte Cristo with a big purple nose.

"A little scrape. Don't worry. I'll be right back."

Molly winces as he heads off in Lucille's direction. She follows at a discreet distance.

Harry approaches Lucille from behind as she's pouring coffee for a table of three kids just beginning their evening of clubbing. Harry taps the red-and-white-striped shoulder, which reminds him of nothing so much as a massive peppermint candy, and says, in his closest approximation of a charming rogue, "So, I hear we had a bit of a problem."

At the sound of his voice, Lucille sets down the coffee pitcher and turns glacially toward Harry, sulfuric bursts flaring in her eyes. "We? No, *we* don't have a problem. *I* have a fucking problem."

Harry fails to notice her knuckles bunching into a fist the size of a small ham. He fails to notice the massive arm cock itself for a blow. All he notices is that, for the second time this day, he's on his back and his nose is a bloody, pulpy mass.

"*Now* 'we' have a problem." Lucille stalks away and Molly rushes to his side. She drops down to her knees beside Harry.

"My God! Are you okay?"

Harry's pleased to have her attention even as he's irritated by what is so obviously a stupid question. Blood streams down his cheeks, his nose approaches Cyrano-esque proportions—of course he's not all right. But he gamely props himself up on his elbows and nods, which is when he notices Molly stifling laughter.

"Are . . . are you laughing at me?"

Molly tries and fails to choke the laughter back with a poorly placed cough. "I'm sorry . . . I know . . . it's terrible of me . . . but . . ."

She trails off helplessly and Harry surprises them both by laughing along with her. It's a genuine laugh, a shared appreciation of the absurd, and for a moment the pain in his nose disappears amid the first unforced connection he's experienced with this woman.

She holds out her hand.

Harry takes it.

She pulls him to his feet and hands him a napkin, which he gingerly dabs at blood streaming from his battered nose.

"What happened?"

"You got your butt kicked is what happened."

"I was actually in the room for that part. I mean what happened to Lucille?"

Molly escorts Harry to the counter—the corner most remote from Lucille's section—wets a clean napkin for him, pours him a cup of weak, lukewarm coffee, which he doesn't touch, and explains how, fortified by Harry's and Molly's prodding, Lucille returned to her landlord to demand new paint, new carpet, and even new appliances (her initiative) or face the combined wrath of the Housing Authority, the Better Business Bureau, and the *Los Angeles Times*. Her landlord listened patiently without comment, and she returned home from her late shift Thursday to find her lock changed and her meager belongings in a heap in front of her door. Lucille's attempt to apologize and backpedal was complicated by the landlord's having already installed a family of Filipino immigrants, who accepted the threadbare apartment without complaint. Since Lucille held Molly to be at least partly responsible, her belongings were being stored at Molly's apartment until further arrangements could be made. And with the words *further arrangements*, Molly looks to Harry expectantly.

"She spent the night on my couch, but you have to do something."

Two damsels in distress.

Two opportunities to come to the rescue.

And so it comes to pass that this unlikely troika—Harry, Lucille, and Molly—should find itself packed into the Jaguar, heading into the bohemian hills of Echo Park, where Molly reposes in what Harry imagines is languid splendor but is in fact a medium-sized studio apartment that—via the addition of a single, well-placed sheet of drywall—her landlord rents as a one-bedroom. It's not an area that Harry knows well, and though he won't go so far as to say he avoids it, he's certainly never frequented it, the tattoo/piercing-per-square-foot ratio being a bit high for his comfort. But Molly is clearly taken with her hood and rhapsodizes about it in between giving just-slightly-past-last-minute directions—"Oops, you wanted to turn there"—and so Harry does his best to give it a fair shake. But in truth he's so awash with anticipation at entering Molly's Lair that he can think of little else, and so he settles for the occasional well-placed appreciative grunt, a habit he honed to perfection with Anna whenever her declamations threatened to intrude on his interior monologues.

Lucille sits silently in the backseat, glowering despite Harry's having secured her a room in a boutique hotel a mere ten blocks from Café Retro. She appears to have little use for Molly's enthusiasms, for her extolling of the area's "multicultural, multiethnic vibe," for anything other than the comfortable bed that's eluding her at the moment. And her silent disapproval is palpable throughout the vehicle, expanding like a lead bubble and fueling Molly's anxious chatter. As these two women engage in a vicious and deepening cycle, poor clueless Harry, squinting at street signs, tries not to smash the Jaguar's fender against the low, crumbling masonry walls that seem to gird so many of the properties as they wind upward through the hills.

Harry notes the distinctly different character of the hills that are home to the two of them. His own hill, farther west in Bel Air, faces the ocean, so clean breezes frequently waft through. The properties are set back from the road, hidden, evasive, obscured from one another's sight lines, backs turned determinedly toward one another. The lawns are neatly clipped, the driveways—where visible—smoothly paved, occasionally glinting with reflected sunlight. Molly's Echo Park hill consists of more ramshackle, urgent, intruding and extruding little boxes, nearly intertwined with one another, or so Harry would swear. Cars fill driveways, spill onto the streets; house paint peels and lawns run wild. The hills couldn't be more different, Harry notes, even as he reflects that they were probably thrust into being by the same jagged fault lines. But geological certainties can't answer the question that's begun to nag at Harry—do the differences in the hills they call home potentially speak to deeper differences still? What, realistically, can the possible outcome of all this be? And underneath it all lies the growing nagging sense that perhaps it's time to stop mucking about with this girl's life and get on with the business of tending to his own. But Harry's not ready to tackle such troubling thoughts. Today's strategy: defer.

"That's the one. Third on the left." Molly points and Harry follows the trajectory of her slender arm, her finger, the tip of her nail, and there's Château Molly. It's little more than a dilapidated box, but Harry's heart is beating the way it did when he first beheld the Hall of

Mirrors when Anna dragged him out to Versailles. Harry noses into the driveway as much as space allows and gets out. He marvels at the quiet of the night, the smell of jasmine in the air—the same silence and smells he gets at home. Molly gets out and waves him along as she heads up to the front door. Lucille doesn't leave the backseat.

Harry catches up with Molly as she fiddles with the key in the lock. He can't pull his eyes from the nape of her neck, gleaming palely in the moonlight.

"Sorry. The place is a total disaster."

"Don't worry about it."

She swings the door open and the sound of television greets them both. Molly rolls her eyes with irritation and bounds in.

"Dammit, Bruce. I told you to call before just showing up."

Dammit, Bruce.

With two words, Harry is torpedoed, a halved *Lusitania* on its way to Davy Jones's locker. He stands there stunned and unmoving as the staccato notes of Molly's irritation mingle with Bruce's bored monotone.

"I called. No one was here."

"Well, didn't that tell you something?"

"Decided to surprise you."

"Well, you did."

Her tone—suggesting the surprise is a sufficiently unhappy one—gives Harry the impetus to begin moving his feet, reaching back into the recesses of memory where the instructions for taking steps are hardwired into place. Even as the evening spins off course, Harry makes the most of the opportunity, taking in the furnishings on an eager hunt for Molly Clues. Her cramped living room is an eclectic catalog, and its unusual entries range from African masks to Kandinsky reproductions. Harry's surprised to find a copy of a glossy rap-music magazine, with the industry's latest wunderkind assuming a menacing pose on the cover.

Molly looks at him with embarrassment. "Sorry about this, Harry."

Bruce, slumped on a gasping sofa, resplendent in his wifebeater and five-o'clock shadow—damn these pretty boys straight to hell, Harry thinks—doesn't even lift his eyes in Harry's direction.

Molly turns to take in the bit of TV programming that has Bruce so captivated and groans. "Jesus fucking Christ, Bruce. You're totally hopeless. I can't believe my lover watches reality TV."

"Dude, I'm not your 'lover' . . . What are you, Danielle fuckin' Steel?"

Molly shields her eyes with exasperation. "You know, I don't have time or energy for this right now. Harry? Let me show you where her stuff is."

Harry nods and crosses the room—making sure to momentarily slow his pace in front of Bruce to maximize view-blocking potential—and follows Molly to the kitchen, where she points to two shabby suit-cases propped in a corner.

"There. That's it."

She reaches into the freezer and pulls out a vodka bottle. She pours herself a shot and lights a cigarette.

"Sorry. Mind if I smoke?"

Harry shakes his head. She holds out the bottle to him, offering. Harry shrugs and nods, and she pours him a shot.

"I know what you're thinking."

Harry surprises himself by saying, "You couldn't possibly know what I'm thinking."

"You're thinking, 'What the hell is this smart woman doing with such an asshole?' Right? Admit it."

Actually, Harry's been thinking about how much he would like to have Molly up on her countertop just now, legs spread open, sliding luxuriously inside her, Bruce's corpse attracting flies in the living room.

"More or less."

"Well, maybe I'm not as smart as either of us think I am."

She inhales deeply and looks to Harry with what he would swear looks like a request for reassurance in her eyes. And although the thought that he doesn't *really* know how smart Molly is does briefly flit

123

across his mind, it's clear, as he's observed before, that it matters deeply to her. The road ahead is clear.

"Well. Even smart people do . . . questionable things sometimes."

Molly nods, trying it on. "Yes, they do, don't they?"

"Yes. And . . ."

"And?"

"And every day is a new chance to . . ."

"Make different choices?"

Harry nods and summons a spandex-clad memory. "And it's not enough to know what you want . . . you have to know why you want it."

Molly smiles, and Harry's heart is screaming, and even though Bruce is sitting on the other side of the door, something whispers inside that he can kiss this woman right now and she won't mind. Harry's never ventured a step of this magnitude, but he knows it would come easily to Dantès and wants very much to see if he can pull it off. Molly's face hasn't moved, her eyes are still turned searchingly and appreciatively in his direction, but before he can plug in all the coordinates and put the dance into motion, the kitchen fills with the harsh blare of the Jaguar's horn. Harry curses and hurries back through the kitchen, back past Bruce, and sticks his head out the door holding his forefinger up to Lucille, who is unmoved and continues to lean on the horn. Harry wags his finger furiously and the horn continues, and now lights are coming on in neighbors' windows, and so he stomps out to the car, opens the door, and gently but firmly pushes Lucille away from the horn and back down into the backseat.

"One. Minute," he says with fury. Like Claire earlier, Lucille smells something in Harry's pores that chokes the retort she'd planned. Harry turns back to find Molly struggling into the doorway with the suitcases. With a last glare at Lucille, he hurries back to help her.

"Sorry about that," Harry says.

"Don't worry. I'll give you a rain check on the drink."

Harry nods and takes the suitcases from her, tossing them hard into the trunk, and pulls off into the night.

"Here you go."

Harry holds open the door to Lucille's room. He's already placed the suitcases inside, made financial arrangements with the front desk, and now all he wants is to go home. She lumbers past him and sits down on the edge of the bed, back turned to Harry.

Harry feels a poke of irritation. Not a thank-you. Nothing. But it's commingled with something else—pity? compassion?—as he watches this woman settle alone into this hotel room that is her only address, with two suitcases that contain the sum of her possessions. He sighs.

"Lucille."

She doesn't turn.

He speaks to her back. "Look, I'm sorry. I didn't think you'd get kicked out like that. It's not fair."

She snorts with derision at the concept. "Fair," she whispers with husky bemusement.

"We'll sort this out. I promise. I'll help you find a new place." He shrugs, the tendrils of Lucille's gloom beginning to pry into the crevasses of his heart. "Maybe it's an opportunity."

Nothing from Lucille. He sets the room key on the bed behind her. "I understand why you're mad."

She turns slowly, looking at him disbelievingly over her shoulder. *You couldn't possibly understand* anything *about me.*

It's under the withering indictment of her glare that he slowly closes the door and leaves her.

When he gets home, two messages are on the answering machine. One from Nicole, calling in sick. Again. And one from Elliott. Asking Harry to call. Just to talk.

Nine

In which our hero crosses the Rubicon

THREE YEARS INTO Harry Rent's marriage to Anna Weldt, on a clear, warm June evening, Harry officially tells his first lie to his wife.

"So who did you pick?" Anna asks.

"Her name is Nicole. Seems like a smart kid," Harry answers. "Some sort of business degree."

Remnants of Friday-evening dinner sit on the dining room table between them. Emptied wineglasses, a pat of warm, misshapen yellow butter. Anna's plate is so clean that an observer could be forgiven for thinking she hasn't eaten yet. Harry's plate, on the other hand, is a mass of bread crumbs and butter smears that have begun to march in formation onto the floral tablecloth, but Harry's too light-headed, too dizzy with fear and shame, to register them. Besides, he knows Anna will expertly sweep them away when the meal is finished in that strange, Harry-erasing fashion she has. He's become convinced that his grand purpose in Anna's life is to provide that which needs to be cleaned up.

"Well, that's good news. You can use the help," Anna says.

126

Harry nods, eyes downcast into the bottom of his wineglass, wondering how sadly transparent he is. A glance up at Anna's departing back—she's begun, as expected, to clear the table—suggests that his feeble gambit has held. He props up the newspaper to give himself some cover as he contemplates what has just unfolded.

I've lied to Anna, Harry thinks, with a growing sense of unreality. *I've lied to my wife, over what? Over a whiff of perfume and a tight pair of jeans? Why the hell did I do that?* Harry assuages his guilt slightly with the notion that it wasn't planned, he hadn't rehearsed a story or anything like that, he'd simply been given his at bat and unaccountably swung at a wild pitch. After all, it's a question of degrees, Harry considers. Harry has his own painful experience with his wife's fixation with advanced degrees, with the academically lettered, and he has lived ever since in the long shadow of his inadequacy, despite his having an M.D. Every time he visits with Anna's family and friends—the Greenwich Cohort, he calls them—he's bewildered by the dizzying array of jumbled vowels and consonants tumbling in anxious pursuit of last names—M.F.A., M.B.A., Ph.D., Psy.D., C.E., D.L.S., L.L.M.—as though the imprimatur of Old Money wasn't enough, but needed additional validation, like parking stickers piled thickly onto a garage exit ticket. (Harry used to tease Claire about her insistence upon introducing herself as "Dr. Weldt" at cocktail parties, whereas he, "an actual doctor with an actual practice and stuff," introduced himself as "Harry." She would shrug and sigh ruefully, "It's a family thing, Harry. I'm damaged." Harry would come to see she wasn't exaggerating, and he never liked her more than when she struggled against the baleful influence of the elder Weldts, although following his own humiliation at their hands, the teasing stopped.)

And so he tells himself that it's not because he's smitten with Nicole—harmlessly smitten, of course (infidelity being something Harry is convinced he's genetically incapable of), but smitten nonetheless—that he's lied to Anna, but rather because he wants to avoid her disapproval with respect to Nicole's unlettered state with all its unpleasant echoes. (It's with a start that Harry remembers her spelling of *assistent* and makes a mental note to deep-six her application.)

As the dining room table is magically restored to its pristine state around him, Harry relaxes a bit, content that he's done his subversive bit to aid the underclass and level the playing field ever so slightly, all the while protecting his wife's academic sensibilities.

Harry's delusion holds precariously until bedtime, but in the quiet darkness of the conjugal bedroom it collapses like a mobile home in an Arkansas twister. Harry gradually becomes aware of his rapid heartbeat, his clammy palms, his shortness of breath.

Anna sleeps on her side, back turned to Harry, and even though he can't see her face, even though the gentle rising and falling of her shoulders tells him she's asleep, Harry feels accused. It's his imagination, of course, a guilty conscience run amok. They've slept in this position for years—Anna with her back turned, waiting for Harry to move up against her and enfold her in his arms. But when he tries to do so tonight, he's struck by how awkward he seems, how self-conscious and empty the gesture feels, how stiff and leaden his arms are. Alarm feeds on itself, spiraling, amplifying. Surely Anna can tell, Harry worries. She must be able to feel that something's wrong, feel his dishonesty vibrating through his pores. As he grows more tense, he becomes hyperalert to any perceived changes in her sleeping rhythms: Was that a sharp breath? Is she moving? *Oh, God, why did I say that?* Harry becomes aware that he's soaked with guilty perspiration, and the more he strains to remain still, the more disruptive he feels himself becoming.

OK. Deep breath. Just relax.

Harry steadies himself and takes a moment to scrutinize Anna, to convince himself that she is, in fact, sleeping. He slides away from her and studies her back. It's relaxed, undulating in its dreams. Harry feels a surge of protective pity for this vulnerable landscape. He places a hand between her shoulder blades, on the spot where he imagines the blade of his first lie has slipped in. He caresses it gently as though his touch might heal the wound, and she stirs sleepily beneath his touch, sighs a contented sigh at the warmth of his palm, and inches closer to him. Harry gently kisses her back and drapes an arm around her, wrist dangling limply over her hip. He'll apologize in the morning and tell her the truth. I'm sorry, I don't know why I did that, it just sort of blurted out. I guess I felt guilty because she's pretty and I didn't want you to think that was why I hired her.

But that's exactly *why you hired her.*

Harry ignores the voice, closes his eyes, and waits for sleep to come.

"So which business school did she go to?" Anna asks over breakfast.

"UCLA, I think," Harry says, the response tumbling out involuntarily, over and done in a flash before he can register what he's saying and get in its way. His mouth is a flapping barn door.

"Really? I wonder if she studied with Carter."

"No idea," Harry says evasively. "I'll have to ask her."

"When does she start?"

"Monday." Harry is relieved to be able to answer something truthfully.

"I'll ask her myself. I'll stop in and say hi, introduce myself. We can reminisce about the old place."

Harry nods as he sips his coffee and fretfully looks through the morning paper. It was *not* supposed to unfold this way. He'd sorted it all out the night before, planned what he was going to say, how he'd say it, and Anna had to go and foul it all up as usual by not giving him the chance to do it his way. Just once, he wishes, she would give him the time, the space to follow his own design. He's quite certain it would have come off well, perhaps even brought them a bit closer in an odd sort of way. Instead, he's thwarted once again, left with another of his usual untenable situations without a glimmer of an idea about what to do when Monday morning rolls around.

Harry still toys with the idea of coming clean, wondering if it's not too late for a full confession, throwing himself on Anna's mercy, but he can't visualize the moves. Excusing one white blurt of a lie seemed doable. But to have slept on it, not come clean, and then lied again bespeaks (mistakenly, Harry's convinced) greater premeditation. The odds of a bounceback seem slim, and Harry's not a gambler, cautious even when the odds favor him, which they presently do not.

Harry's only vaguely aware of Anna's presence around him, going to great lengths to avoid looking at her, catching only fleeting glimpses of her hand wiping the table clean, of dishes stacked on her arm. He's stuck in numb contemplation of this previously uncharted side of himself. He's deeply troubled by the apparent ease of his dishonesty, and he wonders, point-blank, *Am I a liar?*

The reflexive answer is no, despite the freshly minted evidence. He's aware that he's always been rather ploddingly honest in a reliable-if-not-always-terribly-attractive, never-cheating-on-his-taxes sort of way. Anna learned, for example, that questions like "Does this outfit make me look fat?" were best avoided with Harry. But he also knows that it was this quality that made him oddly attractive to her. She'd told him, early in their courtship, "There are no mysteries with you, Harry. I like that." He'd always suspected that it was his uncalculating side that raised his profile above her swarm of Greenwich suitors and their Byzantine rules of courtship and comportment, swaddled as they were in their odd, vestigial prohibitions, arcane codes, and almost cabalistic fetish for ritual.

So wherefrom, then, this hitherto unimagined capacity for deceit? Has it been lying dormant, like an appendix, waiting to burst yellowly to infectious life? Or is it something else, an evolution of things, of their lives together, that has grown in him this new and unwanted appendage? Now he anxiously rewinds the tapes, reviews his mental catalog of their moments together, searching for any telltale precursors, tiny fibs, glib evasions, harbingers of falsehoods to come. But there's nothing, the record is clear, at least insofar as Harry can see. Perhaps this is a freak, an anomaly, a onetime blip. Sui generis.

Harry begins to relax a little, to forgive himself this trespass—a blot, to be sure, but in the grand scheme truly a minor blot. He's still Harry, after all. Harry the Honest. Harry the Plodding. Harry the Slightly

Dull and Predictable—but reliable. One doesn't change as suddenly, as drastically, as all that. He sighs and sets the newspaper down, his body sagging with relief at having passed his own reassessment so resoundingly, determined to find an honorable way out of this mess, when Anna speaks up from the kitchen.

"I've got some time Monday. How about eleven thirty? We can take her to lunch."

"Sounds terrific."

The acrid chemical smell of the printing shop and the rattling cacophony of photocopying machines do little to settle Harry's stomach as he bobs and wobbles nervously at the counter, awaiting his turn. He spreads his materials out and looks them over, reluctant to raise his head and make eye contact with anyone. Presently, ten stubby, ink-stained fingers with nails chewed to nothingness enter his field of vision. Harry contents himself to address the fingers.

"Can you print this"—Harry indicates one pile of materials—"to match this?" he asks, indicating the other. Fingers turns Harry's handiwork toward himself and peruses it.

"Offset?"

"Sure," Harry says, having absolutely no idea what he means.

"Yeah, no problem. What's it for?"

Harry has feared all along that this bit of guerrilla cut-and-paste was likely to prompt questions. Fortunately, he's anticipated this and has a riposte—albeit a feeble one—at hand.

"It's a prop. For a play."

Another day, another lie.

What am I turning into? Harry wonders. Okay, this is a stranger and not his wife. And he's lying to fingers, after all, as opposed to looking into eyes and letting rip. But there's a light-headed ease, coupled with a premeditation absent from his lies to Anna, that rumbles suggestively within like a pre-eruption temblor.

What the hell am I doing?

131

Fingers lifts the document and examines it. What Harry is doing is this: He has obtained an actual UCLA business school diploma. (Max's son Josh was a graduate whose stellar academic performance saw him summoned to Wall Street within hours of his graduation, leaving the reliably cooperative and incurious Max the custodian of his degree.) Using an X-Acto knife, Harry has liberated the document from the confines of its plain black frame, his sloppy and unsteady cuts confirming the wisdom of his choice not to pursue a career in surgery. Matching the diploma's font on his computer, Harry has overlaid Nicole's name and is now poised at the penultimate step, the final stage being a meticulous reframing of the original, as well as the creation of a matching frame for the copy.

Harry's aware of a whole host of logistical concerns that he hasn't even begun to tackle, not the least of which is how to enlist Nicole's aid in this deception. But it's all Harry can do to move forward one step at a time, clinging blindly to a conviction that somehow things will work out and he'll make it if he can just get through today, through this particular problem. And although there's little in Harry's past to give him such limitless faith in his ingenuity, it's all he has at the moment. As is his fashion, Harry makes do.

Fingers sets down the diploma as Harry pulls out his wallet.

"How much?"

"Thirty-five. Plus tax."

A steal. "Great." Harry pulls out two twenties and slides them to Fingers. "Can I wait for it?"

Fingers' sarcastic laugh is the first thing to alert Harry that he's back in that familiar, trouble-strewn landscape known as Harry-land.

"End of next week. Maybe Wednesday."

Harry feels his head in a gradually tightening vise, a deep throb making its way to the surface. The pain finally lifts Harry's head, and his eyes fasten on his torturer. Thin wisps of silver hair, a flattened boxer's nose, a gray smock with a variety of pens and pencils staining his pocket. Unsympathetic, disinterested, precise eyes.

"Um, oh, boy . . . I really need this sooner."

"Sorry. We're jammed up."

"It's really kind of an emergency."

"Important play?" Fingers asks sarcastically.

Harry ignores the gibe, astute though it is. He fights the anxiety rising in his chest. He tries to hold his hand steady as he pulls out his wallet again. "Don't you have some kind of rush fee?"

Fingers shakes his head with disgust. "Why is everyone in such a hurry these days? This shop does quality work. You can't rush that."

Harry considers explaining *exactly* why he's in such a hurry but realizes that Fingers is unlikely to greet his tale with much sympathy, and for an all-too-brief instant Harry considers that he'd probably be right about that. Instead, he places a hundred-dollar bill on the counter.

"Will that help?"

Fingers is unmoved.

A second bill joins the first. "Better?"

Nothing. Fucking artists.

A third bill. Now the money disappears, crumpled into an ink-stained fist.

"Come back in an hour."

Dazed and reeling, Harry stumbles out into the fresh air, unsure how he'll spend the next hour—sitting in his car, probably, driving anxiously around the block. But he's sure of one thing—even at ten times the price, he's gotten a bargain. Mendacity, it appears, is a small-ticket purchase.

It's been an unbearable weekend for Harry, a barely distinguishable blur of queasiness, jitters, and foreboding. His only release has been during the first moments of each morning, when his eyes flutter open and he's granted three or four contented seconds of absolution before he remembers the unfortunate fix he's in, becomes aware of the Damoclean sword barely held in place over his bed, its point pressing against his forehead.

When Monday morning arrives, Harry's eyes are open before the alarm goes off. Anna lies on her side, back to him, her face obscured by her floating mane, and Harry experiences a brief window of serenity. And then he remembers.

Last chance, Harry thinks. But he's too muddled to consider his final out clearly, too carried along by blind momentum, a chill inevitability having taken over, suffusing his limbs with a thick numbness. He creeps out of bed, so as not to disturb Anna, and sleepwalks through his morning preparations. An automaton whose mind has already leapt ahead to what awaits. He showers absently, shaves absently, dresses absently, and there's something miraculous about his safe arrival at the office an hour later, given that his mind hasn't once been directly engaged with the task at hand, including driving.

With oppressive dread he enters the office, switches on the lights, and stands helplessly in the early-morning emptiness, Nicole's diploma stuck ridiculously under his arm. Not even the prospect of Nicole's honeysuckle aroma affords him much relief. He glances at the clock: seven thirty. A full hour early. Thus Harry embarks upon the first of the day's two interminable waits—for the arrivals of Nicole and Anna, respectively.

He dispenses with six minutes and nineteen seconds looking for a hammer and a nail with which to hang Nicole's ersatz MBA before coming up empty and resigning himself to propping it on her desk for the day. That leaves fifty-three minutes and forty-one seconds, which inch past glacially, seeming to Harry to delight in their truculence, although feeling mocked by the elements is nothing new to him. Still, the sentence is a finite one, and as Harry sits—weightlessly, it seems to him—in his chair staring through space, he contents himself with the consolation of the known. This torture will end at eight thirty; Nicole will arrive, and this first gauntlet will be run.

Fifty-two minutes and a desktop littered with bent paper clips, crumpled balls of paper, and doodled Post-its later, Harry lifts his eyes expectantly toward the door, waiting to be delivered from his dry-mouthed prison. But the door remains steadfastly closed, and 8:30 becomes 8:31

and soon blurs with relentless inevitability into 8:35. At which point Harry experiences a blossom of panic, the same panic that always accompanies Harry's forays into the unknown. Now that he's left the perimeter of his negotiated expectations, he's confronted with immeasurable possibility, and too much possibility has always short-circuited Harry's coping mechanisms.

Because he now has no way of knowing how long his torment will last, how strong he has to be, how much stamina he'll need. She might walk in at 8:36 or she might be an hour late or perhaps not coming in altogether, having gotten sick or changed her mind or been spirited away by a handsome Italian exchange student or lost the address and phone number of the practice or somehow bumped into Anna, who's already learned the truth and is plotting revenge or . . .

At 8:50, Nicole apologetically wanders into the office. If Harry could arrest the swoon of longing that the whisper of her perfectly remembered scent sets in motion, if he could wrest his eyes from her skintight jeans disappearing into black, high-heeled leather boots, he might be alarmed by a certain vacancy in her eyes, but he's exhausted by the emotional currency he's spent to get this far.

"Hey," she says brightly, and drops her bag onto what is clearly her desk. She flops into her chair and surveys her surroundings. She lifts the phone handset, pokes at some buttons, sets it back into the cradle. She looks over her computer, at a loss for the power switch, which Harry deftly flips on for her. Her inbox is empty. She nods, leans back, and smiles.

"Yeah. Okay. Cool. I like it."

Harry marvels at the sureness with which she's claimed this space as her own. Her comfort and ease in assuming her surroundings—subsuming them—speaks either of bottomless self-confidence or a total absence of interior life. Either way, it's almost as though the desk is now in another office entirely. Nicole's Lair. And so, it's with a vaguely accusing note in her voice that Nicole asks, "What's that?" pointing a French-manicured index finger at her faux diploma.

Harry's prepared the response and prays that it will fly. "I hope you don't mind. It's really just for the patients. We get a lot of mucky-mucks here, kinda snobby, and they like to feel like they're getting the best of the best. Makes 'em feel like they're getting their money's worth. Our little secret," he adds with a guilty wink.

Gum cracks like a rifle shot between Nicole's gyrating jaws. She raises a dubious eyebrow, and Harry realizes he's underestimated her. She's smart enough to know something's amiss, but she's also smart enough, it appears, to pick her battles.

"Whatever you say, boss." The bargain accepted, she turns to the computer. "You got DSL?" She begins to open up random Web sites.

"Yes, of course. But hang on. There's something else."

She turns to him expectantly, wondering how weird this is going to get.

"Um, actually, why don't you take today off."

Weird, indeed. "Huh?"

"Yeah. Take the day. It's really quiet. We had a bunch of cancellations. I think I'm just gonna close up. We can start for real tomorrow."

"With pay?"

"Of course. With pay."

A shrug. "Okay. Bye." In the years ahead, he will learn to decipher the subtle variations in Nicole's repertoire of shrugs—the affectionate shrug, the impatient one, the concerned one—but for now her gestures might as well be Dead Sea scrolls to Harry, who wonders just how ridiculous he seems to her. He allows himself a brief moment of admiration as she disappears from view, then settles, exhausted, into her chair, still-jittering molecules of her perfume vibrating in his nostrils. Phase One is complete, with relative success. Now begins the longer wait for the more treacherous Phase Two, in which—Harry hopes—Anna will arrive and take note of Nicole's diploma. Harry will advise Anna, in what he swears to himself will be his last lie, that Nicole has called in sick. They'll have a nice lunch, and with any luck, the sight of the diploma will be sufficient to blunt Anna's interest in Nicole, then life can return to its undisturbed state. He just has to ride out the next two hours.

Which turns out not to be at all difficult. After calling his patients and cancelling his appointments, Harry dozes off in Nicole's chair, his sleepless weekend having caught up with him. The ringing phone startles him awake.

It's Anna.

"I'm sorry, love. I can't make lunch after all. I've got a conference call. Hey, how come you're answering the phone yourself?"

"That's okay," Harry says, a trifle groggily but trying to sound awake and alert. "She called in sick anyway."

There. Done. That's it.

"Really?" Anna asks, surprised. "Not a very good first impression, is it?"

"She sounded pretty bad," he says, convincing himself this last fib is really a continuation of the previous one, and anyway now it's to protect Nicole.

"Well, I guess it's just as well then."

"Yeah, all you'd have gotten to see was her degree." Harry can't stop himself from tossing out this flourish, this grace note of self-satisfaction. After all, no small expense and effort went into this little prop; it should be acknowledged. Too late does Harry see the flaw.

"Her degree?"

"Yep. UCLA. MBA. Just last year."

"How is her degree there if she's out sick?"

Shitfuckgoddamnitsonofabitch.

"Oh, she brought it by . . . over the weekend." Harry's glad for the anonymity of the phone, which hides his flushed cheeks and the blossoming stains under his arms.

"The weekend? She has a key?"

"Yeah."

"Really?" Disapproval flecks her voice.

"To open up." Harry becomes conscious of wanting to reply in as few words as possible, as though brevity somehow lessens the lie.

"Yes, I suppose. When did you give it to her?"

"After the interview."

Anna sighs, her familiar sigh. "Harry, really. You need to be more careful. You're always so trusting. You don't know this girl at all. What if she cleaned you out?"

"But she has a degree," Harry says lamely.

"Degrees can be faked, you know. Look, darling, I know you mean well, but promise me you'll get the key back until—I don't know—let's say after the first ninety days? When you're sure you trust her, *then* give her the keys. Okay?"

"Okay. Sure."

"Great. I have to run. I love you. I'll see you tonight."

"Love you, too."

Harry sets down the receiver, contemplating the call. At a minimum, he figures, he'll have to give Nicole a key, then ask for it back, so that reality can be bent to conform to his version of events. Although the possibility of extended gymnastics to keep Anna and Nicole from meeting is enough to prompt him to consider sacking Nicole and abandoning this whole dance. But that would entail more confrontation, the last thing Harry wants. So he determines to ride herd on this bucking, unruly tale until he tames it or until he's trampled underfoot.

Harry sits back to assess the damage. Like a FEMA investigator, he pokes through the rubble of the last few days, conducting his forensic inquiry. From the epicenter of his first, mild fib to Anna—"some sort of business degree"—to the conclusion of their phone call, Harry counts the aftershocks accumulating fast and furiously in its wake, a total of twelve in all, some of them more destructive than the original tremor.

Harry is miserable. He feels soiled, ashamed, as though he's permanently been marked by this sordid little fiasco. He's a man who's never had much beyond his plodding reliability, and now he's sacrificed that, messed around with dangerous and wildly infectious agents for comparatively little gain.

But another dimension to all this is even more disturbing to Harry. As he rises, the last mists of Nicole's perfume still clinging to her chair, he turns to glance at her degree and realizes that he's also mildly thrilled by the whole affair. There's something exhilarating, he realizes, about not getting caught. He's not used to being smarter—or luckier—than everyone else, and although in truth he's been neither, the creaky edifice of his deception has proved sturdier than he imagined. It dawns on Harry that he's actually outsmarted his wife, something of which neither he nor she nor anyone they know would have thought him capable. There's a tiny sense of redress, a slight but palpable balancing of accounts.

Oh, he'll never do it again, of that he's quite certain. It's too much work, too tiring and nerve-racking. Too much to keep track of. But as he wanders back into his own office, he's surprised to feel, sharing space with his gloom, the exuberance of a child with a real secret, one he can never share. This special knowledge makes him feel unique. Particular. Confers a strange and unfamiliar power on him. For a brief moment, Harry feels oddly real, oddly present. Someone to be contended with.

He shudders slightly. Dangerous stuff. Never again.

Ten

In which our hero says the word

FOR YEARS HARRY has kept lists. Things to do. Places to visit. Promises to keep. The lists are haphazard, often overlapping, and he seems to derive more satisfaction from the list-keeping itself than from the accumulation of completed tasks. But, as he crosses another item through, he notes that this is a list unlike any he's ever kept. It's headed "MOLLY/ LUCILLE" and contains about a half dozen items, including:

Arrange Lucille apartment.

~~*Close Lucille hotel bill.*~~

Arrange appliances/furniture.

CD for Molly.

As he sits alone in his office, Nicole being MIA this morning, he crosses out the latest item.

~~*Arrange Lucille apartment.*~~

Once again, Max has stepped in and saved Harry. Through the kind offices of one of Max's property-owning patients, Harry's been able to obtain a nice, clean, rent-stabilized apartment for Lucille—just in time, as her room-service bills were becoming fearsome. Nicole had made a snotty remark to that effect as she'd opened and date-stamped the incoming invoices, and Harry felt a stab of irritation similar to the one he'd experienced when Claire had referred to his "fat waitress." Harry's irritation continues this morning as the phone rings, underscoring Nicole's absence. He picks it up.

"Doctor's office."

"Harry? It's Molly."

Harry's irritation evaporates. "Hey. How are things going?"

"Good, thanks. We've got the appliances and stuff set to be delivered Monday morning."

"Great news." Harry crosses out another item: ~~Arrange appliances/furniture.~~

"I told Lucille we'd help her get it all set up. Is that cool? She doesn't really have anyone else to help her."

"Absolutely."

There's a pause on the line as though Molly is struggling with what to say next. Finally:

"Listen, I just want to say, I've decided that even though this whole arrangement is, well, pretty strange, it doesn't matter. You clearly have your reasons. And I think it's cool."

Harry remains uncharacteristically silent. Molly takes this as encouragement to continue.

"I mean, I guess it's the honorable thing to do. Sort of cleaning up your own mess. Which is great. I mean, everyone should be like that." The tone that drapes this last sentiment clearly invokes Bruce. "But . . . well, I've never met anyone quite like you, Harry."

Harry desperately wants to ask her, *What am I like?* Wants to fix himself somehow, even if it's through someone else's eyes. Because the truth is that, increasingly, he has little idea himself. Things are happening too quickly and not quickly enough. He's finding it difficult to reconcile the struggling widower, a fading but present echo, with whatever this thing he's becoming is, and he can't quite latch onto what he looks like, either from within or without. To be neither here nor there. Departed but not yet arrived. Moving through familiar waters that no longer look the same. It's nothing he can share with Molly, so he settles, instead, for a chuckle.

"Hey, that makes two of us."

Harry notes the unintended honesty of the remark, wondering if Molly will latch onto it, will find it as odd as he does. But she doesn't take it up. She has something else on her mind, which she is only now working around to.

"Listen, there's something else . . . It's not a big deal but . . ."

"Shoot."

She exhales wearily on the other end of the line. "I wanted to apologize about that thing at my place the other night. I'm so—"

"There's no need to apologize to me, Molly. Really."

"No, there is. Bruce was incredibly rude to you."

Harry chances it. "Actually, he was incredibly rude to *you*. He was just indifferent to me."

Harry wishes he could see Molly's face, read her eyes for reaction, gauge her breathing, her stance, determine if this salvo has reached its target, even as he's relieved to have the security of the phone behind which to be so brazen. There's a long pause. Then:

"Yes. You're right."

What follows is one of those silent moments in which two people know precisely what needs to be said, and neither can summon the will to say it yet.

Finally, Molly speaks up. "Well, I'll see you Monday morning."

"Yeah. Take care."

"You, too."

Harry hangs up the phone and adds an item to his list: *Crush Bruce.*

His discomfiting ambivalence dissolves amid rage. Oh, Harry understands about patience. He's learned enough from the adventures of Edmond Dantès to realize that if he bides his time, studies his enemy carefully, and plans in a manner that leaves nothing to chance, victory must surely go to the righteous, whom, in this scenario, he takes to be himself. At the same time, is this whining gnat really so formidable a foe, he wonders, that this level of planning is called for? Can't he just whack the fucker and have done with?

But his rage is short-lived, already dimming, and for reasons he can't fully explain, arranging Lucille's life continues to feel more compelling to him than ridding the world of Bruce once and for all. It isn't that he's ceased desiring Molly. After all, he's still pressing ahead with a plan that, with some hindsight, he can now admit sucks. He's spent a fair amount of money on this pursuit, with no immediate end of expenses in sight. And although the amount is ultimately insignificant when held against his net worth, and although the plan does appear to be lurching forward in its ramshackle fashion, something about the indirection of it all, approaching Molly so obliquely via kindness to Lucille, increasingly strikes Harry as un-Dantès-like. But he's in for a dollar (and then some) and is committed to pressing onward.

Yet there's something else now, something new that eggs him along. He can't forget that last dark look Lucille bestowed upon him in the hotel room. Something about those icy, lonely eyes propels him forward here, as he seeks to understand something . . . something almost familiar? What did he see there—or, more accurately, what did he recognize there?

Harry tears the list from the pad, stuffs it into his pocket, grabs his coat, and heads out. But something stops him at Nicole's empty chair. He pauses at her desk, examining her slipshod work space, the piles of Post-it doodles, the unopened mail, the thin layer of dust on the computer keyboard. Not even the fading wisps of her perfume, which cling to the work space in her absence, can calm the anger that's beginning to roil within. Frustrated and seeking an outlet, he does the one thing within his power at the moment.

He pulls her diploma off the wall and throws it into the garbage.

Then, with a pat of his pocket to check for his keys, he quits the office.

As Molly gives brisk orders to the deliverymen, Harry wanders through the empty apartment. He's struck by its cleanness, the blank canvas of it all, and he wonders if Lucille will be able to perceive the same possibilities that he feels radiating within these bare walls, surging up through the pristine wooden floors. His footfall echoes throughout the space, and he's surprised by the wave of nostalgia that overtakes him as he remembers moving into his first condominium with Anna. (This was before a drunk driver on the Taconic Parkway delivered them Anna's inheritance and Bel Air splendor.) It was larger than this, though not much, and they owned it instead of renting it. But he remembers Anna commandeering the movers and organizing the proceedings with the same cool efficiency Molly is now displaying. And Harry let her, not because she was strong and he was weak, but because he so admired his wife. He reveled in watching her bend the world to her will, and he was in constant admiration of just how sound her judgment and choices always turned out to be. Harry would surely have located the easy chair there under the side window, but when Anna instructed the movers to set it just beyond the fireplace, the room doubled in size. Anna understood scale, she understood proportion, she understood placement. Everything in Anna's world was placed with certainty and permanence. With the exception, it seems, of Harry himself, the one thing in her life that resisted conforming to her will.

Harry winces at the familiar stabbing in his side. He kneads his ribs to little avail.

"Are you okay?" Molly's voice startles Harry.

"Fine," he answers hoarsely. "Why?"

"You're a little flushed."

Harry shrugs. "It's stuffy in here." He crosses the room to open a window and remembers Lucille's squalid alley-facing window. Now he raises the double-paned glass and leans out, looking at the modest but well-tended yard in the rear. No Peeping Toms will be able to roost here, he reflects.

"It's a nice place," Molly says approvingly. Harry nods in agreement and turns to Lucille, seeking her approval as well. But he's surprised by the intensity with which she regards him. There's something like recognition in her eyes, as if in the brief moment that Harry dropped his guard, she beheld someone with a similar capacity for suffering. A birds-of-a-feather look. It makes Harry uncomfortable, and he busies himself checking the windows.

"You'll probably get a little street noise in the front," he explains as he raises the living room windows, "but I think the back rooms will be pretty quiet." He doesn't turn as he still feels Lucille's probing eyes on his back. The throbbing in his side grows worse and he leans against the windowsill for support. Which is when he sees it. Parked across the street. The gray Impala.

Yes. Of course. Claire.

"Son of a bitch," he mutters. The pain lifting as he focuses on the car.

"What?" Molly asks.

Harry shakes his head. "Nothing. Sorry. Just remembered something." He lowers the window and steps away. Finally making eye contact with Lucille. Who clearly knows he's lying. She glances out the window, but if she notes the car, she says nothing, registers nothing. Molly senses something simmering in the room but can't make it out. Harry turns to Lucille brightly, rubbing his hands. Time for a subject change.

"So? What do you think?"

Lucille nods. "Dunno what to say. Nice. Really nice. Thanks. No one ever . . ."

She trails off and waves the sentiment aside brusquely. It's terse but it's real. There's gratitude there, genuine gratitude from Lucille. Something Harry hasn't experienced yet, and he likes it. He's done something good and she's acknowledged it.

145

Harry had a speech planned, words about selflessness and support intended to play to Molly as much as to Lucille. But the moment feels too real to polish with artifice, and so he holds her eyes and says, "You're welcome, Lucille."

She nods again, as Molly glows with admiration and the pain in his side lifts once again. "Well, I guess it's home now," Lucille says, setting out on the coffee table the framed picture of the young boy that Harry had glimpsed through the alley window.

It's a different drive up into the hills of Echo Park this time. It's just Molly and Harry together. Lucille's gloom no longer pervades the evening air. The conversation is friendly and relaxed, and Molly is impressed that Harry remembers the labyrinthine route back to her place. (In fact, he doesn't—he's spent hours memorizing the relevant squares of his *Thomas Guide*.) Harry's been careful to inquire after her studies, and Molly complies expansively, regaling him with a bird's-eye view on the latest developments in postcolonial study. (It takes Harry a good twenty minutes of listening to divine that *postcolonial* has nothing to do with the Revolutionary War, but he nods along gamely.) He even cobbles together a few intelligent questions along the way, which prompt further animated outpourings.

It's knowing more about the crosscurrents of South African literature than he ever imagined possible that he pulls back into her driveway. To his surprise, however, he doesn't stop the car.

"So," he begins.

"So," she replies, with a glance back at her windows. They are reassuringly dark. She turns back to Harry. "I still owe you a drink."

Harry's heart is thumping. Whatever the defects of his plan, it's gotten him this far. But to his vast surprise, he doesn't leap at the offer.

"Yes, you do. Would you mind if we took one more rain check?"

Three reasons for his inaction pop into mind. First, there's the specter of Bruce bobbing around intrusively. The possibility of his sudden unwelcome appearance is quite enough, on its own, to hold Harry in place. There's also the recognition of the value of playing it cool, something Harry has never experienced before. But in this new play-book he's learned about mystery and tension and anticipation, and he decides these all play to his advantage.

But neither of these, he realizes, is the primary reason. No, the lead weight that has attached itself to his ankles and wrists is Lucille. He's experiencing annoying pricks of conscience, an incipient sense that perhaps she's being ill-used as his pawn. That this represents a potential cave-in of the foundation of his Master Plan is not lost on Harry, but it's too much for him to deal with at the moment.

"Sure. Whatever. It's all good."

Molly's clearly surprised at his demurral, maybe a bit disappointed, but there's an intrigued look in her eyes, suggesting that Harry's gam-bit has delivered some modest payoff. In a fit of inspiration, Harry de-livers the coup de grâce. He leans over in the car and kisses her, gently, on the cheek.

"Great. I'll stop by the café tomorrow. Have a little gift for you."

Harry contemplates the many fronts on which he's just advanced. He's probably surprised and intrigued her by not making a move. (He has.) He's pretty sure he's kissed her in a way that's superficially friendly but is just soft and tender enough to suggest an undercurrent of something more. (He has.) And he suspects he's intrigued her with this notion of a gift, which she's trying to square with his exceedingly gentlemanly behavior. (Correct again.) He's kept the ball in play and finds that, for the moment, continuing his advance is more appealing than scoring the goal. Molly nods and smiles, and despite his jumble of mixed emotions, Harry is struck by how affecting her pull on him re-mains.

"Well . . . good night," she says.

Harry nods. "Good—" He's drowned out by the roar of Bruce's Harley, which fills the entire street, rattling the Jaguar's windows.

Molly's eyes roll and she sighs. "I *hate* that bike."

Harry regards her probingly, the question burning his brain: *Then why?* But he won't ask, not tonight, anyway, even as he senses that she'd welcome the chance to answer, or at least to think about it aloud. Molly waves to Harry and gets out of the Jaguar. Bruce walks up the driveway and slips his arm around her waist, escorting her to the door without so much as a glance back at Harry, who waits in the car until they disappear inside. And even as he waits, he wonders, is it because he wants Molly to think him chivalrous? Or because he wants to see if she'll look back at him?

No matter. As they reach the door, she turns back to Harry and smiles. Both ways, he wins.

The next day at Café Retro, Harry hands her the small gift-wrapped package with what he judges to be just the right amount of flourish. He's feeling upbeat about his selection, so when Molly unwraps the CD, it takes him a moment to realize that her enthusiasm and gratitude are meticulously feigned. She's burbling on when Harry interrupts her.

"You don't like it."

Molly protests, intent on not hurting Harry's feelings. But he presses her and she finally shrugs awkwardly.

"It's not really my thing. But it was sweet of you to think of me."

Harry is confused—surely he did his homework carefully. He can't imagine having selected the wrong album, especially since he enlisted the support of the young, tattooed clerk, who nodded approvingly when Harry pointed to the magazine cover—the same magazine he saw on Molly's coffee table—and asked for the album in question. He was even mildly pleased at the salesclerk's obvious approval of this cool-music-purchasing old dude. He's spent the better part of the morning hitting nearly a half dozen music stores around town before finally coming up with the elusive CD. *(Note to self,* he thinks in a desperate moment: *Be sure to have the gift in hand next time before promising delivery.)* How, then, in the wake of all this preparation is it possible that his shot has fallen so wide of the mark?

"But I saw the magazine in your living room." Harry flummoxed.

Molly rolls her eyes and chuckles ruefully. "That's Bruce's, not mine. I don't know how he listens to that stuff." She looks at the CD in her hand. "I guess I could give it to him."

Harry feels prickles of heat and sweat at his temples at the thought of having just bought Bruce a present. But he's afraid of seeming petty, and so he shrugs as nonchalantly as he can, parlaying the misstep into an opportunity.

"Well, it's nothing I'd ever bother listening to. Might as well give it to someone who cares."

Molly nods. "Okay. Thanks, I guess." She grins. "This is kind of weird."

Harry waves off her thanks. "Actually, I'm kind of glad you don't like that stuff," he says, anticipating her objections. "It surprised me when I thought you did—it's violent and degrading to women."

Molly nods in enthusiastic agreement. "Yes! It is! I keep telling him that, keep pointing out some of those disgusting lyrics. He thinks it's just part of a persona, that it's not real and I shouldn't take it seriously. He says it's just a song, it doesn't mean anything."

"*Deutschland über alles* was just a song, too," Harry opines, pushing it, as ever, a bit too far.

"Exactly! Words have consequences. Just as powerful as actions."

Yes, they do, Harry thinks, and for a moment he's gone, lost, about to be carried away by a memory that threatens to steal up and commandeer him. But he holds fast, deflecting images of Greenwich, of Anna's family home, of those half dozen overheard words that changed everything.

"Hey, I have to get back to work. Well, thanks for the CD."

Harry shakes his head. "Forget about it." It's only as Molly departs for her section that the crestfallen look that's been trying to elbow its way onto his face assumes its rightful place. He's feeling sorry for himself when a familiar scent wafts into his nostrils. He glances down at the counter before him, where Lucille has slid a Monte Cristo sandwich under his nose.

"Sorry you crashed and burned there." She shrugs. "She's not so easy to figure out. Honest mistake, I guess. Looked like you could use a little cheering up. You like these, right?"

From something in her voice, something in her eyes, Harry would swear that she knows everything, that she's calling him on it and is giving him the choice of lying to her face or letting her in on his plans. He glances down at the sandwich, but his side has begun to throb again and the thought of wolfing the thing down is beyond him. And so Harry the play-it-safer, Harry the never-gambler, Harry the original-path-of-least-resistancer, decides to double down.

"Actually, I think they're disgusting," he confides sotto voce.

Lucille grins victoriously and turns the plate toward herself, picking up a fork. "Hah. I thought so." She stabs a corner of the sandwich and begins to eat, shaking her head. "When you're twenty-whatever you can eat crap like this and still look like her. Hell, I never looked like her." She glances up from her plate at Harry's worried eyes. "Don't worry, your secret is safe. It's kinda flattering, I guess, you going through all this. And that thing with the CD is pretty funny."

Harry eyes her warily, wondering just how far her understanding of "all this" really extends. He resists the urge to blurt and remains composed. She fills the silence.

"Personally, I've hated that piece of shit from the first day. He's just a bad kid."

Harry shrugs. "His mother probably loves him." Keeping it safe, circular small talk.

"Don't count on it."

"Who knows? I guess some kids just go wrong, no matter what you try."

Lucille snorts with grim familiarity. "Tell me all about it."

Harry raises his eyebrow, inviting her to continue. She contemplates another mouthful of her Monte Cristo before speaking. "I know you seen the picture of my boy. Saw you looking at it."

"I didn't want to pry."

"Yeah. Well, he went about as wrong as you can go, and I still don't know why. I mean, okay, I'm not rich or anything, but I kept him all right. Guess it wasn't enough." She sighs. "I think he was ashamed of me, didn't want people to know about fat mama, you know? Eh, how would you know what that's like?"

Harry feels a gray mist pass over his eyes and experiences an insane urge to tell her, *I know* exactly *what that's like,* but settles for lowering his eyes until the pain in his side passes. Then:

"What happened?"

Lucille shrugs, mopping up her plate with a toast corner. "Gangs. Trouble. He's in the system now. I don't see him. Not for years."

"Don't you want to?" Harry asks sorrowfully.

She shrugs and gets up, brushing the counter clean, taking the plate with her and walking off. But Harry catches a faint whisper:

"What do *you* think?"

Numbly, Harry pulls out his wallet and leaves a bill on the counter. Only later will he realize that he hasn't even glanced at it—it could be a five or a hundred—but for the moment the fog of memory sits upon him, his eyes cloudy and his ears buzzing thickly as though he's awoken in an apiary. Through the din, he hears a familiar voice:

In fact, he graduated Harvard Med.

Harry stumbles out of Café Retro, Anna's words reverberating in his aching head.

It's been a long, rough day, even by Harry's recent standards of activity. But the worst is over, he reasons, as evening crawls into Bel Air, so it's without foreboding that he answers the unexpected knock at his front door.

"Mr. Harry Rent?"

Harry doesn't recognize them at first because, since their last run-in, they've gained a dozen pounds between them and have traded in their uniforms for cheap suits. But Harry finally places Don Quixote and Sancho Panza, taking himself back to that ill-fated day of the Everhappy

Eterna Comfort Band™. And all at once, he realizes whatever brings them here can't be good.

"Yes?"

"May we come inside?"

Harry shakily opens the door and waves them in. "Have a seat. Something to drink? I mean, not booze, I know, but . . ." Harry can't keep the quaver from his voice.

"Nothing, sir. Thank you."

"Okay, then." Harry leans against his dining room table in a pose of studied nonchalance. "What can I do for you guys?"

As before, Quixote takes the lead, while Panza takes in the surroundings with a practiced, jaded eye. "Mr. Rent, this morning we raided an establishment called the Happy Angels Delivery Service. Are you familiar with it?"

Harry feels a splash of red dot his cheeks. "Uh, it rings a bell . . . Can't place it though . . ."

"It's an escort service, Mr. Rent. And your name was found in the files there."

Now, a realization. *They don't recognize me.* And with it a flush of hopefulness. *Can I have changed so much already?*

Panza pauses in his reconnaissance to ask a question. "Is the wife home, Mr. Rent?"

The wife. A long silent moment as the words hang untouched. Harry fastens on them, turning them over in his mind.

Quixote coughs politely. "Mr. Rent? Are you all right?"

"No," Harry replies dully. Then adds: "There is no wife. Anymore." There. It's been said. How long has it taken to get here? Harry wonders. Time has lost its shape for him these days, feeling increasingly like a monochrome jigsaw puzzle. He can't tell how long it's been—days? weeks?—but it's been said aloud to someone, at last, in a manner that's different and more meaningful than the pro forma exchanges with solicitous friends. Does this make Anna more dead? Harry wonders. Or just finally dead?

My wife is dead . . .

Harry tries the words on inside but they still don't seem to fit him properly.

"Mr. Rent? Are you all right?"

Harry nods blankly, returning to the moment. "Yeah. Listen, am I under arrest?"

Sancho and Quixote exchange a weary look, and Quixote shakes his head. "Look, it's the guys who run these rings we care about, not the johns." The last word drips with practiced contempt. "We're just trying to pin down some details. And you'll probably be called to testify."

Testify . . . The word echoes fatally in Harry's brain, the attendant humiliations unspooling before his eyes like newsreel disaster footage: disgraced, his practice ruined, forsaken by his remaining friends, Molly and Lucille abandoning him in disgust. A voice whispers from somewhere deep inside his brain . . .

The count of Monte Cristo does not testify.

Harry pulls himself erect, and assuming the mantle that he increasingly feels he was born to wear, he speaks with a forcefulness that these fuzz would be unable to square with the quivering collar of the past if only he registered in their memories.

"Sorry, boys. Unless you're arresting me, I have nothing to say. And even if you are, I have great lawyers, and I still have nothing to say."

Panza reddens and starts to rise, but Quixote holds him back. Harry's gamble—that this pair is not interested in the bureaucratic ordeal of bringing him in—seems to have been at least half-right.

Quixote, doing his dutiful good cop, speaks with a friendly voice. "Listen, Mr. Rent. This doesn't have to be a whole big deal. It really would be much easier if you just talked to us for a bit."

Harry nods. "Easier for you."

"And for you," snarls Panza.

Harry shrugs and strolls to the front door, which he holds open. "Sorry, guys. I can't help you."

Panza looks to Quixote for direction. Quixote nods, smiling, and heads to the open door. "We'll be back, Mr. Rent. Until then, think about your privacy." With a head flick to Panza, who falls obediently into line, Quixote marches out.

It's only as they leave that the full shock and weight of the encounter descends on Harry, who grabs the doorframe for support. Breathing deeply to settle his heaving stomach, he finally steadies himself enough to close the door. Which is when the phone rings.

Harry sweeps it up furiously, barking into the receiver, "What?"

"Hey, it's me."

"Who is this?"

"It's me. Elliott."

"Oh, for fuck's sake, Elliott, what is it?"

After a surprised silence, Elliott speaks in a small, wounded voice. "Nothing, never mind." He hangs up and Harry feels miserable. Against all of his better instincts, he dials *69, and a moment later Elliott answers, "Hello?"

"Sorry, Elliott. It's been kind of a rough day."

"That's okay, I understand. Want to talk about it?"

"Um, no, Elliott. I don't. But thanks."

"No problem. I just meant, I'm here if you need to talk."

"Okay, I'll remember that. Was there a reason you called?"

"Oh, yeah! Right. Look I just wanted to tell you that I officially do believe you—I checked it out—so I know you were telling the truth. And that I'm grateful—you really helped talk me down from a pretty gnarly spot."

"Well, I'm glad I could help, Elliott," Harry says, wondering how long this is going to take.

Elliott burbles on imperturbably, "And I wanted you to know that you inspired me to get it together and find Katie."

Harry can't imagine how he's been the source of such inspiration but knows better than to ask. "Well, good for you, Elliott. I'm sure it will work out just fine." He's sure of no such thing, of course, but why should he allow his spreading gloom to dampen Elliott's enthusiasm? "You let me know how it all works out."

"Count on it, my friend. Hey, by the way, what's your name?"

Harry sighs, resigned to the unavoidable. "It's Harry, Elliott. My name is Harry."

"Pleased to meet you, Harry."

"Same here, Elliott."

"Although we haven't actually met, I guess, just talked on the phone. But you know what I mean, right?"

"Yes, Elliott, I know what you mean."

"I suppose we could meet if you wanted to. Just to make it official. Would you like to meet?"

"Um, no. Sorry, Elliott—things are bit hectic for me just now."

"Sure. Well, maybe when things quiet down for you." Hopefully.

Harry sits down, as though the weight of Elliott's quiet desperation, coming atop the assault by Panza and Quixote, has finally snapped his legs in two. Just hang up, he tells himself, just set the phone down . . .

"Elliott, I'm going out on a limb here, but do you have any . . . other . . . friends?"

There's a moment of silence and Harry wonders how deeply he's embarrassed his unwelcome protégé. Finally Elliott speaks up unconvincingly, "Yeah, sure. I have friends. I mean, some. You know no one really close but, yeah. Of course . . ."

"That's fine, Elliott . . . I didn't mean anything by it."

"It's only that . . ." Elliott trails off.

Harry sighs. And digs. "It's only what, Elliott?"

"Well . . . it's just I think that you probably sorta saved my life the other night."

"Huh?" Surprised to the core, Harry can only manage a grunt.

"Yeah. I think I was going downhill pretty fast. Tough love, that's what's always worked for me, you know? I mean, it's no big deal, I guess. But I appreciate it."

Harry nonplussed. "Well. Glad to have helped."

"Yeah, so if I can return the favor . . . you know. Anyway, I hope whatever is going on clears up."

"Yeah. Me, too. Good luck, Elliott."

"You, too, Harry."

Harry sets the phone down as he contemplates this last. What, really, can luck offer him? Marley-like, Anna *was* dead. Here's Harry fascinated by the sound of the words, the feel of them as they form on his lips. He turns to the empty room.

"Anna is dead."

Words have arrived. Harry imagined feelings would accompany, at least within a reasonable distance. But the only feeling at the moment is a grim relief that she's not here to witness and be tarred by his impending public humiliation.

Harry wants to feel more. He wants to be riven by heartbreak. He wants to pound his breast and tear his hair. But he feels stuck, emotionally constipated. Defeated, he seeks a familiar refuge.

Down the stairs he wanders, past the curtain-wall windows that open onto the darkening hills of Bel Air. The lights in his neighbors' homes are beginning to glow, but Harry's kept it dark here. He wanders along the lower-level hallway and stops in front of a door that always remains closed. With a last glance back at the cool, clean, minimal grace of his open floor plan, he turns the knob and steps inside.

He hits a switch and the light flickers anxiously to life. Harry wanders amid his possessions, amid the items purchased, enthusiasms abandoned, impulses followed that Anna would eventually quietly relegate here, to their final resting place, like an immune system defeating and ejecting an intruding organism. There are the Paris street-sign plaques, hung haphazardly along the far wall. Harry had hoped to put one or two in their bedroom, but they failed the option period. Over in the corner are the chess sets, a half dozen of them of increasingly superior design and materials. He was surprised that Anna didn't take to chess. It seemed quiet and patrician enough to appeal to her old-money sensibilities. Of course, it might also have been that Harry never really learned to play particularly well. He was a frustrating and unpredictable opponent, launching all sorts of foolish gambits and absurd openings, the sort of behavior that drives any true chess player to distraction. But he loved the boards, glittering and inlaid, and the pieces, solid and substantial in his palm, and now here they were piled with all the rest of him. Banished by Anna. Yes, banished. There's no other word for it.

Harry glances across the room, surveying his past passions, his past selves, all represented and rejected. The guitar phase—three vintage guitars sit propped in stands, forlorn under a thin coating of dust. He picks up each one, gingerly wipes them clean, and strums the three or four power chords in his repertoire before returning them to their stands.

He wanders amid the comfort of his abandoned selves and wonders how his latest self will fare without Anna to render judgment, without accessories to store. (This Edmond Dantès travels light, he reflects.) He looks around the rubble and considers this strange, in-between state of their lives—Anna gone but still vitally in evidence throughout their home, and Harry present but invisible, all evidence of his existence buried below, out of sight. Above all, he wonders why none of it satisfied his wife, why she was unable to accept the slightest, harmless expression of self, and he wonders just how tawdry she really found him.

He can't stop the anger from rising, and before he knows it, his fury has carried him out of his secret room and into Anna's walk-in closet, and now, with a thumping heart and shaking hands, he tears her clothing off the hangers, grabbing thick wads of fabrics carelessly and throwing them into a single pile in the center of the closet. This bit of petty vandalism doesn't spend his rage, and so he dashes into the kitchen and, knocking items from shelves in a blind search, locates a box of heavy-duty, green garbage bags. It takes him ten minutes of frantic, frenzied stuffing to fill enough bags to empty the closet of any trace of Anna. He stands in the middle of the denuded closet panting over the filled bags, and at last his energy flags, the taut set of his mouth begins to sag, but he isn't finished. One by one, he slings the bags over his shoulder and takes them downstairs, down to his room of secrets, and he hurls them into a pile in one of the corners. Only when this is done does he allow himself to sink, trembling, into an easy chair.

Just as his hands have stopped shaking, the phone rings again. Harry sighs and picks up the extension.

"What is it, Elliott?"

"It's not Elliott, Harry. It's Claire. And before you hang up on me, you should know this: I know everything. The hookers. The details. The raid. I have it all. You had the chance to tell me your way. You could have admitted that it was your cheating that drove Anna under the knife. Now the world will find out my way, and you can do what you like with what remains of your life. I just have to decide who I give it to first. The AMA? Your patients? Or maybe that Molly waitress person. Good night, Harry."

Eleven

In which our hero bounces back

HARRY SITS ON the toilet in a daze. He's numb, entirely out of body in the wake of Claire's phone call. It began with the familiar stabbing sensation in his side. (A visit to the doddering family doctor uncovered no medical reason for the persistent ache. Coming up empty, old Dr. Barrett had diagnosed, "Stress," and muttered something about time off. Harry wasn't sure which of them he was talking about.) Then his legs began to wobble and weaken. Now he's waiting for his bodily functions to desert him in predictably angry rapid lockstep. But the usual exodus of innards doesn't come. Try as he might, grunting, straining forcefully, veins in his neck bulging, he's plugged up tight. It's a trembling, sweating hulk that hunches on the toilet praying for some release, contemplating his various futures, each one grimmer than the next. And all point back to one inescapable truth:

Everyone is going to find out. Everyone. Claire will make it her business to tell the world. His patients. His friends. Everyone who looked upon him so sorrowfully at Anna's funeral will now look at him with loathing. Max. How will his old friend take this news?

And then there's his new life. Claire's made the threat clear. Molly is going to find out. Lucille, too, he realizes—a prospect that is only slightly less unappealing. Harry knows he shouldn't be worried about them when there's so much more at stake, but he can't seem to help himself. How thoroughly does he have his priorities boogered up, he wonders, noting that his cathartic cleanse of Anna's closet was the first time in days that Molly and Lucille had been absent from his thoughts.

What does it matter now? Claire is determined to bring it all down around his ears. But when? Where? How? Clearly, she'll do it in a manner calculated to maximize humiliation. Through the nauseated haze that clouds his perceptions, a voice whispers insistently in his ear:

What would Dantès do?

Well, Dantès would *not* be cowering on the toilet, for starters. So Harry pulls himself shakily to his feet and steps out uncertainly into the bedroom. He throws open the window and breathes in the crisp, cold midnight air. It's laced with the spiced scent of burning pine, and Harry finds it mildly restorative. Gulping his breaths greedily, Harry decides that Dantès would be able to anticipate Claire's next move. To know one's enemy, to plan for his or her actions, that's where the upper hand lies. And once Harry begins to think this way, it's with surprisingly little effort that the answer, so obvious, makes itself known to him.

Anna's will reading. That's where she'll do it. In front of family, in front of friends not seen since the funeral. Of course, that leaves the business of Molly and his patients and her other threats. The question is when. The deeply devious or sadistic would wait, stretch out the anticipation and the anxiety and the dread for as long as possible, torturing the web-snared fly. But Harry knows Claire is far too undisciplined, ruled by her appetites. She's always demanded instant gratification. And although it doesn't occur to Harry that Claire hasn't assigned the same obsessive primacy to Molly that he has, he concludes that—if it isn't already too late—he probably has slightly less than twenty-four hours to get to Molly first.

To do what? The only answer to present itself is wildly unpalatable to Harry. But as he turns his dilemma over, examining it from every quarter, he sees no alternative.

The truth. Harry is going to have to tell her the truth.

It's the ultimate Hail Mary pass. Harry calculates that the great likelihood is that she'll be disgusted by him, and his quest will come to a shattering end. But he sees no other choice. He might be able to discredit Claire, but discrediting her private investigators and the LAPD is more than this Dantès can manage. Perhaps if Molly hears it first from him, the right words, spoken in the right way, there's a possibility, however slight, that she might not revile him.

And now, once more, the familiar wobbles and aches and weaves of the old Harry, the self he'd thought he'd left behind, begin to assert themselves, and a hysterical wail roils within his throat. Breaking down, clutching his impacted gut, Harry screeches into the empty room, into the night:

"I'm not Edmond fucking Dantès! Goddammit!"

He collapses into a heap at the dining room table, pounding the tabletop with despair. What a ruse, what a sham. *I've been kidding myself,* Harry thinks, *what's the matter with me?* Why has this non-tryst with a woman half his age overshadowed all his other impulses? And suddenly, a brief bolt of clarity cuts through the despair and Harry is granted a fleeting insight: Can it be that it's become so important to tell Molly the truth because that—he can now begin to admit, far, far too late—is what he failed to do with Anna? It feels incomplete, this shard of self-knowledge, but that's part of it, surely. Hunched over the gnarled and knotted oak table, he remembers that morning with Anna all those years ago, that first careless lie about Nicole's degree, and all the subsequent ones accumulated in its wake. But this one, he suspects, will not so easily be disposed of. A wave of ineffable sorrow washes over him. He can feel the creaking edifice of his alter ego preparing to topple down upon him in a final, dusty, suffocating heap.

As Harry feels himself sinking into helplessness, the doorbell rings. He freezes, his blood skidding to a halt in his veins.

This can't possibly be good news.

He can't conceive who might be at his door at this ungodly hour . . . Sancho and Quixote? Claire? *Bruce?* . . . He's now genuinely terrified, swamped by uncertainty. But the bell rings a second time and Harry's legs involuntarily move—quietly, so as not to betray his presence— toward the eyepiece. What he sees causes his brain to reboot. Through the scratched, cloudy fish-eye, Harry can make out Molly, standing on his stoop.

He doesn't understand this, not one bit. And although opening the door would move him immeasurably closer to clarifying the situation, he's paralyzed. It occurs to him that perhaps Claire has already gotten to her, and she's come up here to confront him. But how? How does she know where he lives? How has she found him?

Whether it's the shadow that slices the threshold or the staccato intake of Harry's breath, Molly begins to look curiously into the eyepiece. She speaks softly but urgently.

"Harry? Is that you? Are you in there? It's Molly. I have your wallet."

Wallet? For a moment, the word might as well be in Urdu. Then it connects. Despite his incomprehension of the circumstances, Harry allows himself a bit of hysterical relief. *Oh. My wallet. She has my wallet. That's why she's here. Knocking on my front door. At one o'clock in the morning.* He swings the door open in a wild release of nerves.

"Hi!" he says almost ridiculously brightly.

"Um . . . hey. I hope you don't mind my coming by. I would have called but you're not listed."

"No, I'm not, am I?" Harry says with irrational glee. An involuntary cackle escapes his lips, frightening Molly slightly.

"Look, this is a bad time, obviously. It's just—you left your wallet. It was on my way home so I figured I'd bring it by." She holds out Harry's wallet, which he only now realizes he must have left on the counter in his daze. Harry stands there dumbly, making no move toward it. Molly sighs with a bit of exasperation. "Hello? Anyone home? Here, take it."

Her tone snaps Harry back to the moment like a splash of cold water. If an iota of Dantès is still to be found in Harry's depleted system, he needs it now. He reaches for the wallet and puts his hand on it, covering her smaller hand and gently guiding her inside.

"It's cold. Come in."

She steps into the hallway, cautious and uncertain at first, but as the cavernous dimensions of the home begin to reveal themselves, she finds herself awed by the space, stepping deeper inside.

"Wow . . . This is amazing."

"You think so? Thanks."

"My God, yes. I've never been inside a Bel Air mansion."

Harry laughs. "It's not exactly a mansion—it's only got four bedrooms."

"You saw where I live. This is a mansion."

Harry nods as Dantès resumes possession of corpus Rent. "Fair enough. Come on. Let me make you some tea and then I'll give you a tour of the mansion."

It takes Harry a bit of searching to locate where Anna's put the tea assortment, but once he finds it, he's impressed yet again with her thoroughness—a dozen varieties, sealed airtight, just awaiting boiling water. Harry finds something strangely bittersweet about the carefully tended racks. Molly seems impressed by the variety, and Harry halfheartedly takes credit for it, though doing so feels like yet another infidelity. As they walk through the empty house, Harry notes that Molly holds her decaf green tea in the palms of both hands, something he finds almost unbearably lovely.

"Well, you've seen the kitchen. Here's the dining room."

"I love the view."

Harry nods. "Breakfasts are nice, looking out into the canyon."

"I'll bet."

They continue on through the living room, the library, the study. Harry waves vaguely in the direction of the master bedroom, not confident enough to march her into the room, with all its sexual intimations. In room after room, Molly takes in the cool elegance of the space, the crisp, stark minimalist lines. He watches her eagerly for reactions, and she nods appreciatively if politely.

"Then there's the downstairs."

"There's more? Sure is a lot for one person."

Harry momentarily sidesteps the implied question. "Mostly guest rooms and the like. Follow me."

Harry guides her down the stairs, and they walk along the carpeted lower corridor, lined by picture windows on the left and bedrooms on the right. Harry points out the pair of guest rooms. "For guests, obviously," he says a bit lamely.

Molly nods. "It's a nice place, Harry."

There's something in her tone—not insincerity, but a sense of something held back. As earlier, with the CD.

Harry stops and turns to face her. "But?"

Molly smiles and shrugs. "No but."

"Come on. We're friends now. It won't hurt my feelings."

Molly hesitates for a moment. Then: "It doesn't really feel very . . . lived in, does it? There's a chill to everything . . . it's elegant but . . . I don't know, it's not very welcoming. It's just my taste, I like a bit of a mess. As you've seen," she adds with a hint of embarrassment.

Yes! Harry thinks, and blurts out before he can stop himself, "My wife decorated it. I never liked it. She's dead now."

For a moment, the throbbing in his side subsides. Harry feels a bit dizzy, made light-headed by this scandalous admission. An appropriately awkward moment of silence follows.

"Harry, I'm so sorry—"

"No, don't. I don't mean that. I mean . . . I just mean, it's not me, all this."

Molly nods. "Okay. I understand."

It's an awkward moment, and Harry struggles to absorb the implication of this unexpected, electric admission, this shockingly icy exhalation of truth, when he glances down to the end of the hallway, where the door to his room of discards remains open. He hurries down and closes it before Molly can see inside.

She comes over to join him. "What's that?"

Harry pauses, wanting desperately to invite her in, wanting to show her what's inside, show her the accumulation that *is* him. He's come a long way, but not quite far enough.

"Nothing. Just a storeroom."

The couple repairs to the dining room table and falls into conversation, and something unprecedented happens. Harry spends nearly three hours with Molly without once imagining her naked.

Molly's tea cools, then cools again, and soon even Harry has poured himself a mug, and still they talk. Harry hasn't talked so openly in years, though he suspects it's more commonplace for Molly.

They talk about Bruce, about his thefts, about what it will take for her to divest herself of him. (She's not sure; something big and unpleasant, she imagines.) They talk about books they've read (well, about books *she's* read; Harry's contributions are limited to a surprisingly detailed knowledge of *The Count of Monte Cristo*). They talk about their childhoods. They talk about the places they've traveled. They talk about Molly's plans for the future. They even talk about Anna.

And having released himself from the notion of any romantic or sexual future (since she's sure to reject him once the truth of his affairs comes out), Harry's free to attend her without pressures and finds that he actually likes this woman, even with her flaws. Flaws he's only begun to notice. Yet he doesn't mind that she's a bit naïve, occasionally didactic, and a touch self-absorbed. Somehow, in the space of their hours together, she has become more real to him. This person is more palpable, as though the object of Harry's fantasies has dissolved to reveal this infinitely more interesting human being in her wake. Finally, they turn to the subject of Lucille, which Molly brings up tentatively.

"Listen, there's something I've been meaning to talk to you about."

"Shoot."

Molly nods, clearly uncomfortable. She rubs her forehead and dives in. "This whole business with Lucille. What's up with that, really?"

I'm doing it to impress you. "What do you mean?"

"I don't know. I've been thinking about it. At first I thought it was cool, but I don't know. I mean, here you are, this upper-class white male—let's face it, you're a classic patriarchal-power figure—and you're kind of playing God with this low-income, uneducated woman. I mean, you say you mean well, but I don't know, maybe it's some weird power thing for you?"

"Jesus, Molly, no. It's not—"

"I mean, what are you going to do, support her forever? You're going to stop at some point and then what? Will she be any better off for all of this?"

Harry glances at his toes, ashamed to admit he hasn't really thought past the next few weeks.

"I don't know, Harry. I go back and forth between liking you and being creeped out by you."

The hurt must be apparent on Harry's face because Molly's features soften slightly.

"I mean, I'd much rather like you. But I feel like there's a reason you're doing all this that maybe you're not being honest about."

Harry nods, impressed—how little credit he's given Molly, he realizes. He gets up and refills his tea and hers, collecting himself, steadying his nerves. He returns to Molly, hands her the mug and inhales deeply.

"Well, maybe I have some making up to do."

Molly listens, waiting for more.

"And maybe I'm taking a look at who I've been and who I'd like to be?" His tone is tentative, almost querying.

"Maybe?"

Harry answers with a smile and then a question of his own. "Do you think people can change, Molly? I mean, really change? Become someone entirely new?"

Molly finds the question a bit odd, a bit grand, a bit larger in scope than she'd expected, and she struggles to return this power serve. "I don't know. Maybe . . ."

"Maybe?"

"Well, what do you really mean? 'Entirely new'? You mean like a lie, like a new persona? Or changing qualities or traits or behavior? Or—"

"Yes. All of them. I mean, what if you decide you don't like who you were, and so now you want to be someone new? Someone, for example, who might help someone like Lucille."

Molly thinks for a long moment before answering. Then: "I suppose that would depend on why you—someone—was trying to change."

Harry sets his mug down and prays he won't throw up. "Listen, Molly. I have something I need to tell you."

The tone of his voice alarms her and her face registers concern. "Sure."

"The thing is . . . it's not a good thing and I think you're probably not going to like me much once you hear it. But I want you to hear this from me. And maybe it will help you understand me a little better."

"Okay," she says tentatively.

Harry's surprised at how outside his own body he feels, as though he's sitting in a movie-theater seat, watching someone else's story unspool before him. The distance gives him a bit of courage, and all the usual Harry uncertainties—perspiration, quavering voice, downcast eyes—are miraculously absent. And he begins to tell her a story, a story that shares its shape with the truth and, he supposes, is, in terms of facts, not entirely unlike the truth. How his relationship with his wife had cooled over the years, that he'd begun to sense that his wife was ashamed of him. How he found himself increasingly lonely and isolated. How, never being especially smooth or confident with women, he found himself gravitating toward women who traded their companionship for money. How he felt pathetic and sullied each time out but couldn't navigate the loneliness of his marriage. How he's not the man he was— how distant and unfamiliar that shameful, downtrodden creature seems to him now—but, as much as he would like to disown his past, he can't lie (though he can make amends). And now, there have been busts, arrests, and his name is sure to splash across this affair.

As he tells the story, he's aware of his redactions, the shifts of emphasis, the resemblance to the facts—truth's doppelgänger. But it's close enough to how it was that it allows Harry to feel honest, to convince himself of his sincerity, even as it spares Molly (and himself) the least flattering details. And as he speaks, he can't help but register a sad truth he's avoided—that he never gave his wife the opportunity that Molly is giving him now; surely Anna must have felt much the same under the weight of her transgression as Harry feels now under his. How much, he wonders, did this missed opportunity cost them?

Is his tale to Molly the truth? Is it honest? Well, it's as close to honesty as Harry has traveled in years, and he marvels at how it feels. As Molly nods sympathetically and takes Harry's hand, he thinks back to the array of lies he employed with Anna to keep the Rube Goldberg apparatus of his life in constant spinning operation. And he finds himself regretting his irresponsible self, wishing he'd tried a bit harder, forgiven Anna for Greenwich. Wishing that he'd had enough faith in her to give her another chance to greet the truth. To know him.

"Wow."

"Yeah. Wow."

Molly weighs her words. "Well. I think you made a mistake and now you're trying to fix it. You seem sincere to me, Harry."

Yes, that's it, Harry thinks with nearly tearful relief. I made a mistake and I want to fix it. Even as he wonders if "seeming sincere" is enough, he marvels that the expulsion of this hidden truth has made him feel better than all of the bodily explosions of the past few days, better than the trails of vomit and blood and shit and semen abandoning him at every turn, when really, all he needed to expel was the infection of these lies.

"You don't hate me?"

"No, Harry. I don't hate you."

The phone rings a third time, and Harry glares through his open office door at Nicole, who sits at her desk, locked in earnest conversation with a friend, phone tucked under her ear. Harry folds his arms, suppressing anger, willing Nicole to feel his angry eyes upon her, hang up the damn phone, and answer this call. It's an epic battle of wills, but as the fifth ring commences, Harry hits the limits of his telepathic gifts, and he balks, answering the phone.

It's the police. The call is brief. Harry's services will not be required, and LAPD apologizes for any inconvenience. His name will not appear in connection with this affair. Harry lowers the phone numbly, dazed at the rapid turnaround of events.

It was Molly who suggested that Lucille might be able to help him with his troubles. She's quite friendly with the cops who make Café Retro their nightly hangout, and they've helped her once or twice before in matters with her son's incarceration, she explained. (She also thought that Lucille's assistance might go some way to addressing the inherent gender/power imbalances of their relationship, and although Harry didn't really give a rat's ass about gender/power imbalances, it was clearly important to Molly, and so he embraced her reasoning.) Molly even offered to explain the situation to Lucille to spare Harry any further embarrassment. Harry accepted, expecting little, so it was a great surprise when Lucille called him to let him know that his problems were going to go away. But not until the police call does Harry finally believe it's true. And now he's left contrasting the bloodless efficiency of this coffee shop waitress with the incapacity of his assistant, who seems unable to do so much as answer a ringing phone.

A wave of giddy relief swamps Harry. He's certainly not out of the woods yet, not by a bit. Claire is sure to make mischief for him, with or without the imprimatur of the LAPD. There's still the will reading to contend with. But he's got time now, there's a bit of breathing space where the night before there was only bleakness. He sinks back into his chair trying to restrain this largely illusory sense of well-being that's rising within him, a euphoria that's led him into all sorts of trouble in the past. But he knows that, at a bare minimum, he needs—no, he *wants*—to do something nice for Lucille. Something that will express his gratitude, that can give some form to the odd affection and kindness he's feeling toward his charge, even as he notes the ironic reversal of roles. Perhaps there's something to this gender-imbalance business after all, Harry thinks, because he's all too aware of having had his skin saved by the one he's set out to save. It's all confusing but not entirely un-pleasant, especially as Harry has the perfect idea about how to thank Lucille for her intervention.

Harry doesn't even look for Molly as he bounds through the doors of Café Retro. Rather, he hurries to Lucille's section, where she's presently taking a complicated order from a senior citizen that's riddled with "on the side" 's. Harry taps his foot impatiently, a shoebox tucked under his right arm. He's so focused on Lucille that he doesn't notice that Molly has appeared at his side.

"Hey."

"Oh! Hi."

"What's up?"

"Um, came to thank Lucille. She was great. Just like you said."

Molly nods, smiling. "What's in the box?"

Harry winks and motions toward Lucille. "Surprise. Thank-you gift."

Harry doesn't notice the minute occlusion of Molly's smile because Lucille has turned from Mr. On the Side, sighing heavily, and shuffles toward them. Harry lights up and waves excitedly.

"Hey! Lucille!"

She nods gruffly in his direction, but Harry bolts toward her like a straining dog unleashed and throws his arms as far around her as he can manage, about as far as her shoulder blades. "Thank you *so* much," he whispers in her ear.

She pushes him away firmly but not unkindly and smoothes out her uniform. "Was nothing. Just a couple'a calls."

"Well, it was a big deal to me. Here. For you." He hands her the shoebox.

"What is it?" Lucille asks, taking the box warily.

"A thank-you gift. Go ahead, check it out," Harry says with child-like eagerness.

Lucille opens the box to find a utilitarian-looking pair of shoes. She's not sure what to make of it. "Shoes. Okay. Thanks. Kinda ugly . . ."

Harry nods happily. "Yeah. I know. But you have to try them on."

Lucille closes the box. "Sure, I'll try 'em later. Thanks, Harry."

"No, no, no. Try them now. Please."

"Harry, I can't—"

"Trust me. Please."

Lucille sighs, looks around furtively, and shuffles behind the counter. She drops the new shoes to the floor. As she shifts her bulk, Harry imagines the battered feet and bruised toes she's gone behind the counter to hide, slipping into the new shoes. As they do, the expression on Lucille's face changes to one of incomprehension.

Harry grins like a madman. "Amazing, huh?"

Lucille nods, stunned. "My God. They're incredible."

"They're special orthopedic shoes. Max had them designed for you—he had all the details from your visit."

Lucille stares at Harry, speechless.

"I tried to think of something that I could do for you that would mean as much, and although this isn't even close, I figured what could be better for someone who has to stand all day. I hope you like them."

Lucille nods slowly and hurries into the back, a slight film clouding her eyes. Harry is standing there holding the empty shoebox, wondering if he's made a mistake, when Molly taps his shoulder.

"Hm?" He turns to face her.

"That was really, *really* nice." She reaches up and kisses him on the cheek, then wanders off to tend to her section. Harry rubs his cheek gently as he takes this in, noting that Molly's reaction to Lucille's shoes far outstripped her response to her own CD. Now Harry has something new to think about, and he can't help but note that it's the genuine gift, bought out of authentic appreciation, that scored the mark, whereas the bauble designed to manipulate fell short.

Harry's left wanting to do more. After all, Lucille has so comprehensively saved his ass that he feels a mere pair of shoes is hardly equal reward. There must be something more he can do, something bigger and appropriately life altering. There's also the desire to continue riding this newfound wave of authenticity, and even though Harry senses that the desire to do so is somehow inherently contradictory to the spirit of the thing—might, in fact, make it downright impossible—his cheek is still glowing, and the glow is spreading. He likes the image of himself as a man capable of a true gesture, and he suspects that the cultivation of this self might guide him to where he's hoping to end up. He likes, at the very least, seeming sincere. Yes, he's not Edmond Dantès, not yet anyway, he can admit that. But he's no longer Harry Rent 1.0 either, and he's eager to move through this in-between space to claim the prize of his new and fully evolved self. And so he feels disposed to the grand gesture.

The idea, when it arrives, comes in so quietly, so matter-of-factly, that Harry almost fails to recognize it as the grand gesture he seeks. But as he turns over the idea, he begins to get excited, and as he watches Lucille move from section to section, seeming to glide on her new shoes, he's at last convinced that he can change her life in a manner worthy of the count of Monte Cristo.

Her son. He'll reunite her with her son. Just like in the book.

He'll do it to surprise—she's sure to demur if he offers. But he can see it now, the joyous family reunion, Lucille's tearful gratitude. It'll take a little doing, but how hard can it be? If private investigators worked so well for Claire, why not for him? He's so excited about getting to work that he begins to hurry from the café without saying good-bye to Molly or Lucille, and he almost fails to notice that the shoulder that's just body-checked him belongs to the Evil Bruce. It's only the pain of the contact that brings Harry roughly back into the moment, and he turns to find Bruce's receding back.

Harry continues out of the café, then turns back to regard the scene through the window, like watching players in a silent movie, as he tries to understand what it is that draws Molly to Bruce. He hovers over her, bobbing impatiently as she tries to take an order, and she's finally forced to guide him over to the counter and sit him down with what appears to be an admonishment to "stay." She returns to her customers, and Bruce fidgets, bored and irritated, when his eyes alight on a table of teenage girls. One of the girls, a bare-midriffed blonde with a belly piercing, catches his eye and smiles provocatively at him. Bruce glances furtively to Molly, busy with customers, back turned. He returns his attention to the blonde and smiles at the girl, and all at once, Harry feels the serenity that only comes with the knowledge of certain, total triumph.

That's it. I've got you now, you bastard.

As he turns to walk off into the night, Harry resolves that Lucille's is not the only life he intends to change.

Back at home, Harry settles in, contented by the efforts of a day well spent. He tallies his victories and his losses, and for a change, the victories outstrip the losses. The success of the shoes, both with Molly and with Lucille. His inspired plan to reunite Lucille with her son. The devilish wit of his plan to finish off Bruce: Taking his cues right from the pages of Dumas, apt pupil Harry will utilize his foe's weaknesses to provide his undoing. Working the phones, he's put both balls into motion. In a more relaxed state than he's been in for weeks, he takes his

copy of *The Count of Monte Cristo* (Puffin Classics, abridged) out onto
the balcony to wrap up the final chapters of his hero's adventure.

But as Harry winds through the last thirty pages of the book, a sense
of foreboding washes over him. Even as Dantès dispatches his rivals
left, right, and center, emerging seemingly unscathed, there's a growing
sense that revenge has not only failed to satisfy but that it's tarnished his
soul in some fashion. It's reading to Harry like a classic case of Beware
of What You Ask For, and it's giving him some pause with respect to
his own grand design, as he wonders now if he's been taking direction
from the best of quarters. He's especially struck by the farewell letter
Dantès leaves behind before heading off to sea without his great love,
Mercédès, in the final pages of the book:

> *Tell the angel who will watch over your future destiny, Morrel, to pray*
> *sometimes for a man, who like Satan thought himself for an instant*
> *equal to God, but who now acknowledges with Christian humility*
> *that God alone possesses supreme power and infinite wisdom. Perhaps*
> *those prayers may soften the remorse he feels in his heart. As for you,*
> *Morrel, this is the secret of my conduct towards you. There is neither*
> *happiness nor misery in the world; there is only the comparison of one*
> *state with another, nothing more. He who has felt the deepest grief is*
> *best able to experience supreme happiness. We must have felt what it is*
> *to die, Morrel, that we may appreciate the enjoyments of living.*

Dammit. Harry doesn't like this, hadn't reckoned on ambiguity. He
likes happy endings, he wants to see heroes get their due and villains get
their just deserts. And although the villains have, to a man, paid the
price in Dumas's tale, still this Dantès is laden with sorrow.

Harry is annoyed and a little fearful. He doesn't understand this and
wishes he did. It feels important for what's to follow.

Twelve

In which our hero disappears

ONE YEAR INTO Harry Rent's marriage to Anna Weldt, a reckoning is at hand. The second broken wineglass of the weekend should have alerted him. The first might rationally have been excused, a fluke, a slipup. But for the normally graceful Anna to shatter two wineglasses in the sink—the second inscribing the heel of her palm with an angry red slash—this was surely a sign that all was not well.

Harry sits at the dining room table, sipping black coffee and thumbing through the newspaper, the couple having taken up residence in Anna's condominium after the wedding. The small space is sparsely furnished, gleaming with bare surfaces of wood, polished metal and glass, off of which the crack of the wineglass reverberates.

Unfortunately, Harry has no greater gift for reading between the lines as a husband than he did during their courtship, so all he can think to ask is "Are you okay?" He satisfies himself with Anna's terse "I'm fine." And although he suspects she's not, he's willing to leave it untouched. And there's no real need for him to extend himself since, as always, Anna can be counted on to do the heavy lifting.

"Listen, we're going to need to go see my parents," Anna says a few minutes later as she dries the last of the dishes.

"Really?" Harry asks with surprise, the broken wineglasses explained.

Anna nods. "My mother does this annual clambake fund-raiser thing for the Maritime Museum." She shrugs. "It's her big thing, we can't miss it."

"Sounds good. It'll be nice to spend some time with them."

"I guess there's no choice. It's something she actually cares about. Attendance is mandatory."

Harry had come to find it odd that more than a year of marriage had elapsed with so little time spent in the presence of her parents. But their newlywed year had otherwise unfolded so smoothly and pleasantly—a blur of travel, dining, friends, and, above all, laughter; constant, joyful laughter—that Harry felt uncompelled to address its single peculiar omission. Harry's mother was long gone and his father was living in China with a mail-order bride (having fouled up the order of operations on that one), so that absence made sense, and, in truth, Harry had become used to a life without parents.

But Anna's family was just a flight away, and every time Harry had brought up the possibility of a get-together, something seemed to prevent it. Father's work schedule, Mother's charity work, their international travel. Other than a visit during a brief stopover in New York en route to their London honeymoon, Harry had virtually no exposure to the Weldts. Contact between Anna and her parents was rare and brief. They seldom spoke on the phone, and although sensible floral arrangements arrived on Anna's and Harry's birthdays and on their anniversary, the cards were florist boilerplate with nothing more than "Mom and Dad" appended.

Harry couldn't help noticing the way the normally graceful Anna would stiffen at the mention of her parents, a brittleness creeping into her aspect. At first, he developed an incomplete and indirect picture of the couple, distant and forbidding, living coldly amid their Connecticut wealth. He could never even quite pin down what Anna's father did. Managing the family money seemed to consume most of their energies. "Old-money stuff," Anna had initially demurred when asked.

During their brief New York visit—an absurdly expensive, quiet, formal dinner in a restaurant Harry dimly knew by its international reputation—Harry developed a slightly better sense of the Weldts. It became immediately clear to him that Barbara was the force in the family. Elegant but controlled to the point of rigidity, she radiated a forbidding iciness that not even her rare smiles could melt. Behind her eyes, Harry felt he could discern a perpetually running adding machine, forever toting up the rare pluses and far more frequent minuses of everything she beheld. Arthur, in contrast, seemed affable if malleable, content to cede all authority to his wife. His role in the marriage was to confirm her judgments, to lend her a support that she scarcely needed.

After their first and only meeting, Anna became slightly more expansive about them, about her struggles growing up "in that house," and Harry could detect a genuine affection for her kind if feckless father. Anna's relationship with her mother was, on the other hand, nothing short of disastrous, a source of considerable anxiety and resentment.

In truth, Harry was himself sufficiently intimidated by Mrs. Weldt that he never protested her absence from their lives. Now, the prospect of seeing her again alarms him, as does the thought of being back among the swarm of Anna's youthful suitors, with particular insecurity reserved for Jeremy, her onetime cyclist beau who had haunted their courtship. Harry can't help but wonder if perhaps the broken wineglasses bespeak some uneasiness about facing Jeremy for the first time. And as he is wont to do, he fills the space of uncertainty with the worst possible answers. Surely, Anna is feeling buyer's remorse over her choice of spouse and dreads the possibility of facing the life that might have been. Lord knows, he would.

That night, Harry overhears Anna in hushed telephone conversation with Claire. He pauses for a moment in front of her study door, tells himself he's really not eavesdropping, he's just making sure she's okay. But he stands and he listens.

"Claire, I don't care . . . it doesn't matter what she thinks, she hates everyone. He's my husband and I don't have to explain that or apologize to anyone. You guys like each other, that's all I really care about. Anyway, isn't it time we both stood our ground? I've had it. I swear to God, Claire, it's going to be different this time."

Harry's heard enough and shuffles down the hall toward the bedroom. He sits down on the bed and takes stock. On the one hand, his fear about Jeremy is allayed, at least for the moment. On the other hand, he's troubled by the certainty of his impending rejection by Mrs. Weldt. Despite Anna's confidence, there's a hint of a wobble in her voice, suggesting a more threatening undertaking is at hand. And so he resolves that he is going to do nothing at all to make this homecoming difficult for his wife, even as he acknowledges his propensity for clumsy gestures. Her parents might not find that trait especially endearing, but he hasn't married the parents, he's married the daughter, and as long as her devotion remains intact, he can face anything.

Anna is uncharacteristically subdued for much of the journey to Greenwich. She says little at the airport check-in, where she's normally particular about her seating. She doesn't say much more during the flight, where she's normally garrulous to ease her boredom. She says nothing at all at the rental car pickup, where she's normally particular about getting a nonsmoking vehicle. In fact, the only substantive words spoken by Anna on this trip thus far have been her several requests to her flight attendant for more liquor.

Harry misses the energy of his wife's conversation. It's a sound track

Harry adores, and now he feels lonely and worried amid the silenced music, awkwardly aware that the gap she's left is more than he can hope to fill. In the car, Harry watches Anna for reaction as the highways begin to fall away, and the green, manicured lanes of Greenwich begin to snake by. He'd expected some signs of recognition, even hints of dread, but there's nothing. Anna stares vacantly out the window. Harry reaches over to take her hand, which she acknowledges with a squeeze. She looks at Harry as he drives and smiles a slightly intoxicated, lopsided smile.

"I love you, Harry Rent. You know that, right?"

Harry nods, careful to keep his eyes on the road. He kisses the back of her hand, and she drapes her arms around his shoulders. A kiss aimed for his cheek wetly grazes his ear.

"Don't let my mom get to you," she whispers as though worried that Mrs. Weldt might hear her even now. Harry nods even though he knows from that familiar wobble in Anna's voice that the admonition is intended more for her than for him.

Finally, she points ahead. "It's that one."

"That one" is little more than a pair of stone gates that open onto a serpentine paved path. Harry drives slowly up the drive, which is bounded by towering oaks, and at length a house—"that house," in Anna's dismissive words—comes into view.

Harry gasps at the scale of the mansion. He's no architecture buff, but he guesses it must be well over 150 years old, a mighty monument of brick and stone, all eaves and cornices and shuttered windows. Beyond the portico, two wings, three stories apiece, extend. If there are limits to the property, they're not apparent to Harry, as the landscaping of the football-field-long yard appears to give way almost seamlessly to the woods that surround the building and cast long and slightly menacing shadows across the property.

"Holy shit" is all Harry can think to say.

"Yup," Anna answers glumly. She gives Harry's hand a final squeeze and opens the door and steps out. Harry begins to do the same, but as

179

he opens his door, a black-and-white blur flies into the car and obscures his vision. Harry can make out shouts and barks and what feels like a dog's paw crushing his balls, and before he has time to react, a name is shouted across the property.

"Igor!"

The Old English sheepdog that has leapt into the car, taking up every available inch of space, snaps its head up at the sound of his name and, as quickly as he appeared, bolts. Dazed and wounded, Harry staggers out of the car, his clothes a welter of muddy footprints. He looks down at his ruined outfit helplessly.

The servant who summoned the dog addresses Anna. "Your parents are with the party planners. They should be done by dinner." He takes in Harry with mild disdain and opens the trunk, hoists the two bags out, and disappears into the house.

Anna shakes her head. "Typical. *They* don't keep their animal tied up, and somehow it's *your* fault." An urgency creeps into her voice. "Come on, we need to get you changed out of that quickly before anyone sees you."

Harry forces a grin, remembering his promise to himself not to make waves. "Oh, it's not that bad. Don't worry. I just want to take this all in for a—"

"Harry," Anna pleads, fear creeping into her voice. "They can't see you like this. You *need* to change. Come on." She takes him by the arm and drags him toward the house.

Inside the grand house, Harry is surprised by how dark he finds everything, as if the family has conspired to keep the sun out. Or perhaps they bring the darkness with them wherever they go. But even in the dim half-light, the contours of the Weldts' wealth are impossible to overlook. The worn bottoms of Harry's loafers slip precariously on the marble entry staircase, and he clutches the cold banister tightly as he follows Anna. Portraits line the stairway, the varnish cracked and brown as stern Weldt ancestors scrutinize Harry's march upward. Everywhere he turns there's fine porcelain, gilt, faded silks, all carelessly arrayed as if to disavow their value.

Anna and Harry's guest bedroom is larger than their condominium.

The air is thick with musty neglect. Claw-foot Chippendale dressers brood in the dark space. A matching Chippendale escritoire sits beneath a tightly shuttered window. Thick feathered bedding covers a massive four-post bed.

"Dinner is served at seven," Alexander, the butler, mutters as he closes the door discreetly behind the couple. Anna hurries to the shutters and throws them open with surprising force. Harry squints at the flood of light that fills the room. She opens the window and leans out, panting.

"I can't breathe in this place."

Harry comes over and gently touches her back. "We'll be fine. It's just a weekend. It doesn't seem that bad."

Anna shakes her head. "Would it have killed them to greet us? It's always exactly the same here."

Unsure how to comfort his wife, Harry kisses the back of her head. "I'm going to change."

She nods.

Precisely at seven, Harry and Anna proceed back down the master staircase, walk down a long, carpeted hallway, and step through a pair of swinging doors into the dining room, where the Weldts are waiting to receive them.

Harry observes, as he did at their first meeting, that Anna is the result of the best parts of both. From Barbara Weldt, she's inherited strong facial features and her sculpted jawline, but Claire is the more obvious descendant of her mother, sharing her inclination to chubby limbs. It's in conjunction with Anna's tall, angular father, Arthur, that the sculpted marvel that is his wife can be explained. But neither of them accounts for Anna's personality. Whereas there's a glassy, flat sheen in Arthur's gray eyes, the icy brittleness in Barbara's eyes strikes Harry, as before, as potentially dangerous.

Harry dons his best bedside manner and approaches the Weldts.

"Barbara. Arthur. It's good to see you again. You look terrific." He holds out his hand, first to Arthur, who accepts it limply, and then to Barbara, who, after a moment's hesitation, takes it into her crushing grip.

"Harry," Barbara says, speaking for her husband.

"It's quite a home you have here. Amazing place. I'm a little over-whelmed."

Barbara looks around at the room as if seeking to confirm Harry's impressions, but her indifference to her possessions is clear. "Thank you."

"Hello, Mother," Anna says, stepping forward and lightly kissing her mother's offered cheek.

"Hello, dear. You traveled well?"

Anna nods. "Thank you."

"Welcome home, Anna," Arthur offers with a sweetness in his voice that surprises Harry. Anna winks and presses her father's arm.

"Are you hungry?" Barbara asks. "Sit. Is it my imagination or have you put on a little weight, Anna?"

Harry looks at his svelte bride, agog.

She reddens. "I don't think so."

"Something seems different."

"Well . . . I'm married."

Barbara lets the remark pass without comment, while Arthur smiles stiffly as Alexander appears with a tray of gin martinis. Barbara scoops one up with alacrity. Arthur demurs and whispers to his wife, "Easy, dear."

But she ignores him and sits down at the head of the table, taking a long, authoritative pull from her glass. Anna and Harry decline their drinks and join Barbara. Arthur waits for them to sit, then takes his place at the table. It's a long, handsome hunk of mahogany, but it feels like an unbalanced seesaw at the moment with the four of them clustered together at one end. It's been impeccably laid with a bewildering array of implements, and Harry contents himself that, if nothing else, he'll get a decent meal out of it. But by the third course of the dinner, Harry is starved both for food and for conversation.

The courses have been few and small—a salad of wan iceberg lettuce; an oily consommé; a small plate of tough, dry beef accompanied by brussels sprouts soaked in butter—and he's hungry and confused. On top of it all, out somewhere in the evening, Igor has been barking plaintively, his unacknowledged wails echoing through the drafty halls of the mansion.

Harry whispers to Anna, "Is the dog okay?"

She shrugs helplessly.

The arid small talk continues. Harry notices that they've made no more than token efforts to ask about him or his family, and his attempts to ask about the Weldts have politely been glossed. Arthur has, a few times, seemed about to open up new conversational byways, until Barbara pointedly redirects him. Finally, limbered up by a few more martinis, the brittleness in Barbara's eyes begins to smolder.

Anna, unknowingly, rushes headlong into the beast. "Where's Claire? I expected to see her here."

"She's decided to join us tomorrow, only," Barbara reports. "Keeping contact with us at a minimum, it appears. She got fired again. She seems to cultivate enemies. Not a smart move for a fat, depressed girl." She briskly sets her empty glass aside, discarding it with apparent ease, and Harry feels a pang of sympathy for the similarly discarded Claire, and it begins to dawn on him that he's no chance at all with Anna's mother if this is how she disdains her own flesh and blood. (Arthur has the good grace to appear pained by Barbara's remarks, even if he says nothing to contradict her.) Harry finds himself admiring Claire's apparent wisdom in keeping away from this reunion until the last possible moment.

"How are things at work, Anna?" Arthur asks, hoping to change the subject.

"She's *not* fat," Anna says to her mother before turning to her father. "Things are fine. A little slow right now, the markets are kind of soft."

"Ah," Barbara replies flatly, and although Harry's not sure what the tone means, the sight of Anna stiffening in his peripheral vision suggests that buttons are being pressed.

He tries to help out. "She's right. Everything's in dicey shape right now."

Barbara doesn't address Harry's remark as she speaks to Anna. "One person's downturn is another person's opportunity, don't you think?" Barbara's tone hasn't wavered—she could be discussing menu options for the clambake. "Whatever the conditions of the market, dear, my experience is that people who have a reason why they haven't excelled are the people who don't excel."

Anna stares down at her cutlery, unwilling to make eye contact with her mother during this rebuke.

Despite Barbara's trademark equilibrium, Harry senses that something has her boiling, and she continues, "You come from a long distinguished line, you and your sister. The best schools. The best opportunities. It has always been my hope that you would fulfill your promise and be exceptional." This last said with a glance in Harry's direction. Harry can't read the glimpse—it's too brief, too guarded—and he's unsure what to say next but feels compelled to say something, if only to draw the fire away from his wife.

"Your dog is barking."

Holding back an appreciative smile, Anna clutches Harry's hand gratefully beneath the table.

"That's what they do, Harry," Barbara says. "They bark. If we go running every time they bark, we're just rewarding bad behavior."

Igor barks on into the night. Harry tries for a subject change. "Fair enough. So, tell me about this clambake," he says brightly.

Barbara dutifully obliges. "It's to raise operating funds for the

Maritime Museum. We are a seafaring people, Harry, since the first of us came over nearly four hundred years ago. And this family believes in service and looks for ways to give back to the community."

"Really? How much are the clambake tickets? I'd like to buy a few and contribute."

The room petrifies at once. Anna's hands slides from Harry's grasp. Even Igor stops barking.

"We don't discuss money at dinner, Harry," Arthur says as gently as he can under Barbara's hawklike visage.

"No, of course not," Harry stammers, aware of the tremendous faux pas. "I didn't mean . . . I only . . . Well, you know. Later, obviously."

Igor begins to bark again. Harry feels an unbearable heat in his ears as a bead of sweat trickles down his temple. Beside him, Anna has begun to drink.

Anna had forgiven him the moment they were alone—"I know you meant well, sweetheart"—but it's clear the transgression isn't minor, and an undeniable curtain of tension has settled upon his wife, and she warns Harry against similar overreaching at the party. "Don't try too hard, honey. Let me do the talking, and we'll survive the weekend." And so Harry tossed nervously through the night, hoping fervently that the following day's festivities would lighten the mood and allow him to effect the necessary repairs.

Fortunately, the morning holds the promise to wash away the ills of the night before. Barbara's clambake has transformed the landscape, filling the dark and forbidding property with color, sound, and life. Overnight, the Clambake Clan Catering Company has laid out dozens of long tables, impeccably appointed with blue-checkered tablecloths beneath billowing tents. Everything is a model of quiet good taste, from the whitewashed folding chairs to the hydrangeas in the floral arrangements to sounds of the string quartet that drift into the air via meticulously placed speakers.

Harry takes in the crowd that has materialized for the affair and reflects that he's never seen so much khaki and so many loafers in one place. By comparison, he appears downright rakish in gray slacks and his starched, pin-striped dress shirt, even though Anna vetted his sartorial choices. He's further struck by the general sameness of the attendees—mostly silver-haired, ruddy-cheeked, and murmuring quietly. Even the kids seem old, teenagers subdued and disinterested as they sit around secretly sipping from mixed drinks poured by accommodating bartenders.

The banner for the Maritime Museum flutters overhead, and four speakers now have stepped up to the microphone and, in halting, ill-prepared remarks, lauded the importance of preserving Connecticut's seafaring heritage. And, of course, they all praise the hosts of the event, praise that's greeted with an appropriately modest, nearly imperceptible nod from Barbara and a slightly more effusive wave from Arthur.

Harry hasn't made any blunders yet, nor has he connected with any of the people he's met. Anna is unfailingly gracious, holding Harry's arm and introducing him to couple after couple, all of whom have blended in Harry's mind into one rich, dour supercouple. His mind drifts, imagining a nearby factory that clones these rich types, turning them out with assembly-line precision, made to order for events such as these, provided, perhaps, as a service courtesy of the Clambake Clan Catering Company. Claire's arrival has been his one bright spot, but she's making her own rounds, dispensing with her mingling duties. Harry watches her garish, tipsy stumbling from afar, amused and impressed anew by how unwilling she is to assume the Weldt mold.

Anna's footing among her peers, in contrast, is sure. As she engages with them, it's scarcely the first time that Harry finds himself admiring her seemingly unshakable sense of place, of self. How drawn he remains to this most attractive, essential of her qualities, this remarkable solidity in moments she claims fully as her own. He's content to cede center stage to her and drift more and more fully into the background. Perhaps, he muses, this is as it should be. Perhaps that's where I can do her the most good. Certainly nothing beyond his wife engages him with this event. And so he opts for disengagement, mentally drifting away and slowly disappearing from where he's not needed. Not even Claire's increasingly drunken attempts to hang herself on a well-tended but uninterested youth a third of her age provides him much amusement.

"Harry, this is Jeremy. Jeremy, Harry."

Harry has so divested himself from the moment that he's totally unprepared for the one introduction he's been dreading. Startled and lost, all he can do for the moment is gape at Jeremy, who is considerably taller than Harry had expected, and whose good looks are filled out with a slight post–Tour de France weight gain.

Harry recovers and takes Jeremy's proffered hand with feigned good cheer. He's had his opening line prepared for days.

"Nice to meet you, Jeremy."

"How do you do, Rent?"

"Hey, saw you on the Tour. Thought you looked better than, what was it, one thirty-two?"

Jeremy grins with surprising charm. "That makes two of us." He turns his attention to Anna. "You look absolutely magnificent, Anna."

Anna dismisses the compliment. "Thank you, Jeremy. Nice of you to come back."

"Miss Barbara's clambake? I'd be blacklisted for years to follow."

"Yes, you would," Anna chuckles. "How's your training?"

Anna and Jeremy begin to talk in technical terms only vaguely familiar to Harry from his time spent watching the Tour de France with Anna during their courtship, something about lactic threshold, anaerobic tolerance, and watts per pedal. Harry tunes out the content and studies his rival, dismayed to find how easily he wears his wealth, his privilege, his status—none of which hide just how deeply smitten he is. In that light, Anna's own poise and certainty, so lovingly admired only moments ago, takes on a worrisome edge, and he wonders, for neither the first nor the last time, if she really married the man she was meant for.

Harry's not the only one thinking it.

"Shame on me for not marrying you when I could have, Anna," Jeremy says carelessly.

Anna shakes her head. "Try to behave yourself, Jeremy."

Jeremy remembers himself and turns to Harry, aghast. "Harry, forgive me. I didn't mean it the way it sounded. I've had one glass of champagne too many. A stupid thing to say, and I'm genuinely pleased for the both of you."

Harry tries to be the better man. "I understand. I'd be kicking myself in your shoes, too."

As the conversation continues, Jeremy goes out of his way to include Harry, to do his best to reassure that nothing grave lies behind his slip of the tongue. And Harry appreciates Jeremy's efforts, finds that he's growing to like him, feels ashamed of his rehearsed gibe, even as he begins to accept proffered flutes of champagne to dull his shame. He does his best to participate, but he's all too aware that he's a third wheel here, that Anna and Jeremy are bound by their shared wealth and privilege, and with a sadness that he realizes is probably foolish and petty, he excuses himself and wanders tipsily off.

The Jeremy incident has confirmed for Harry how completely out of place he is here. He's determined to keep a low profile and stay out of harm's way until it's time to leave. So he avoids groups, keeps away from the food table, doesn't return to his seat. But even this fading into the background isn't enough to remove Harry from the scene as much as he'd like. He can still feel, or imagines he feels, inquiring and disapproving eyes on him, and so he looks around the grounds for a place in which to lose himself more definitively.

His rescue comes in the form of a ramshackle toolshed at the far southern end of the yard, away from the revelers, unlikely to garner much notice. Tucking the remnants of a stray bottle of champagne under his arm, he makes his way to it, taking care to be as unobtrusive as possible, until he nears the door, when he bolts for the shed and darts inside.

Harry closes the door quickly behind him, panting, hoping no one has noticed his erratic behavior. It takes his eyes a moment to adjust to the darkness, although shafts of light penetrate from between slats of plywood hammered over holes in the structure. The muffled sounds of the clambake seem less overwhelming in here, distant and benign. He drains the final drops from the slippery, glistening bottle.

Harry takes the measure of the shed, finding it well stocked and well maintained. Rows of screwdrivers lined up according to size hang from a wall-mounted Peg-Board. Jars ranging from baby food to mason sit on the shelves, also scrupulously arranged by size, containing all manner of screws, washers, nuts, and bolts. A workbench with a large green vise attached to its corner takes up nearly half the shed. Harry fiddles with the vise, opening and closing the jaws, momentarily mesmerized by the tool.

His reverie is shattered by the sound of the door flopping wildly open and then slamming shut again.

"Hey, Bro," Claire giggles drunkenly. "What are you doing in here?"

Startled, Harry turns to face Claire, who stumbles in his direction, in her cups. She loses her footing and one of the folds of her dress catches in the vise. A long, loud tearing sound fills the small space. Harry moves to catch Claire, but she's frozen in place and winces.

"Oops," she blurts, and dissolves into wild laughter. She examines the shredded fabric. "Okay. That was expensive once." She turns to Harry and shrugs. She notes the champagne bottle, picks it up hopefully, only to darken at its emptiness. "Anything to drink in here?"

A bit woozy himself, Harry looks at the rows of tools hanging on the wall. "I can offer you a screwdriver."

"That's pretty good," she snorts, taking one down. She sighs and regards it pitifully, along with the rows of size-arranged tools along the wall. "Poor castrated bastard," she mutters. She lowers herself to the ground and sits with her back braced against one of the walls. Harry sits down beside her, and she can't keep the anger out of her voice.

"This is where he hides from her, you know. His only respite from the Gargoyle of Greenwich." She shakes her head. "Look around, Harry. Meet my father. This is all of him, right here. Since he's not allowed to assert himself in the house."

Harry looks around the tiny shack from this curiously childlike vantage point, craning his neck upward to take it all in. It's so alien to him, impossible for him to fully comprehend, this notion of such total relegation, and he can't help but feel sorry for his father-in-law even as he breathes a momentary sigh of relief that this is yet another parental trait Anna hasn't inherited. He can't imagine her ever banishing him in this way, and the thought fills him with a moment of love and gratitude and leaves him feeling slightly ashamed of his disappearing act.

Claire seems to read his mind. "I overheard that stuff with Jeremy. Is that why you came in here?"

Harry hesitates, then nods uncomfortably.

"It really doesn't mean anything, Harry. Repressed rich people, they talk a whole different language, full of codes and strange subtext, and half the time they don't even know what the fuck they really mean. But I know Anna adores you. You know that, too, right, Harry?"

Thick-tongued with champagne, Harry doesn't answer quickly enough for Claire's taste. He picks up a monkey wrench that's fallen to the ground near them and begins to fiddle with it.

"Harry! You *do* know that? Do *not* let the Arthur-Barbara poison actually infect you. If you doubt that, the terrorists have won."

At length, he nods, but neither of them are fully convinced.

The alcohol, however, continues to commandeer Claire, who yawns. "Attaboy. Fuck, I'm tired." She looks around the shed. "This is a nice place. I think I could settle down here."

She sets her head against Harry's shoulder, and to his surprise, she's asleep within seconds, her rattling snore utterly unlike Anna's diminutive dream whimpers. A few moments pass, then a few more, as Claire slides into a deeper sleep. Harry carefully twists his head to take her in, and he can't recall ever seeing Claire so peaceful. She's usually in constant motion, always urgently on the move to or from something. He hasn't the heart to disturb her. And so he sits beside her, still and silent, his own tipsy eyes closing slowly.

Hours later, Anna's voice: "Harry? Are you all right?"

Harry stirs disagreeably, his stiff neck protesting. Beside him, Claire raises her head, groaning. He rubs his eyes and opens them to find Anna and her parents standing in the doorway of the shed. Night has fallen. The guests have gone.

"Oh. Hi."

"Claire?" Anna asks with ill-concealed disbelief. "Harry, what are you doing in here? We've been looking for you for hours."

Harry fumbles with the monkey wrench that's fallen from his sleepy grasp. "Um. Needed a wrench?"

Claire staggers to her feet, and Anna and her parents note her tattered dress. Arthur fidgets with embarrassment, unsure what to do. It's Barbara's glacial "Ah," followed by her abrupt departure, that seems to grant him permission to react. He looks with concern at his daughter and then, with trepidation, sets out after his wife, leaving a pained Anna in the doorway, rubbing her forehead, unsure what to make of the tableau before her.

"Anna, don't go all nutso," Claire tries. "It's nothing."

Anna ignores her. "Oh, Harry . . ."

"Anna, I'm sorry. I—"

"Please. Don't say anything."

Hereinafter, he will follow Anna's request to the letter.

Once again, en route to his room, Harry overhears Anna. And as before, he stops to listen. But now heated voices rather than hushed ones rise from within Arthur's study.

191

"What a scandal," Barbara mutters with resignation.

"Don't go overboard, Mother. It's not what it looks like. And you know Claire. It was probably all her doing."

Harry looks up to see Claire enter the hallway en route to her room. Caught in the act, he makes no pretense. He holds his index finger to his lips. Claire leans in toward the door with interest.

"I mean, really, Anna, what on earth are we supposed to say?" Barbara continues. "We don't hear from you for months, and then you announce you've married this Harry person about whom we know nothing."

"Anna, you should have spoken to your mother," Arthur offers dutifully.

"Yes. You should have," Barbara affirms. "I expect this kind of thing from Claire, but you've been relatively sane most of your life. Why didn't you seek me out before marrying that man? 'I'd like to buy a clambake ticket.' Really."

The pain must be evident in his eyes because Claire silently takes Harry's hands and shakes her head. *They don't matter,* she wants to say.

"Anna," Barbara pleads. "An *X-ray* practice? Why didn't you talk to me? I could have helped you."

Speak up anytime, Harry thinks. *Tell them you love me.*

"Help? Me? Maybe I didn't need or want your help," Anna says. "That's all you really care about, isn't it? That I didn't come to you first. You're punishing us both because I didn't get Mother's permission to be an adult."

"Oh, Anna!" Barbara exclaims with contempt. "Don't be a child. How do we know it's not our money he's after? Just another public-school graduate looking to trade up?"

"Is that all that matters to you? You haven't the slightest idea who he is."

At last.

"Well, enlighten us, Anna. It's not as though we haven't asked."

Here it comes. Harry wills his wife to feel his love through the walls of the study, conveying images of their madcap week in London, racing between museums and theater; of Anna's tonsillectomy, when Harry plied her with gelato; of the hilarity of moving Harry's apartment of clutter first into her condo and then into their storage space. A year of love. Of glue. Of strength. *Use this. Use it all. Use me.*

"In fact, he graduated Harvard Med."

Six words. Separating the before and the after.

There's a moment of silence. Then Barbara asks, "He did?"

"Really?" seconds Arthur with barely concealed delight.

"Why didn't you tell us this?" Barbara demands. "We had no idea."

"He doesn't like to talk about himself. Surely *you* can appreciate that."

Harry breaks free from a shocked Claire's hand and wanders numbly down the hall, whatever follows lost to him. He knows in the Grand Scheme it's a small enough thing. But it confirms what he's always feared—that he's not good enough for his wife. And now they both know it.

Harry can't sleep. Igor's barking fills the night but it's not what's keeping him awake. Anna's interview with her parents, his inflated CV, it all rings in his ears and prevents sleep from overtaking him although every limb insistently whispers its exhaustion.

As he views the replay incessantly, Harry is struck by the sheer desperation in Anna's voice. He can't disavow the painful truth the interview has revealed. Yet he finds that, in spite of the twisting pain in his chest that keeps him awake, he can somehow understand her desperate ploy. She was fending off an attack of killer bees, angry stings jabbing her everywhere, and in a quintessential fight-or-flight moment, she fought back and defended herself the best way she knew how. Mortified by Claire's report, she apologized profusely to Harry and promised to explain everything and make amends once they got home, and Harry felt it would be churlish to refuse her. He realizes that he's collateral damage in this ongoing skirmish between mother and child.

But the hurt and disappointment sear. He's left weighing his catalog of memories, what he perceived as the happiness of their first year (how foolish he feels now), against this betrayal—yes, that's the only word for it—and he doesn't know which to believe, which represents his wife and their life together. This heartbreak of certainty lost and swept away by doubt keeps him awake, restless. Finally, Harry throws back the heavy covers and swings out of bed. Anna, mildly tranquilized, sleeps fitfully. And so he slips on his coat and slippers as quietly as possible. He tiptoes out of the bedroom and into the musty foyer, dimly lit by candle-shaped lightbulbs, their single filament burning low. He pauses before Claire's door, but her rococo snores make clear she's sleeping off her hangover. Igor's barking grows more plaintive, and Harry makes his way to the front door. He's about to step outside when something catches his attention.

In the drawing room, Arthur dozes in a large armchair before a dwindling fire. Harry regards him for a moment, taking in his tattered robe, the faded fabric of the armrests, when Arthur's eyes flutter open, as if the pressure of Harry's attention has awakened him. He looks over sleepily in his direction and his eyes widen slightly. The two men hold each other's stare for a moment, and perhaps he's just imagining it, but Harry can swear Arthur's trying to tell him something. He can't quite make out the wordless communiqué. Perhaps he's explaining that it's a difficult place to live, this constellation of formidable, unpredictable Weldt women; or perhaps he's commiserating with Harry, hinting that he himself has been judged in this household; or perhaps he's simply trying to apologize, something he daren't do within Barbara's sphere of influence. Most disquieting to Harry, though, is the sense that perhaps he's being warned about what lies ahead. Harry experiences a mild shudder of revulsion and pity for the deflated sack of a man sitting before him in refuge from his own bed, nods politely, and continues out into the warm Connecticut evening.

The damp grass tickles the parts of his feet left uncovered by his slippers. He walks past the debris from the clambake, back past the toolshed, and he finds Igor trying to paw his way into some sealed trash cans. At the sound of Harry's footsteps, he freezes, turns his attention to Harry, and bounds toward him, a great lumbering cloud. He jumps up onto Harry and begins licking his face excitedly. Harry smiles his first smile of the day.

"Hey, Igor. Easy, boy. Easy."

He crouches down and gives the dog a vigorous scratching.

"Well, someone in this family appreciates me."

Harry looks back to the darkened house. He stares at what he believes is the window of the guest bedroom. He looks into the darkness and hopes that Anna will stir. That a light will come on. That she'll appear at the window and beckon him back to bed. He stares hard at the window, trying to will her awake. But the room remains stubbornly dark and still.

Harry rises and is about to turn back to the house when Igor walks a few feet in the opposite direction, stops, turns back to Harry, and barks once.

"What?"

Igor takes a few more steps away from Harry and barks again.

"What, you want to show me something? Is that it?" He approaches Igor, who continues a few more feet ahead, pauses, and looks back at Harry. Harry approaches Igor, who moves on again.

This bit of follow the leader continues for some distance. Gradually, they enter the woods that line the perimeter of the Weldt property, and the path becomes more difficult to follow. Dirt and loose rock replace the manicured footpaths, and Harry huffs a bit as he climbs over some fallen logs. Each time, Igor pauses, waits for Harry to safely reach his side, then carries on.

After a considerable distance, Igor stops and looks up to Harry, confused.

"What? Where are we going?"

Igor looks from side to side, uncertain, and barks.

"Are we lost?"

Igor continues to scan the landscape uncertainly, and so Harry takes charge. He follows the sound of running water a few hundred yards in the distance. This time, he pauses along the way to make sure Igor is keeping pace with him. At length, they arrive at a clear brook that rushes over cracked boulders, and Harry sits down at the water's edge. Igor sits beside him. Man and dog behold the water and one another. Having arrived together.

In the house, Anna has awakened and can't find Harry.

Thirteen

In which our hero begins to put the pieces together

HARRY SITS IN FRONT of a glass partition waiting for Lucille's son to be brought to him. He's impressed by this juvenile facility—it's all new construction: blue glass, steel and cool gray stone, surprisingly modern and streamlined, at least from the outside. Once inside, there's a good deal of cinder block and linoleum, but it's considerably more civilized and comfortable than Harry expected. As he waits, his eyes wander down the row of other visits taking place, and he feels conspicuously out of place as tearful meetings unfold almost entirely between young mothers and their younger sons.

It was surprisingly easy for Harry to locate Lucille's son in the system. Easy enough that Harry can't understand how Lucille should have failed to find him on her own. One phone call was all it took, that first call to the investigators. A day later, a copy of Lucille's son's file sat open before him, and Harry was unnerved by the boy's prodigious criminality. At fifteen, the young man had never met a petty crime he could refuse—robbery, assault, car theft. Lucille wasn't exaggerating. Carl really had gone about as bad as a kid could go.

Harry found himself considering the child he and Anna never had. It was to have come later, but first there was her career to attend to. How would a child of theirs have fared, he wondered. Even with privilege, with opportunity, who's to say their offspring might not have ended up right here? Was there something that both Anna and Harry suspected or feared that prevented either from ever forcefully pushing the question? Some inherent Rent/Weldt defect that both despaired of passing on? After Anna's death, Harry was relieved that there was no child to raise without a mother, although, as he teased the question out more, he wondered if a child might have been capable of redirecting what increasingly seemed like the inevitability of their estrangement. Would Harry have dallied with whores had he been a father? He's reasonably certain he wouldn't have. But after the death of her parents, Anna all but stopped talking about the possibility of children. And then she was gone.

Returning his attention to Carl's file, Harry was surprised by the photo. Harry imagined Carl as an obese, surly teen with pockmarked skin and greasy hair. (Why the skin and hair, he's not sure, but the image took shape of its own volition in Harry's febrile imagination.) Instead, the face that greeted him in the file was lean and angelic, startling in its good looks, and Harry wondered if the investigators had found the right kid. But all the other documentation matched up, and Lucille's signature was in evidence all throughout the intake paperwork.

The visitor log showed she hadn't seen the boy in just over two years.

Harry nervously rehearses his pitch, hoping to appeal to any remnants of conscience the kid might have, but failing that, he has a backup plan. Finally, after nearly twenty minutes, Carl is brought to Harry and sits down facing him. He's dressed in an orange jumper like the rest of the boys. There's such feline grace to him, such a deeply polished nonchalance, that Harry once again doubts his lineage.

Carl appraises Harry suspiciously. "You're not my cousin."

"I know. But they only let family visit. Thanks for seeing me any-way. I figured you might."

"Why'd you figure that?"

"Well, you don't get a lot of visitors. Company is company, right?"

"Whatever. Who the fuck are you?"

"My name's Harry. I'm a friend of your mother's."

Carl snorts with disbelief.

"What's so funny?"

"You don't look like the kind of guy who'd do my mom."

Harry reddens with embarrassment as his mind momentarily skitters back to that evening in the alley, that moment when he beheld Lucille in all of her majestic and mountainous nakedness.

"Do? Who said 'do'? I said I was a friend."

"Yeah, right, whatever. You got any cigarettes?"

"I don't smoke."

Carl dismisses him with a single, well-practiced flicker of the eyes. "Well, what do you want?"

Harry's pretty sure he's not going to get anywhere appealing to this kid, so he might as well get right to the point. "I want you to see your mother."

Carl's face twists into a grimace of distaste. "Fuck that shit. No way."

"Why not?"

"Have you *seen* her? She's, like, as big as a fucking planet. That shit's disgusting. No way." Carl leans back in his chair, arms crossed.

Harry can't quite believe what he's hearing. "But she's your *mother!*"

"Not my fault." Bored. Uncomprehending. Irritated.

Harry sinks back into his chair, struggling to hold back the wave of anger that threatens to engulf him. It's too much to bear, this spectacle of shame, of one turning away in embarrassment from family, this pub-lic humiliation of the Calculus of Not Good Enough, of being tallied up and found wanting, this withdrawal of love from those most entitled to and deserving of it. He aches for Lucille, living in this too familiar echo of crushing disavowal. Harry can't help himself, and now he's dizzy with rage, so furious he has to grasp the chair to steady himself. When he can finally pry a few words out, they fall in livid clumps.

"You arrogant . . . miserable . . . piece of shit." Harry's eyes fill with angry tears.

"Fuck you, dude. I'm outta here." Carl starts to rise.

"You sit the fuck down. Right now." Harry speaks in this powerful new voice that's become so readily available.

Carl flips him off and steps away from the table. Harry, increasingly aware of curious eyes on him, eyes questioning this tableau between man and boy in a room full of mothers and sons, speaks up for all to hear.

"Don't be mad, baby . . . What about that night at your house? In the garage. Remember?"

Carl's eyes widen with surprise and he pales as the other boys turn interested, dark eyes his way.

"What the fuck are you doing?"

Harry leans in, sick with anxiety even as he's impressed by his ballsy improvisation. "Sit down and I'll stop." A guard approaches Carl curiously, but Carl waves him off and slowly returns to his chair.

"Do you know what they'll do to me in here if—?"

"I have a pretty good idea. Now shut up and listen." Harry is light-headed with power, and the words tumble out in a dizzying, panicked rush. "You're going to do exactly what I tell you to do and have a nice visit with your mother and make her feel good. You do that, and there will be a pile of money waiting for you when you get out of here. You don't, and you get to spend the next two years . . . with a lot of new boyfriends. It's your call."

Carl seems not to have heard the last part—at the mention of money, his mercenary instincts roar to life. "Money? How much?"

Harry cites a generous figure.

Carl whistles and cackles. "Shit, I'd make nice with Osama bin Laden for that." He turns suspicious. "How you gonna give it to me?"

"You have a savings account?"

Carl nods. "My mom made one for me."

Again anger. Of course she did. "I'll deposit it. It'll be waiting when you're out."

"How will I know?"

"I'll show you the deposit receipt."

Carl grins. "Fuck. Bring it on."

Behind the wheel of the Jaguar, in its silent, leather-lined, climate-controlled cocoon, Harry is shaking with rage, the fury nearly overwhelming. But it's not Carl and Lucille that fills his thoughts, try as he does to force them back to point.

Jesus, Anna.

Is that why you died? To escape me?

But beneath the rage there's a second insistent voice, a voice reverberating with guilt, a barely discernible voice that can only whisper, *I'm sorry.*

Through red-rimmed eyes, a shard of an image in the rearview draws his notice. It's the gray Impala, parked two car lengths behind him.

And now Harry's mind and heart empty out, and everything is replaced with a single purpose. He pulls the Jaguar away from the curb and the Impala follows. Without any warning, Harry throws the car into reverse and pounds the accelerator. The Jaguar offers up a wheel-spinning screech of protest before hurtling backward and tearing through the grille of the Impala. The entire front section of the car compresses like a bellows cramp, and a pair of deployed air bags obscure the undoubtedly shocked expressions of Harry's pursuers.

A wave of euphoria sweeps through Harry, and only the sound of sirens in the distance focuses him enough to put the car into drive. It takes some aggressive back-and-forth before the mélange of chrome and steel finally releases its grip on the Jaguar, tearing the trunk lid off and leaving it impaled on the hood of the Impala. Harry speeds the wounded vehicle away, turning into a warren of small side streets, where he promptly gets completely lost.

"What happened to your car?" Molly squints through the glare reflecting on Café Retro's window to where the wounded Jaguar sags in the parking lot.

Harry shrugs. "Fender bender."

Molly raises an eyebrow. "Fender ender is more like it."

Harry's voice is small, distant, as though addressing someone not present. "You know, I never really liked that car. It was my wife's idea. Thought my patients would like it. But she was always too concerned about what other people thought."

Harry can't stop the last from coming out, riding out the attendant stab of guilt as it blossoms into anger. But he shoves all distractions aside and focuses on his mission. And, for a moment, he registers that he can, in fact, push distractions aside—something previously entirely beyond his gifts—before he realizes that he's stuck in a bit of a tautological cul-de-sac, and so he returns his focus to the moment, to Lucille.

"I've got news for Lucille."

"More shoes?"

"No. Bigger than shoes." He waves at Lucille, busy in her section. She nods at Harry and continues taking an order. As soon as she's done, she walks over, and Harry is delighted to note the ease with which she moves—there's a newfound grace, as though having just learned how to use her feet, she's now somehow graduated to ballet lessons. She can't keep the grin off her face.

"Holy crap. These shoes . . ." She's at a loss for words.

Harry nods. "Max is a magician. But come here, sit down. I have some news."

Lucille looks to Molly for a clue, but Molly shrugs. "He won't tell me."

Lucille nervously balances atop a stool and a half, and Harry briefly wonders what it will take for this woman to trust him, to stop assuming a hunted-animal mien every time he hands her another life-changing card.

"Okay. What's up?"

Harry takes a deep breath and smiles. "I found your son."

Lucille pales, looks at him uncomprehendingly. "What?"

"Your son! I found him. He wants to see you."

Harry's too thrilled with himself to note the look of dark concern moving across Molly's face, but he's troubled by Lucille's trepidation—this is not the result he was expecting. He gamely presses forward.

"I'm telling you. He wants you to visit him. I found him. It was so easy, I'm sure you could have found him, too . . ."

Of course she could have. She doesn't want to see him.

Too late, as ever, Harry figures it out and the words die on his lips. The trio sits in silence as Harry looks desperately to Molly. Molly inhales helplessly, but before she can speak Lucille rises.

"Thanks, Harry. That was nice of you. But I don't think so." With a sad attempt at a smile, she lumbers off to wait on her section.

Harry sinks into her abandoned stool like a collapsing parade float.

Molly puts a hand on his shoulder and sits beside him, shaking her head. "Harry . . . what . . . what were you thinking?" She says it gently but there's no escaping her mortification.

Dazed, Harry shakes his head. "I don't know. I wasn't. I mean, I saw her pictures and she said . . ." He turns to Molly plaintively. "I just wanted to help."

Molly takes his hand, searches his eyes, and Harry's heart skips a beat, as he feels scrutinized, exposed. Beheld.

"Help who?"

Harry looks at Molly with surprise, regards his hand in hers. What can she possibly know? How could she have figured out the humiliating bond that ties him to Lucille, when he's only beginning to understand it himself?

And there's that flicker of anger again. Now he remembers his thoughts back at Café Retro on the afternoon of Anna's funeral, as he reflected on how little Anna gave him to "rail angrily" about . . . only that's not true, is it? It's been there all along, the great unspoken truth of their marriage, their shared two-way failure of shame (hers) and accommodation (his), and the rage has been suppressed until now, but it's finally starting to come out—and this is all bound up in easing Lucille's humiliation in ways that Anna never extended to him.

None of this can he say to Molly, as terribly as he wants to.

"Well, her, of course. Who else?"

Harry's office was empty when he arrived, Nicole being late again, as usual, as always. Harry hurried through the front office, headed straight for his darkened sanctuary, and that's where he sits now, alone and in the dark, the viewing boxes bare and unlit. The giant, crooked arm of the X-ray apparatus sits dormant before him. Harry sits huddled in the corner, paralyzed by confusion, unable to decide what to do next, unable even to determine his choices.

Apologize to Lucille for interfering? Abandon his plan with Carl? Go back and tell Molly everything? Stop visiting Café Retro altogether? The more Harry worries, the more anxieties pile up, constricting him. What will come of the will reading? What kind of a mess am I going to be in? Can I pull the plug on Bruce's planned doom?

Where do I go from here?

What am I supposed to do now?

The sudden and unexpected thump of blaring hip-hop from Nicole's desk jolts him from his paralysis. Again, anger surges.

"Hey! I'm trying to *think* in here!"

Harry's shout has no effect as it's drowned out by the music. With thickening fury, he gets up and steps out of his chamber, to find Nicole at her desk playing computer solitaire.

"Hey!"

The force in Harry's voice surprises the normally imperturbable Nicole, who turns to face her boss.

"Do you mind?" Harry indicates the music.

Nicole, not fully comprehending the sudden shift in the balance of power, reluctantly turns the music down.

"Thank you," Harry sighs exasperatedly, and starts to turn away, then something gets the better of him. The accumulated weight of unanswered calls, unmailed bills. Unmet expectations.

"Hey, Nicole. You know what? You're fired."

The words are easier to say than Harry ever imagined they might be, and the loss of the sight and smell of Nicole no longer strikes him as remotely difficult to bear. Discarding her diploma is no longer enough—all at once he wants to be rid of her.

In what has been and will continue to be a day full of surprises, Nicole hands him another but not the last:

"Good for you. It took you long enough."

She smiles at Harry with what he swears is affection before shutting off her computer and leaving the office for good.

There's something indecent, Harry feels, about the mound of freshly overturned earth that covers Anna's grave. Not that he'd expected anything different. It hasn't been that long, after all. Days, right? Or weeks? Harry's unnerved at how thoroughly he has lost track of time.

He's not even sure what's brought him here, as the sun begins to sink from view. He'd wandered without purpose, and some internal compass delivered him here, without his knowledge. At first he thought it was the need for a quiet place to think. But as soon as his eyes fell on the headstone, the jumble of woe that had been plaguing him disappeared, as if the conductor of his chaos had suddenly, dramatically silenced his orchestra.

Sure, part of what brings him here is obligation, the understanding that the newly bereft are supposed to make their pilgrimages of mourning. But something else is nagging at Harry, something that's begun to take shape ever since his interview with Carl. A sense of something left unsaid. But it's all too amorphous for Harry to get his arms around. It's just a dull, relentless nagging in the pit of his stomach. Something to set right.

He stands there dumbly, feeling heavy and clumsy in his limbs, and just as he's about to give up giving voice to this nameless urge that's plaguing him, he notices it, sitting unobtrusively against the headstone.

It's a simple floral bouquet. A spring selection of daisies and daffodils. There's no card. And it strikes Harry with an irresistible force: He's not the first person to leave flowers for Anna. The husband of the deceased, the devastated widower, isn't the first person to pay tribute to the departed.

Jesus God, Harry thinks, *how is this possible?* He leans against the headstone, barely able to hold himself upright. What has he been doing all this time? How has he been spending his days, his energy, his feelings? Dispersing them all in every conceivable direction except where they most belong. The quiet, understated bouquet cuts through his heart worse than anything he's felt since he heard the words *Harvard Med*.

He's been stuck on a roller coaster, carried along, mostly willingly, he admits, by the sheer momentum of what he's put into play. And even now, as he wants for the first time to stop everything he's begun, he still feels committed to keeping his balls in the air, even as he's certain now that they are destined to come down around his ears.

Flowers. Why didn't I think to stop for flowers?

Late the next morning, Harry shifts uncomfortably on a settee in the lobby of the Stiles Hotel. Max sits across a low coffee table, talking, drink in hand, but Harry isn't listening. Divided to the end, he's chiding himself for being too weak to stop this charade even as he's taking in his surroundings, fixing in memory the tableau of Bruce's Last Stand.

The lobby is bustling but discreet, lined with trendy furnishings. Striped fabrics clash and intersect with low, hard seating surfaces. Harry realizes that he and Max probably raise the median age of the room by about twenty years, and he wonders how unusual Max found the suggestion to meet here.

Harry had been worrying about how he could be present for the fall without its seeming too obvious. Positioning, he knew, was key, and he needed to be in place to pick up the pieces. But how to do that in a fashion that would not beggar disbelief had Harry completely stumped, when Max called to say he wanted to talk. Harry jumped at the opportunity to use the hotel bar for cover, and now Max is speechifying in that portentous way he has, and Harry suspects he should be listening, if only he could stop scanning the lobby for Molly's arrival. Bruce has already gone up to the room, which suggests that the reborn Happy Angels Delivery Service—now dispatching women under the moniker Candyland Companions—has followed his instructions to the letter, deploying one of their girls (described carefully to meet Bruce's predilections) directly in Bruce's path, making herself fully available to him and leading him back to this hotel. He only wishes that he could somehow be in the room at the moment when Molly enters—summoned by a "message" from Bruce delivered to Café Retro, and a key left at the front desk—to find Bruce in the arms of "Felicia"; to see the flying glassware, the flying fists; to experience firsthand the moment he's been waiting for, the moment Molly can see Bruce for what he really is and finally tells him to go fuck himself and never, ever, ever call her again. And despite the mounting anticipation at the approaching denouement, he's not without qualms over his role in contriving this moment.

Now Harry spots Molly, who has just entered the hotel. She proceeds to the front desk, collects a key, and heads expectantly to the elevator. Harry angles himself away from her to avoid being seen, although he's sure she can hear the anxious thumping of his heart. She steps into the elevator and disappears behind the closing doors. Minutes now, Harry thinks.

"Hey. Are you listening to me?"

Harry turns his focus back to Max. "Um, yeah. Of course."

"Well? Don't you have anything to say?"

"About what?"

Max shakes his head. "Okay, I'll try again. I've made a decision. I'm retiring. It's official."

"You're kidding."

"Nope. I'm done with the shit and I'm outta here. Off to Florida at last. I can bake in the sun, crisp slowly, and die among my people."

"Come on, Max. How many more times are we going to have this conversation?"

"Zero more times. I'm not fucking around, Harry. This is it. I've already referred my patients to that jackass Roth. I'm out."

Harry wishes that the hard settee beneath his ass was a comfortable padded armchair, so he could slowly sink into it in disbelief. For a moment, thoughts of Molly and the drama surely unfolding floors above are banished.

"You're . . . you're leaving? Really?"

Max nods. "Really."

"To Florida?"

"Yeah. Fuckin' Florida."

Harry blinks back unexpected tears and nods. Max sighs and fiddles with his drink, uncomfortable.

"You knew I was gonna go eventually."

"Yeah. Eventually. It's just . . . well . . . you talked about it so much but it never happened, so I guess I thought it was just talk."

"You calling me a bullshitter?" Max asks with a grin.

Harry shakes his head sadly. "You're my best friend."

My only friend. My only friend left.

Max sets down his drink and puts his hand on Harry's arm. When he speaks, his voice is flecked with pity. "I know. Thing is, thing I ask myself, and don't take this wrong, is what did our friendship really amount to? I mean, yeah, we're pals, we golf, we're kinda confidants and crap, but—especially at our age—don't you think that stuff is maybe somewhere else? What about Anna? Wasn't *she* your best friend?"

She should have been.

But Harry thinks back with distaste to the man who brought call girls into hotel rooms, the man who told dozens of lies, big and small. Is that how you treat a best friend? But then, was Greenwich how you treat a best friend? Of course it wasn't. It all seems so much clearer to him now, as though everything has been washed away by this collapsing spiral of deceit and solitude, and now Harry Rent 2.0, the new and improved Harry Rent, this year's model Harry Rent, sits in a lobby feeling completely alone for the first time in his life.

Max steps into the silence. "Listen, as long as we're unloading all the unpleasant shit, I just need to say one more thing. Take it or leave it, as always. I don't know what's up with you and the fat waitress, but I don't like it."

Harry raises his head dully and looks at Max.

"You can't mess around with people's lives, kid. They're not toys, this isn't some fucking game. You're clearly going through some shit right now, and maybe it's not all bad, maybe you're figuring some crap out. But don't get some crazy idea that you can control people, because that will bite you on the fucking ass so hard that you'll carry those teeth marks around for the rest of your goddamn life."

How quickly and easily Harry feels his house of cards brought down around him. This is surely not the day he envisioned, having imagined himself basking in triumph and adoration, not soaking in misery and self-loathing. He's been so busy, so occupied with plans, charting his little victories and setbacks, keeping his balls in motion, all the while failing to notice the widening void around him. Playing his performance of Edmond Dantès to an empty house.

"When do you leave?" is all Harry can ask.

Max shakes his head. "Soon. Day after the will reading."

Harry nods blankly.

"It's not all bad, Harry. At least, it doesn't need to be."

And almost on cue, Molly emerges from the elevator and rushes toward the exit. Her flushed cheeks and determined expression tell Harry that things have gone more or less according to plan. For a moment, he contemplates simply letting her go, allowing her life to step out of the shadow of his manipulations and resume its own course. For both of their sakes. But although his heart is no longer in it, he can't quite stop himself from rising to follow her.

"Max, gimme a sec, okay?"

Before Max can reply, Harry is on Molly's tail. He follows her out onto the street where she's fumbling through her purse for a cigarette.

"Molly? Is that you?" *More fucking games.*

Molly turns and registers surprise to see Harry behind her, but she's too flustered to convert it into suspicion.

"Harry? What are you doing here?"

He indicates the lobby. "I was meeting a friend for a drink." He re-presses a rueful chuckle at Max's unanticipated complication. "What's going on? Are you okay?"

"No, no, I'm not." She locates a cigarette. She lights it with trembling hands and turns to face Harry. "That son of a bitch! I can't believe this shit!"

"What shit? What are you talking about?"

"That bastard! That lying bastard! I caught him—in the act!—with some bleached-blond slut."

"You're kidding." It's a workmanlike performance. Harry has lost all enthusiasm for his script but he's a professional and the show must go on.

"I can't believe it. After all this, after everything—I mean, what does that asshole want?"

"What did you do?"

"I told him to fuck himself. We're through. I'm done."

So there it is. The moment Harry has been waiting for, working to-ward. And he doesn't feel a goddamned thing. It's completely empty. There's no sense of triumph. No satisfaction. Nothing at all. He is about to say something when Bruce bounds out the front doors of the hotel.

"Molly. Wait up."

"Don't you 'wait up' me! Leave me alone."

Bruce grabs her hand and Harry finds that the one emotion still working is anger. He steps up and, to everyone's surprise, grabs Bruce's hand and pulls it away. He pushes Bruce from Molly and steps in between them.

"Did you hear her? She said to leave her alone."

"Who the fuck are you? Get out of my way."

Bruce menacingly approaches Harry, whose mind flashes back to that day in Max's yard, and Bruce is on the ground clutching his nose before Harry realizes that he's thrown his first punch.

"You crazy old fuck!"

"Oh my God! Harry!"

But there's no stopping Harry now, and with the blood pounding in his ears, he bends over, grabs Bruce's shirt, and hoists him to his feet. Harry speaks softly but with unmistakable gravity.

"I'm sick of you. So is she. You're going to fuck off now."

Bruce snatches his shirt from Harry's grip and, with a final bird flipped to them both, staggers on down the street. Harry turns to Molly and speaks with an authority that surprises her.

"I'm sorry, Molly. I shouldn't have done that. I guess I'm done, too."

Molly looks up at him, vaguely uncomprehending. She's overloaded by emotion and by the morning's dramatic events, but Harry thinks for a moment he can detect a glimmer of admiration amid the noise in her eyes.

"You deserve better than that."

The glimmer is snuffed out as she nods and, to Harry's surprise, begins to weep. Moving like a robot, he takes her into his arms, stunned by her reaction.

"Why . . . why, Harry . . . why are men such . . . jerks?"

He holds her, devastated. He imagined she'd be relieved, angry, sure, but ultimately celebratory, recognizing she was better off. He never allowed himself to consider she might feel pain. That he might cause her pain. He was only trying to help, to get her to that point she knew she was headed for. But now this. The victory is as dry as sand in his mouth. The nothingness was better.

"I don't know, Molly. I don't know."

Looking through the doors of the hotel lobby, Harry notes that the bar is empty. Max is gone. Molly is in his arms and he's alone.

It's Lucille who delivers the final surprise.

Harry lies in bed, poking at the carcass of the day. He supposes Max is right. Theirs was a friendship that never ran all that deep. So why does he feel so lousy? Because, one by one, the fixed points in his life are giving way, dissolving, and he's left wondering why any of it mattered to begin with. Why all the deception? Why all the oblique loops and feints and ridiculously convoluted travels? Looking back at the last few years of his life, he can find no two points connected by a single, straight line, and now an ineffable sadness at the time wasted, the opportunities missed, takes hold, and he's afraid that this perpetual indirection is all he knows. The direct approach, Max had advised. How might the direct approach have saved him and Anna?

The bedside phone startles him, relieving him from the terror of further contemplation of that horrible question.

Molly?

Max?

Anna?

"Hello?"

"I don't know how you did it, but congrats." Lucille. A little drunk, by the sound.

"What do you mean?"

"I know you pulled it off. She might have all those fancy letters after her name but that doesn't make her smart. I'm no dummy and I don't believe in coincidences."

Harry hesitates. "Maybe I helped it along."

"Maybe you shoved it along."

"Look, people are who they are. Bruce was going to do it sooner or later. I just set the stage."

"Like you're doing with me and my kid?"

"That's different."

"How?"

Yes, how? "I don't know, Lucille. It just is. You're not Bruce. You're . . . a friend."

"So you keep saying. Okay, let's do it."

"Really?"

"Hey, if you can get her to dump that loser, maybe you really can work miracles." The alcohol can't dampen the strain of hope in her voice.

Harry sits up. "When can you go?"

"How about Tuesday?"

"I can't—that's Anna's will reading. Can you do Monday?"

"Lemme see, but I think I can work it out."

Harry hangs up the phone. Max's parting warning rings in his ears, and Harry knows this isn't the ideal approach, but he clings to the chance to set all right with a final stroke. Perhaps this last success will blot out the misfires of the day, will finally set straight all the books, reconcile the accounting and allow everyone to start anew.

It's not ideal. But it's in motion, it bears promise, and with a hand atop Penguin, unabridged, Harry swears to Dantès that this is the last time, the last round. It will end after this, no more cheats, no more shortcuts, no more deceptions. Like Max, he'll take himself out of the game.

Just this one time, and then—truly—never again.

Fourteen

In which our hero fatally miscalculates

LUCILLE MOVES with such unfamiliarity through the department store that Harry finds himself wondering if she's ever been shopping before. She stares wide-eyed at the wares on display from the four-hundred-thread-count sheets to the espresso machines to the Versace pantsuits. She avoids making eye contact with the sales staff, brusquely shakes her head when approached, and wears a steadily pained expression as they leave men's footwear and head up to consumer electronics.

The stop is Harry's idea and it took a bit of coaxing. Lucille was already struggling with her indebtedness to him ("I don't like you doin' so much for me all the time"), but his suggestion that they not show up empty-handed was hard to argue with. He reminded her of her little shrine of clippings—the sneakers, the iPod, the photo-collage shopping list he'd glimpsed in her apartment—and convinced her it could all be handled in a single, painless stop. And now, with a pair of Nike Shox underarm—Lucille took a flier on the size, guessing about a 10½—they're hunched over the electronics counter looking at the state of the art in digital music technology.

Harry takes in Lucille, who has made an effort to appear presentable for the big day, an effort that only underscores her dire straits. Her blouse is faded, thinning almost to the point of transparency at the elbows. The pale brown outlines of a too-often-cleaned stain whisper stubbornly through the wan fabric of her skirt. Her dress shoes are scuffed, her bag is frayed, and Harry remembers Molly's question— what's going to happen to this person when he's done with her?

Lucille is still reeling from the price tags on the Nikes—she couldn't conceive of spending $125 on a pair of sneakers, didn't seem able to grasp the moment of transaction, but Harry stepped into the void, gold card extended, and now the sneakers are hers. Still, her freshly minted status as an American Consumer does nothing to ease the blow of iPod prices.

"Holy shit! Is that three *hundred* dollars?"

Harry nods. "On sale." He holds his card out to the clerk. "We'll take one."

The clerk, a plump, bespectacled boy of nineteen, reaches for Harry's card, but Lucille speaks up.

"No!"

"What?"

"This is too much. I can't. You can't. No. No more."

The clerk looks questioningly at Harry, who hands him his card, nods, and turns Lucille to face him.

"Look, I know this seems like a lot, but it's not. Not for me. Besides, don't forget what a huge favor you did for me. I mean, this doesn't scratch the surface of what you saved me in lawyers' fees alone. And let's not even talk about the humiliation, the public embarrassment you spared me. So really. It's okay. This is nothing next to that."

This is all true, and Harry means every word, but what he doesn't admit, what nags at his conscience, is the additional thought that the more booty she brings along, the less likely Carl is to reject her. Clearly, the boy can be bought, and Harry's taking no chances. He takes the shopping bag containing the iPod from the clerk and puts it in her hands.

"Come on. You haven't seen him in years. Make it special."

Lucille considers it for a moment and then nods. "Okay, but we're done. Nothing else. I don't want the kid to like me just because I bring him stuff. Okay?"

"Okay." Harry nods, his stomach lurching, amazed at how Lucille always seems one step ahead of him somehow, seeing through him almost continually. And, once again, he wants to back out, abandon ship, pull the plug on the plan. He knows this isn't right, this manipulation, pulling the strings of someone else's life, but he knows he's raised Lucille's hopes and finds himself thinking yet again, *Just one more day . . . I just have to get through this one more day. After that, everything will be all right.*

As he shuffles toward the exit in a dreamlike state, he notices a saleslady in the cosmetics department. He takes Lucille's elbow and guides her toward her. "Hey. Come here for a minute."

"What?" Lucille asks with alarm at the prospect of entering so feminized a zone.

Harry presents Lucille to the saleslady—her name tag reads KRISTIN—whose eyes momentarily widen at the forbidding sight of Lucille. But within a microsecond, Kristin accepts the challenge and dons her Super Sales Smile.

"Well, hello there. And who do we have here?"

"This is Lucille," Harry says. "She has a big day today. She's going to visit her son."

"I see," Kristin says. "Well, let's make you up extra-special for your son, what do you say?"

She guides Lucille onto a stool—Harry's seen happier faces in a dentist's chair—and busies herself applying base. Lucille is too terrified to resist.

"Yes," Harry says. "Make her extra-special. Whatever it takes, it's on me."

Harry can't take his eyes off Lucille.

They sit in silence in the crippled Jaguar just outside the juvenile hall, and Harry can't help but marvel at What Kristin Hath Wrought. Henry Higgins has nothing on this minimum-wage salesclerk, who has transformed Lucille, softening her edges and crags considerably. It's as if she's painted away the scowl from Lucille's lips. Deprived of the armor of her grim visage, Harry worries that she seems ill-protected from the predatory beasts that circle her. Including, above all, himself.

"I can't do this."

"What?" Harry is startled back to the moment—even the sound of her voice seems softened by Kristin's magic.

"I can't do this, Harry." She speaks softly, eyes downcast.

"Why not?"

"I'm scared."

"Don't be scared." *I have your insurance policy in my pocket.* He fingers the deposit slip.

"My kid, he don't like me very much."

"Two years is a long time to go without a mother."

"He's gone longer than that."

She looks down in her lap, twiddling with the handles of her shopping bag, which sits between her legs, wanting to crawl out of her freshly madeup skin. And before he knows what he's saying, Harry offers her an out.

"Look. If you really are uncomfortable, you don't have to do this. I mean, it's supposed to be nice for you. If it isn't, we can forget about it. Really."

He says the last a bit too hopefully, but now he's praying she'll nod and they'll turn the car away and he can deposit her in safer waters with nary a predator in sight. Where she can repose and bask in her new home, her new face, her new life. *Yes, that's it Lucille. Let's just get out of here. There's some bad shit in the air.*

Lucille sighs. "Thanks, Harry. But we're here, right?" She hoists the shopping bag and unlocks the door. "What am I gonna do with a pair of ten-and-a-half Shox? Let's get it over with."

They step out of the car and head to the entrance.

The first setback occurs at the check-in desk.

"No gifts for the inmates."

Harry and Lucille exchange a worried look. Harry speaks up.

"This is the boy's mother. You can search everything." He hands over the bag, smiling, trying a bit of humor. "There's no nail file in here."

The guard repeats himself, unmoved. "No gifts for the inmates."

No entreaties can budge the guard, and now Lucille is left conspicuously holding a shopping bag that she can't hand over. "What the fuck am I gonna do with this stuff?" she mutters.

"Don't worry. We'll get it to him somehow," Harry says confidently without the slightest clue as to how to make that happen.

The second setback occurs as they sit before the glass window, waiting for Carl to be brought to them.

Harry watches Lucille watching the meetings taking place around her, young boys and their mothers, and somehow Harry is certain that Lucille is judging herself a co-conspirator in failure with these other women, women whose sons somehow got away from them, mothers who failed, boys who failed, failure pressing in from all the walls, whispering from beneath the chairs, prodding from the doorways, a silently deafening din of failure. And though he's not a mother, Harry doesn't feel as out of place as he'd like, his own failures pricking insistently at his conscience.

Harry had prepared Lucille for the likelihood of a wait, having himself waited twenty minutes for Carl to be brought up. But twenty minutes is going on sixty, and a gloom has begun to overtake them both, even as Lucille sits in stoic humiliation, waiting before the only empty pane of glass in the place.

218

Finally Carl steps into the hall, his body language screaming resistance. The guards have his arm and Harry swears they're actually pulling him in, against his will.

Carl sulks into his chair, hands thrust deep into his pockets, eyes fixed on his sneakers. Look up, you bastard, Harry thinks. Just give her one smile. But Carl's previous fluid grace has dissolved into a pantomime of sludgy resentment. Harry regards Lucille, whose eyes glow hopefully. She's too moved laying eyes on the boy to feel wounded by his rudeness.

"Hey, kid," she says softly, with a tenderness Harry's never heard.

Carl shrugs in reply. Lucille desperately drinks in his every gesture, however alienating.

"Long time no see," she whispers. "How've ya been?"

Carl rolls his eyes with irritation.

"Listen, I . . . sorry, *we* got you some stuff, but the guards won't let me give it to you." She pulls the sneakers and the iPod from the shopping bag to show him.

"Then why the fuck are you showing me it?"

"Well, Harry said we'd figure out a way to get it to ya. Thought you might like it."

"Yeah? How's Harry gonna do that?" Carl asks skeptically.

"We'll figure something out," Harry says.

"Yeah. Right." Smart kid, Harry thinks with bitter admiration. Less gullible than his mother.

Reddening and flustered, Lucille helplessly packs the items back into the bag and hands the bag back to Harry. She turns back to Carl.

"Sorry. Thought you'd like that stuff."

"Whatever."

The trio lapses into awkward silence, which is punctuated by the sound of the boy next to Carl snorting like a pig. Carl lashes out and smacks the boy's head and the guard hurries over.

"Pull that shit again, and you're out of here," the guard warns. Carl ignores the guard, sulking.

Lucille tries to fill the awkward space. "You look good, Carl. Always had the looks in the family." Her voice still never above a whisper.

Carl stares off blankly into space, arms folded.

Lucille tries again. "What kind of stuff they have you doing in there?" No reply.

"Carl. Your mother is talking to you," Harry says forcefully.

"Yeah, I can hear. What the fuck do you want from me? Why are you here?"

Confusion crosses Lucille's face. She glances sideways at Harry.

"I thought you wanted to see me."

Now the boy beside Carl, leaving the window and his visitor, does a full-throated pig impression in Lucille's direction, and the boys sitting around him begin to laugh and join in.

Carl reddens and kicks the chair away. "Fuck this shit." He looks to Harry. "You can't pay me enough for this shit, man."

And Carl is gone, and the window is empty once again, and Harry stares at Lucille, whose makeup has taken on the aspect of a sad clown, and as strains of *Pagliacci* inexplicably fill Harry's head, Lucille stares back at Harry, and finally a single, uncomprehending word pierces the aria screaming in his brain.

"Pay?"

Harry's made the effort, gone back inside, tried to get Carl brought back up, if only to remind him of their deal and brandish his deposit receipt under his nose, but it's hopeless. Carl has disappeared into the bowels of the facility, and even as Harry tries to convince the guard to retrieve the boy, he knows he won't see him again. After thirty minutes of unsuccessful cajoling ("Are you trying to bribe a state official, sir?"), Harry returns to the waiting area to find Lucille gone. Got a taxi, the guard explains. Left this for you.

He hands Harry back the shopping bag.

"She doesn't have money for a taxi," Harry explains helplessly to the guard. The guard shrugs, disinterested, unmoved. Carl's spirit brother.

Harry walks to his car in the late-afternoon sun, numb, dejected, and now he's convinced that he sees Carls everywhere, that the world all around him is peopled with Carls-in-waiting. From the dull, incompetent eyes of Nicole, to Claire's bewildered fury, to Anastasia the hooker's insouciant cynicism, to Bruce's bored, impatient mien, to the guard sitting right there, to the irritated visitors all around him, he feels outnumbered, overwhelmed. A stray thought pierces the gloom.

Anna was different. Once. At the beginning.

The beginning. How very long it's been, Harry realizes, since he's thought back to their earliest days together, to those two other people he can no longer recognize.

He's pretty much hit the bottom and knows it, and yet his heart is empty, his soul feels dead to him, and he wonders if it isn't too late, if he's become a Carl himself. It's as though the weight of the despair he feels is so crushing—the horror at the thought of what he's done to Lucille's life, Molly's life, and, above all, to Anna's life—that he can't feel it at all. The numbness that precedes death. Harry's done. Or he wants to be.

The Jaguar resists ignition but finally turns over and lurches slowly out of the parking lot, coughing and protesting along the way.

Two tortuous hours later, the mortally wounded Jaguar finally expires. It's close enough to home that Harry can walk the remaining distance, but it's all uphill, and his calves strain under the effort of the climb. Head down, he plods purposefully up the darkening street, a single, forlorn figure among multimillion-dollar driveways. A neighborhood-watch patrol vehicle drives past him and shines a light on his face. Harry winces and slowly flips off the driver.

"Mr. Rent? Is that you?"

"Fuck off, rent-a-cop."

He continues trudging up on his way. The rent-a-cop hesitates for a moment, then switches off his search beacon and drives on.

Exhausted, sweating, and trembling, Harry crosses his threshold. He staggers to his bed and falls on it, face-up. He suspects he won't sleep

221

tonight, wonders if he'll ever sleep again. He just wants to suffer, finally. He wants the dam to break, for the pain that he's endlessly, busily been deferring to finally fill him, for the numbness to end. He knows he's wrecked it all, Lucille's life, Molly's life, and of course his own. *One more day,* he kept thinking, *just get me through one more day.* But he's run out of the days, and he knows it.

Please. Just crush me already and have done with.

He notes the blinking light on the answering machine. One message. Trancelike, he presses Play.

"Hi, Harry. It's Elliott. Listen, I have some news—"

Elliott never finishes his sentence, as Harry brings his fist crashing down on the machine. He pounds it again and again, splintering plastic and bits of wire, and the heel of his palm is gashed and bleeding, but still he pounds the machine until it's nearly dust, then he swipes the debris from the table. He falls back into the bed, blood staining the sheets.

He won't sleep tonight. He doesn't deserve it. For Harry, this evening, there is only purgatory. Numb, endless purgatory. The hours stretch out before him like armed foes on the march, and Harry can't imagine how he'll get through the night. But he makes one decision. There's one thing he's absolutely sure of, with a certainty unlike any he's ever felt:

Tomorrow he will tell Molly everything. The truth, every last word, nothing left out. He will let her go, but at least he'll do it properly.

And you can go, too, he thinks, as he nudges Edmond Dantès—abridged and unabridged—off the nightstand and into the bedside trash can.

Harry is strangely calm as fingers of morning light tug at his top sheet. As expected, he hasn't slept, but against all expectations, he feels refreshed. His head is clear, his limbs feel light, and his mind is sharp and focused. Not even the pain from the cuts in his hand, encrusted with dried blood, dulls his purpose. It's as though the decision to tell the truth has lifted this terrible weight that's been filling his pockets, his stomach, his heart. He's going to go to Anna's will reading today (how close he'd come to forgetting that!), and after that he's going to come clean, tell the truth to Molly, apologize and make amends to Lucille, and even though it means that he'll probably lose them both from his life, he'll finally be able to move on to . . .

To what? To this thing he's supposed to have become? This new and better person? An honest man. A changed man.

Not much comfort there, Harry reflects.

He's washing his hands, gently soaping the edges of his cuts, when the phone rings.

"Harry? Is that you? It's Molly."

"Oh. Hi. Yes. It's me." Resolution wavers at the sound of her voice. Heartbeat speeds up and anxiety washes over Harry. But he'll entertain no thoughts of changing course.

"Hey, what happened yesterday?"

Harry finds the urgency in her voice troubling. "Um. It didn't go that well. Listen, I need to talk to you—"

"Is Lucille with you?"

What a risible notion. "With me? God, no. Why?"

"She's not here. She doesn't answer her phone."

Neither would I, Harry thinks. "Maybe she's taking a day to herself."

"Harry. Lucille never takes a day to herself. *Never.* Not once in three years."

"Well, maybe she's starting today."

"Harry, you saw her work with an ingrown toenail. I'm telling you, something's wrong. What happened yesterday?"

Harry sighs. "He didn't want to see her."

"What? But I thought—"

"He didn't want to see her, Molly." The finality of Harry's tone does not invite further comment.

"Harry, I'm really worried. We need to get over there."

"Molly, you're overreacting. Anyway, I can't. My car, it's dead."

"Harry, please. I have a terrible feeling. I'll come get you."

The contagion of dread leaks from Molly's voice, across the handset, and into Harry's ear.

"No, I'll get a cab and meet you there."

When the taxi deposits Harry at Lucille's doorstep, Molly is already there, pounding on the door.

She looks at Harry desperately, helplessly. "She's not answering, Harry!"

"Maybe she's out." Harry's protestations ring hollowly in his ears. He takes Molly's place pounding on the door. "Lucille! Lucille, are you there? Open up!"

After a moment of frustrating silence, Harry makes his way around the building. As he works his way toward the back, looking in the windows along the way, he can't help but remember his evening in the alleyway behind Lucille's apartment, the first time he intruded upon her life. He fights back a wave of shame and self-loathing as he circles back to the bedroom window, an anxious Molly clinging to his side. At last he peers in the bedroom window, through which Lucille's mountainous bulk can be discerned in repose on the bed.

"She's in there," Harry says.

"Is she okay? What is she doing? Is she sleeping?"

"I can't tell."

He cups his hands and presses them against the glass to shield his eyes from the reflection. Once his eyes adjust to the difference in light, he can make out the tableau before him: the empty pill bottle, the note, the trail of vomit. He's seen this scene rendered so many times that it's imprinted on his subconscious, and he immediately recognizes the position as a chess player understands a position, without fully grasping what he's seeing. So it's instinct that drives Harry to shatter the window with his elbow.

Molly shrieks at the shock of the breaking glass. "Harry! What is it?"

But Harry is working the window open and climbing inside. "Get your car around the front! Hurry!"

A tearful Molly nods and stumbles off. Harry steps through broken glass and hurries to Lucille's bedside, suddenly brought up short by a detail.

The note beside her is addressed to him.

"Oh, no . . . No, no, you don't . . . Don't do this!"

Harry opens her eyelid, notes the pupil's fixed, dilated state. He presses his fingers to her throat. It takes him a moment to detect a pulse, faint, irregular. Fading.

"No, Lucille! Goddammit! *No!*"

He brushes the vomit from her lips, pinches her nose, and breathes into her mouth. The full force of his lungs barely budges her bulk. Harry pulls his vomit-flecked face from hers.

"You are not going to die!"

Harry runs to the front door and opens it. Molly's car is idling out front.

"Open the back door!"

He runs back into the house, back into her bedroom. He grabs the empty pill bottle and the note, stuffs them both into his pocket, then heaves Lucille off the bed.

It's a Herculean effort, and twice she slips from his grasp, thudding to the floor like a fish on a deck. But Harry grabs her arms, entwines them around his neck, and hoists her upon his back. He stumbles through the apartment with his load, sweat stinging his eyes, his muscles burning with exhaustion, and his heart pounding into his mouth. The distance to the car seems insurmountable, and Harry feels his strength ebbing by the living room, the lack of sleep buzzing in his muscles, when Lucille gives a muffled groan. The groan fortifies Harry, encourages him, and he repositions his human cargo and stomps down the front steps, past agape neighbors. With Molly's help, he loads Lucille in the backseat and commandeers the wheel as they head to the emergency room, tires wailing.

Fifteen

In which our hero gets the girl

THEIR STORY BEGINS with a crash.

A hot July afternoon. Two pairs of panicked eyes. A dropped cell phone. Quick and sudden pressure on the brakes. A bicycle skidding across a layer of windswept gravel. Impact. The bicycle clattering over the hood of the SUV. Bruises, scrapes, and an arm swollen and possibly broken.

The arm belongs to a woman, thirty-five, a slender, dark-haired beauty with polished cheekbones and hungry eyes. Her name is Anna Weldt, and the possibility of a broken arm is serious enough for her primary-care physician to refer her for an immediate X-ray, just down the hall to a well-meaning if feckless radiologist named Harry Rent, who's just set up shop and has been pleading for referrals.

Harry finds himself short of breath, his chest squeezing tightly, as he prepares Anna for her X-ray. The proximity of beautiful women has always made him nervous, and there's something intimate about the dark

226

and quiet space as he positions Anna's arm on the X-ray table and moves the lens into position above it. He's trying hard not to stare, settling for furtive glances that he's reasonably confident can be read as a normal part of the examination. Still, he can't imagine that his mien doesn't completely give him away. He's got a bit of a wandering eye, a soft spot for a pretty face, but this is something altogether different, something considerably more intense and powerful. Anna's appearance in his office, battered and struggling to regain her composure, shifted something within Harry, and he stepped in to perform these tasks that he usually relegates to his technician. A dichotomy informs this woman, an admixture of post-trauma vulnerability and an inexplicable centeredness that comes off Anna in waves. Harry finds her riveting, totally fascinating, and being the lousy poker player he is, he's certain he's completely transparent. But if he is, Anna doesn't seem to notice. She's got her head down and she's trembling.

"Are you cold in here?" Harry asks.

She shakes her head and the trembling intensifies, and now Harry can hear choked sobs coming from his patient. He kneels before her.

"Hey. It's okay. You're fine now. Here."

He takes off his lab coat and drapes it around her shoulders. She pulls it tight around her.

Harry touches her shoulder gently. "You're fine. You're in one piece. It's all going to be fine. Okay?"

To his surprise, she takes his hand and holds it tightly. "There was a car . . . I didn't see it . . ."

He answers the squeeze with comforting pressure, and soon the trembling stops and Harry can feel Anna's body slacken. He's struck by the battle going on inside this woman between the need to remain composed and the urge to let her emotions run amok. *I know how you feel,* Harry wants to say, but doesn't. He continues preparing the X-ray in silence, smiling at Anna. She returns the smile with a grateful nod, and something about the wordlessness of the exchange is immediately comforting and enticing to them both, their having almost immediately stepped into a space beyond words. For Harry, too many words, too many conversations, only distract him from his inner monologue, and he's always found himself more than adequately absorbing. For Anna, it's a break from the insistent, pleading din that normally follows her around, from men trying to woo, to win, to impress. And so they settle comfortably into this contented silence, like an affectionate, old married couple.

Harry gives her a once-over and nods, satisfied. "If you've got any metal in your pockets, you should probably give it to me."

Anna nods and reaches into the pocket of her shorts. She extracts a Swiss Army knife—for emergencies, she shrugs—which she hands to Harry, who pockets it and leaves the room.

Anna's Swiss Army knife sits on the desk before him as Harry dials the phone.

He's spent the last half hour daydreaming, spinning out dozens of scenarios in which Anna is swept away by his charm, succumbing to his wit and verve. Fortified by his imaginings, he's finally worked up the nerve to make the actual phone call.

"Hello?"

"Hello, Ms. Weldt? This is Dr. Rent."

"Hi. How are you? And please call me Anna." Her voice is steady, confident, healed. The battle for control won.

"I'm fine, thanks. Anna," Harry adds nervously, trying it on. "Um, listen, I still have your knife." Considerably less suave than imagined.

"I know."

"You do?"

"Yes. I figured you were keeping it so you'd have an excuse to call me."

Harry reddens at once. The truth is, he's not so calculating as all that. He's just a bit absentminded, although when he discovered the knife in his gown pocket, he was glad to have it for precisely the reason Anna has suggested.

"Ah. Oh. I see." He hangs on the line, flustered.

Anna helpfully fills in the silence. "Well, it *would* be nice to get it back."

Harry clears his throat. "For emergencies."

"Exactly."

"Would you like to meet somewhere? Or should I send it to you?" Always careful to leave the honorable out.

"Oh, let's meet. I miss my knife."

Arrangements made, Harry hangs up the phone, pleased with himself for taking the plunge. He considers Anna's voice, the way she inhabits each word, her language an extension of a great stillness emanating from deep within her. There's something deeply rooted, anchored and anchoring, in her voice that he finds irresistibly attractive.

He's wholly unaware of Anna's family's vast fortune, of her Greenwich pedigree, of the storm of suitors seeking their grand payout that Anna parries almost daily. The knowledge of any one of which would paralyze Harry into heartbroken inaction.

First date. Only it's not really a date, is it? It's one of those adumbrated almost-dates. The interest is there. The spark is there. Everything's there but the Date Itself, which lingers behind, held in abeyance, seeking some sort of confirmation before asserting itself in all its jubilant datehood.

Harry sits nervously at the bar, fiddling with Anna's knife in his clammy hands, turning it over, examining it. It's scuffed from the accident, the white cross flecked with grit. Harry envies the knife, imagining it pressed against Anna's warm thigh. Her appearance in the doorway of the bar rouses him from his daydream, and he hurriedly wipes the damp knife against his trousers as he gets up to greet her.

"Hi," he says a bit dumbly, he fears.

"Hi," she says, and Harry marvels at how a single word—the same word he's just tossed carelessly across the bar—can resonate so much more fully, so much more meaningfully, coming from her mouth.

She sits, and Harry hands her the knife.

"For you."

"Thank you."

She looks it over, delighted, as Harry examines Anna, out here in the light, out in the open. Her sprained arm is in a cast, which charms Harry. Her immobilized limb is lovely in its helplessness, and he wants to take it into his arms and protect it. He wants to reach out and touch it—gently, as one might stroke a wounded bird—but he'll do no such thing.

Anna's examination of the knife complete, she puts it into her pocket.

"Listen, Harry. I've been thinking about you for days. I wanted to thank you."

"It's nothing really, it's just a knife—"

"No, not for this. For that day in your office. I was terrified, scared to death. Somehow, I don't know how you did it, you calmed me down. Made it all seem all right."

Harry blushes mildly. "Oh, just being the good doctor, you know."

Anna shakes her head. "No. When you took my hand, I felt . . . kindness. Something real . . . that's more than bedside manner. It felt sort of familiar . . ."

Harry shrugs uncomfortably. "I was worried about you."

"Yeah. I know," Anna says with a smile. "Thank you."

Harry surprises himself by holding her eyes. "You're welcome."

They order drinks and fall into easy conversation. She seems genuinely interested in Harry's nascent practice, in how he chose his specialty, in Harry's opinions on a variety of subjects including but not limited to Los Angeles sports teams, one-hit wonders of the 1970s, and obscure chess openings. For his part, Harry can't remember the last time a woman sought to engage him so thoroughly, and he finds himself chattering on contentedly, his inner monologue turned outward for once. Soon, though, he remembers his manners and turns the attention back to Anna, learning of her interest in—among other things—cubism (synthetic), renewable energy sources, and yoga. She makes a passing reference to a strained relationship with her family, although Harry can detect her affection for her father. She's also, it turns out, a devoted cyclist who trains regularly and makes mention of some guru coach of hers named Geerchyk.

"And speaking of cycling, would you mind terribly . . ."

Anna waves the bartender over, commandeers the bar TV, and after much searching lands on the Tour de France. She's immediately enrapt, but all Harry sees is an undulating mass of colored spandex surging through the countryside.

"Great, we didn't miss the end."

Anna studies the set intently, reading the cryptic markings along the bottom that convey the riders' standings and other race particulars. Her eyes light up with delight.

"Oooo! Jeremy is leading the breakaway!"

"Jeremy? Breakaway?" Harry stammers, afraid that he sounds as bad as he sounds.

Anna nods excitedly. "Umm, a breakaway is when a bunch of riders ride out ahead of the peloton—that's the main group of riders—in an attempt to win that day's stage. My friend Jeremy is at the front of the breakaway."

Harry turns to examine the set. It's hard to make out much more of Jeremy than a whippet-thin wisp of Technicolor spandex.

"They're pretty skinny, aren't they?"

Anna nods. "You have to be for climbing some of those mountains." She glances over at Harry. "Actually, you have a great sprinter's physique. They're a bit bigger and more powerful than the climbers." She smiles, and Harry feels a warm flush wash over him. Now he leans in and watches the stage carefully with Anna.

"How much longer to go?"

"About ten kilometers."

"What happens next?"

"Well, the peloton is already closing the gap. They can't let the break-away get too far, and now it's time to reel them in. They'll probably pick one of the teams to chase them down and tire them out. But there's a chance that Jeremy can hold off the challenge—he's amazingly fast. *If he doesn't let his cockiness get the better of him. Big if.*"

Harry frowns, pricked by jealousy. "So who is this Jeremy?" he asks with studied nonchalance.

"Family friend. Known him for years." Equally nonchalant.

Anna offers up nothing more about Jeremy, so it's not without a dose of schadenfreude that Harry watches his breakaway hopes dashed a few moments later, leaving him crossing the finish line twenty-third. Anna sighs with disappointment.

Harry does a fine impersonation of generosity. "Too bad. He looked pretty good. He should have won it."

Anna looks at Harry's serious expression and smiles a conspiratorial, inclusive smile, into which he promptly and permanently tumbles.

"He's an arrogant overreacher who got exactly what he deserves. And you've got a good heart."

She places her hand on Harry's arm, and there's such kindness in her eyes that Harry actually feels seen—beheld past his usual clumsiness. And the real marvel is that she appears to like him all the same. She seems to embrace that in him which has usually been rejected. Someone has come along who has perceived him fully, and the experience is so singular and powerful that he knows this is the woman he wants to marry. The only hurdle will be convincing her. He'll have to watch for the opportunity for his own breakaway.

Together, they watch all three weeks of the Tour de France. Harry turns up dutifully night after night at the bar. He's even grabbed a book about cycling and read it—well, skimmed it really. But he picked up enough to appear to talk knowledgeably about breakaways and *domestiques*, even as he sensed that Anna saw through him from the beginning but was too kind to embarrass him. Her grin is touched and flattered as she listens to his opinions on the day's stage or the time differences in the general classification. At worst, Harry assumes she appreciates the effort, and she rewards him by overlooking all but his most obvious errors.

As the Tour progresses, Harry wrestles with conflicting impulses: On the one hand, he doesn't want to appear too eager. On the other, the Tour runs nightly for three weeks (minus two rest days), which gives him an extraordinary amount of captive time with Anna, and Harry's not good at moderation. He should probably make himself unavailable for at least a stage or two, if only for appearance's sake. But the sinister prospect of leaving Anna to commune with Jeremy in his absence gets the better of him. Any pretense of savoir faire goes out the window early on, and Harry becomes a nightly fixture at Anna's side.

After a week, they move to her living room to watch more comfortably as the mountain stages begin. Her condominium is streamlined but furnished in expensive good taste, awash with glass and aluminum and black leather. Harry admires her cool sense of order, a decided contrast to his hopeless clutter. The only discordant note to the décor is her twisted bike frame, which leans against a far wall, untouched since her accident. Anna notes Harry's eyes fall on it.

"I haven't had the nerve to get back on yet."

Harry watches as Jeremy's overall standing drops from twenty-third to fifty-sixth—the result of a spectacular crash in a sprint finish—but not even the good news of Jeremy's flameout eases Harry's nerves. The more he learns, the less he likes him. As he suspected, Jeremy and Anna once dated, and although she maintains he was far too self-involved to have ever been husband potential, the way she speaks about him, how even her forbidding parents—who hover offstage in perpetual frowning disapproval—seemed to like him, sets Harry on jealous edge. As the parameters of Anna's family wealth begin to come into dim focus, Harry can't help wondering if Jeremy is the man Anna is meant to marry.

Now, in the mountains, Jeremy has decided to make a move to regain lost time. He powers up the hill, passing other riders, and Anna grows visibly excited, cheering him on as he takes his place at the front of the latest breakaway.

Harry's irritation grows, and he can't help himself. "I thought you said he was an arrogant overreacher."

Anna smiles. "I did. He is. But he's also an old friend, and this is a remarkable display of athleticism." She looks at Harry curiously. "Harry. Are you jealous?"

Harry shrugs uncomfortably for a moment.

"Of Jeremy? Really?"

"Yes! Of Jeremy! For God's sake, he's Mr. Tour de France athlete, born on the right side of the tracks, and he's handsome to boot. Of course I'm jealous."

Without taking her eyes off Harry, she clicks the remote control, shutting off the TV.

"What are you doing? What about the stage?"

"Who cares about the stage?"

"You do."

"I care about this—about you—more. May I point something out to you?"

Harry nods warily.

"Jeremy is out there, on a bike, on a mountain in France. You are here. In my living room."

Harry reddens at having to have the obvious spelled out to him. "That's true." He's not sure what to say next.

Anna breaks the awkward silence. "You know what my favorite part of cycling is? It's called 'drafting' . . . The idea is that you ride up close to the rider in front of you, and you're pulled along." She moves closer to Harry. "You're being protected by those around you. Until you're ready to make your move. You don't worry about the rest of the pack— their presence just helps you."

"Drafting. Got it," he mumbles.

Harry realizes he's learned something. As he's watched Jeremy and his fellow cyclists climb up thousands of feet, one pedal stroke at a time, he's developed a sense of the focus required, the sheer commitment to get on the bike and climb up that mountain no matter how hard it seems. No matter how steep the climb. No matter how many specta-tors crowd the roads. No matter what the competition.

I'm climbing. I'm going to the top.

"So what are you going to do about it?"

Harry leans over and gives his first kiss to the woman he's going to marry.

The Tour is over (Jeremy's final position in the overall classification was 132nd, a glorious wipeout), and somehow the couple has sustained a post-Tour phase. Harry was terrified that without the common bond of the Tour to bring them together, they'd drift apart, but he surprised himself by persevering without the excuse of meeting to watch a stage.

Harry sits in the doctor's waiting room, flipping through magazines as Anna's cast is being removed in the back. His heart is pounding with anticipation, the surprise he has in store has been torturing him for weeks. Harry's never been good at keeping secrets and his impatience is legendary, but just this once he's held it all together for what he hopes will be a dramatic presentation.

Anna's voice can be heard thanking the doctor, and moments later she steps into the waiting room, where she registers surprise at Harry's presence. Again, that irresistible mixture of vulnerability and assurance.

"Harry? You're here?" she says disbelievingly, and Harry detects a slight mist in her eyes.

"Of course I'm here. Where else would I be?" he asks, confused.

She takes his hand with her good arm. Harry runs his fingertips along her slender forearm, atrophied from lack of use—something he's waited weeks to do.

"Yeah." She nods. "Where else?"

She surprises Harry with a tight, almost desperate hug. "Thanks," she whispers.

Harry pulls her back and looks at her questioningly. "Hey. Is every-thing all right?"

She nods. "Better than all right."

"Okay. Then come with me, because I have a surprise for you."

Anna follows Harry to the parking lot, where he opens the trunk of his battered station wagon and extracts a gleaming bicycle.

"My bike! You fixed my bike?"

Harry clears his throat, embarrassed. "Actually, I replaced it. I wanted to fix it but I couldn't do that without giving away the surprise."

She takes the bike and looks it over, stunned. "But . . . but this is all the same equipment. The same brakes . . . the same—"

"The same everything. Took some doing, but we got it all." He shrugs. "A fresh start, you know?" He hands her a helmet.

She takes it warily. "Harry, I'm speechless. This is just amazing. But I'm not ready—"

"Sure you are."

"But, Harry—"

"Come on. Pretend it's one of those mountains in France. There's no choice. You have to get back on." Then: "I'll be right here, Anna."

Anna nods and brusquely presses her knuckles into her tears. She puts the helmet on, climbs onto the bike, and Harry watches as she pedals tentatively around the parking lot. He follows so that he's never more than a dozen steps from her as she circles, and he watches her fear slowly melt away and her pedal strokes become more confident, and now she's smiling and picking up speed, and before they know it she's laughing and then shouts to Harry as she rides.

"Hooray! This is great! I love this! Thank you, Harry! Thank you, thank you! I love riding again! I love it!"

She brings the bike to an unexpected stop in front of Harry's feet, flushed with joy.

"I love *you*, Harry."

And so it comes to pass that Harry Rent finally wins a stage.

"Prepare, what's to prepare? You ask, she answers. Wham bam, don't make a federal case."

Months later, Harry has decided he's ready to propose to Anna. But he's got no idea how to approach it, can't visualize the moment, and so he does what he always does with important decisions. He punts. In this case, to Max.

"Max, she comes from big money. There's formality and ritual and history and you don't just walk up to a woman like that and say, 'Hey, what say we get hitched?'"

"No, only an asshole would say, 'Hey, what say we get hitched?' But you're not—at last check—such an asshole. 'Anna, will you marry me?' kinda hits all the bases."

"I just want it to be special."

"You're asking a woman to marry you. It doesn't get more special than that. Just be yourself. She can get the bells and whistles from the Playboy Brigade. Punch your weight, kid."

Harry darkens at the expression.

"What, what is it? What did I say?"

"My weight . . . Max, am I out of my depth here? That Jeremy guy, you know he's got the right résumé."

"What, that cycling pooftah?"

"He's no pooftah, Max. He can climb an alp on his bike."

"Please. Cyclists are a bunch of skinny pooftahs. You can beat his time."

In the end, Harry followed Max's advice to the letter. Mostly.

It was a rare rainy Sunday morning in Los Angeles. The rhythm of the raindrops produced a mildly narcotic effect that left Harry and Anna lounging in her bed far later than usual. He'd been carrying the ring around for days, waiting for the right moment to ask, nearly asking a dozen times and then backing off, resolve wavering. Now they'd finished making love so sweetly, so warmly, that Harry felt there was no better moment, and so he excused himself. He climbed out of bed and stepped out to the hall closet, where he pulled the ring box from the pocket of his coat. Then he crossed over to the bathroom where he brushed his teeth, straightened his hair, and steadied his nerves. He pulled the ring—a modest platinum band studded with small diamonds—from its box and, for safekeeping, slipped it onto his right pinkie, where it came to rest just beneath his first knuckle. He braced himself. An emergency pit stop to empty his nervous bladder and then he would take the plunge.

Harry flushed the toilet, and it took him a moment to place the dull metallic *clunk* that preceded the bowl's emptying itself. But in that agonizingly brief slice of time, Anna's engagement ring was already on its way to sea.

"No," Harry whispered as it dawned on him. Then, more frantically: "No! *No!*"

"Harry? Are you all right?"

He ignored her concerned voice and immediately dropped to his knees and, without thinking, plunged his arm into the toilet, up well past his elbow. He fished around desperately, tears of rage and embarrassment forming.

"Goddamn it! Please . . ."

Anna found him in this deranged configuration, desperately snaking his arm through her plumbing, thrashing helplessly on her tile bathroom floor.

"Jesus . . . Harry? What are you doing?"

Harry froze, mortified. He smiled weakly.

"Harry. Why do you have your arm in my toilet?"

And Harry groaned, a weary, defeated groan that seemed to carry his soul, his hopes, away with it. He extracted his dripping arm from Anna's toilet and slowly, tearfully pulled himself to his feet.

"I . . . I . . ." He looked helplessly at the empty bowl and lowered his head into his hands. "I had a ring . . . for you . . . it fell in." He pointed at the toilet. "It's gone." He dropped down on the open seat. "I'm *such* an idiot, Anna."

It took Anna only a few seconds to collect herself and approach

Harry. She gently kissed his forehead, took his hand, and dropped to her knees before him.

"Was there something you wanted to ask me, Harry?"

Harry laughed a humorless laugh. "Yeah. But . . . I can't . . . It's . . ."

"Harry," Anna interrupted meaningfully. "Was there something you wanted to ask me?"

Harry was certain that his graceless, not to mention unhygienic, performance had irreparably damaged his standing. But even now, Max was right.

"Anna, will you marry me?" Ringless. With Anna on her knees.

"I thought you'd never ask."

It only occurred to Harry much later that she might not have been joking.

Harry and Anna married without fanfare. Harry was sure she'd want a more formal wedding, but Anna seemed eager to begin their new lives at once. So they hustled down to city hall, where Max and Claire stood as witnesses for the new couple. Harry had only met Claire a month earlier—she'd been emotionally convalescing from her most recent breakup, an ill-advised affair with the latest in her long string of married employers—but the two got on reasonably well. Claire found him sweet in an unprepossessing way, and Harry admired her concern for Anna's happiness.

"Just keep my sister happy," she'd said as she kissed his cheek, "and we'll be ducky. Welcome to the family."

Harry promised that he would. As Claire departed, he overheard a sotto voce exchange between the sisters.

"When will you tell them?"

"Don't rush me." Anna grinned.

Claire chuckled, nodding. "Good luck." Then: "I like him, Anna."

The exchange causes Harry to spend the first night of their marriage wide-awake.

239

Despite her endorsement, Claire's words have infected him, crawled under his skin and taken up residence, where they now poke and prod at him. He's all too aware of the divides that separate them. Harry's never been comfortable around money, and he suspects that the vast wealth of the Weldt family could buy his own humble beginnings several dozen times over. He lacks the physical grace that seems to come naturally to these country-club types. And although he's no dummy, his conversation certainly doesn't gleam, isn't rife with allusion and steeped in learning. Now the prospect of heading home to meet the family, to be splayed out for the disapproving scrutiny of all, including Jeremy 132 (as Harry now refers to him), is more than he can bear.

He leans over and strokes the hair of his sleeping wife. His wife. How much he likes the sound of that. He places his palm against the flat of her hip, feels the warmth of her against his hand. She's undoubtedly real, undoubtedly his. But he quietly whispers the question that nags at him:

"Oh, honey. Why did you marry me?"

The following morning, the dawn of their first full day as man and wife, Anna is already sitting at the dining room table when Harry pads out in his underwear, yawning and rubbing his eyes. She watches him expectantly, and he only gradually becomes aware of her stare. He sniffles, coughs with embarrassment, and waves.

"Good morning, Mrs. Rent." He grins foolishly.

"Good morning, Mr. Rent," she responds with affection. "Sit down?" She points to a chair. Harry shuffles into it. Anna quits the table, returning with a robe and coffee. She drapes the robe across his shoulders, kissing his earlobe, and pours the coffee into a sleek, black mug. She sits back down and pours herself some coffee.

"Sleep okay?" she asks.

"Mostly."

"I'd like to tell you a story. Are you awake enough?"

Harry nods, his stomach sinking, wondering if she was awake and heard his nocturnal question. Hands trembling, he lifts his coffee.

"When I was about five, I hurt myself on the playground. It's one of my earliest memories. I was standing in front of the seesaw, about to get on, when Alex Moore pushed down his end, and my end rose up unexpectedly and caught me in the chin. I bit through my tongue, and I stood there screaming, blood running down my face. It was a horrible mess—your tongue bleeds a lot, apparently. Did you know that? Anyway, Nancy, my nanny, rushed me to the hospital, and they had to sew me up—it took seven stitches—and it ached for days and I spoke like I had some kind of speech defect, but that wasn't the worst."

She takes a sip of her coffee before continuing. Her voice never wavers, never loses that profound stillness that Harry loves so.

"The worst of it was that my father was in Zurich on business, and my mother was drying out for the fourth, but not last, time. So what I learned at five was that you were more or less on your own. That you couldn't really expect much help when you got into trouble. And that's exactly what I went through my life believing until the day I met you. But you'd have been there, Harry. You'd have made everything seem all right, wouldn't you?"

Harry nods sheepishly.

"I know you would have. Of all the men I've met in my life, you're the first . . . good man I have ever known. I love that goodness, and I tell you, it's worth twenty family fortunes. You shouldn't ask why I married you—I should ask why you chose me.

"But if you really need an answer, I married you because I believe you'd never leave anyone bleeding on a seesaw. And I can only hope you believe that I'll always be there for you, too, whatever happens, whenever you need me. That's what family does, right?

"But just in case you're ever in a bind . . ."

She offers Harry a small, bright red gift box, wrapped in a single white ribbon. Curiously, Harry pulls on the end of the ribbon and lets it fall away. He lifts the lid, and sitting on a bed of white cotton is Anna's Swiss Army knife.

Anna smiles warmly at Harry. "For emergencies."

Harry nods. "Emergencies." He takes the knife out of the box, weighs it in the palm of his hand, and slowly wraps his fingers around it. With his other hand, he holds Anna's warm cheek as he studies her closely, drinking her in. He fixes this face, this moment, her beautiful smile, permanently in memory. A moment he's certain he will always remember. A moment he never wants to forget.

Sixteen

In which our hero comes clean at last

HARRY HADN'T RECKONED on finding himself back at the same hospital where Anna died, hadn't thought it through, and as they stood outside the entrance to the emergency room and watched Lucille being loaded onto a stretcher, Harry suddenly found himself unwilling and unable to enter the building, fearing any reminder of that horrible interview. The prospect of returning to these hallways, of encountering Dr. Couteau, remote as that might be, froze Harry's feet into place. As Lucille disappeared through the automatic doors, Molly gently took Harry's arm.

"Harry? What is it? You're pale."

Harry's throat was too dry to reply.

"She's going to be okay," Molly soothed, misinterpreting the moment. "Come on." And she led Harry into the emergency room, where they took a seat in the waiting area. Which is where they sit now, where they've sat for the last forty-five minutes, wordlessly awaiting news of Lucille.

Molly fidgets beside Harry, discomfited by the pain and the damaged bodies that surround her in the waiting area, compound fractures jutting at unnatural angles, protruding through rent flesh; muted sniffles and groans filling the air, untended by the brisk doctors and nurses, all perpetually en route elsewhere. Harry's aware of Molly's distress, but he's even more aware of another strange shift in his feelings. Until today, Anna's death and its aftermath have felt strangely surreal and distant to him, whereas Lucille's plight and his adventures with Molly have felt more immediate and concrete. But now, as he's directly confronted with unavoidable memories, that's no longer the case. The feelings stirred by returning to these environs have made his current predicament seem almost laughably abstract. The loss of Anna and the growing awareness of the shambles of his life are beginning to feel real to him at last, revivifying with each passing minute. He's worked so diligently to protect himself from all of this, but the narcotic haze is wearing off and the great shredding pain is patiently waiting its turn. How at home among the wounded he is, he considers.

Harry's elbow brushes against the pocket of his coat, and the stiffness of the envelope crammed within reminds him. He pulls the note from his pocket and stares at it. Molly notices, grateful for the distraction, but too well-mannered to say anything. Feeling that there's nothing more that can possibly surprise him, Harry tears open the envelope. Lucille's penmanship is childlike, the note scrawled in pencil:

Dear Harry,

Thanks for trying. With Carl, with me, for everything. Thing is, nothing really changes, right? People are who they are. You can dress them up nice but it don't mater. I'm always gonna be a poor, fat waitress whos son hates her and that's just how it is. I know why you done all this Harry.

I know you like Molly and that this stuff makes you look like a good guy and she likes that. But you know to me you kind of were a good guy. No one was ever that nice to me so whyever you did I guess it don't mater so much. Its what you <u>do</u> that counts right? Anyways, it was nice and I liked it.

Thanks.
Lucille

"Mr. Rent?"

The voice of the emergency room attendant startles Harry back to the moment. He stuffs the note in his pocket, ignoring Molly's curious eyes. Not again, Harry thinks. Not another doctor bringing me word of another death. *Please.*

And then he notices the floor. And he remembers the somber carpeting of Dr. Couteau's office. And he cracks a madman's grin.

"Linoleum . . . ," Harry mutters happily.

Molly regards him with concern. "Harry?"

The young doctor—can he be over thirty, Harry wonders—fixes him with a similar look. "Are you all right, Mr. Rent?"

"Linoleum. You're here on the linoleum. Not on carpeting. She's going to be all right."

The doctor looks mildly disappointed to have been denied his dramatic announcement, but nods with a smile.

"Yeah. Barely. She threw most of it up—that happens more often than you'd think. But you probably saved her life, Mr. Rent."

Molly hugs him tearfully, and only Harry knows he's done no such thing.

"She's asking to see you."

Harry nods weakly. "Okay." He turns to Molly. "Would you mind waiting for a minute?"

Molly can't conceal her surprise but nods. "I'll be right here."

"Thanks."

She watches as Harry disappears with the doctor.

Harry steps into the hospital room, and the first thing he's struck by is how clean Lucille looks. Purged, somehow. Cleansed, perhaps, by all she's been through. Maybe it's just the attention of the nurses, but Harry feels as though layers have been scrubbed away from this woman. She fiddles with embarrassment at the sight of him and shrugs.

"Guess it's not over till the fat waitress sings."

"Jesus, Lucille. I'm . . . I'm sorry. I didn't mean . . . didn't mean for all this." Harry can't speak above a hoarse whisper.

"I know. You found my note?"

Harry nods shamefacedly. "Lucille . . ."

"It's okay. I won't tell. You don't have to say nothin'. I understand."

"No. No, you don't. Look, you're part . . . mostly right. But the stuff with Carl. That wasn't for anyone else. It was supposed to be for you. I just got it wrong. It was a terrible idea but I thought it would make you happy." These may be the most honest words Harry has spoken since forging Nicole's MBA all those wasted years ago.

"Yeah. It would have," Lucille says, blinking back tears. "Thanks for trying."

Harry nods, and he takes her hand, his own disappearing within it.

"So, do you think we could just be friends now?" Lucille asks, her voice breaking.

"Definitely," Harry whispers, his own voice shaking.

Shell-shocked and closing down from lack of sleep, Harry has lapsed into abstracted silence, "Will reading" having been the last words he muttered to Molly back at the hospital. From there it was all limp nods or shakes of the head as Molly asked her questions: Do you have a way to get there? (Shake.) Do you want me to take you? (Nods.) Can you give me the address? (Nods. Scribble.) On and on went this navigational catechism until they now find themselves idling in front of a

Century City skyscraper. Harry doesn't even look at the building from the car window. The weight of responsibility of all he's set in motion is so heavy he can't budge from beneath it.

"Harry. We're here."

Harry stares ahead dully.

"Harry. You have to go. You're already late."

No response.

Molly sighs. "Harry, I don't know what to do here. You have to help me out."

Harry robotically moves to open his door and begins to step out. He turns back and looks at Molly with a gauzy-eyed gaze that shocks her with its unabashed plea.

"Do . . . do you want me to come with you? Is that what you want?"

Nods.

"Harry, why won't you say something?"

Nothing.

"Okay. Let me park the car."

Harry remains silent through the lobby, through the hushed elevator ride to the thirty-second floor, as he walks past the receptionist at Newton, Ruland, Kobat and Clarke, Anna's family's blue-chip law firm, and into the conference room, already full of expectant people. As one, they turn toward the door and behold a disheveled, wide-eyed Harry Rent. Harry makes no attempt to acknowledge their stares. He simply moves past them, to the open seat reserved for him at the end of the long conference table. Molly tiptoes in, striving for invisibility and failing, past eyes trying to perform the bit of mental calculus that somehow results in this haunted apparition entering with so youthful a vision of beauty. Molly lowers her eyes and sinks into a comfortable chair on the perimeter of the room, away from the table.

Now Harry's eyes travel along the table as he takes in all the familiar faces, most not seen since Anna's funeral. The squat, compact Beatrice, perpetually frowning . . . lumbering Aaron and his tiny wife,

Mia . . . neighbors Regina and Howard . . . Italianate Deb and the others . . . even lithe Geerchyk sits at the end of the table in signature black . . . stalwart Max, as ever . . . and finally, Claire. She holds his eyes calmly, with a sureness that Harry finds surprisingly soothing, and he notices the manila file that sits beneath her left hand. He knows what's sure to follow, and he waits for the blow to land.

And he doesn't care. She fails to stir even a fillip of anxiety.

Instead, he regards the table sadly, taking in the history represented by these people, and he can finally perceive that the single filament that tied him to these people—Anna—is gone, and with it went his association with all of them. It seems absurd to him that the possibility of their judgment could have so upset him, could have motivated him to these grave and wrongheaded moves he's made to get here. What a waste, all of it, these foolish steps to impress this lot, none of whom— not even Max, he notes with regret—he feels any ties to. It shouldn't have mattered what any of them thought, he chides himself. It only mattered what Anna thought, and *you know exactly what she thought, don't you?* All the rest has been noise, distraction. The fog that has obscured this truth for longer than Harry can admit to himself has finally begun to lift. Not fully, not yet, but shards of truth have begun poking out insistently through the clouds, and Harry isn't looking away anymore. And the first, unavoidable truth, confirmed by the printouts and photos he knows lie nestled in Claire's manila file, is that he's the reason his wife is dead.

"Well, now that we're all here, if there are no objections, I'd like to begin." The reproachful baritone of Richard Bannister, Anna's lawyer—which made him, by extension, by force of will, Harry's lawyer, too. The contempt for Harry that Bannister barely managed to conceal while Anna was alive floats freely above the conference-room table now. Molly winces but Harry pays it no mind.

"Very well. We are assembled in the matter of the last will and testament of Anna Rent, and we . . ."

Harry tunes out Bannister's careful recitation and regards Claire, wondering when she'll make her dramatic announcement. Her hand continues to rest on the file. She sits quietly, hesitating, it seems, in silent argument with herself. What does he see when he looks at his sister-in-law? She's still the same Claire who fell asleep on his shoulder, who stood beside him at his wedding. Of this he's sure. But he can scarcely recognize her anymore. Her body remains pudgy but her spirit is etiolated, and Harry's gaze seems to pass through her. Something has gone out of her, and he beholds the one person who is even more lost than he is, and he feels sorrier for her than he can possibly feel for himself.

Bannister reads on, and Anna's last wishes are executed, every friend appropriately acknowledged. As expected, the vast majority of her estate—real estate, investments, cash—is bequeathed to her husband. And still Claire sits silently. Before Harry fully realizes it's over, Bannister has handed him a file and left the room. Friends have filed out, pausing to give Harry brief, respectful wishes, leaving Claire, Harry, and Molly alone.

Claire and Harry look at each other wordlessly. It's a long silence, stretched impossibly thin, a look filled with history, regret, and recrimination, and Molly watches the silent exchange with confusion but at a respectful distance. Finally, Claire rises. She crosses over to Harry and hands him the file.

He looks down at it. "You didn't say anything."

Claire nods, and it takes a moment before she can reply. "I was going to. I was furious. Am."

"Why didn't you?"

She shakes her head, looking somewhere off into the distance, at something Harry understands she can no longer see. "What good would it do anyone?" Then she lowers her voice and asks a question of her own. "Do you think you killed her, Harry?"

Harry swallows. Tears beginning to glitter. He tries to whisper but it's a hoarse croak. "Yes." He nods gravely.

There's something Claire wants to say, this same thing she's been struggling with, but the words don't come. She shakes her head sadly and exits the room, leaving Molly and Harry alone.

"Oh, Harry. I'm sorry."

"She's right."

"No, she isn't." Molly repeats herself forcefully. "She isn't. You've changed, Harry. She doesn't know you anymore. You're not who you were. You're different. I know that. So do you."

But what Harry really knows is that without his meddling, Lucille would never have taken those pills . . . that without his interference, Molly and Bruce would still be together . . . that without his philandering, Anna would not have gone under the knife. That he's already had his second chance and blown it, which is why he's sitting here now, clutching a folder that has bestowed a considerable fortune on him, ashamed and heartsick, unworthy of this heartfelt defense.

The drive home was brief and quiet. After the will reading, Harry and Molly made a brief stop at the hospital to look in on Lucille. Reassured that she was resting comfortably, Molly insisted on taking a visibly exhausted Harry home and putting him to bed, and so she drove him through the twisting Bel Air hills toward his home.

How strange, he thinks, gazing dully out the windows into the night, to have Molly steering him through these roads, his roads, his familiar, restorative route. But as she dips the car down into the drops, that reassuring answering drop in the pit of Harry's stomach is silent. And Harry understands that the comforting safety of home that would greet him, that would charge the drive home, was never about the drive but about what awaited him at its end. He's no longer approaching a home; it's merely an empty house.

Molly parks the car and within minutes Harry is splayed in a near vegetative state on the couch as she busies herself in the kitchen preparing tea. As he watches her pour, he finds, as with Claire, he's not at all nervous about what's to come. Perhaps it's the exhaustion. But he thinks not. More likely, it's this unfamiliar serenity of being released once and for all from deception. And he's figured out the best possible way to do it.

"Here you go," she says. "Try the green tea. The antioxidants are good for you."

Harry nods and sips from the mug, smiling weakly at Molly. "Thanks."

"He speaks."

"He does. He will."

Molly looks at him inquiringly. "What will he say?"

"Come with me?"

It's a question. Molly nods. He rises, holds out his hand, and she takes it. He walks her to the second level of the house, back to the closed door of his room.

"I want to show you something."

"This is your storeroom, right?"

His answer is to push the door open slowly and flip on the light. He guides Molly into the space, and her eyes widen as she takes in the Ghosts of Harry Past. It's a moment before the wonder lifts enough for her to speak.

"Wow . . . how cool! What is this stuff?"

Harry doesn't answer right away. He watches her as she moves through the room, randomly touching chess pieces and street signs. She plucks a guitar string.

"This is, like, the world's coolest garage sale." She turns to Harry, grinning. "What is it?"

"It's me." He picks up the guitar and tunes the low E-string. "All of this. I'm really not the guy you've known the last few weeks. I mean, I partly am, but this is the stuff inside. The stuff that should have been outside. Upstairs." Then: "Only it embarrassed my wife. And I never stood up to her."

Molly thinks for a moment, sensing how important an admission this is, then nods and grabs his hands. "Let's take it up."

"What?"

251

"Let's put it all out where it belongs. Where everyone can see it. See you."

"Molly, listen. First, there's something I have tell you. Sit down."

He guides her to his favorite armchair. And he begins to talk. And, at last, he tells her everything. From the beginning. From Greenwich to this moment. He tells her about Lucille. He tells her about Claire. He tells her about the count of Monte Cristo. He even tells her about Bruce. He doesn't leave a single detail out. At long last, Harry Rent tells the truth, the whole truth, and nothing but the truth.

When he finishes his tale, Molly is silent for a long time. Cold tea in her hands. She's trying to control her emotions, but Harry can see the tremor in her hands, the slight heaving of her shoulders.

"Why are you telling me this?" Her voice a low whisper.

"Because you deserve it. I'm done lying. Max was right. You can't play with people's lives." Harry watches intently as Molly's intelligent, angry eyes churn through the events.

"So all this . . . all the time it was you . . ."

Harry nods.

"Everything. Even Bruce . . ."

"I didn't make him sleep with anyone. He made his own choice. But I did set the stage for him."

Molly sighs with an unbearable heaviness. "Just like Edmond Dantès."

"Just like Edmond Dantès."

She stands up and sets her tea down. She won't cry, not in front of him. He knows this. "You know, Edmond Dantès lost everything in the end," she whispers. "Everything that mattered." With a final, disappointed look at Harry, she lets herself out.

Harry collapses into his armchair and lingers in the deserted room, absorbing what he knows is his deserved fate, one final discard for the pile. It could have ended no other way, he realizes. That much was clear to a storyteller of Dumas's genius. If Harry was half the student he thought himself to be, he'd have seen that much earlier. But, of course, if he were half the student he thought himself to be, it would all be different, wouldn't it? So the question of what he *has* been all these years is all that's left for him to answer, and there's no longer any mystery there.

But now, after a moment of sitting alone, Harry realizes he hasn't heard the sound of Molly's car starting up. Curious, he walks outside to find her sitting in her car, hands on the wheel, tears streaking her face. He should leave her alone, he knows. Give her some dignity, some privacy. He walks up to the car, and after an indecisive moment, she lowers the window, openly angry at last.

"You lied to me, Harry. You manipulated me."

"I know. Everything I did was wrong." He shrugs. "But you convinced me that people change. I guess I just changed too late."

They stand in the kitchen, nursing warmed teacups. Sitting in silence—how vulnerable and intimate Harry found this unexpected longueur—Molly's anger gradually melted away, leaving bemusement in its wake.

"Harry, why didn't you just ask me? Why all the drama?"

"Is there the remotest chance you would have said yes?"

She hesitates. Her "Yes" is unconvincing. Then she falters. "Probably not. Well, not at first. But . . ." She sighs, confused. "Well, it's kind of flattering, you know. Weirdly flattering. But flattering. I mean, no one's ever gone to that kind of trouble over me."

"Really?"

"Really. I have to admit, when you punched out Bruce, I mean part of me was appalled by such retrograde macho posturing . . . but part of me liked being defended that way. It was . . . curiously romantic. And not at all what I'm used to. Very Dumas." At last, she smiles at Harry over the rising steam from her mug.

Harry's grateful for the smile, a smile he doesn't really deserve. "I'm sorry, Molly. Really sorry. More than you can realize."

She nods. "I know you are, Harry," she says kindly.

"Do you know how many times I've wanted to kiss you?" It's an honest question. The direct route, at last, even as something within him knows it's all too late.

She nods. "Yeah. Did you know that I wanted you to?"

Harry shakes his head helplessly. "I'm not very good at picking up on that stuff."

"Well, let me help you."

She places down her tea, pushes herself snugly against Harry's chest, and offers up her lips.

"Now," she whispers.

The first kiss led to a second, the second to a longer, deeper third, and before Harry knew it, Molly was moving Harry toward the bedroom. As he stands at the threshold of his long-sought-after, once-remote fantasy, those puerile imaginings of his former self now feel preordained, somehow inevitable and within reach. Yet Harry can't escape the matter-of-fact emptiness he feels at the prospect of his triumph.

Molly has discarded her blouse, and at last her much-fantasized-about tattoo hovers inches from him. But Harry's interior fog is continuing to lift, and something is holding him back. When his eyes fall on the open closet door and gap left by Anna's discarded clothing, the emptiness fills with sorrow, and Harry can stand it no longer. He pulls himself away from Molly.

"Harry? What is it?"

"I'm sorry, Molly." He sits on the edge of his bed. "I can't do this." Laughing in disbelief, he looks around the vast, empty space of his home and finds he feels diminished and strangely incomplete.

Molly's eyes follow his around the room and to the emptied closet. "She's here, isn't she?"

Is that it? Harry wonders. Is it these traces of Anna, her presence inhabiting every abandoned corner, that restrain him, his desire dampened by these permanently fixed echoes, echoes of spices and liquor bottles and carefully laid writing pads? Harry considers this for a moment before shaking his head.

"No. She's gone. That's the problem."

Molly nods with a sympathetic understanding that, for a moment, reminds Harry of Anna. Harry watches vaguely as she pulls her clothes back on, and at length he escorts her to the door, where she considers him with the same sort of fondness Nicole bestowed upon him at the end.

"Forgive me?" he asks.

Molly smiles. "You're all right, Harry. A little screwed up. But all right." She gently kisses him on the lips, allowing what they both know to be their last gaze to linger. Then she steps out into the night, and a moment later he hears her drive off. He settles into his living room chair, the one with the best view of the hills, from which the fog has all but disappeared. He feels estranged, floating freely as if somehow unanchored, cut loose from his pier, truly a permanent exile, a wanderer, whatever his phone number. Like his friend Edmond Dantès. And he remembers his closing lines from his farewell letter:

We must have felt what it is to die . . . that we may appreciate the enjoyments of living.

Harry sits in the armchair, trembling violently when the phone rings. Harry looks to the answering machine to screen the call, then remembers pounding the device into oblivion. He considers simply letting it ring but finally picks up the phone.

"Hello?"

"Hi, Harry! It's Elliott. How are you doing?"

"Fine, Elliott."

"Really? You sound tired, Harry. Am I disturbing you?"

"No, Elliott, you're not disturbing me. What can I do for you?"

"Wow. You really do sound tired, Harry. Maybe I should call back."

"I'll probably be tired then, too, Elliott. What's up?"

"Okay, I'll make it quick. I have someone I want you to say hello to. Okay?"

The precedents for such randomness from Elliott are so well established that Harry can't find the grounds to say no. "Sure."

"Say hello to Harry, honey."

"Hi, Harry. This is Katie."

Despite his exhaustion, Harry can't help but be surprised and interested. Her voice is a bit deeper and sturdier than he'd imagined. Not that he ever expected to hear it.

"Um. Hi, Katie."

"Listen, I wanted to thank you. All that stuff you said to Elliott, well, he really seemed to get it."

Elliott interrupts, irrepressible. "We're getting back together, Harry! I did it, I found her, and she took me back."

"And we're getting married," Katie sighs contentedly. "I love this man so much."

"And I love you, too, baby. With all of my heart. Anyway, this is all thanks to you, Harry. You were right. Every word you said to me."

"Wonderful," Harry says, not remembering what he said, only remembering he said it to get rid of Elliott.

Fortunately, Elliott obliges. "You told me that things improve and you get through the dark times. Remember? And the best thing you said was about just going through the dark times to get through them. Well, I did, and you were right."

"Oh, baby, I love you so much!"

"I love you, too, honey. Anyway, Harry doesn't need to hear us gush. We should go. You really do sound tired, Harry. Take care of yourself, okay?"

"Okay."

Harry returns the receiver to the cradle. He can't help but compare the great love that the hapless Elliott has secured with this resonant emptiness that surrounds him. Heart racing, Harry crosses to the bedroom, reaches to his nightstand drawer, and opens it. He plunges his hand in and withdraws the Swiss Army knife. The tremor that shakes his body seems to originate somewhere below his groin and races upward like the expanding bubble of a massive underwater explosion. It breaks the surface and a tsunami of loss floods Harry with images—the

X-ray, the first date, the morning after their wedding, the gift box, the white ribbon, and now Anna's words echo:

For emergencies.

Emergencies. The rush is more than Harry can bear, holding this bit of red plastic that—along with a drawerful of whispering objects—is all that remains of his wife. He squeezes the knife tighter and tighter, hoping the effort will stanch his tears—his first real tears—which stream down his face in burning rivulets. Clutching the knife to his chest, he buries his face into his pillow to muffle the wails that shake his body as the fundamental reality of his marriage finally takes full possession of him. At last, that awful night, the one great conflagration of their marriage in which the unspoken was briefly spoken, after which Anna would be lying dead in a hospital, unfurls in Harry's memory despite every safeguard he has erected to keep him from reliving this moment, from accepting its unbearable truths.

Harry had been hiding out down in his room of clutter when Anna informed him of her decision. Since the Everhappy Eterna Comfort Band™ affair, he'd fled to these quarters, where he spent most of his time avoiding the fallout of his actions. Anna's initial shock and disbelief had gradually been replaced by her usual cool pragmatism, and to a casual observer, all might have seemed normal, but Harry was sure something had shifted, some crucial stage had been skipped, and he'd anxiously been waiting for it to catch up with him. Harry was fiddling with one of his guitars, plucking forlornly at random notes, when Anna appeared in the doorway of his sanctuary. She seemed to be measuring her words even more carefully than normal, something Harry would not have imagined was possible, when she finally spoke up.

"I've made an appointment with Dr. Couteau."

Harry knew the name from Anna's stable of specialists. He'd handled a few minor cosmetic procedures for her.

"Okay. What for?"

Anna hesitated, then described the procedure she had in mind. It was the last thing Harry expected to hear. He stopped plucking at the guitar.

"What? Are you nuts?"

She folded her arms and shook her head, leaning into his doorway.

"I don't understand, Anna."

And something realigned in Anna in that moment, and she addressed him as never before.

"No, Harry, you never understand, do you? I think you don't want to understand."

Harry was shocked by her bluntness. A long-standing agreement to talk around difficulty had been nullified in a single stroke.

"Anna, what's going on?"

She wrapped her arms around her shoulders as if cold. In a low voice, she told him, "That's what you like, isn't it? Those girls . . ."

And Harry felt the anger rise, anger that, after all these years, he no longer believed existed, anger he'd been unable to summon. But there it was, ready and at hand, and all he needed to do, all he'd ever needed to do, was open the tap.

"Oh, no. Don't you dare. If you want to butcher yourself, go ahead, but don't do it on my account."

"I thought you'd be happy."

"You thought I'd be happy?"

"I thought . . . I thought it might help," she said with frustrated helplessness.

Harry couldn't fully read the moment, couldn't decide if she was simply trying to make him feel guilty or if it really was some sincere attempt to resuscitate their marriage. But it didn't matter—the buttons were raw and too easily pressed and it had been a long time coming.

"That's what you think, isn't it? That you can just . . . make a change so you can fit into someone else's idea of who you're supposed to be? And if you can't change it, you can hide it away. Like this room, Anna. Change and hide. Hide and change."

"Harry, please—"

"That's what you've wanted from me all along, isn't it? Admit it. You've been waiting for me to change. All these years. You're still waiting for it."

"No—"

"Admit it—"

"It's not true, Harry! I love you."

"Harvard Med, Anna? What about *Harvard fucking Med*?"

"Jesus, Harry! Still? After all these years? I apologized to you for that!"

"But you never stopped being ashamed of me. That's it, isn't it," Harry insisted, his body beginning to deflate as long-corralled truths escaped him. "Why won't you just admit it? I know already."

And finally, prodded to the limit, Anna lost it. "Ashamed? Of course I'm ashamed, you son of a bitch. You cheated on me, Harry! With *whores*!"

Anna's exclamation sailed into Harry's gut like a sucker punch, but he ignored his own shame and pushed on. He looked down to avoid her eyes.

"You were ashamed of me long before that."

"So it's my fault? Is that what you're saying?" To his surprise, Anna began to weep. "Can't you even apologize? Harry, you broke my heart with what you did! Don't look down. Look at me. Look at me!"

Harry raised his head and was shocked and revolted at the sight of Anna, her face contorted by rage and dripping tears, snot and fury. Suddenly there was something piteous about her, and Harry realized heartbreak is ugly, horrible to behold.

"This is me! I'm your Anna! You're my Harry! Look what you did to me! Your best friend. How could you? To *me*."

Bewildered, unable to bear any more, she hurried out of the room, leaving a numb, diminished Harry, red-eyed in her wake.

What we did to each other, he thought, alone in his space. *What we did to each other.*

And now, Harry stands back in the doorway of his room, as Anna herself stood there only a few short weeks ago. He'd thought he was alone then, and in a way he was, but he knows now, finally, what it truly means to be alone. The room reverberates before him with their shouts, as if the fight had only taken place moments earlier, the space electric with the thrumming vibrations of their conflict. Of course, she was right, he realizes now. It's taken him this long, but he can see it. Even as he can see that she was wrong. Did she ever see that, he wondered. Would she have had the time to work it out before the knives cut her open?

She'd had time for nothing. He knows that with sickening certainty. And he didn't apologize. And she went ahead with her plans. And weeks later, she was dead, and he'd never have another chance to apologize for the awful wrong he'd done her. This misery, this everlasting regret, would be his to bear forever, and he supposes it's exactly what he deserves.

He surveys the room and its forlorn contents with self-loathing. Guitars? Chess? Such foolishness from a man his age. Of course she was ashamed of him. Who wouldn't have been? What could he have been expecting? How differently might things have played out, Harry wonders, if instead of seven years later, they'd had their big fight that very night in Greenwich? Damn the Weldts, let them hear it, wake the whole household. If he'd given full voice to his feelings of betrayal, given Anna her chance to see what she'd done and to apologize—to *really* apologize—what a different couple would have left Greenwich that July weekend. It's not too difficult to follow a chain of cause and effect in which Harry never calls an escort service, and in which Anna, as a result, never goes under a knife. And she'd be here now. And this room wouldn't exist.

Shadows. Dreams. Too late now.

Harry takes a key from his pocket and locks the door. He's about to throw the key out over the balcony into the woods and canyon outside his window when his doorbell rings. For a moment, he worries that Molly has come back, but the view from the peephole startles him. Claire bobs uncertainly on his doorstep. After a moment's hesitation, he opens the door for her.

"Hey," she says, her heavy eyelids betraying her elevated blood alcohol level.

"Claire. Are you drunk?"

Shrugs. "A little. Situation normal," she slurs. "You going to invite me in?"

Harry takes her arm and escorts her to the sofa, upon which she flops with relief. He appraises her with wonder and fetches her a glass of water before sitting down beside her. She looks around the empty space and sniffs disapprovingly at the water.

"I don't want water, Harry."

"Claire—"

"I don't want water," she says firmly. Harry sighs with resignation and pours her a vodka tonic, her usual.

"We're—I'm out of lemons," he says, handing her the drink.

"I'll live." Claire drinks up gratefully and nods at Harry. "Thank you."

Harry says nothing, regarding her with wary confusion.

She sighs and gazes off toward the hills. "She didn't approve, either. She couldn't let it be." Claire shrugs at Harry. "I drink. She should get over it."

Harry doesn't correct the tense.

At length, Claire sighs awkwardly. "Bet you're surprised to see me," she says, slightly amused with herself.

"You'd win that bet."

She nods. "Had something I wanted to tell you. Something I didn't say at the lawyers'. But I don't think I had it all figured out. Still not sure I do."

Harry waits, dreading whatever's likely to follow.

"You asked why I didn't say anything. I wanted to. Believe me. I was so fucking angry, Harry."

"I can relate."

She looks at him carefully, and for a moment there's a trace of the old Claire in her eyes. Harry can almost swear that he's caught a glimpse of

261

his old friend. "I think you can. Because the thing is, I realized, it wasn't just you I was angry at. Oh, I'm plenty angry at you, don't get me wrong. What you did to Anna was shitty and disgusting. But . . ." She hesitates.

"But?" Harry prods her gently after the silence grows awkward.

Tears materialize in Claire's eyes. She doesn't wipe them away. "But we both know that there's someone else to be angry at. I know what she did to you, Harry."

"That was one night."

"All of it, Harry. Not just Greenwich. I know who my sister was. She could be a warm, wonderful person. And she could be a controlling bitch. I was her sister, she did it to me, too."

Harry nods, awash with gratitude. Then, barely audible, his own eyes filling with tears: "I never told her I was sorry, Claire. For what I did."

Claire nods. "Neither did she, Harry."

Harry considers this and knows it to be true. Oh, the words might have been spoken, for form's sake. But the life of slights that followed spoke louder than any apology. No apology could ever convince because her shame was always there.

"She was ashamed of me," Harry says, voice breaking.

"She loved you."

"But I embarrassed her. She loved me *and* I embarrassed her. Both of them. From the beginning to the end. That's the truth. We both know that, too."

Claire finally wipes her tears away, faces Harry, and nods. "Yeah."

She takes his hand and grips it tightly, as Harry fiddles sadly with the Swiss Army knife in his free palm.

After a moment of pained silence, she yawns drunkenly. "Fuck, I'm tired."

She rests her head on Harry's shoulder, and in a moment she's asleep, snoring raucously once more, as ever, and not even Harry's tears can disturb her rest.

Acknowledgments

When a first novel is written in one's forties, debts have accrued and accounts must be settled. I would like to extend heartfelt thanks to the following:

To friends and loved ones: Cheryl Arutt, Eric Brown, Steve Burkow, Gabriel Carras, Lauren Cerand, Suzanne Cole, Christopher DeLeo, Jack Dettis, Jeannie Elias and David Derge, Nikki Furrer (for getting me over the transom), Yanina Gotsulsky, Catherine Jones, Joe Kuhr, Sean Loughlin, Jon Marks, Larry Mathews, Scott O'Connor (for the mechanics of throwing a punch), Marc Parent, Paul Terwelp and Dana Glover, Chris Tallon, Luci Tyndall, Ned Vaughn, David Warden, Steve White, Alex Yera, and the memory of Steven Corbin.

To early readers and workshoppers: The gang at the Monday-night workshop guided Harry into the world, chapter by chapter, and prevented many early missteps—Bella Mahaya Carter, Sarah Kate Levy,

Bhargavi C. Mandava, and Richard Wadholm. Leslie Schwartz helped me figure out the structure and was Harry's earliest champion.

For dear friendship and thoughtful close reads of the finished manuscript: Laila Lalami, Tod Goldberg, and David Francis, whose weekly lunches keep me sane.

To all the readers of The Elegant Variation: I am impressed anew each day by your civility, intelligence, passion, and taste.

At Bloomsbury: My wonderful editor, Colin Dickerman, whose aim is true, Karen Rinaldi, Sara Mercurio, Peter Miller, Elizabeth Peters, Carrie Majer, and Miles Doyle. Thanks, too, to Steven Boldt for the careful copyedit.

At Writers House: Special thanks to the magnificent Simon Lipskar for guiding me safely through the thicket and loving Harry from Day One. Thanks also to Dan Conaway for the greatest letter ever and Josh Getzler for keeping the trains running on time.

Extra-special thanks are owed to the following three people: My cycling coach, Gary Kobat, who taught me the secret to finishing strong, a secret that comes in handy with surprising frequency. Any resemblance to Robby Geerchyk is purely affectionate. Jim Ruland lashed me to the mast to keep me on point when my attention wandered and gave me my most important early note. And without the sustained, daily encouragement from my dear friend Maud Newton, this book would surely not exist today.

Above all, thanks to my family: My parents, Michael and Eva Sarvas, to whom this book is dedicated; my sister, Monika, her husband, Brian Wolfe, and my niece and nephew, Jordan and Zachary. And finally, my beloved wife, Kathy, who miraculously tolerates it all.

A Note on the Author

Mark Sarvas is the founder of the popular litblog The Elegant Variation, which *Forbes* and the *Guardian* have named one of the best blogs on the Web. A member of the National Book Critics Circle, he's written reviews for the *New York Times Book Review*, the *Threepenny Review*, and the *Philadelphia Inquirer.* This is his first novel. He lives in Los Angeles with his wife.